Rogue

Kari Nichols

Rogue

Copyright © 2014 by Kari Nichols
All rights reserved

First Edition

ISBN: 978-0-9906123-2-2 (Paperback)
ISBN: 978-0-9906123-0-8 (EPUB)
ISBN: 978-0-9906123-1-5 (MOBI)

This is a work of fiction. Names, characters, organizations, places, events, and incidents are either products of the author's imagination or are used fictitiously.

All rights reserved. In accordance with the U.S. Copyright Act of 1976, the scanning, uploading, and electronic sharing of any part of this book without the permission of the publisher is unlawful piracy and theft of an author's intellectual property except in the case of brief quotations embodied in critical articles and reviews.

The scanning, uploading, and distribution of this book via the internet or any other means without the permission of the publisher is illegal and punishable by law. Please purchase only authorized editions, and do not participate in or encourage electronic piracy of copyrighted materials. Your support of the author's rights is appreciated.

Edited by Melissa Harlow
Proofread by Julia Gibbs
Cover design by Kari Nichols

Author photograph by Cottonwood Studios (http://www.cottonwoodstudiosworldwide.com)
Signet design by Nadine Pau (http://nadinepau-stock.deviantart.com/)
Title font: US Declaration by Tomasz Skowronski
Name/Chapter font: Mailart Rubberstamp by K-Type (http://www.k-type.com/fonts/mailart-rubberstamp/)
Handwriting font (Matthew): Bolívar by César Puertas (http://www.myfonts.com/fonts/cepuertas/bolivar/)
Handwriting font (Carvajal): Toms Handwriting by Omega Font Labs

For more information about Kari Nichols, please visit:
www.KariNichols.com

For Caleb.

Your encouragement made this possible.

Thank you for making every day an adventure.

One has to pay dearly for immortality; one has to die several times
while one is still alive.

-Friedrich Nietzsche

ONE

New York City, Present Day

HE DRESSED in one of his Armanis today. A custom gray suit, paisley bow tie, and his favorite cufflinks would be perfect for this meeting. It was always difficult picking out exactly the right look for each encounter. Because let's be honest—it's not every day you get to meet with a dead man, or with a soon-to-be-dead man, to be more specific. And Gregory Stein *would* be dead within forty-eight hours. The outfit needed to speak clearly to the target—'I have money to spare. I'm happy to entrust you with all my money. I am not a threat'. But the addition of the bow tie to this outfit also gave a little eccentric flair to the ensemble. The kind of eccentricity that would lend itself to the 'I have more money than I know what to do with' persona that he would be wearing with the accompanying suit. Yes, this look would do the trick.

Rogue once felt sorry for his targets. He could remember a time where he would envision the lives they could have led and the families they were leaving behind. What if his target was not a real threat to anyone? What if the target was a normal guy going about his business? But that kind of thinking led to serious complications in his past—thus earning him his nickname: Rogue. Laughable really, that his nickname should imply he actually 'went rogue'. He supposed defiance had a small role in earning his nickname, but if he could go back and make the same choices all over again, he would not change one thing. His grandfather started calling him Rogue shortly after the incident, and the rest of the Family soon after accepted the nickname as a permanent fixture.

No. He would never again defy the Family. He was a grandson of the first immortal. From a young age, he had always striven to please the Family. He had begun his training at an earlier age than any of his brothers or cousins. He worked harder and longer than anyone else to master the most difficult skills.

He had shown more promise than any of the Family since the beginning. And he had ultimately let one thing stand in the way of becoming one of the 'greats'. He'd decided long ago to quietly and respectfully fulfill his duties, if only to keep the peace among the Family for as long as possible. There was no need to evoke further provocation for dissention amongst the ranks. Lately, the assassins seemed to be growing more and more restless with leadership and the decisions of Saint and Priest. Contracts accepted by the Family's leaders had always blurred the lines of right vs. wrong and good vs. evil. For millennia the ambiguity had not bothered any of the assassins. But over the past few centuries, the contracts grew less blurred and more, well, outright evil. The Family was beginning to take note—especially those who followed strict religious practices. If they continued down this trajectory for much longer, there would be no more Family.

But that was not where Rogue's thoughts needed to be right now. This was a day of possibility for an exciting new investment in a successful company. And with the amount he was offering to invest, there was only one man he would be speaking with today—Gregory Stein, founder and CEO of Stein Securities. Of course, his true purpose in meeting was to get a lay of Gregory's office, as well as the building, security cameras and guards. Gregory would be blissfully ignorant of his true intentions and only too happy to show 'Mr. Matthew McCloud' around to secure the patronage of an investor offering a forty million dollar investment to his company.

Rogue vaguely wondered about the nature of the contract. He always made up scenarios about the reasons behind them. He imagined there was an elaborate story revolving around a slighted employee or a jilted lover. In this scenario, with his knowledge of the company's recent changes to their investment structure, he imagined there was a disgruntled competitor who feared their business would lose millions of dollars if Stein Securities was successful in their restructuring.

As a general rule, the reasoning behind each contract was fairly easy to decipher. Money problems accounted for about forty percent of the assassin's contracts, jealousy for about thirty percent, a change in leadership accounted for around twenty percent, and lovers' quarrels for most of the remaining ten percent.

As Rogue finished straightening his bow tie, he practiced his introduction a few times.

"Hi, I am Matthew McCloud. You must be Mr. Stein—or can I call you Gregory? *(Carefree laughter)*." Was that insultingly casual?

God, it was strange using his actual name. He had been going by Rogue for over two hundred years now, and the use of Matthew (or Mattia, as he had been named at birth) always made him feel uneasy.

"Hello, Mr. Stein. I am Mr. McCloud. It is a pleasure to finally meet you."

Way too formal for McCloud, Rogue thought. He decided to land somewhere between the two, but would wing it when he got into the meeting so he could determine the formality depending on how Gregory Stein was dressed.

He eyed himself in the mirror: dark hair gelled to the side with a perfect part, clean shaven by his personal barber, three thousand dollar custom-designed gray suit. *Yeah,* he thought, *I definitely play the billionaire role to a 't' ... I guess that happens when a billionaire plays the role of a billionaire.* He chuckled softly and shook his head at his little joke.

He picked up the copy of the Wall Street Journal he had grabbed a few weeks earlier. A writer for the Journal had done considerable legwork on Gregory Stein for an article that had been published about Stein Securities earlier that month. Rogue had read and re-read the article in the past weeks, but one last time couldn't hurt. *Thank you again, Mr. Luce,* he thought smugly toward the writer who unwittingly aided this assassination.

"Alright," Rogue said as he put the paper back down, "let's get this over with."

He grabbed his keys and headed to his elevator. On his trip down the forty floors that stood between his penthouse and his garage, he pondered the life he was able to maintain. After centuries of having unlimited resources and amassing wealth beyond a person's wildest dreams, he had certainly grown accustomed to the finer things in life. *Like buying an entire apartment complex so you don't have to share the garage with anyone else*, he thought, and laughed again.

He stepped off the elevator into the garage and smiled widely. Today he would have the pleasure of driving his favorite car. Usually he kept a low profile, which is why he would normally drive away from his apartment in his Boxster or Escalade—both black of course. Fortunately he only kept flats in major cities where his mid-range cars—the Boxters, the BMW M3, the Lotus Evora and the Tesla Model S—would be considered standard fare: LA, New York, Paris, Tokyo, and Dubai. Of course, in order to do recon work, he always kept a black SUV in his garage. And just in case he needed to show off a little, he figured he needed to keep a *really* nice car at each home. That's why he would be driving his 2014 Aston Martin Vanquish today. This one was green; his other, in Dubai was a perfect shade of deep orange. If you owned a car like this, you wanted to be seen, so naturally he ordered his luxury cars in flashy colors.

"Hello, beautiful," he whispered to the magnificent piece of technology waiting for him. "It has been far too long. Let's go on a little date."

As he listened to the purr of the engine, he allowed his doubts about the contract to drift away.

"This is what you do," he told himself again on the drive downtown. "This is what you have always done."

His little pep talk set his mind at ease as he reluctantly handed over his keys to a valet who looked like he should still be in diapers. *Why on earth do they hire children for this job?* he mused with a twinge of anger. Of course it would not have mattered if the valet was twenty or forty or sixty; handing over the keys of his Vanquish to anyone at all made his stomach churn with distress. He was not a man prone to violence—violence outside of his job, that is—but the idea of a child hurting his Vanquish in any way seemed to pull anger out of him from somewhere deep inside.

"If you get a scratch on her or lay a finger anywhere besides the door handle, key, gear shift or steering wheel, I will have you murdered in your sleep," Rogue thought aloud—not quite accidentally—with a tight smile.

The valet coughed a laugh, but his expression quickly turned to horror when he realized the man in front of him might actually have the resources to follow through with his threat. As Rogue turned and walked away with a smirk on his face, the valet yelled after him,

"I won't, sir! I promise!"

Two

ROGUE QUICKLY snapped some images of the lobby on his phone while acting like he was trying to find a signal.

"My God, the cell service downtown is awful with all these buildings around. What provider do you have to use to get a good signal in here?"

The receptionist laughed at Rogue's flamboyant movements to 'find service' and asked,

"Can I get your I.D., Mr. … ?"

"McCloud," he quickly finished.

"Thank you, Mr. McCloud." She checked his I.D. and handed it back to him. "Ms. Renaud is Mr. Stein's executive assistant; she'll be waiting for you on the forty-fifth floor."

At one time, this had been difficult for him—surveying the landscape, mapping out entrances and exits, finding the best entry points for various types of kills. Now he barely needed to think as he mentally noted where everything was. He knew he would be able go back to his penthouse after this meeting and draw a perfect map of each part of the building. He knew there were security cameras in every corner of the lobby—one facing the center of the room, two keyed in on the entry, and one fixed on the receptionist's desk. He also knew there were twelve large windows lining the front of the building, and four the same size on the east side. There were two main staircases accessible in the back corners of the room and most likely a third in the back hallway for maintenance. Of the six total elevators, only four were in working condition. After the time he put into this job, it came as easily to him as breathing. Still, with the technology available, it would not hurt to have a photo map along with his mental one. He took a few more photos of the building for reference as he walked towards the elevators. This building had standard security—basic camera surveillance and two lightly-armed security guards on the ground floor

—which meant nothing extraordinary was going on here. Why on earth would the Family have accepted this contract?

As he rose to the forty-fifth floor of the building, he straightened his tie and checked his hair and teeth in the reflection of the elevator doors. As the doors opened and he stepped out he decided to continue the 'looking for cell service' act so he could take a few photos of the surrounding buildings.

"Aha! I guess you have to come up to the forty-fifth floor to get a signal downtown. Do you mind if I make a quick call?"

Stein's executive assistant barely glanced up from her paperwork and waved a hand of agreement from her desk. Rogue walked to the windows and took note of the closest buildings with the best rooftop vantage points of Mr. Stein's office. If he had to be taken out with a sniper, then Rogue would note which buildings were the best to take the shot from. He loudly finished his fake call and walked back to Ms. Renaud's desk. As she looked up to greet him with a courteous smile, Rogue stopped on his heels. *How is this possible?* he wondered, shock clouding his mind. His head began to swim and his mind grew fuzzy. *What is this feeling?* he thought, right before he realized he was looking up at the lights overhead. Ms. Renaud let out a panicked cry for help, though Rogue could not understand why.

That was when he hit the floor.

Three

Madrid, 1749

Mattia stumbled toward the door as the knock sounded for the third time.

"Who the hell knocks on a door at four in the morn'?" he yelled as he made his way through the pitch black house. He stubbed two of his toes on the leg of the table that stood in his gathering room and another on the wall that jutted slightly out between his kitchen and the entry. By the time he made it to the door, he had yelled a curse at almost every piece of furniture he owned and every wall in the house in case they, too, decided to jump out and further brutalize his body. He yanked open the heavy wooden door with a fiery anger.

His father stood on the other side, looking at him with more concern than Mattia had ever seen on his face.

"Sorry, Father," Mattia quickly apologized. "Please come in," he added as he stepped aside to allow his father's entry. He felt even worse now than when he kicked the wall a moment before. He not only put on a rather loud display of anger for his father to hear, but was also incredibly drunk and weary. This was not the way he ever wanted his father to see him.

His father rushed in without a word and sat down at the large dining table, his expression never changing from one of sickened concern. Mattia struck a match to light the candles on his dining table, sat down quietly across from him and waited until he gathered his thoughts. Sometimes this would take hours. Mattia sent a quick prayer up that his father would be swift so he could get back to sleep. The night before he had attended one of the greatest parties of his life and drunk far too much wine. He arrived home only one hour before and had barely fallen asleep when his father knocked on the door. The headache he now suffered from because of the wine could easily rival the pain of the blow to the head he received during the brawl he had been in a few hours prior. Yet here he sat awaiting his father's discourse on he knew not what.

His father's face looked drawn and tired. He looked as if he had been dreading this conversation so much that he had not slept in weeks. His brown hair was matted to his head, which was not a common sight for anyone in the Family. With the wealth they had amassed over the past millennia, the Family could afford to live in opulence. The man sitting across from him looked distraught, and tired. He no longer looked like a man in his late twenties; he looked more like a man in his late thirties. What in the world was going on here? Mattia was about to ask him when his father finally spoke.

"Mattia," his father began, "I have heard from Priest."

"Oh," Mattia responded with a dejected sigh.

His heart sank. The look on his father's face could only mean one thing. Once again, a contract was going to be given to another in the Family. He had been training for this since he could swing a sword. After one hundred seventy-four years of life, he thought his own grandfather would have enough faith in him to grant him his first contract. This must be why his father looked like such a wreck. He finally had broken down at the prospect of Mattia never becoming an assassin. This was horrible! Now he would have to juggle his worry for his father's mental state along with his devastation for his own predicament. This whole situation was ridiculous to begin with. He was better than his cousins at every form of assassination—even better than some of his uncles. He knew that everyone else in the Family envied his brothers' and his natural abilities and advantages over their peers. But it seemed that because he was young, they were going to keep him away from the action, and he was simply unwilling to abide it. He sat quietly, knowing that if he opened his mouth a string of profanity and angry desperation would engulf the entire room, and his father would likely have to knock him out to restrain him. His father started talking again,

"He has informed me that the next contract will be given to you."

Mattia's eyes grew to twice their normal size. He knew the only reason he heard what he *thought* his father said was because he was still drunk from the night before. *Snap out of it, Mattia! Sober yourself and listen*, he sternly thought to himself.

"Did you hear me, Mattia? The next contract is yours."

What? Why was his father's demeanor so grim? This was the best news he had heard in decades!

"Why do you look as if someone has died, Father?" Mattia asked. "'Tis the best news of my life!"

But still his father sat quietly with his concerned eyes affixed to Mattia's face. Mattia had never felt such relief. The greatest accomplishment to this point in his life was when he acquired an audience with both Priest and Saint to be officially inducted into the Family so he could begin his training. He had been given his own unique mark and matching signet ring. That was the year he turned twenty-eight—the year he stopped aging. In the one hundred forty-six years that followed he had been honing his skills, learning every assassination technique possible, and gaining wisdom from the other assassins on how to scout a location for entry points, map out exits, and take down targets in the most unobtrusive ways. Of course there were always contracts that included specific instructions for how the target was to be killed—which were almost always the most gruesome deaths imaginable. Only a lunatic would force an assassin to brutally kill a target, which, if Mattia thought about it, was a befitting descriptor of any person willing to hire an assassin to kill another person. But it was not his place to judge. Saint and Priest always reviewed the proposed contracts and decided which ones the Family would accept and which they would decline. They also assigned each contract to a specific assassin or group of assassins to match the contract perfectly. Mattia knew, without a doubt, that this contract would be perfectly suited for him. He had been hearing the stories of triumph and glorious assassinations since he was a child. He would sneak into the dining hall late at night, hiding under tables and behind curtains, to listen to his uncles and cousins boasting of their triumphs. Every assassin wore their contracts like a badge of honor, and he would be no different.

His father finally stood, looked up at him and said,

"The contract has not been made official yet. All we know is that it is connected to the treaty that King Ferdinand is trying to sign with King John."

Mattia finally understood—his father assumed he would be sent to kill a king on his very first contract. Mattia furrowed his brow with the thought of all the planning that would have to go into an assassination of a royal target, but he would be happy to do the work when the official word came in. He vaguely wondered if another assassin would be joining him or if he would be going solo. He desperately hoped it would be him alone so he could have bragging rights of such a high-caliber target on his very first contract.

His father turned to leave and added, "We think the contract will be settled within the month. So be prepared, practice your technique every day, and stop drinking every night like a drunken wretch."

He slammed the door so hard behind him as he left that the wind from the door blew the candles out. But no amount of disapproval or door slamming could dampen Mattia's mood tonight. Tonight marked the beginning of the rest of his life.

Four

JOSE DE CARVAJAL Y LANCASTER sat in the small office in his home and contemplated his position in life. He had been writing and rewriting this treaty for what felt like a decade. Ever since his appointment as First Secretary of State by King Ferdinand three years ago, the land negotiations between Spain and Portugal had neither ceased nor progressed. He had poured his entire life into a single contract that neither king seemed to care about. *This feels like a waste of time! There are so many other matters that the Crown is attending right now.* He sat at his desk, staring at the naked wooden wall in front of him. Between the tax reform, the census, increasing the strength of the Spanish Navy, colonization in the Americas, and smoothing over the never-ending trouble with the Church, it seemed that he had been assigned the least important task in the entirety of Spain. That bastard Ensenada had King Ferdinand's full support and financial backing. He had the king's ear. And it seemed that any time Carvajal took a step toward finishing this treaty, Ensenada had a reason to avert the king's attention elsewhere.

"Stop!" he yelled at himself. "This is not healthy. Stop thinking like this or you are going to become a madman, looking over your shoulder every minute of every day. You are not a victim. Everyone is simply fulfilling their assignments here. And moreover, how interesting it is that you call Ensenada a bastard when you yourself are the bastard of a dead king. It is a wonder that you have any position in society at all! Calm down, and for God's sake, stop talking to yourself!"

He took a deep breath and tried to stop thinking about everything for a short moment. He looked around at the lack of décor in the room: one desk, one chair, and an endless supply of parchment and ink. He thought of the sad state of the rest of his house, and it was a stark reminder of the lack of a woman in his life. Unfortunately, when he stopped thinking about his political obligations, there was only one thing that occupied his mind—Anamaria Serrano.

Anamaria had been the only other subject on his mind since he had seen her a year earlier. He spent every free moment thinking of ways to see her, even if it was only a glance as she passed by. He attended parties and festivals he never before would have attended just to watch her interacting with her friends. Her lips were the perfect shade of pink, her eyes the deepest brown he had ever seen, and her lovely skin had the most beautiful natural hint of tan, though it was clear she had never been subjected to the harshness of the sun. When she smiled, *oh, when she smiled*, she stirred up feelings in him that he had not imagined he could possess. And when she laughed, he felt that he could scarcely take another breath until he heard her laugh again. He was fully devoted to this magnificent woman, and he had begun talking with her father, Marquis de Francisco Pérez Serrano, about the possibility of marriage. The problem was that Serrano was a wealthy owner of a mine that was highly profitable for the King, and he claimed he was uncertain that the marriage of his oldest daughter to the bastard son of a former king would be in his best interest. He kept saying things like, "I believe that my Anamaria might have other worthy men in pursuit of her hand in addition to you." Carvajal worried he could lose her and hoped she could not do better than himself. He continually reminded Serrano that he was the Secretary of State and a trusted advisor to the king (though it often did not seem that way). But to his dismay, Serrano made excuses about urgent business at the mine each time the matter was readdressed. Carvajal would have to find a way to corner Serrano into a decision quickly. This matter was beginning to interfere with his work, and that simply would not do.

He found an unsullied piece of parchment and wrote yet another letter to Serrano—

> Marqués de Francisco Perez Serrano,
>
> I feel the time has come to tell you that if I have not received consent within a fortnight to begin courtship with your daughter, Anamaria, I will relinquish my petition for her hand. Many wealthy fathers of beautiful young women have addressed the possibility of my entering into courtship with their daughters. I would be a fool to delay in responding to these fine offers that have been laid at my own doorstep to wait for a rejection from an offer that I have most generously laid before that of another. Make haste with your response as you are aware of the suitability of this match and can truly have no objection to my offer.
>
> Sincerely,
>
> Jose de Carvajal y Lancaster

Boldness. Yes. That was what Serrano must be looking for in a suitor for his daughter—boldness. Up to this point it seemed that he had done more begging than demanding. The time for asking had passed and he needed his answer. Anamaria *would* be his wife.

He looked at the letter sitting atop his work. This was truly the most important document on the desk. He called for his housemaid and instructed her to take the letter directly to the courier assigned to him by the king in hopes it would be delivered as quickly as possible. Royal business was always handled with expediency, and as far as the courier knew, this was royal business. He sealed the letter and handed it to the maid. For good measure, he sent a prayer up to the Blessed Virgin that she might bless the manner in which his letter was received and provide a prompt yet merry response. He reclined in his chair and hoped that he had done enough.

Five

Mattia practiced his introduction for his brothers.

"Hello. My name is Conte Mattia de Trapani, but you can call me Mattia."

His brothers simultaneously burst into uncontrollable laughter. Mattia waited for minutes, angrily wringing his hands together, while they picked themselves up off the floor and dried their tears.

"You are already practicing your introduction to the ladies at the party!" Antonio was barely able to say as he began laughing again.

"You are the most flirtatious individual I have ever known, little brother," Marcus added as the laughter picked up again.

"Your stance, your face, even your intonation—it is as if you are planning on taking every woman you meet back to your bed," Antonio finished with a chuckle.

His brothers grew quiet as they saw the flash of expression on Mattia's face at the accusation. It was not a face of offense, nor one of surprise. It was of … *recognition*.

"You cannot keep living this way," Marcus chided in the most somber tone Mattia had ever heard from his eldest brother's voice. His golden-brown eyes looked as if they were burning with intensity as he continued, "You have a contract coming in a matter of weeks, and if you continue to act like a drunken, lecherous lout it will be given away to another in the Family."

"You know this!" Antonio nearly yelled, his black hair flapping up and down in sync with the flail of his arms.

Having grown up the youngest of three boys, Mattia had always been given more flexibility, fewer reprimands, and far fewer rules than his brothers and cousins. He had never had anyone besides his father and grandfather demand maturity from him. Until now. Something in his brothers snapped in that moment. They were no longer joking with him, but looking at him with absolute solemnity. Instantaneously, Mattia felt the gravity of the situation at hand. They were looking at him not as a little brother, but as a fellow assassin. Though they were only three and seven years older than him, they had been fulfilling contracts for well over forty years—one of the reasons he was so bothered by the fact that he had not yet received his first. But standing here, face-to-face with them, he finally understood why. In order to be treated as an adult, he needed to act as such. How had this thought eluded him for so many years? He supposed he had found too much enjoyment bedding loose women and drinking himself into a stupor at parties with other boisterous men. He had learned all the skills necessary to become an assassin without ever learning how to behave with the maturity of one. Tonight, at this party, he would introduce himself as a true gentleman—not a child playing dress-up. He would behave accordingly and make his brothers see he truly was an adult, ready for the responsibilities that Priest and Saint were planning to place on his shoulders.

"I will not disappoint you, my brothers," Mattia stated with as much sincerity and resolve as he could muster.

His brothers looked at him for a short time to be sure his promise was genuine before offering nods of approval.

As he dressed for the evening, he thought about the closet full of fine clothes. *'Tis not far from the truth that I might be a count*. His mother had been the daughter of an Italian count and countess, though the title passed to her brothers and not to her. But the Family had been fulfilling contracts for so many centuries that it seemed there was more coin in the Family vaults than one knew what to do with. He had witnessed many a title purchased by coin. If he desired an actual title, he need only buy one from the right politician in the king's favor. But for this contract, a fake title would do. Moreover, without a real title, he would leave no evidence of his existence once the contract was fulfilled and he moved on to a new city to await his next. That is, of course, assuming he fulfilled this contract to the best of his ability, and the Family saw fit to award him another. A pit abruptly formed in his stomach at the thought of failure. This would be his chance to prove once and for all that he was ready to join the other assassins in immortalized glory.

He stepped into the party and quickly surveyed the large gathering. Antonio was in the back left corner speaking with a few land owners in the area. Marcus was directly to his right entertaining a few of the king's naval officers with jokes at the expense of some of the city's richest citizens.

The room that housed the party was massive, and the owners of the home obviously had connections with some outstanding artists. Every inch of the ceiling was painted in the most amazing mural of heaven. Cherubs draped in white linens lined the center of the mural from left to right—some flying with smiles on their faces, some sitting together on clouds playing harps and singing. The adult-sized angels were painted with a paintbrush that must have been infused with life itself; because if you looked at them for long enough, you could almost see them flying and laughing together. The feminine angels had long flowing hair with robes that flowed around them as if the very wind in the sky were causing them to stay perfectly in place. The male angels had a slight look of protectiveness written across their faces. A massive gold and crystal chandelier hung from the twenty-foot-high ceiling, lighting the mural almost as if sunlight were coming up through small holes in the clouds beneath the angels' feet. The placement of angels around the ceiling with their lifelike quality mixed with the lighting from the giant chandelier made the room almost feel ... holy. The walls were draped in opulent blue cloths, and the parts of the walls that peeked out in between the drapes were covered in gold. It was as if this room belonged in the king's palace.

Mattia walked with the gait of a count, and every woman who glanced his way took notice. The new handsome count dressed in the finest cloth at the party was receiving as much attention as he had hoped for merely hours ago. Now he was annoyed by the consideration because it only provided a distraction to the task at hand. He gave short, uninterested nods to the women staring at him and decided he cared not whether it offended them. He made his way to the back of the room where the politician he had come to speak with was standing.

Marcus had arranged for one of the noblemen to introduce Mattia to whomever he needed to become acquainted with at the party. Mattia had chosen his mark after a long and careful consideration. The noble walked beside Mattia, greeting those at the party with ease.

"May I present Conte Mattia de Trapani of Italia," he said with a small bow and gesture toward Mattia.

Mattia nodded his thanks and dismissal to the nobleman before turning and saying, "Buona sera, Jose de Carvajal y Lancaster. I hoped you would be here this evening."

Six

This Italian count certainly has a way with words, Carvajal thought as he listened to the count drone on and on about financial investments and his new business ventures in Madrid. He keyed in on a few things the count said about political stances and loyalty to the Vatican, but truly the only reason Carvajal had come tonight was to see his beautiful Anamaria. The man talking to him was providing just enough distraction to keep his attention split between this conversation and his love, which was frustrating him to no end.

"I apologize, Signore Carvajal," the count interjected, "Am I keeping you from another engagement?"

The count was utterly sincere and not even slightly upset with the obvious divide in attention. Carvajal immediately felt horrible for his lapse in attention. He was a statesman first and foremost and should be getting to know the king's subjects and visitors alike when he attended parties such as these.

"No, no, Conte Trapani. I must beg your forgiveness. There is a matter that I have been dwelling on for some time and it distracts me in a most unpleasant way at all the most inopportune times," Carvajal apologized.

"Please call me Mattia. My title was inherited from my horrible father, and I am happy to have a friend in the king's court," Mattia added with a smile.

Carvajal was instantly put at ease by the conte's disclosure. It was clear he was not seeking position. He was simply trying to get to know people in the king's court. What a refreshing attitude. Carvajal wished there were more gentlemen in the court that shared Mattia's unaffected outlook on life.

"Thank you, Mattia. Please feel free to call me Carvajal—all my friends do."

The conversation grew deeper over the next several hours and covered everything from the state of the economic turmoil with the new monetary systems being installed into the Spanish political structure, to the differences in the latest male fashion trends of Spain and Italy. By the time the party ended both men were genuinely happy to have made the other's acquaintance. Carvajal had not spent four hours standing like a dunce in the corner staring longingly at his Anamaria. Mattia had neither flirted with every woman in the room nor missed out on multiple opportunities to make strong political connections. The party had been a success for both men, and Mattia felt an urge to ask if he would be at the gathering the next night. Carvajal agreed he would be there and would look forward to more conversation about politics and style.

As Mattia turned and made his way toward the door to leave, a woman's laughter on his left caught his attention. The sound was so sweet that he wondered if one of the angels from the mural overhead had not made the sound. *No.* He rebuked himself for even thinking of looking over to take a quick peek at the beautiful sound. He instead searched in the opposite direction for his older brothers, gave them each a subtle nod, and left.

When his brothers arrived home an hour later, he could see they approved of his actions that evening.

"Well played, little brother," Antonio smiled. "Making friends with the Secretary of State is not exactly the kind of political leap we thought you would be taking tonight, but it is brilliant. It looked as if the two of you were lifelong friends," Marcus added.

"I do actually think we shall be friends of a sort," Mattia replied. "He clearly has a lot on his mind, and it seemed as if no one at the party had any interest in coming to greet him. So I will make it my goal for the next few weeks to gain access to the king by way of becoming friends with his Secretary of State."

"Perfect," Marcus said with a sense of finality. "And now that you are home at a decent hour, we shall all share some wine, cook some food, and talk about the latest news from the Family. I received a letter from Uncle Claudius this very day."

By the time his brothers left him, Mattia's head hurt as badly as it had the night his father woke him with the news of his imminent contract. He supposed it was not that his brothers did not want him to drink; it was that they only wanted him to drink under the supervision of another immortal. If he drank unsupervised, he would have dulled senses and impaired judgment, which, in his case, was a bad combination when mixed with his tendency to produce an impassioned temper when drinking. He realized his brothers feared for his life. As immortals, they were not impervious to death by mortal wound, only death by disease or old age. Once again—twice on the same day no less—he came to a realization he should have comprehended a hundred years earlier, but he had previously been too impulsive to think clearly on the matter. If he was going to drink, from now on, he would have the protection and supervision of at least one other in the Family, or he would not drink at all.

As he lay in bed trying to fall asleep, he considered the connection he made that night. His brothers were quite right. It was brilliant. Only two or three other males in the entire country had the same kind of access to the king that Carvajal possessed. If King Ferdinand was the target of his contract, there would be no stopping him now. It almost saddened him to know that if he disappeared after the king's death, Carvajal would certainly be tried as a traitor and killed. But it was all in a day's work, and he would not allow himself to get attached to a pawn in the perfect plan of his very first contract.

When he closed his eyes and tried to clear his mind so he might actually sleep, the only sound he remembered hearing before he gave in to slumber was the sound of laughter ... beautiful, angelic laughter.

Seven

Anamaria had an idea of how the conversation with her father would play out tonight. She also knew that she had absolutely no interest whatsoever in being a part of it. Her father was doing his best to convince her to marry either the Marqués de la Ensenada or Jose de Carvajal y Lancaster. She carried no desires toward either. Ensenada wrote once to her father, expressing interest in the match, but did not request a courtship with her. In contrast, Carvajal essentially asked her father's permission to marry her without having ever spoken a word to her.

Ensenada was an old man—nearly fifty years of age—and it showed. He wore a horrible powdered wig at all times to hide his baldness (or so she had been told by ladies in the King's court). He was quite rotund, but only around his midsection. His body and looks were not ugly, but Anamaria found herself always feeling slightly perplexed by his features. It seemed to her that all his different parts and features were taken from other men and awkwardly pieced together to create one rather confusing man. Beyond that, he was so buried in work that he rarely attended parties or gatherings, and when he did it was only to make connections with the other men. He never spared a glance for her, or any other woman for that matter. When her father told her of the letters he received from both men, the one from Ensenada baffled her more than she could remember feeling in the whole of her life.

The letter from Carvajal, on the other hand, she had been expecting for months. She had first seen him a year earlier at a gala the queen had thrown. She noticed him staring pointedly at her throughout the evening. Her friends began making fun of her, and the whole idea that a man was staring at her had brought her to tears—from laughter. It was so odd for a man of his station to act so inappropriately. Over time, the staring continued and he began showing up at every party she attended. The humor she once found in his shameless obsession grew to resentment. He never approached her. Not once. He had not the courage to speak to her, introduce himself, or even walk by her. She spent many hours considering what sort of man he must be. While he was nearly fifty like Ensenada, he did not look a day over thirty. He was tall, slender, and could boast a handsome face. His strong jaw and perfect teeth were uncommon for a man of his age, and he always looked as if he slept and worked exactly the right amount to maintain his health. And though he wore a powdered wig (as most men over the age of forty did) his dark brown hair would be a complement to his other fine features. She knew of his hair because it sometimes slipped out from under his wig while he walked. If he had not become such an annoyance to her social life, she would happily have accepted his offer of courtship. But in the last six months, she thought of him only as the pest that followed her around to every party and stared at her like a skulking coward from the corner of every room.

This conversation would *not* be pleasant.

"Anamaria, I think we must make a decision," her father proclaimed before she even sat down in the chair across from him. He always kept to the library when he was making difficult decisions about financial or family matters. She loved the smell of this room. Her favorite pieces of literature lined the ten foot walls on every side of her. Thousands of books wrapped in leathers, deeply colored cloths and ancient parchments surrounded her—she felt as if this room was her safe place. This should not be the room in which she and her father discussed this unpleasant matter. Perhaps the sight and smell of her favorite companions would blanket her in comfort while she cried to her father about how despicable both men were.

"You have to choose one of them, Anamaria," he continued. *No*, she told herself. *Nothing will be able to comfort you after this conversation.*

She quietly collected her thoughts before responding. Her father was doing her a great service by including her in this discussion. Most of her friends were *told* whom they were going to marry rather than *asked*. But she and her father had been close since she was young. He read books to her far above a normal child's comprehension and explained their meanings at length. As she grew, they discussed literature and politics together as equals—each hearing the other's opinion and responding in kind. He took her on secret outings into the woods to teach her archery and marksmanship. She had never been a 'normal' young lady like her sister, Isabel—she did not run around gossiping about boys or talking about the newest stock of gowns in town. She indulged her sister by listening and feigning interest, but her true passion was for literature and the outdoors. Her father—God bless him—had not even told her mother about the proposals. If he had, Anamaria would already be at her second fitting for her wedding apparel.

"Father," she began, "you cannot seriously be considering either of these men! They will be dead before I could even have a chance of bearing a child. Ensenada may not be as old as you, but his disposition makes him appear *far* older. And I refuse to marry someone as apprehensive as Carvajal. He attended party after party over the past year just to stand in a corner and stare at me. Not once did he speak so much as a 'hello' to make pleasantries with me. A man like that can have no ability to be a proper husband. I must refuse both."

Her father's face had grown from one of concern at the start of her discourse to one of vexation by the end. "You know you are an old soul, Anamaria. You have not the patience for young men, and you would be well-matched to the intelligence of either of these suitors."

She could not deny his arguments. She knew he was right, but she remained unmoved. She would not agree to an old man as a husband. Though it was clear this would not be the end of the discussion, she boldly stood, turned and exited the library without a word.

Her father stared at her, his face contorted in frustration, but he remained silent. When she closed the doors behind her she heard him release a grunt of exasperation. But at least he knew how she felt about both men now. It made her feel as if a weight had been lifted from her shoulders. Her father adored her most of all his children. She was the eldest of three, and her sister and brother were both younger and more obliging than she. Father always adored her spirit and her will. He might not like it right now, but she knew he would understand her opinions of the men and agree with her sentiments. At twenty-three years of age, she was perfectly capable of finding a younger man with vision. She did not need an old, established man to hold her hand through the rest of his short life. She needed a man whom she could grow old with—someone to go on adventures with. Old men had already experienced all the adventures they would ever want to have, and she could not live a life free of adventure.

She walked through their large home and admired the beauty her mother had surrounded them with. Artwork hung on every wall in the home, curtains on every window. The money from her father's mines allowed them a comfortable lifestyle and allowed her to have private tutors her entire life. She was well versed in art, literature, politics, economics, and writing. She loved to paint, draw, sew and dance. But above all, she loved to read. She walked through the long hallway, past her mother's sitting room on the right and the grand dining hall on the left. She ran her fingers along the deep red wallpapers and the ivory draperies that balanced out the dark walls at even intervals. She made her way up the wide staircase and entered her room on the left at the top of the stairs. She needed to sit and think for a moment to clear her head of this most unpleasant situation.

As she walked into her room, she shook her head at the new décor her mother had arranged for her. The walls had been refinished in cream paint with rose colored fabric panels and curtains around the entire room. Brightly colored floral patterns were strategically placed on the pillows, paintings, and furniture. Anamaria did not mind the floral patterns at all—they made her feel like she was in a garden out of doors, which always put her at ease. The cream dressing table, chest and chairs were laced with gold and rose accents. She knew the redecorating was her mother's way of attempting to make her more like her sister. Anamaria would have been exceedingly happy to have a room that resembled her father's library. But she knew better than to raise any objections to her mother's designs. She felt no ill-will towards her sweet mother. She merely felt as if the woman had never even tried to understand her. She had never said as much, but in her heart Anamaria knew her mother wished she was more like her sister. Isabel's love of fashion, gossip and boys far surpassed her love of reading and the outdoors. Anamaria loved her sister with her whole heart, but she simply did not understand the obsessions her sister had for the more 'appropriately feminine' things in life. Anamaria was not offended by her mother's feelings; her father had more than made up for her mother's lack of understanding. She smiled a little at the thought.

She walked to her bed and lay down. She thought about the kind of man who could really make her happy in life. *What do I really want?* she wondered absently. What she really wanted was one of the heroes from her books. A little known fact that she rarely admitted, even to herself, was that the books she read which were about great romances were her favorites. Men that would put aside their family's approval for the woman they loved, men who would go to great lengths to secure their beloved's happiness, and men who performed grand acts of chivalry—those were the kind of men Anamaria was looking for. She did not want an old man devoid of passion and romance and life. *Surely there is a man in the world for me,* she thought with a sigh.

She was shaken from her daydreams when her door flew open, and she was accosted by her sister.

"Oh, Ana! I could not wait to tell you what I have just heard from Lucia!"

"Isabel, please. I have recently finished a most vexing discussion with father, and all I need right now is to be alone with my thoughts," Anamaria pleaded.

"No, my sister. This news is too astonishing to wait! I have been awaiting this moment all day, so you must sit up and listen to me," Isabel demanded.

"Alright," Anamaria conceded with exasperation, "What is this news you have heard?"

"There is a new Italian count in Madrid. He is young—most assuredly in his twenties—but exceedingly wealthy. None know where he is staying, but he was seen a few nights ago at a party speaking with Jose de Carvajal y Lancaster at great length. They have been spotted together since then as well. *Everyone* is talking about him. Rumors are that his name is Conte de Trapani, but no one is certain because the Secretary is so private in all his social dealings. The one thing that everyone *does* know is that the conte is the most handsome man that has ever set foot in the city. He is supposedly very tall, though I have not yet seen him. And he is said to be well built, though I am not certain on that either. But what is *most* intriguing about him is that women all over the city have been throwing themselves at him, yet he has not spared a glance their way! Is it not a splendid mystery, sister?"

Anamaria marveled at how much her sister said without stopping for breath. Isabel spoke so quickly and passionately about this man, it made Anamaria intrigued enough to want to catch a glimpse of this woman-ignoring enigma that had the entire city talking.

"Maybe he will attend the king's gala this evening," Anamaria mused aloud.

"I knew you would be as mystified as I!" Isabel yelled as she ran out of the room, impassioned by Anamaria's interest.

A young, handsome, rich man in Madrid? Anamaria thought. *The women of this city will undoubtedly break his focus and weasel their way into his coffers.*

As Anamaria dressed for the gala that evening, she did not think once of seeing the mysterious gentleman.

Eight

Mattia's new residence fit the lifestyle of a rich Italian conte perfectly: cavernous rooms, expensive furnishings, ceilings covered in frescos, touches of gold throughout. He cared not about the house but for the appearance it lent to his persona. He would have been happy to stay in the comfortable wooden home on the outskirts of the city, but his brothers convinced him to have Carvajal suggest a residence to occupy while he was in town. So here he was. He used only two of the rooms in the monstrous home—the smallest bedroom upstairs—which was still very large—and the kitchen. Of course, the home had come with a housemaid who lived in the servants' wing. He did not want or need a maid. This house was one more obstacle in the way of his contract. With a house like this, it was far too tempting to bring women home from parties. He knew they would only be further drawn to him by learning of his wealth— and anyone occupying a residence this large would assuredly boast extravagant wealth.

His relationship with Carvajal could not have been more successful. His invitation to the king's gala tonight was assuredly by recommendation of Carvajal— and would allow him to be properly introduced to the entire court. More invitations would undoubtedly follow, and popularity among the richest families would allow him greater access to the king when the time came to fulfill his contract.

He dressed in his finest clothes—a long dark green coat with wide cuffs and gold and brown floral trim down the center, matching breeches, golden colored stockings and black shoes with square buckles. He enjoyed having nice clothes, but even more than that, he enjoyed having a reason to wear them. His long brown hair was neatly tied back with a ribbon the exact shade of his coat, and the sides were perfectly—and naturally—curled. Topped off with his hat, he looked stately. His introduction to the court was sure to be memorable.

Carvajal generously sent his carriage over to collect Mattia for the gathering, and it arrived right on time. The driver knocked on the front door of the estate at exactly half past seven. *Time for the show to begin*, Mattia thought as the carriage made its way through town.

He stepped out of the carriage into a wall of silence. Hundreds of people milled about outside the castle doors in the fresh evening air, but one could have heard a bird tweet a mile away with the stillness of the party. Apparently, word had gotten out that he would be arriving in Carvajal's carriage, because everyone was staring at him with anticipation. Carvajal walked up to Mattia, slightly uneasy with the unfamiliarity of the situation, and welcomed his friend to the gala. Mattia smiled, grasped his friend's shoulder and thanked him for the carriage and the welcome. At that, it was as if an explosion had sounded. The party erupted back into its former state of loud celebration, laughter and conversation. Everyone still watched Mattia from the corners of their eyes, but he was happy to see no groups of desperate women had yet approached him.

Anamaria dressed in her favorite gown for the gala—a three-quarter sleeved, golden-colored silk gown with a full skirt and cream lace trim. Though she was not as conventionally feminine as her sister, she still loved to dress up for a party. The gown she wore this evening accentuated all the right parts of her figure and set her father on edge. It was perfect.

As Carvajal's carriage approached the entry, Isabel ran over to Anamaria and whispered, "This is him, Ana! Are you as nervous as I?"

"Why on earth should I be nervous? It is not as if he is here for the purpose of meeting me," Anamaria quietly countered.

"But perhaps he will see you or me and be swept away by our beauty!" Isabel giggled.

It was true; the sisters—only two years apart in age—were nearly identical in looks. Isabel had lighter hair, was slightly taller, and was not as full in figure as Anamaria, but anyone could see clearly they were sisters.

As the carriage came to a halt, it seemed everyone was as anxious for the arrival of the conte as Isabel.

When the door opened and the Italian emerged, Anamaria felt as though she had been transported to a different time and place. This man—this tall, handsome man—dressed in the most beautiful clothes, was the only person that existed in the universe. He towered over Carvajal—who Anamaria had previously thought a fine height for any man. His muscular build was evident by the bulge of muscles that stretched the fabric at the arms of his coat. His silky brown hair fell in a long singular curl over his right shoulder. His face was a lesson in perfection—chiseled jawline, smooth skin, brilliant green eyes, and a smile that could not be properly set to paper even by the most accomplished of artists. He was a living, breathing archetype of 'the perfect man'. Anamaria shook herself back to reality and glanced sideways at her sister, then at the other guests attending the gala. It seemed she was not the only woman presently living out a fantasy in her mind.

Just as Mattia expected, the partygoers were thrilled to meet him. He walked around greeting each family Carvajal introduced him to. *This must have been how he made his rise to Secretary of State*, Mattia pondered. *He is charismatic and charming tonight. I wonder what changed him into the distracted, sulking figure I met at the party a few days ago.*

"And this is Marqués de Francisco Perez Serrano, owner of many valuable mines in the towns surrounding Madrid." Carvajal smiled widely at the gentleman as he introduced Mattia. "This is Conte Mattia de Trapani of Italy," he continued with pride. It seemed Carvajal had something to gain from this relationship with Mattia after all. *Maybe Serrano has something interesting to offer,* Mattia noted mentally.

"It is an honor to meet you, Conte Trapani. Please let me introduce you to my three children: my eldest, Anamaria, her younger sister, Isabel, and my only son, Salviano."

"It is a pleasure." Mattia bowed slightly, his eyes lowered to avoid looking at either daughter's face. Out of the corner of his eye, he saw Carvajal stiffen during the introduction to Serrano's children and relax slightly as Mattia bowed and turned to show he was moving on. *Also interesting*, Mattia noted.

As the two men began walking away, the angelic laughter that had been singing him to sleep for the past three nights rang in his ears—the very laughter he had heard as he was leaving the party three days prior. Without thinking, he jerked his head around to find the source and immediately regretted the reaction. Before him stood an angel cloaked in gold. The laughter made her beautiful face even more breathtaking with a perfect smile and a flush in her cheeks. Her black hair was swept back into a cascade of curls beginning at the crown of her head, ending all the way down at her waist. She abruptly stopped laughing when her sister roughly jabbed an elbow into her side; she snapped her head to the left to look at him with wide eyes. When their eyes met, Mattia thought surely his heart had exploded from his body. Her golden gown made her deep brown eyes glow like embers. He soon realized he lingered far too long on her exquisite face and turned to carry on with introductions to the other guests. When he glanced at Carvajal, the look of pain that swept over the man's face was palpable.

"Are you feeling well, friend?" Mattia asked quietly.

"No, Mattia. Not well at all. You must excuse me," Carvajal apologized.

As the man turned and hurried away, Mattia could not fathom what sickness had befallen his friend. Another guest hurried to take over Carvajal's duties and continued introducing Mattia to the other guests. He stole quick glances at Anamaria throughout the evening to make sure she was enjoying herself. He realized he felt responsible for her happiness and was unsure where those feelings had come from and how he felt about having them. He knew it was foolish to dwell on this woman he had never even spoken to and tried, unsuccessfully, to force her from his mind.

When the evening was finally over, though he met hundreds of guests at the gala, he remembered only one: Anamaria Serrano.

For the next six days, Mattia thought of nothing but Anamaria. When he slept, he dreamt of her smile and deep brown eyes. When he woke he thought of ways he might be able to make her laugh. *Oh, to hear her laugh again!* When he ate, he wished she was at his side so he could speak with her about her day. When he got into bed at night, he wished she was crawling in beside him so he could hold her as she slept. The idea of another man holding *his* woman —or even looking upon her face for that matter—made his stomach churn with dread. *This is ridiculous. You have not even spoken with this woman. You know nothing about her!* He knew he mustn't long for Anamaria this way. He was going to fulfill his contract and leave Madrid for at least fifty years—the Family never allowed an assassin to take contracts in the same city without fifty years' interruption. If a citizen happened to recognize him somehow, not only would the Family be at risk of discovery, but the assassin would be at risk of being marked as the culprit for both murders. *Stop thinking about her,* Mattia commanded himself. He knew it was of no use, but he would try to put her out of his mind nonetheless.

Nine

ANAMARIA AWOKE with a dreadful headache. Between her sister's jumping, squealing and plans of matchmaking in the past six days since the gala, it was a wonder Anamaria had gotten any sleep at all this week. Every night when Isabel left her for the evening, Anamaria had lain awake for hours thinking about the intensity in Conte Trapani's green eyes as they met hers in that brief moment. He had not looked at a single other woman the entire evening—she knew because Isabel had followed him around for the rest of the evening to make sure. But according to her overzealous sister, he glanced in Anamaria's direction many more times throughout the evening. *Oh, Isabel*, she thought, *why did you have to put these silly thoughts into my head?* It was impossible for her to think of anything else now that she knew there *might* be a possibility that the handsome conte could be interested in her.

She stole away to the forest nearly every day this week to escape to a fantasy world where the conte would secretly rendezvous with her. They would sit and talk for hours. He would always tell her that he loved her and that she was the most beautiful woman he had ever seen. *You are hopeless*, Anamaria scolded herself. *He gave no evidence that he was even interested in knowing your name. So why would he ever fall in love with you?*

Anamaria grew up thinking of romance in the most practical way: marriage was simply a bargaining chip for a title or land. But ever since her own future became a topic of interest, she had become a hopeless romantic. Each time she read a love story in her beloved books, the scenario took shape in her imagination—she became the beautiful woman in the story, and the handsome protagonist always wanted her alone. *This is real life*, she cautioned herself, *and the handsome Conte Trapani does not even know you exist. Stop this now or you will break your own heart.*

"Anamaria!" her mother called from below, "Are you ready to go into town? We will be late for our gown fittings if we do not leave soon! You need to look your finest for the Marqués de la Ensenada's party next week. Make haste and ready yourself."

Ah. Ensenada. Anamaria roused herself from the fantasy she had been having about the conte and climbed from her bed to ready herself for the day. She was acutely aware of the proposal of courtship that Ensenada planned to present her with at the party. She had wanted nothing to do with him before. Now, after meeting the Conte Mattia de Trapani, she wanted to avoid the party altogether. Maybe she could feign an illness.

"What is taking you so long?" Isabel questioned as she entered the room without knocking. "Why are you still in your nightshirt!" she whined. "We are going to have to leave without you, or we will miss the appointment. Come as soon as you are dressed or mother will be furious," she added, as she swept out of the room and down the stairs.

Anamaria dressed in a simple light blue afternoon dress and tied her hair back with a matching ribbon. The weather this spring was unseasonably dry, so there was no need for a cloak. She picked up a book from atop her dressing table without looking and headed out her door and down the stairs.

"You will have some catching up to do," her father called from his library. "They left over twenty minutes ago."

She did not want to ruin this walk by being hurried—the weather was far too beautiful to waste this day with rushing. *The appointments for mother and Isabel will take hours*, she decided. *I will take the long way through town,* she thought with a smile. She looked at the book she had grabbed in her hurry—*Romeo and Juliet.* She began laughing that the fates would have blessed her with this tale of lovers' woe at precisely this time in her life. Ensenada, Carvajal, and Mattia. Three men: two old and unwanted asking for her courtship; one young and handsome—and likely already spoken for. *What a horrible situation to be in*, she pondered.

She looked down at her book. And as she began reading, she drifted back into her fantasy world—she was Juliet and the conte was Romeo. The story took on a whole new meaning when her sweet Romeo had the face of the conte. No longer was she saddened by the outcome of the story—it devastated her. She was on the verge of weeping when she realized she had been paying no attention to her surroundings. She heard a second set of footsteps on the ground behind her and quickly glanced to the side to make sure she was not in the passerby's way. What she saw stopped her dead in her tracks. *The conte!* Her mind screamed in horror. *Am I still daydreaming? No, of course not. If you were still dreaming, your hair would be properly fixed. You should have paid more attention when you were dressing this morning*, she scolded herself inwardly. *You look like you barely rolled out of bed! He is talking to you, you fool! Shut up and listen!*

"Signorina Serrano," Mattia greeted her with a bow. "I hope I did not startle you. I noticed you were deeply engrossed in your book, and I became concerned you might fall on an uneven section of the path; so I decided to be watchful in case you needed assistance," he finished.

He had not meant to happen upon her, but their homes were in the same part of the city. It seemed fate was forcing him to be near Anamaria, or he would not have headed for the city center just at the moment she left her own home. *Wonderful*, he thought with a twinge of sarcasm. *Now I know where she lives as well.*

He realized she was giving him a look of distress. Dear God, he had terrified her! "I am so sorry, signorina. I did not mean to frighten you!" The longer she stared at him the more concerned he grew that she may not be an intelligent sort. *Perhaps she is of low intellect. But no, of course not, she is* reading Shakespeare! *A woman with knowledge of books cannot be simpleminded. Perhaps she is socially inept ... though she gave no sign of such at the party last night. Stop overthinking this, Mattia.*

"Uh ... umm ... No. No. I am sorry. I was lost in my book and taken by surprise. Thank you for your concern for my well-being, sir. It is most graciously received," she finished with a slight curtsey.

He knew he should not, but she was so breathtakingly beautiful *and* articulate that he could not help himself. "Could I accompany you to your destination?"

Anamaria was having trouble breathing. Even after she stood like a dunce for minutes, staring at this model of perfection, he still offered to accompany her to the seamstress. It was likely he was only trying to be a gentleman. *Do not read into it*, she scolded herself.

"Thank you, yes. I am on my way to a dress fitting for the Marqués de la Ensenada's gala next week. Are you planning to attend?" she asked.

"I was planning on it, yes," he responded. "And I will certainly be attending now, knowing that you will be there wearing a new gown," he finished with a flirtatious smile.

Anamaria nearly fainted at the conclusion of that sentence. *Did I hear that correctly? He toyed with my emotions very noticeably. Surely I could not have misinterpreted his meaning. And now I will have to live with that line repeating in my head for the rest of my life.*

"You flatter me, sir," she responded with nervous modesty.

"Not at all," he quickly countered as he stopped walking and turned to look directly at her.

No male had ever spoken to her this way. She decided to match his directness with equanimity and an audaciousness she had only previously displayed in the presence of her father. She turned to face him directly and asked without hesitation, "So will you be asking my father for his permission to court me? Or do you speak with all young ladies in this flirtatious manner?"

Mattia was unsure of how to respond to her questions. He had flirted with hundreds of women, none of whom he ever truly wanted to know. But none had ever been as quick-witted and direct as this Anamaria. They usually smiled and blushed until he flattered them more. He was visibly shaken and could tell from her smirk she enjoyed his discomfort.

"It appears, Conte, that you are unaccustomed to dealing with women who speak their minds," Anamaria surmised correctly.

Mattia opened his mouth to speak, but words escaped him. *What kind of woman is this?* Mattia thought with slight consternation at the feeling of ineptitude. He was normally equipped with a witty retort—without pause. This woman would be his ruin.

Anamaria laughed, "I fear I have struck you dumb, Conte. Have I offended you with my conjecture?"

"No, not at all!" Mattia quickly replied, "But I must admit most women have neither the wit nor the self-assurance that you clearly possess. In all my years I have not come across one like you."

Anamaria rolled her eyes at his use of the phrase 'in all my years'.

"I am sure you have met many simple women, Conte. Simple women who would do anything to secure a mere glance from you. They laugh at your jokes to ensure your attentions for a few moments, am I right? A simple woman is as easy to find in this world as a pebble on the ground."

"You have very low opinions of other women, signorina," Mattia teased. "Tell me, do you have any friends?"

He could tell he had hit a sore spot with that question, and he immediately regretted asking. Her face flushed slightly with embarrassment but quickly shifted to determination.

"The friends I hold dearest to my heart are bound in leather. They have neither the words to wound me as you so clearly wish to do, nor the gall to make presumptuous conjectures about how I live my life. They keep me company when I am lonely and fill me with wisdom when I need such. Apart from my books, I count my sister and father my closest friends. They seem to understand my whims and moods more clearly than any others I have known. So pardon me if I choose to be more selective with the company I keep than most women my age." She took a deep breath and turned her eyes downward. Sadness was the only emotion he could discern in her expression.

"My father calls me an 'old soul' and wishes to marry me off to men over twice my age. I cannot give him a reason to reject the offers, yet I know I would be miserable in either situation. You have proven you are a presumptuous sort of man. Surely you can concoct a reason I should be tamed by a life tethered to an old man. Or are you now silent? Have my 'wit and self-assurance' finally scared you off? Or do you yet wish for more?" she asked quietly, with an oddly defiant expression.

Mattia's jaw had dropped open at some point in her discourse. How many questions did she leave open for him to answer? He thought for a short moment before responding. "I appreciate that you are selective with your friends, and I too count my books as some of my closest companions. I am never far from a stocked library if I can help it. I, too, keep only my family in my closest confidence as they have proven time and time again to be the only trustworthy souls in my life. It is clear your father is correct about your 'old soul' as he calls it, but what a waste your life would be in the company of a withering, old man. You deserve to find a fellow soul to match yours—one to bring out the youth that lies beneath your beautiful surface. You are full of passion and vigor and *life*; to waste all those lovely traits on someone who cannot even travel for fear of death would certainly be a waste of what could be a life of great adventure. I can think of only one reason you should not marry either of those old men, and I am standing before you. I *am* presumptuous, but only because in all my years of existence you are the first exception to the rule, the first color in a world of beige, the first light in a world of dark. Colorless and gloomy has been my life until this moment. And of your wit and pointed opinions—they are a test of mind that I am honored to meet face-to-face. I have ne'er encountered a woman who would challenge me so. And if you think that I could ever be persuaded to run from you, you are thoroughly mistaken. I will always wish for more of you, you lovely, passionate creature. *Always*," he finished, slightly out of breath.

Anamaria looked invigorated and appeased by his discourse. He responded to every part of her speech, and still she looked as if she had more to say. "Then ask not permission to court me, sir."

Mattia felt as if she had trampled his heart with a thousand bulls. This was certainly not the response he expected.

She continued with a smile at his dejected expression, "I know this may seem peculiar, and forgive me if I exceed the boundaries of what is acceptable from a lady; but if you spoke truthfully from your heart, I would request that you tell my father it is your intention to marry me. It makes no sense in my head, yet I know I need no further proof of where and with whom my life should be spent. I do not ask for a quick engagement. I would love nothing more than to know you more intimately, but my father is set on marrying me off to an older gentleman as soon as possible. If you were amenable to a marriage, I would not only spend the rest of my life at your side but be free of a most unwelcome match."

Mattia nearly fell to his knees before her at that petition. This was the woman he had been waiting for since his birth. No woman had ever looked him so directly in the eyes nor addressed him with such intensity—or lack of formality for that matter. She was made for him, and he for her. He knew without doubt there would never be another woman for him—not for the rest of his immortal existence.

He closed the distance between them, gently grasped both her shoulders and declared with fervor, "If your father asked me to slay armies or become a servant in his household or toil for years in his mines to but look upon your perfect face from a distance each day, my answer would be 'yes'. I am terrified of what lengths I might travel to have your hand in marriage."

She smiled the most incredible smile as she dropped her book to the ground, placed both her hands over his, and stared into his eyes without speaking. He studied every part of her face: memorized the curve of her brow, the crinkle of skin next to her smiling brown eyes, the way her dark curls fell gently on her temple. She was *his*. Truly, this woman was his. After a few quiet moments, he grabbed both of her hands, brought them to his lips, and placed a lingering kiss on each of her palms. When he released them, she bent to pick up her book and turned to carry on down the road. She waited until he stepped to her side before continuing the walk. They exchanged smiling glances the whole way to the seamstress's shop, but had no further conversation. Everything that needed to be spoken between them had been. When they arrived, Mattia grabbed and kissed her hand softly, reluctantly let it go, and turned to walk away from what he knew was the only woman he would ever love.

Ten

MATTIA FELT his nerves churning inside his entire body with every step he took in the direction of the Serrano home. He knew it was customary to write a letter asking for a father's permission to court a young lady. But because his intention was set on marriage, he felt a personal visit was necessary.

As he approached the door, he stopped for a moment to consider the implications of this course of action. He would be asking permission to marry a woman he barely knew. A woman who had no idea that he was immortal—or that he was an assassin for that matter. She might fear him when he told her the truth about his Family. He hoped she would allow him to explain. But this engagement was *her* idea. *My brothers are going to kill me.* He swallowed his fears, approached the door, and knocked.

"Conte Trapani!" Signore Serrano said as he opened the door. "What an unexpected surprise! How can I help you?" he asked as he stepped aside and waved Mattia into the house.

"I am sorry I did not send notice, signore, but I am here to speak with you about a delicate matter. I thought it best if I came directly to you," Mattia said nervously.

"Of course," Signore Serrano said, confusion thick in his tone. "Please sit down. My wife and daughters are in town and my son is away for the day."

The man nodded to Mattia, encouraging him to begin, yet Mattia had no idea how to broach the issue.

"I came to inquire," he paused, cleared his throat, and began again. "I came to ask you if it might be possible ...." The break in formalities of what he was about to ask Anamaria's father was enough to induce vomiting. He was petrified to ask the man sitting in front of him for his daughter's hand in marriage for fear of rejection. And Mattia was never afraid of anything.

"Please, be at ease," Signore Serrano said gently. "I can see you are troubled. I may be wealthy, but there is no need for formality in this home. Take comfort. You need not worry."

Mattia sighed deeply, closed his eyes, and spoke with what he hoped came out as fervor.

"I wish to marry Anamaria. She is the most beautiful creature I have ever beheld. She carries herself with dignity and grace. And since meeting her at the gala, I can think of nothing else. She has no match," he said as he opened his eyes to peek at her father.

The man sat absolutely still, his face unreadable. Mattia searched for any hint of emotion—anger, excitement, agony, joy—but found none. It was several minutes before the man's eyes met Mattia's in a thoughtful stare.

"Does Anamaria have any idea of your intentions?" he asked solemnly.

"She does," Mattia responded, not wishing to harm Anamaria by telling her father that the concocting of the plan was, in fact, entirely her doing.

"And she seems happy to go along with this engagement?" Serrano asked, bewildered.

"Yes, signore. She seemed immensely happy at the prospect," Mattia said, with a smirk he could not hide.

"Then I shall have some words with my daughter when she returns home. I will give my answer only after I have spoken with her," Serrano said with finality.

"Thank you, signore," Mattia said with an outstretched hand. Signore Serrano grasped the hand firmly and smiled.

"I have been hoping that a young man would come into her life," he admitted. "She has already refused offers from older men. She is too full of life to be wasted on a man my age. But before you, it seemed no young men were interested." Serrano paused, looking Mattia over for a moment. "What is your living? Where do you intend to reside? Can you provide for her if she accepts your offer?" he asked.

"My living is my family business. My father and his father before him built a successful business dealing in trades. My uncles, brothers and cousins are all a part of it. We're quite successful around the world—we even trade in the Americas and the Indies. We have large estates in Milan and Florence. My intention would be to split our time between my home in Italy and your home here—if we are welcome, of course," Mattia paused for an answer.

"Of course, of course," Serrano quickly agreed.

"Then we shall see your family often, I hope. I cannot promise that we shall never be taken far away for business, but at present, I have no plans to make a permanent home away from Italy. And I can assure you, I am prepared financially for a wife. My family will shout for joy when they see I have finally chosen a wife. I believe they feared I would never find someone to settle down with," he laughed. "I would ask that if she accepts, we may enjoy a private engagement period. I am ready to be wed to her tomorrow, but I believe she will be happier to wait and keep the relationship private for a time. Whenever she feels ready, I will be happy to make the betrothal a public affair," Mattia said carefully. He would run around the city, shouting the news to the heavens if it were not for his brothers and his upcoming contract. But subtlety and discretion would be key if he wanted to fulfill his contract without suspicion.

"We will leave everything up to Anamaria. I will only announce the engagement once she has told me it is her desire for others to know. She is a mature young woman. I would never give my approval so quickly to a man that Isabel selected. But if Anamaria believes you are worthy of her hand, far be it from me to object," Serrano smiled. "I will warn you—she is extremely hard-headed. She is compelling and quick-witted. And you will likely walk away from all your quarrels wondering how you once again lost to a woman so decidedly." Signore Serrano began laughing at the idea of Mattia trying to win an argument with his daughter.

Little does he know, Mattia thought smugly. He was just as hard-headed as Anamaria—which he knew from their earlier conversation. It simply took an equally quick-witted and compelling response to disarm her.

"I am sure you are right," Mattia replied with a smirk. "I hereby relinquish my rights to winning quarrels if it means securing her happiness." He had spoken the words in jest until the realization of their truth struck him—he would do anything to make her happy.

"Good. Good," Serrano chuckled as he poured them both glasses of wine. They remained in the study, laughing and talking, while Mattia perused Serrano's library until they heard the front doors open.

"Father?" Anamaria called.

"I am in my study," Serrano called back.

"Has anyone been by to see you today?" she asked as she burst through the door, her face flush with color. Mattia was standing in the corner, looking at a rare collection of ancient books, and she had not yet noticed him. He turned to watch the exchange and remained silent.

"Indeed," Serrano replied with a smirk. "Someone has recently been by to have a most interesting conversation concerning you, actually." He tried to act as if there were important documents on his desk that warranted more attention than the subject at hand. Anamaria cleared her throat impatiently, fully aware that her father was teasing her. "I understand you have made your own arrangements for marriage?" he said, scolding her with a teasing tone.

"Well," she sighed with a twinkle in her eye, "he is the most handsome man I have ever seen. From the first time my eyes beheld him, I knew he was different from any other man I had ever seen. He carries himself with the dignity of a nobleman, without any of the pride most nobles think is their right."

Mattia was surprised by the words of adoration. Their earlier discourse had been passionate—and at times hostile—but he could see her affections ran deeper than she had allowed him to know that morning. He hung on every pause, every sigh, every flush of her cheeks. He desperately wanted to ask her to continue—with each word he fell further under her spell. He forced himself to remain still so she could continue undisturbed.

"He has looked at no other woman in Madrid since his arrival—I am sure of this because Isabel kept her eyes trained on him. She had her friends following him around the city and reporting back to her. Of course, I tried to get her to stop that absurdity, but I must admit I am astonished and flattered by his devotion. With every report of his actions, I lost more of my heart. And when we were finally able to speak, he was direct and unflappable. I scolded him, and he did not run away. He met my discourse with vigor. He is well-educated and … please, Father. Please tell me you are considering him," she pleaded.

Signore Serrano let out a small giggle.

"Why are you laughing at me? I know I have not been romantic for the whole of my life, but once I was forced to consider my own future, romance seemed the only thing that mattered. Do you find me so ridiculous that I should fall in love with an attractive man? And you know he has wealth, though I would care not if he were poor. But I know you want me to marry a man with a secure future," she added.

The Signore broke into a full laugh, and Mattia could not help but smile at his amusement. Anamaria grew more anxious with every burst of laughter from her father. Her eyes narrowed as she demanded that he explain himself.

"My dearest daughter," Serrano said between laughs, "You have my permission and my blessing. Now turn around and embrace your dear conte," he barely got out as he broke into laughter once more.

Anamaria's face turned bright red as she slowly turned to her right. Her eyes were massive as they found Mattia standing in the corner. Mattia, afraid that she might storm out of the room in embarrassment, closed the gap between them and scooped her up into his arms. He kissed her cheek and her forehead and whispered in her ear, "I cannot wait to call you my wife." Her returning embrace was confirmation of her own excitement.

Mattia had met his match. Finally, after one hundred seventy-four years on this earth, he found a woman he could truly love. He released her from the embrace and looked into her eyes. The excitement he saw was a perfect reflection of his own feelings. She fit perfectly in his arms, and he wondered how he had overlooked her incredible body before this moment. He had done a full study of her exquisite facial features the first time he beheld her beauty, but her body was equally wonderful. It was proportionately correct in every way: her waist not too skinny yet not too large, her bosom full enough for any man's liking, her shoulders just the right width to maintain a feminine form without appearing slight. He was used to towering over the people around him, but Anamaria's spirited personality somehow made her seem taller than her actual height. He smiled blissfully for a moment before addressing her father.

"May I steal your daughter away for a walk, signore?" Mattia asked as he reached for Anamaria's delicate hand.

"Yes, yes. I am certain there will be plenty of romantic outings and dialogues and goings-on now. See that she is safe," Serrano said with a dismissive wave of his hand. As they exited the study, they could still hear her father's laughter.

Anamaria was astonished that this was not a dream. In less than a week, her life was transformed from a battle against her father over which old man she would be marrying, to a victorious celebration over her new engagement. Conte Mattia de Trapani would be her husband! She looked up at her betrothed and smiled widely. The look he gave her instantly melted her heart. He adored her. He was hers. Her fantasy of being swept off her feet by a hero worthy of one of her books was coming to fruition. She could not believe it was true.

"Come, let us walk together," she heard him say through the foggy haze of bliss that clouded her mind. He allowed her to lead him out the back of the house into the large family garden. They walked hand in hand for hours, saying very little.

"I wanted to ask: would it be possible for us to keep our engagement private until I have had an opportunity to speak with my family? I do not wish you to believe I am unwilling to spread the good news. I only know that my family would prefer the news to come directly from me," he said, hopeful Anamaria would agree.

"It is all happening so quickly, I am sure we would be the center of all gossip if we announced it immediately. We shall remain silent on the matter until we both agree the time is right," she said with finality.

Over the course of the next fortnight, Anamaria and Mattia stole away together whenever possible. They would meet in the forest behind Mattia's home for quiet picnics where they would discuss literature at great lengths. They strolled through the town together, mindlessly browsing through shops. They spent evenings with Anamaria's family in her home so her parents would know they were respecting all the boundaries that an unwed couple should adhere to.

They asked each other countless questions about how they were raised, their likes and dislikes, favorite books, and childhood memories. Every night they said their goodbyes, each bemoaned the parting, counting the hours until they would see one another again.

Mattia felt a constant nagging in the back of his mind to tell his love about his true, immortal nature and the family business. But the timing was always wrong for one reason or another. He tried to distract himself by focusing on more pleasant matters—which he considered of equal importance.

He spent hours staring at Anamaria's lips. He wanted to know how they felt under the pressure of his own. He had been careful to maintain a respectful physical distance until the marriage, but he did not know how much longer he could resist the urge to carry her away and make love to her. They had already declared their intentions to be married; he was ready to publicly announce the upcoming marriage in front of God and everyone.

"I am going to speak with my family today," he said during one of their picnics. A gleam of excitement lit his eyes. "I do not want to wait any longer to marry you."

Anamaria's expression changed from joy to exhilaration as he spoke. She nodded vigorously and clutched him in an enormous hug as her eyes filled with tears. She did not speak, but her body shook with sobs of joy as she held him closely.

Mattia was delighted that she shared his feelings so strongly. He kissed her gently on the cheek and hurriedly packed up their things so he could walk her back to her home.

"I will return as soon as I have spoken with my family. I do not know how long it will take. But know that I am thinking of you—my dearest love—every minute we are separated," he said as he kissed her forehead and turned to leave.

"Do not tarry, my love," Anamaria called after him as she watched him depart.

ELEVEN

MATTIA NEARLY RAN to the home outside of town where his brothers were staying. He could not believe after so many years of living, he had actually found a woman of true worth. He thought of nothing but her angelic beauty night and day. He knocked once on the door before entering.

His mood abruptly changed when he saw his brothers' faces. They were ready for work—for death; he was ready to confess his undying love for the woman of his dreams. His brothers were confused by his jovial appearance, but Marcus solemnly handed over the sealed document.

"Your contract arrived by courier not ten minutes ago," Marcus said proudly. Antonio quickly added, "You can open it in private if you choose."

Mattia took the envelope from his brother, nodded silently to both, and turned to leave the house without a word. This was neither the time nor place to tell his brothers of his upcoming marriage, and had he opened his mouth he feared jubilant love songs would come pouring out. He had a job to do, and he would complete the contract with expediency so he could get back to marrying Anamaria.

He walked home with a slight swagger in his step. His first contract made his position in the Family official. He would finally be free to call himself an assassin, a true member of the Family. The few members of the Family that were not assassins held positions in strategizing, reconnaissance, and reviewing possible contracts—all important positions. But prior to today, Mattia held no position at all. He was simply an 'assassin-in-training'.

He arrived home to a man at his front door. Mattia walked towards the man and realized it was Carvajal.

"Hello there!" Mattia yelled from a distance. Carvajal turned and smiled when he heard the sound.

"Hello, Mattia," Carvajal responded when he was closer, "May I speak with you?"

"Of course, friend," Mattia answered with false enthusiasm. His only goal right now was to break the seal of the contract in his coat and begin planning the assassination of a king. But he decided to be a gentleman and accommodate his friend's visit. "What brings you to my house this fine evening?" he asked.

"I wanted to apologize about my behavior at the gala a fortnight ago," Carvajal began. "It would appear you have shown interest in the woman I have loved for the past year," he said with a look of resignation. "I know she is the most beautiful woman in the world. And if you are interested, she will surely be more amenable to you. But I must warn you there are other men trying to win her heart as well."

Mattia's heart broke. For as surely as he was immortal, this man—his friend—had come to offer Anamaria to him. To turn in his resignation from her pursuit. *And*, to warn him of her other suitors. "You give up too easily, my friend," Mattia countered. "You are a man of worth; a man of great intellect, social ability and work ethic. You have no reason to lack confidence, yet I see that you do! What woman has wounded you so deeply that you fear them all now?"

Carvajal was visibly surprised at this turn in conversation. He had evidently come here only to confirm his suspicions, not to be reinvigorated in his affections. He stood for a moment, thinking before responding, "I have never met a beauty before Anamaria who could handle herself with the same maturity and poise in any situation. She is the only one. I am sure of this."

Mattia nodded solemnly. He knew Carvajal was right. And Mattia knew Anamaria wanted only to be wed to him. She had mentioned older suitors in her first discourse with him—though he did not previously know of whom she spoke. Carvajal possessed more life than any other mortal fifty year-old he had met. He had much more life in him yet. But Anamaria would not be a part of it. "I am sorry, my friend," Mattia offered. "Had I known of your affections, I would never have endeavored to introduce myself to her."

Carvajal knew he spoke the truth. The look on his face was one of best wishes and friendship. "I do hope you make her happy, my friend," Carvajal said with a resigned finality. With his declaration of support, accompanied by the overwhelming sadness of defeat, he walked silently away.

Mattia could not believe how rapidly his day had changed since his lunchtime picnic. How amazing it was that a day could bring so many twists and turns.

He remembered the contract, and ran inside and up the large staircase to sit down on the edge of his bed. He removed his coat and retrieved the contract from the inner pocket where it was stowed away. A sense of pride washed over him when he saw the seal of Priest on the parchment. He was going to slay a king. He broke the seal and unrolled the paper.

As he read the words written on the page, the pride and honor he had felt for his position and Family only seconds before melted away. He could hardly comprehend the emotions which rapidly overcame his entire being. Horror and astonishment seeped up from his chest and washed across his face like a cloud of black smoke rising over a city, covering everything in a dreadful, impenetrable cloud. This had to be a mistake. This could not be an actual contract sent from the Family. "No!" he screamed. He paced around the room, reading and re-reading the words that should never have been written. He let the contract fall to the floor along with his hot angry tears. "No! No! No! No! No!" he continued to wail. He stormed through his house, breaking everything in sight. He smashed the dining room chairs over the table until there was nothing left but splinters of wood. He ripped the curtains from every window, and used a knife to slash through every painting. No matter what he did to his broken home, nothing could quell the suffering in his heart. He walked back to his room, shoulders hunched, head hung, and picked up the contract from the floor. "No." he whispered with finality as he lay back on his bed and drifted into a calm state of determination. This would not be his first contract. This would not be a contract at all.

Twelve

Mattia's fury knew no bounds. He marched to his brothers' home and entered without knocking.

"Are you aware of the content of this contract?" he roared, as he threw the contract on the table where they were eating supper.

The brothers looked at each other in astonished confusion then carefully reached for the contract as if Mattia might strike them if they made any sudden movements. Antonio wore an expression of confusion and sadness as he read the contract, Marcus one of anger.

"The whole family?" Antonio asked.

Mattia nodded silently.

"This is indeed a strange request. I have never heard of someone placing a contract on an entire family," Marcus added.

Mattia allowed his brothers to continue reading. When they came to the end of the document, each raised their eyebrows at the last few sentences. The assassinations were to be carried out in a specific way. This was not a simple assassination. This was a massacre, and he was supposed to be framing an innocent man for the entire slaughter.

"Who would approve this contract?" Antonio questioned. "Surely this was not sent by Priest or Saint?"

"Look at the seal," Marcus said as he held up the scroll and pointed. "It is the seal of Priest."

"This is madness!" Mattia yelled. "If this is what I must do to be a part of this Family, I would rather leave and find a different life!" he screamed with an anguish his brothers had not heard from him before.

"Tell me, brother, where is this anguish coming from? Is there more to this story you are not telling us?" Antonio asked.

"Yes, my brothers. Yes. Much more," Mattia conceded.

He spent the next two hours telling Marcus and Antonio all the events since the night he met Carvajal. He spared no detail, omitted no emotion. His brothers' faces acknowledged each part of the story with vivid expressions: impressed by his initial self-control, angry that he allowed himself to be distracted by a woman, confused over his feelings of adoration toward a complete stranger, amused at Anamaria's scolding, happy at the prospect of Mattia finally settling down, and anguished at the possible loss of his future bride. They felt as he felt because they knew him better than any others in existence.

When Mattia completed the story, Marcus grabbed his shoulders firmly and proclaimed with vigor,

"We will fight this together, little brother. We will petition the Council to come, and we will stand with you and tell them this is not a contract of worth, no matter how much was paid for its completion. We will overturn it together.

"I will not allow you to be forced to assassinate the woman you love and her entire family, only to have your friend framed for the murders. This shall not come to pass."

Thirteen

Mattia's brothers and father arrived first for the gathering. Marcus and Antonio relayed to their father the particulars of the situation before their arrival. The expression he wore on his face each time he looked at Mattia was a mix of concern and sorrow. No father would want their child to be in this situation, but Mattia was sure it was worse in this case because of the bond he and his brothers shared with their father. His father was a moral man, a brilliant teacher, and as close to a perfect father as any son could wish for. But because of the centuries they had spent as adults together, they had grown closer still as brothers. Mattia and his brothers came to their father for advice as much as he came to them. More than the blood that ran through their veins, it was a deep bond of brotherhood that connected the four men.

Within five days' time, Mattia's grandfather and nine uncles joined the assembly at Mattia's mansion. Although he was happy to be one step closer to overturning the acceptance of this contract, he was *not* happy about his grandfather's presence in his home. Mattia was determined to keep his gaze from even glancing over his grandfather's face. He was certain this situation would surely end the goodwill he once felt for the ancient one.

His grandfather—whom the entire family simply called Priest—looked older somehow despite his fixed age of thirty-five years. Mattia had never seen the man look so drawn. It had been nearly fifty years since he last met with Priest, and in the time since, something had changed. Priest had an aura of ... *is it bitterness?* Mattia tried to figure out the change as he watched his grandfather interacting with his uncles and father. Surely this was not the same man who taught him how to swing a sword and draw a bow, and told him and his brothers stories of ancient rulers and battles in kingdoms long gone. The man before him was nothing more than a whisper—a shadow. He was a man who had seen too much, lost too much, and given up his will to survive.

Priest summoned the assassins into the room to begin the meeting. "Sergius," Priest called to his eldest son, "please attend to the issue we earlier discussed." Sergius nodded and left the home without a word. The rest of the assassins sat around the giant dining table. There was a formality even in the arrangement of the assassins out of millennia of tradition. To the right of Priest, where Sergius usually sat, was the second eldest, Paulus, then Gregorius and Elias—the twins, then his father, Thomas, followed by Claudius, Felix, Alexander, Demetrius, and Samuel—Priest had fathered all his sons during the rule of the Roman Empire. Finally, Mattia and his brothers sat—Marcus first, then Antonio and Mattia. Age was honored in this family above all else. Mattia had always found it humorous that despite being over two thousand years of age, his grandfather looked no older than a man in his thirties. And he and all his uncles had stopped aging around twenty-seven or twenty-eight years. They looked like brothers rather than men who were born centuries apart.

"I call this meeting of the Council to order," Priest announced loudly, to end any conversation that had been in progress.

All fourteen men spoke together:

> "We stand united, Family of Immortals. Plagued by life. Cursed by the hand of God. We pledge our lives to the Family, the Priest and the Saint."

Priest sat silently for a few moments, all eyes affixed to his face, before speaking. He looked directly into Mattia's eyes, took a deep breath, and began quietly.

"You have disgraced the Family. Since our beginning, no assassin has refused a contract. Nor has one had the audacity to call a Council meeting to discuss the merits of such. You, who are the least of us, the youngest of us, the only unproven of your brothers, think you have a right to question your first contract? I thought my beloved Thomas raised assassins, not spineless children of entitlement. What reason have I to address this issue?" By the time he finished speaking, he was yelling, face deep red with anger.

Mattia's father spoke up quickly, "My great father—*I* called this meeting only after my eldest son spoke to me of the situation. *I* was the one who thought this matter merited a meeting of the Council. If you will only hear the story in full," he turned to look at each of the brothers around the table, "you, too, will call for this contract to be rejected."

The men around the table each nodded slightly to show their approval of further discussion. Mattia sighed in relief and relaxed a bit. If they took the time to hear his justification, surely they would allow him this refusal without penalty or resentment. He realized everyone was waiting for his explanation.

He told them the same story he had told his brothers two nights prior. He spared no details. These men did not shy away from emotion as Mattia had witnessed in other men he encountered. They were not embarrassed by Mattia's confession of love for Anamaria. Many of them had experienced similar feelings throughout their lives—some many times over. When one is an immortal, the mortal loves you have in life last but a breath in an endless life. Some of his uncles found a new love each century. Mattia was certain he would never love again, but he hoped Anamaria's life would be long enough to enjoy at least one lifetime of peaceful happiness. Perhaps they would even have children together. He smiled at the thought of Anamaria carrying his sons. By the time he reached the part of the story where he revealed that the contract directed him to kill not only his fiancée as well as her entire family, but *also* frame his friend for their murders, his uncles all wore looks of concern.

Paulus spoke up, "Priest, I request a full review of the contract. Please convey unto us everything you know about it." The men around the table all voiced their agreement and looked at Priest to begin.

Though he was visibly angry at having to explain his acceptance of the contract, Priest acquiesced to his sons' request.

"Several months ago, I was contacted by a man named the Marqués de la

Ensenada. He heard of our Family through an Italian friend who knew of his situation. When I received the letter, his appeal was fairly vague. He wrote that there was another in his government who put his relations with the Portuguese queen at risk. When I asked for further explanation he illuminated the situation. The man—Jose de Carvajal y Lancaster—was authoring a contract which would settle a disagreement with the Portuguese over land in the Americas. The treaty would provide Spain with more land in Brazil than the Portuguese, but Ensenada requires the support of the Portuguese queen to stay in power. He fears this treaty will destroy him." Priest paused to catch his breath.

"Why, then, kill the Serrano family?" Paulus interjected.

Priest continued, "Because he needs to ruin Jose de Carvajal y Lancaster fully. He, like Mattia here, is smitten with the Serrano girl. Ensenada knows this and set Anamaria's father on a path which made him believe Ensenada, too, would be pursuing his daughter's hand in marriage. Ensenada's plan is to have the entire Serrano family murdered. He will then go, brokenhearted, to the king to reveal that he himself loved the Serrano girl, and that upon his confession of this love to his 'friend' Jose de Carvajal y Lancaster, Carvajal killed the entire family out of jealousy and hatred. I thought nothing of the contract. I still think nothing of it. It is for political gain; which, as all of you know, many of our contracts are hinged upon. Would you have declined the contract, my sons?" Priest finished with an expression of absolute innocence.

"We have never accepted a contract to kill an entire family, Father," Mattia's father vehemently said. "Especially not in a situation where the family does not pose a direct threat to the parties involved in the dispute. I move that this contract be cancelled."

Some of the men around the table were visibly shaken by the story. Mattia was not the only man upset by this blatant break in Family protocol. He could see dissention in the Family's future. Authority would be questioned now— something that had never been done since the beginning. The men around the table began voicing their agreement with Mattia's plea for the contract's cancellation until every man sponsored his cause.

Mattia noted that his grandfather wore an odd look upon his face. It almost looked like … triumph? But his contract was overturned by his own sons. Mattia could not fathom why Priest was unmoved.

At that moment, Sergius barged in the door and stomped to a halt next to Priest. "It is done," Sergius reported.

The men around the table looked at each other questioningly. They had not thought anything of Sergius having been sent on an assignment until this moment.

"Good," Priest said with a smirk. "And who was home?"

"The mother, son, and one daughter," he answered without hesitation.

"Wait," Mattia jumped out of his seat and yelled. "What have you done?" he asked Sergius, fearful of the answer. "What have you done?" he screamed at Priest angrily. He looked back and forth between his confused uncle and smug grandfather, desperate for an answer.

"The contract is fulfilled to the best of our ability. There shall be no more discussion here today," Priest said with a delighted air of finality.

"No!" Mattia let out a savage scream as he sprinted out the door and down the path to Anamaria's house. He vaguely heard angry shouts coming from the house behind him. This would put a chasm in the Family—the likes of which they had never seen.

Fourteen

Mattia arrived at the Serrano house in time to hear shrieks of agony coming from inside. He burst through the front door, shouting for Anamaria. He followed the screaming sobs up the stairs and approached a room covered in blood. He walked into the room and had to grab the wall to keep himself upright.

On the floor in front of him, Signore Serrano was cradling his wife's dead body, rocking back and forth, staring at his dead children. Tears streamed down his grimacing face. Next to him, Isabel sat on the ground, holding her knees tightly to her chest. She alternated wailing, sobbing and screaming while looking around at the scene.

Mattia understood their pain. His own face was already covered in tears.

"No," he gasped.

The two looked up at him with grief-stricken eyes. Signore Serrano shook his head as a confirmation of Anamaria's death. Mattia rushed to her beautiful limp body as her sister shrieked in anguish.

Mattia had never wept this way. He had never cherished a mortal, never yearned for the intimacy of a shared life, and never loved another so completely in his long life. The pain was too great for him to bear.

He pushed his forehead against her cold cheek and whispered, "You cannot be dead. This cannot be. Come back. Please. Come back to me."

Fifteen

New York City, Present Day

ROGUE SNAPPED back into consciousness. *What the hell was that?* he thought, taking in his surroundings. He had just vividly relived the part of his life he had been trying to forget for the last two hundred years.

He glanced around at his surroundings and saw Ms. Renaud on the phone with 911 while Mr. Stein was running around the office grabbing pillows off lobby couches to place under his head. *The woman on the phone cannot exist!* he thought with distress. *And I cannot risk paramedics coming here and delaying this whole operation.*

Rogue jumped up in a swift move and grabbed the phone from Ms. Renaud's hand. She looked at him in shock while he spoke to the 911 operator. "I am perfectly fine," he promised. "I have low blood sugar, and I am going to eat a piece of candy and be completely fine," he added as he grabbed a handful of candy out of the bowl on Ms. Renaud's desk. He hung up the phone and looked back and forth between Ms. Renaud and Mr. Stein. They both looked as if he had died and come back to life. "Did my heart stop beating while I was out?" he joked. They didn't look appeased, and he worried about the length of his blackout. "How long was I out?"

"About three minutes," Mr. Stein replied, his face regaining some color. "We thought our biggest investor was going to die right before our eyes. Please, never come to the office without eating a big meal beforehand," he added with a slight joke in his tone. "Come on into my office and sit down," he motioned to the open door.

Rogue walked through the doorway and immediately surveyed the room for weaknesses. Four floor-to-ceiling windows lined one entire wall. Two more floor-to-ceiling windows were situated on the back wall behind the desk. There were at least three surrounding buildings with perfect vantage points of this office. He hoped the weapon of choice would be a sniper rifle. The rest of the office was clean and modern—the only table in the room was a sleek black desk with a glass top. All the chairs were white with rounded backs. The floors were made of large white marble tiles with black streaks running through them. Even the walls were white with a single small black stripe painted around the entire room about waist high. Across the room from the desk was a small seating area with one black, leather, high-back chair and a chrome floor lamp. The bookcases on the wall next to the seating area were oriented in a unique way—the books sat at an angle instead of straight up and down. *The decorator of this room is incredible*, Rogue thought.

"It seems I am going to have to get your decorator's phone number," he mused aloud.

"No need," Mr. Stein countered. "Ms. Renaud, my assistant, did all the decorating. Amazing, isn't she?" he asked.

"Indeed she is." Rogue wanted to move on from that subject. "I'm sorry we were not formally introduced before I decided to take a nap on your lobby floor. I am Matthew McCloud," he said as he offered his hand to Mr. Stein.

"And I'm Gregory Stein. We're informal over here at Stein Securities, so feel free to call me Greg," he added as he shook Rogue's hand. "Why don't you sit down and tell me what prompted your interest in my company?"

"Well," Rogue began, "My family's money has been invested and reinvested hundreds of times over the past years by different firms and in various types of investment schemes. It seems to me that it's finally time to settle down and find a secure investment where we can place a large portion of our money while maintaining the security of knowing we will have a lucrative return. And with the announcement of your company's new streamlined systems, it appears that you are offering the biggest return on investment with the greatest long-term security. With this investment, I feel that even my great-great-grandchildren will be taken care of for the rest of their lives. Am I correct?"

The two talked for hours about the various options for investments, ideas for diversifying the McCloud portfolio, and the average percentage of return offered by Stein Securities.

Rogue had played the part to perfection. Stein was fully convinced that he was ready to invest. As the meeting came to a close, Rogue thanked him for his time and stood to leave.

"I'm looking forward to working with you in the upcoming months and years," Stein said as he escorted Rogue back to the lobby.

Not likely, Rogue thought. "Absolutely," he said aloud.

Sixteen

"Please talk to Ms. Renaud about the paperwork we're going to need you to fill out. With an investment this large I'm sure you understand how long this process can take," Stein said with a smile as he showed Rogue out of his office. They shook hands one last time. "I look forward to hearing from you, Mr. McCloud," he said formally as he turned and shut the door to his office.

Rogue had been dreading this conversation from the moment he glanced at Ms. Renaud's beautiful, haunting face. He sucked in a deep breath, gathered his courage, and made his way to her desk.

As she looked up and smiled, Rogue nearly fainted a second time. She was the spitting image of Anamaria. *Focus on the differences*, he commanded himself. Her hair was straight and smooth instead of the curls Anamaria had worn. Her eyes were a brilliant deep blue rather than the dark brown Anamaria's had been. Apart from that, he could find no other discernible differences. *This is madness. No such woman should exist in the world*, he thought with a twinge of resentment. He decided at that moment that he had to understand how this was possible. He had to get to know Ms. Renaud.

"Let me get all the paperwork together for you, Mr. McCloud," Ms. Renaud said as she collected papers from her desk drawers and printer. "I just have a few more documents to print off before you can be on your way."

When she looked at him, a spark flared in his head that made him desperate to know if this woman was a reincarnation of his Anamaria. "Could I take you out for a drink after you get off work tonight?" Rogue asked, before he realized what he was doing. *Why, in God's name, did you just ask her out on a date? Are you this desperate to be tormented by your past that you would submit yourself to hours of longing and reminiscing?* He was surprised at his idiocy.

The woman looked shocked. She opened her mouth, but Rogue suddenly realized he could not bear it if her voice matched Anamaria's. He hadn't been paying close attention before when she spoke—the first time he was still in shock from his fainting episode, the second, he was distracted by how much she resembled his Anamaria. He cut her off before any words escaped her beautiful mouth; "Look, you don't have to answer now. I will be at Little Branch on 7th and Leroy." She looked slightly bewildered by his invitation, and he knew by her expression she would never show up to the bar.

She handed him the paperwork with a strange look on her face. As he turned and began walking away, she cleared her throat and quietly said, "I guess I'll see you at seven."

Seventeen

"Oh my God, oh my God, oh my God, oh my God," Lissie Renaud chanted as she walked to the subway to head home. "What did you do, Lissie?" she asked herself with a twinge of panic. She had said 'yes' to a date. *Only because he's an investor*, she thought—trying to come up with any possible explanation for her temporary insanity. Lissie had not been on a date since college. And who would really consider fast food tacos and a trip to the dollar store a date? *This is a disaster*, she thought as she walked down the stairs to hop on the 1 train. She had moved to a modest apartment near Lincoln Center after she had scored the job as Gregory Stein's executive assistant. Her college education had lent her nothing in the way of qualifications for secretarial work, but it seemed just having the worthless piece of paper that showed she had a degree and logging enough internship hours with well-known corporations was all she had really needed to get a job in the corporate world. 'Executive assistant' was a far cry from the CEO she had always dreamed of becoming. "But hey, you've gotta start somewhere," she told herself each time she felt her hopes and dreams spiraling down the drain called 'real life'.

Lissie had asked to leave work early because of this stupid date. Of course, after all the long hours she worked without complaint, Mr. Stein had readily agreed. "Why couldn't he have found a reason to keep me longer today?" she said aloud, forgetting she was on a subway surrounded by dozens of work-weary travelers. *Great*, she thought, *and now I'm the 'lunatic on the subway'*. She spared a glance around to see how many people turned to look at her like she was mentally ill, but no one even batted an eyelid.

This had been a bizarre day. This morning she had to deal with an angry phone call from Mrs. Stein about the mess her husband had left in their kitchen after breakfast. Nothing Lissie said had appeased the woman. Then, the company's largest private investor to date had come in and passed out without warning. She screamed for Mr. Stein to help and called 911. Next, the incredibly tall, dark and handsome billionaire asked her out on a date ... and she had accepted! *Madness*, she thought to herself. *This is a day of madness.*

She exited the subway and rushed toward her apartment. When she first moved to New York from Missouri six years earlier, she hadn't expected to find an apartment she could afford on her own. Friends and family had prepared her for years of roommate living, shared bathrooms, and grungy small apartments in New Jersey or the Bronx. But she had happened upon the cutest one bedroom apartment in a beautiful building on 67th Street. The place cost her less than three hundred thousand dollars (a steal for anything bigger than three hundred square feet in Manhattan). It was a total gut-job, but it was hers. She was initially apprehensive about the music school across the street, but had been happy to discover that the street noise was almost nonexistent from the eighth floor where her apartment was situated.

When she entered her building and saw her doorman, Roger, smiling at her, she was immediately at ease. "Hello, Ms. Renaud, did you have a nice day?"

"Not quite what I would call nice," she replied with a wary smile.

"I'm sure tomorrow will be better," he assured her as the elevator doors slid shut.

When she unlocked her door and stepped inside her renovated six hundred square foot space, she heaved a sigh of relief. *Home*, she smiled as she sank into her new sofa. She had spent extra time and money to maintain the historical aspects of the apartment during the renovation. She was especially careful with the original hardwood floors, built-in bookcases and arched entryways throughout the space. It took her five and a half years of penny-pinching to finish it, but now she could finally relax in her own, customized space. This modern gray sofa was the final installation in her masterpiece.

Lissie's parents had been incredibly generous with her financially—they had taken care of all her student loans so she could start her post-college life debt-free. She had always been a frugal child. From the age of six, she saved every dollar she received from her birthdays, Christmases and allowances. By the time she was sixteen she had saved over three thousand dollars in her bank account. Once she hit sixteen, her parents allowed her to get a part-time job as long as her grades didn't suffer. Her incomparable work ethic allowed her to keep her retail job for the remainder of her high school years. Perfect attendance and grades and a business-like personality made her a favorite with both her teachers and employers alike. When she was accepted into University of Missouri on a full academic scholarship, she secured a full-time job as a receptionist for a small law firm in town. She worked all year—only taking off a week for Thanksgiving and Christmas—and stayed every summer to ensure she wasn't replaced by someone else. She invested her money in various stocks starting at age fourteen—and the returns had been lucrative. By the time she finished her four-year degree, she had accumulated over two hundred thousand dollars to take with her to New York. Her social life and sleeping schedule suffered greatly because of the choices she made, but when she looked around her apartment, she knew it had all been worth it. She owned an apartment in New York City that would easily turn a huge profit after the updates she had made.

Stop stalling! she reprimanded herself as she got up to change her clothes. The whole reason she'd asked to get off work early was to ensure she would have adequate time to get home, change into something a little less 'workplace', and touch up her makeup. Now she had approximately ten minutes to do all that and get back to the subway with enough time to make it to the bar by seven o'clock.

"What to wear, what to wear," she chanted as she looked through her clothing selection. Ninety-five percent of her clothes were either for work or for lounging around the house. She pulled her only little black dress—which was still not quite right for a date—out of the closet and sighed. "I guess you're gonna have to do." She dressed quickly, threw on a gorgeous pair of black high heels, grabbed her purse, and headed out. She hadn't even had time to look at herself in the mirror—so much for checking the makeup.

On her way back downtown, a pit of dread began building in her stomach. Not only was she inexperienced at dating, she was a horrible conversationalist outside of the workplace. If she was talking about paperwork, contracts, or scheduling appointments, she was dynamite. But when it came to talking about herself ... forget it. *Why are you torturing yourself, Lissie? This is going to be a disaster,* she thought with a trepidation she hadn't felt since she put the offer in on her apartment six years earlier.

She reached for her phone and made a quick call; it unfortunately went straight to voicemail. "It's just like you to have your phone off in my time of dire need, you little brat," she said playfully. "Well don't call back when you get this. I'll call you as soon as I can, but I'll have you know I'm going on a date. Okay, okay. I know you're either going into cardiac arrest or shock, but I'll tell you about it later. Love you, brother," she said as she hit 'end' on the phone. She had desperately hoped her brother could give her some words of advice—dating was his area of expertise. Her nerves kicked into high gear once again.

When she arrived at the address Mr. McCloud had given her, she worried that she was in the wrong place. The building was narrow and run-down on the outside. When she looked at the nondescript brown door closely, she realized there was a small engraved plaque mounted above a doorbell that told her she had found the bar. *I wonder if the inside is as awful as the outside.* She thought for a moment about turning around and heading straight back to her cozy, safe apartment—free from the panic and angst she was currently feeling. Her phone vibrated in her pocket and she was thankful for an excuse to delay her entry into the bar. She hoped that the text message from her brother would bring news of some tragic event that would prevent her from going on this date.

> In a meeting. Got your message. You're right—I did almost go into cardiac arrest. But I have a feeling you're second-guessing yourself right now. Stop it this

The message cut off in the middle, and Lissie worried about what else he had to say. She stared at the phone, willing it to receive the rest of the text. When she felt it vibrate, she exhaled a breath she didn't know she had been holding.

> instant and get your ass in there. It's about time you have some fun! If you chicken out, I'll disown you ;)

Traitor, she thought. He was supposed to be on her side—even if she was being a chicken. *God, I hate it when he's right.* Her heart began racing at the realization she was about to go on a date with the richest man she had ever met. She took a deep breath, closed her eyes, and grabbed the handle of the door.

"You cannot do this. I have absolutely no faith in you whatsoever," she told herself as she turned the knob and headed inside.

Eighteen

She walked down the stairs into a gorgeous 1920s speakeasy. The rules from the original establishment were still posted and enforced—which was perfect for Lissie. She had no desire to go to a bar where a bunch of drunken twenty-one year-olds were yelling, laughing loudly and spilling drinks all over the floor; she had been dragged to too many bars like that by her college roommates. Every time she had gone out, she ended up having to babysit them, drive everyone home, and hold their hair back while they evacuated their stomachs into the toilet—it sucked to be the only responsible person in her dormitory. Most of the time she was too tired from her studies and full time job to go out, but she often succumbed to their begging because she feared for their lives otherwise.

She looked around the dimly lit bar and smiled a little at the feel of the place. Though the bar had just opened for the night and no patrons had yet arrived, she could tell the bartenders had already been working for hours to chop fresh fruit, grind up spices, and prepare the garnishes for each drink. They were dressed as if they had been transported from another era; and honestly, the ambiance made Lissie feel like she had stepped back in time.

The bathroom door opened, and Mr. McCloud walked to his table. He turned towards the front door with a look of apprehension in his eyes, which seemed odd to Lissie. His eyes flashed a look of worry or surprise—Lissie couldn't discern which in the low lighting—but he quickly masked it with a welcoming smile.

"Ms. Renaud!" he said with arms wide, "I'm happy you could make it."

"Mr. McCloud," Lissie replied formally, with a hand straight out for a handshake.

The man looked amused at her extended hand and gently took it, lifted it to his lips, and kissed it. The look he wore on his face when he kissed it was utter agony. Lissie was totally confused. She decided to chalk it up to his eccentricity and wealth—because weren't all billionaires allowed to be a little crazy?

"Please, come sit down," he gestured toward his table.

Lissie briskly walked to the table and sat down in the chair Mr. McCloud pulled out for her. She was thinking of this as more of a client meeting than a date, to keep herself from panicking. As he pushed her chair in, she could've sworn she heard him chuckle. *Why is he laughing at me?* she thought angrily. *I may not be good at this dating thing, but you don't have to make me feel like a joke!* She moaned dejectedly in her head. Oh, if only she had the courage to voice her thoughts. But that had never boded well for her—not when she had finally unleashed her wrath on the chemistry professor that saw fit to give her a 'B'—*A NONSENSICALLY UNDESERVED 'B'*—after she completed all of her assignments on time with special attention given to every detail; or when the boy upstairs tried to kiss her after a fast food date, and she announced in no uncertain terms that he had no right to act inappropriately after spending approximately two dollars on her. *Nope,* she thought, *keep it all inside. This might end pleasantly if you refrain from lecturing him. Just try to get through the night without giving him a reason to think you're a lunatic.* This was her version of a pep talk? *God, I'm a disaster.*

"Tell me how you like working for Greg," Mr. McCloud asked ... or maybe demanded? She wasn't sure what to make of that.

Maybe this isn't a date ... maybe he really wants to know more about the company he's going to give a chunk of his money to. I can work with this. Lissie mused before she spoke.

"Stein Securities has been at the forefront of investing for almost twenty years. Mr. Stein provides personal attention to all his major investors—something I'm sure you haven't seen from any other investment firms' CEOs. Would you like to know more about Mr. Stein's personal life? Or just the company itself?" she asked.

Rogue couldn't help himself this time. He let out a quiet laugh, and she glared at him with an expression he could not quite understand.

"I'm sorry, but you're an ass." she said in an indignant whisper.

"You misunderstand me," he countered as she continued to glare angrily. "I asked you here on a date. You know, a date? Chocolate? Flowers? Drinks and dinner? And when I asked you how you feel about your job, you started reciting the Stein Securities investment brochure. Did you think this was a business meeting?"

Confusion flashed across her face before she answered. "I was originally under the impression that you asked me out on a date, but your question seemed more work related," she said in a serious tone.

This is going to be interesting. This woman is less an incarnation of my Anamaria and more of 'The Ice Queen', he realized without humor. Whenever he thought of Anamaria, he could only remember her beautiful face, her passion for life, literature and love, and her adorable stubbornness. At a glance, Ms. Renaud seemed only to possess a beautiful face and a frosty disposition. *Maybe I should approach this differently,* he mused.

"Well," he began carefully, "as of this moment, the only thing I know about you is that your last name is 'Renaud' and you work for Stein Securities. I thought it appropriate to ask you about one of the only two things I know."

She looked either relieved or appeased, but because she was difficult to read, he was not sure which.

"Oh," she replied with an apologetic tone. "Well, I believe I owe you an apology for calling you an 'ass'. My name is Lisette Anamaria Renaud, but I go by Lissie. People often mistakenly call me Lizzy. But no 'z' sound. I can't stand it when people call me Lizzy."

He knew that his face could only convey grief in this moment. This was worse than he had feared. He could feel his emotions welling up inside and was worried that tears would begin to flow out of his eyes if he dwelled any longer on her name. *Say something, damn it. You are staring at her like she's a ghost ... and undoubtedly she is a ghost sent to haunt you.*

He cleared his throat and spoke again, "Lisette Anamaria. Huh. Is that a family name?" *What the hell? You are going to continue down this path? You are an absolute moron*, he yelled angrily in his mind.

Her confusion could not have been written more clearly on her face. His emotions had changed from humor to horror to polite curiosity in a matter of seconds. *She must think I'm a complete dunce.* But rather than get up and run out of the restaurant, she stayed planted in her seat and kindly answered the question.

"It is, actually. My father is originally from France. Lisette was his grandmother's name. And my mother's family is originally from Spain. The name Anamaria has been in my family for centuries," she said, as Mr. McCloud's eyes gleamed with some kind of masked emotion. She didn't know why, but suddenly she felt the urge to continue the explanation.

"It's really pretty interesting. When I was in high school I did this class project to trace my family tree. My grandparents kept some really intensive records that went all the way back to the 1600s. The name "Anamaria" came from an aunt in the 1700s that was mysteriously killed. I was fairly disturbed after learning I was named after a victim of murder, but I've since gotten over it," she said with a smile.

Lissie could not believe how easily she had just given up that bit of family history. She was a fairly private person, even with her own family. Even more surprising was the look of outright sorrow on Mr. McCloud's face. Lissie had been here for no more than five minutes and already she thought Mr. McCloud was either overly sensitive, insane, or just plain bizarre.

"I am very sorry," Mr. McCloud said after several moments, "I have a very similar story of a murdered loved one in my ... family history ... and it brings me grief to know you, also, endured that kind of pain."

"It was a distant ancestor. So please don't worry, I didn't endure it. And on top of that, there doesn't seem to be any historical record of the murder. I'm honestly not affected by it in any way. Why would I be?"

Lissie could have sworn Mr. McCloud murmured something like, "If only you knew," under his breath but had not heard him clearly enough to decipher what words he had actually spoken.

"Well, if I may be so bold, what is your first name?" Lissie asked with a smirk. She was hoping to convey to him that she did, in fact, have a cute sense of humor when she wasn't being made fun of.

Mr. McCloud smiled and said, "Of course, my name is Matthew. My parents never gave me a middle name. That was not something people did when ... I mean ... where I came from."

"And your family is originally from ... ?" she asked.

"My mother was born in Italy and insisted my brothers and I be named according to her heritage. My father is a mix of Middle Eastern and European. My grandfather is from the Middle East. We are not really sure who my father's mother was because my grandfather refuses to talk about his past, but it's obvious my father has European features. We have come to accept that he has no past, and that is good enough for us," he said with a laugh.

Lissie couldn't believe how comfortable she felt talking to this man. She was having no trouble coming up with questions to ask him. And despite the strangeness of the evening up to this point, she realized she was enjoying herself more than she had in quite some time.

"So where is your family now?" she asked, happy that the conversation was now flowing with ease.

"My brothers travel all over for business but both have permanent homes in Italy. I honestly have no idea where either of them is right now. The rest of my family is scattered across Europe. They have homes all over and rarely stay in one place for long," he replied.

"Sounds like a busy life. Tell me about your brothers; are they married? Do they have children?" she asked, happy to keep the conversation trained on him as long as possible.

"Well, I am the youngest. But we are all very close in age."

He seemed to find some sort of humor in that sentiment, but quickly continued.

"My mother was not able to have any more children after me. Marcus, my oldest brother, was married for a while. His wife passed away but gave him two children before she died. In a way, he did not fully lose her because of the kids, you know?"

She didn't know. Not one bit. But she nodded her head regardless to keep him talking.

"My other brother, Antonio, is only a few years older than me. He has never had a wife, but he has children from several different women. Like I said, he travels all over the world. And when you're as rich and handsome as the three of us are," he said with a flirtatious smile, "it is hard for women to resist."

Uh oh, Lissie thought with a grimace. 'Playboy billionaire' was taking on a whole new meaning before her very eyes. Time for some pointed questions now.

"And what about you, Matthew? Do you have women and children all over the world?" she asked with as much courage as she could muster.

"None," he replied with such graveness in his eyes, she felt as if she might become emotional.

She could tell that there would be no further explanation on that subject and decided to move on to happier topics.

"So tell me about your life. Where do you live? What do you do for fun?" She hoped that would keep him talking for a while.

"Well," he said and then paused to think for a moment, "I live in a penthouse in Chelsea when I'm in New York. But I also have several apartments around the world. I found it is easier for me to travel when I have a place to call 'home' in most of the cities I frequent for business."

He kept talking, but Lissie started to zone out of the conversation. This man had asked her out on a date. He was a billionaire. She was an assistant to a CEO. Did he think she would be an easy lay? How could she convince him that she didn't want to go home with a stranger—who was very much living up to the 'strange' part of that word? Or did she want to go home with him? He *was* incredibly handsome. And it was about time for her to let her hair down and start getting out there. She looked closely at all his features. He was visibly muscular in his arms and shoulders. In fact, upon further examination, he was pleasing in every way. His bright green eyes burned with intensity; even in the low light of the bar, she could see that he was a passionate man. Sad. Wounded, even. But passionate. When he spoke about travelling for his work, he almost looked conflicted. His chiseled jaw would clench and relax while he talked about the things that made him happy or displeased. He was essentially an emotionally open book. He made no attempt to hide anything—which Lissie found quite endearing for some reason. His skin paid homage to his parentage —the tone was clearly from the Middle Eastern heritage mixed with Italian, *and maybe some Spanish?* she wondered.

Lissie realized he had finished answering her previous questions. "So, do you have one city in particular that you think of as more of a home than the others?"

"No, no, no," he replied with a playful smile and a raised hand. "You have had your fair share of questions. Now it's my turn."

Nineteen

Rogue hoped that his candidness would prove fruitful with this woman. He hoped he could get ample information out of her now that he had answered all her questions first.

"Why don't you tell me about your family?" he said.

She sighed as if she were uncomfortable talking about herself at any length and began, "Parents are still married, and I have one brother."

"Really?" he laughed. "That is all you are going give me here? Details, please."

She seemed to contemplate her answer for a bit before speaking. Her expression was mischievous as she began. "You want details? Alright. As I said earlier, my mother is from Spanish descent, but her grandparents came over from Europe in the early 1900s. My father's family has been in the U.S. since the 1800s, and they're all from France." She smiled teasingly; a triumphant expression gleamed in her eyes. She was going to be more difficult to crack than he had hoped.

Rogue tried his best to think of a way to question Lissie that would force her to open up about herself. But as he looked into her beautiful blue eyes, he began to drown in the ocean he saw there. *It really is incredible,* he thought. *Another, equally beautiful Anamaria.* He quickly looked away to avoid the emotions that were dangerously close to breaking through his carefully built walls.

The bar was starting to fill up with patrons and they had yet to order any drinks. He had frequented this speakeasy enough that the bartenders knew he would tip several hundred dollars even if he only ordered a drink or two, but he decided to call one over to take their orders.

"I'm not finished with you—I want to know more. But first, what would you like to drink?" he asked Lissie as the bartender walked over to take their orders.

"I'm actually not much of a drinker. So why don't you just bring me something alcoholic that doesn't really taste like alcohol," she said, as if she were embarrassed.

Rogue looked up and added, "Why don't you make six or seven drinks of your choice, and we'll see what the lady prefers." The bartender smiled at the challenge and immediately turned to get to work.

"Thank you for that," Lissie timidly said. "I really have no idea what I'm doing when it comes to alcohol." She giggled a little and added softly, "Or men."

Rogue watched as her face turned deep red. She slowly turned her wide eyes up to meet his and added, "I cannot believe I just said that. That was an inner dialogue gone very wrong."

She looked down and around and anywhere but his face. He could not help but let out a small laugh before replying, "Believe me, you do not want to hear the tormented inner dialogue that is happening in my head. It seems we are both a mess in this department." He smiled as she looked back at him. He hoped she could read the sincerity on his face. He had not even looked at another woman this way since he lost his Anamaria.

"If you don't mind me asking, why are you rusty in the dating department?" he asked her with an encouraging smile.

Oh God. She knew she was going to answer all his questions. He'd already made her feel much less awkward about her inexperience. She didn't believe a word he said about his own dating life being a mess. *Look at him!* she marveled silently. *He's a god. He's probably got women crawling to him on their knees, trying to kiss his feet.* But it was sweet of him to make her feel better about her own issues.

"I'm a loner. I'm too goal-oriented," she blurted out, "A bona fide geek. I took studying way too seriously growing up. I didn't have many friends because I was always doing some extracurricular activity that would make my transcripts look better. I decided to start saving all my money when I was six years old, and I never stopped. I never wanted to go to the movies with kids from school because it would mean spending money that I was saving for my future. When I graduated from high school, my mom took me on a trip to New York, and I knew this was where I wanted to be. I worked part-time during high school and full-time while I was in college. I didn't have time to go on dates with the schedule I maintained. And once I got my degree and moved up here, all I made time to do was work and finish remodeling my apartment. I spent all the money I saved growing up on a cute little apartment in the Upper West Side, but it was a total gut-job. It took me five and a half years to finish the remodel. And consequently, my social life is nonexistent. My co-workers don't even ask me to go out with them for drinks anymore because my answer for five and a half years was, 'No, I have to get back to work on the apartment', or, 'No, I have to put every cent I make into my remodel'. So now I'm stuck with a beautiful apartment that I absolutely love and no friends to share it with. And I am so sorry I just unloaded on you like that!" she added, despite the fact that she was happy to have gotten it off her chest after so long.

"I'm happy you did," he replied kindly. "It is nice to know I'm not the only one alone in this city."

Oh no. You're actually going to fall for that mushy crap, aren't you? He's totally full of it! But you're going to choose to believe him? This will not end well. But honestly, what's the real harm in getting attached to a tall, handsome billionaire who claims to be lonely? Nothing. She made her mind up. She would ride out this wave and throw caution to the wind.

The bartender arrived with a tray full of beautiful drinks in all different glasses. He pointed out what each one was, and left them to try the drinks in peace. Lissie sipped each drink suspiciously. There was one that tasted more like a spicy sauce than a drink. Matthew laughed at her disgusted expression and happily took it away from her to finish it. After tasting all the drinks, she decided there were two she liked best—one that had hints of raspberry and ginger (which she was certain was a virgin, because it did *not* taste like there was any alcohol in there) and another that tasted like strawberry and mint. No less than two minutes from her first sip, she could already feel her mental capacities begin to slow. Thankfully, the conversation stuck to the drinks while she figured out her favorites. Despite her protests, Matthew ordered another round of her favorites after she finished her first two glasses. She knew she would regret drinking them in the morning, but they were too good to pass up. Matthew seemed content to sip on the drinks she hadn't liked. *Not too picky,* she thought. That could be a good quality to have. *Or he's an alcoholic. Please don't be an alcoholic!*

"And you have a brother?" he asked.

"I do. A younger brother named John—after my father. He's really the only person in my family that I keep up with. We're really close. I've never been very close with my parents. They knew that I was a good kid, and they were happy to support me in my studies. But beyond that, I didn't have much time for them," she answered, surprised by her ability to complete full sentences when she felt this tipsy.

He continued to ask her questions about her family for some time. She felt herself falling into an easy pattern of answering without hesitation or fear of his reactions. It had been too long since she allowed herself to enjoy life—but it had taken spending an evening out with a sexy billionaire to realize how much she missed these kinds of interactions.

"Now," Matthew leaned forward with a very serious look on his face. *Uh oh. What's this about?* Lissie worried. "I have seen your decorating skills, and I'm not going to lie," he paused as she grew apprehensive about what might follow, "you are absolutely amazing. Please, will you come to my apartment and help me decorate it? I'm absolutely worthless with that kind of endeavor, and the guy I hired to decorate did not capture what I wanted *at all*."

Lissie smiled widely at his praise. "Wow. Yeah, okay. I'll come take a look and see what I can do." She could tell he was being honest, and she was too excited to refuse his request or consider the repercussions if he didn't ask her on a second date. Decorating was one of the activities she had always loved to do. She'd even considered getting her degree in interior design, but had quickly dismissed the idea. Her dream of becoming the CEO of a Fortune 500 company was far too ingrained into her psyche to allow that drastic of a change for her future. While she was in the process of remodeling her own apartment, she had felt deep regret that she hadn't gone with her gut and changed her degree. She was the kind of person who made decisions once and never looked back—and her degree choice was one of the first decisions she ever regretted. But there was nothing to be done now. She was just going to stick with her job at Stein Securities because it was stable. And her entire life plan was based on stability.

When she was in middle school, her parents sat her down to discuss their crumbling marriage. They talked with her for hours about how bad things had gotten and how worried they were about their friends and family finding out. Lissie listened closely to the discussion and as they told her they were going to stick through the rough patch so she and her brother would have stability. They put such a huge emphasis on the necessity of stability in Lissie and John's lives, that she began making decisions about her future and sticking to them in order to show her parents how stable her life had become. They seemed happy enough with the way she turned out, and after she and her brother graduated from high school, her parents ended up staying happily married.

"I would love to see your own remodel if you would let me," he added.

"Absolutely," she said with a light head. "Oh my. I think these drinks are a little stronger than I realized."

Matthew let out a quiet laugh. "You want to grab something to eat? It's getting pretty crowded in here anyway."

She looked around at the swarms of people she'd failed to notice before that moment. There were people standing at the bar, and more standing near the entry waiting for tables to clear. "Wow, I hadn't even noticed how crazy it is in here. Yeah, let's go grab some food." She glanced at her watch and couldn't believe it was after ten. They had been here for over three hours though it felt like they had only been talking for a few moments.

Matthew paid the check, and from the number of bills he handed the bartender, she was pretty sure he had left a several-hundred-dollar tip.

He turned to face her and put out his hand in an offer to hold hers. She grabbed it with a smile and allowed him to lead her out into the crowded streets of a Friday night in Manhattan.

Twenty

When they emerged from the dark bar, the warm summer air washed over them, and they both breathed deeply. They exchanged smiles at their simultaneous act and turned to leave the bar. Lissie was under the impression they would be grabbing a slice of pizza from one of the ubiquitous dollar slice places around town—that was what she did whenever she was hungry.

"What kind of food do you like?" Matthew stopped and asked.

"Well, I've never been the adventurous type—not in any part of my life really. I usually eat diner food, burgers, pizza, salads, Mexican or Italian," she replied guiltily. "We can just grab a slice of pizza."

Matthew waved his finger in her face while 'tsk-ing' her. "For shame, young lady. Have you never tried Indian food? Sushi? Thai? Vietnamese? Greek? Fusion?" She shook her head 'no' to each type of food, and could see his expression grow more horrified with each answer. "Then tonight I will begin your food education. You have been missing out on an entire world of flavor, and I feel it's my duty to expand your horizons. Tonight, I am taking you to Takashi. Now get in," he demanded.

She was confused by his command. *Get in what?* she wondered. She turned to her left to see he had opened the door to a bright green car that looked ridiculously expensive, though she had no idea what it was. "Wow," she breathed as she slid in. She had never sat in such a luxurious vehicle. In fact, it had been years since she sat in any car. She sold her '96 Camry when she moved to New York in 2007, and she had been working so hard since the move, she hadn't even gone home to see her family during holidays. She video-chatted with her parents periodically, but only to make sure they were still healthy and happy. Every time she had seen her brother, it had either been over video chat, or he had been the one to visit her. She felt a pang of guilt about the way she neglected her family but quickly drew her attention back to the present.

"What kind of car is this?" she asked as Matthew slid into the driver's seat and started up the engine.

"An Aston Martin Vanquish," he replied with a tone of love and honor. "I am in love with this mechanical wonder," he added. And she believed every word.

I would die if he ever looked at me or talked about me that way, she thought. *Did I really just think that? Oh my gosh! Am I so desperate for this man's attention that I'm jealous of his car? WHO ARE YOU, LISSIE? This is not the girl I know!* She finished her mental beating and turned back to Matthew. He was staring at her with an odd look on his face.

"What?" she asked timidly, worrying that she had spoken her thoughts aloud again.

"This weekend I am devoting myself to changing your world from 'Plain Jane' to 'Culinary Connoisseur'," he declared with a look of resolve.

Lissie gulped with trepidation. She was not adventurous. She mostly liked to watch romantic comedies—and you don't even need a preview to figure out the end of those. She liked that her job was stable—she never had to wonder about what task Mr. Stein would ask her to do next. She never travelled—she didn't like the idea of getting left by a train or having her passport stolen and being stranded in a foreign country—nor could she stand the idea of not knowing the language somewhere. She liked shopping at the same stores for her clothes—Banana Republic and Anne Taylor—because she knew exactly what sizes would fit and that everything would be appropriate for her work attire. Nothing adventurous. Ever.

The car pulled to a stop outside the restaurant, and Matthew walked around the car to open her door. *Whoa. He's a big time gentleman. Opening the door to get in the car is one thing. Opening it to get out is an entirely new level of amazing,* she thought happily.

"You are getting the royal treatment for the next …" he looked at his watch, "… forty-nine hours. I claim you until Sunday night at eleven fifty-nine p.m."

He set an alarm to go off at precisely eleven fifty-nine p.m. on Sunday. Lissie laughed. Harder than she could remember laughing since high school … maybe even middle school. Matthew looked like she had kicked him in the gut—like he was physically in pain.

"Are you okay?" she asked quickly, her laugh coming to an abrupt halt.

"Yes … yes. I'm sorry for that absurd reaction. I have to tell you that you really remind me of someone that meant a great deal to me a long ago. And you should take that as a compliment. She was an extraordinary woman … with an angelic laugh—like yours," he finished as he walked back around his car to go park.

Lissie wasn't sure what to make of that. She thought Matthew might be interested in her—*in a romantic way*, she hoped. But he was still hung up on some other woman. *Well then*, she decided, *it's up to you to help him forget the past.*

"Are you ready for an adventure?" he asked as he walked up with his arm extended toward the restaurant.

"I most certainly am," she answered with a smile as she walked through the open door.

Twenty-One

BY THE TIME dinner ended, Rogue had watched Lissie try six different kinds of beef—each one cooked to perfection. She put her foot down when he ordered the tongue, but mustered up enough courage to take a bite of the heart—which was one of his favorite dishes. He introduce her to Chef Takashi—who was thrilled to see him eating with a woman and let her know as much. Rogue had lived long enough that embarrassment was a rare occurrence, but when the chef made a big deal about his bringing Lissie, he couldn't help but get a little red in the face.

The dinner was wonderful, and the conversation continued to flow with ease. He felt strange each time she called him by his birth name. Only his immediate family called him 'Mattia'. His grandfather, uncles, cousins and nephews all called him by the name his grandfather had branded him with so long ago. He hoped maybe, over time, Lissie would help him once again become accustomed to thinking of himself as 'Matthew'. Rogue was certain that he was not falling in love with Lissie the way he had with Anamaria, but the fact that he was planning to spend his entire weekend with her spoke volumes about his feelings for the woman.

"What kind of food would you like to explore tomorrow?" he asked as he opened the passenger door of his car for Lissie to enter.

"I'm going to let you decide that," she said with a smile. "You obviously have excellent taste in cuisine, so I'm leaving it up to you. And that was amazing, by the way. Thank you so much for taking me there."

When she smiled at him like that, he had the urge to grab her hand, pull her close, wrap his arms around her body and kiss her beautiful mouth. But this was neither the time nor the place. A gentleman would never behave that brashly on a first date.

"Can I drive you home?" he asked.

"Yes, thank you. I'm on 67th between Broadway and Amsterdam," she said.

The drive home was quiet. Rogue did not want the night to end, but he didn't think it was appropriate to ask if he could come up to her apartment. Lissie was staring ahead, looking ... *is determined the expression she's wearing? Yes. She's looking determined.*

Lissie made up her mind. This weekend was an adventure for every aspect of her life—she was dating, trying new foods, opening up about her personal life, and doing her best to try to let loose. She was going to ask Matthew to come upstairs. *Oh my God, you can't do that! This is the first date. He's going to think you're slutty. Except for the part where you basically told him you haven't dated since college, or really ever for that matter. Man up!* she demanded of herself. *You can do this.* Her heart was racing and her hands were shaking, but she had made up her mind.

"So ..." she began, "... I only have white wine in my apartment. Do we need to stop so I can grab you a bottle of red? Or are you okay with white?"

I may have been wrong earlier. It's possible I am falling in love, Rogue told himself. He hoped the shocked look that was plastered on his face was not making her feel as if he wanted to say no. He was simply trying to decide whether he wanted to take the time to stop for wine or get to her apartment as quickly as the speed limit and stop lights would allow.

"I'm sorry," she started. "Is that too forward? You don't have to come up at all. I just had such a great time tonight ..."

"Stop that," he interrupted. "I'm not upset that you asked me up. I'm trying to decide if stopping for wine is worth delaying our arrival at your apartment," he finished with a smirk.

She broke into a massive smile, the kind of smile that reached every part of her face. Her eyes crinkled—and sparkled with the city lights reflecting in them. *God, she's gorgeous*, Rogue realized for the hundredth time.

"I think I'll skip the red wine tonight," he decided.

Lissie hadn't felt this nervous since it was time to take her SATs in high school. And she actually prepared for that test. This was a whole different ballgame: one she was absolutely unequipped for.

Matthew parked his car in a secured lot nearby—only eighty dollars for the night—and walked hand in hand with Lissie to her apartment. The nighttime doorman had to ask her for her ID due to the fact that she was never out past eight p.m.—which meant he had never seen her before.

When they entered the elevator, Lissie could feel her pulse quicken and her breathing speed up. *Oh no. Please don't pass out or something weird like that*, she begged herself. When the elevator stopped on the eighth floor she nervously said, "Well ... this is us!" *You. Are. So. Awkward.* She inwardly scolded herself. She almost dropped her keys twice on the way to her door. She decided to focus on showing Matthew how she decorated her apartment, which immediately put her at ease.

"Well," she said as she opened the door wide and flipped on the lights, "this is it!"

Rogue walked around the apartment paying attention to every detail. He hoped it would give him more insight into who Lissie really was. As he looked around, he realized how magnificent her apartment renovation actually was. It was obvious how much time she had spent thinking about the way the end product would look. Upon entering, the kitchen was directly to the right. She had knocked down the wall between the kitchen and living room to make one large living space. The lights she had chosen were made from old, rusty wire, but they somehow still felt modern. Her dark countertops contrasted well with the light gray cabinetry. All the original hardwood floors had been flawlessly refinished. The arches in the hallways to the left leading to the bedroom and bathroom gave the apartment a cozy feel without making the modern design feel out of place. There was a low-profile modern, gray sofa that sat in the large living room and set the mood for a comfortable yet stylish area. The original built-in bookcases that spanned the entire left wall of the living room had been refinished in a flat black and filled with hundreds of books. She had taken out the shelves of the center bookcase to mount a TV so it would fade into the black of the shelf when not in use. There were gold pieces of décor splashed around the room to add a little sparkle to the neutral colors she had used in the rest of the room.

"This is incredible," he breathed.

"Really? You really think it's good?" she asked excitedly.

"Yes. I really do. Why didn't you make a career out of decorating?" he asked, confused as to why she would be a glorified secretary when she had such a rare gift.

"It just wasn't on the career path that I set for myself from a young age. And by the time I realized this was what I loved, I was too far into my degree to switch. It would've been a horrible waste of money," she said with a twinge of sadness.

"Well, I can honestly say I don't think you needed a degree to make a career out of decorating. You're already leaps and bounds better than the idiot I hired to do my place," he snorted with frustration merely thinking about the price he had paid—not that the money was an issue. But it was the principle of the matter. "Please. Please tell me you'll try to fix what the last guy did. You can have as much money as you need, and of course I'll pay you for your labor," he begged.

Lissie laughed with delight at the request. "Of course I'll fix your apartment. We can't have you living in a space you hate! And I could never take money for it. I already know I'll enjoy doing the redecorating so much it will be like you're giving me a gift."

Rogue suddenly realized that he was alone with a woman. In her apartment. Nerves overtook him, and he went to her bookshelves to distract himself from the question, *what do we do now?*

"You have a wonderful selection of books," he remarked.

Lissie poured them both glasses of wine. She came over to stand by him and handed him his glass.

"Yes," she replied, "some of them have been passed down in my family for hundreds of years. This is my favorite," she said as she withdrew a simple leather book that looked like it belonged in the library Rogue kept at his apartment in Paris.

"And which one is that?" he asked absentmindedly.

"*Romeo and Juliet*," she answered with a pleasant tone to her voice.

Rogue refused to look at the book. He had avoided *Romeo and Juliet* ever since Anamaria carried it with her the day they had confessed their love for one other. He felt sick that it should be both Lissie *and* Anamaria's favorite book. There were simply too many connections between them. One more might change his mind and force him to leave Lissie without a backward glance. He turned and walked toward the couch.

"Would you like to sit down and talk some more?" he asked as he sat.

"Thank you, yes," she replied.

Lissie couldn't remember the last time she felt this happy. It was obvious that Matthew harbored painful memories of the past that involved another woman, but she would be foolish to let the past stand in her way. "The past is the past, you can only move forward," she had often told herself. She glanced at Matthew and decided maybe he needed to hear it too. She walked over to him, sat down as closely as she could without sitting on top of him, and looked him in the eyes.

"I hope it's alright for me to say this, but I feel like you need to know that the past is the past, Matthew. You can only ever move forward."

His eyes glassed over with the threat of tears. He grabbed her shoulders and pulled her in for a tight hug. Lissie had not been embraced by anyone this way for so long, she had forgotten how wonderful a hug could be.

"Thank you," Matthew choked out, "You have no idea how much I needed to hear those words."

Lissie sat back and stared into Matthew's beautiful green eyes. She wanted to stare for much longer, but she was interrupted by Matthew's hands caressing both sides of her face and pushing their way through her hair. He pulled her face towards his without any resistance from her, and placed a single, gentle kiss on her lips. She wanted to cheer. She wanted to get up and dance around the apartment. She wanted it to last much, much longer. It was what a kiss should feel like—not just sparks, but full-on fireworks and missiles exploding.

He pulled back from her mouth with a smile on his face, still holding her face with both hands. She was so breathless she had to lay her forehead against his to keep from falling backwards.

"Wow," she muttered.

"That is exactly what I was thinking," Matthew agreed.

"Can we please do that again?" she asked.

Without a word, Matthew drew her back towards his lips and kissed her much more passionately this time. When they broke apart a few moments later, Lissie was certain that she was dead. Feelings like this only existed in heaven, right? But when she opened her eyes and Matthew was staring at her like she was the most beautiful person he had ever seen, she nearly passed out.

"You are the most beautiful woman on the earth," he said. And she knew he was speaking honestly. His face was the easiest book she had ever read, and it was wonderful knowing what he was feeling.

"I feel the same way," Lissie replied. Matthew let out a long laugh which Lissie was confused about until he added, "I am so happy you know you are the most beautiful woman on the earth!"

He continued to laugh until Lissie punched him in the shoulder. "You know exactly what I meant, and you had to go and ruin a moment by correcting my grammatical error? Seriously?"

Matthew now laughed even harder, and despite how she tried, Lissie couldn't resist joining him. When their stomachs grew sore from the exertion, they tried quieting their laughter, but they were thrown back into it even more at the effort.

Lissie looked at her watch and became serious. "It's three a.m., Matthew. I would like it if you would stay with me tonight. I mean ... not for ... sex or anything. Just stay with me. After the evening we've spent together, I don't know if I could bear the thought of you leaving right now."

"I'll stay," Matthew replied with a quiet seriousness.

Then he kissed her gently for the last time that night.

Twenty-Two

THE NEXT MORNING Lissie woke up to the snores of someone sleeping next to her in her bed. *Oh my God*, she thought, *Matthew actually stayed.* She half expected him to be gone when she woke up—she had asked a man to stay with her and they both remained fully clothed without any physical benefits. Didn't that somehow go against the grain of most men's thought processes? She slowly crawled out of bed so she wouldn't wake him. After inching herself out from beneath the covers, she tiptoed to the kitchen to make a pot of coffee.

Okay. That was kind of wonderful. He just ... spent the night. He actually slept in his dress pants and undershirt and didn't try anything. Apart from holding her hand until they fell asleep, he hadn't even touched her the rest of the night. She hadn't slept that well in years. She knew he didn't have a criminal history because he passed the initial background check with Stein Securities; she wasn't fearful that he would hurt her. But still, this was a big step outside of the stable, normal, controlled lifestyle she had so carefully constructed for herself.

She grabbed two mugs from her cabinet and filled them with the delicious smelling coffee that had finished brewing. She always used a flavored creamer in her coffee to tone down the bite a little. She had no idea how he took his coffee, so she decided to wake him up and ask.

"Good morning," she said softly as she reentered her room with both mugs in hand.

Matthew moved a little before falling back into a still, deep sleep. They had slept for over seven hours, and she still had another thirty-seven-and-a-half hours of promised adventures to look forward to. She was determined to get him out of bed and filled with caffeine so their day could begin.

"Matthew," she said a little louder.

This time his eyes opened slightly as he looked around in confusion, then he snapped to full attention. He sprang from the bed, grabbing the small knife he left on the side table, opened it, and got in—what looked like—a defensive position. It seemed he was ready for attackers.

Lissie burst into laughter while trying not to spill hot coffee from the mugs she held in her hands.

"What in the world were you expecting?" she inquired, still laughing. His expression went from suspicion, to surprise to acknowledgement of his surroundings in a matter of seconds. He closed and dropped the knife back on the table rapidly and came over to greet his hostess with a quick kiss.

"Sorry about that," he apologized, "I'm not used to waking up in strange places with beautiful women offering me cups of coffee. I thought surely someone had kidnapped me and thrown me into the most wonderful prison of all time." He joined Lissie in a short laugh and took the coffee mug from her hand.

"How do you like your coffee? I have milk, sugar or French vanilla creamer," she said.

"I'll take a little creamer if you don't mind sharing," he replied as he slipped a hand around her waist and walked with her toward the kitchen.

"What's on the adventure agenda for the day?" she asked as she poured the creamer in his mug.

"Hmmm. I don't know. There are innumerable choices because of your complete inexperience with all things 'fun'," he prodded her playfully. "Why don't we start by running to my apartment so I can get cleaned up and you can see the blank canvas that awaits your decorating expertise?"

"That sounds wonderful. Give me ten minutes and I'll be ready," she said, as she chugged the rest of her coffee and rushed into her room, closing the door behind her. "What should I be wearing for this adventure?" she yelled into the other room.

"Something casual will be fine, I think—probably jeans," Matthew yelled back.

Lissie couldn't help but smile. He was so *normal* for a billionaire. She didn't really know what she had expected, but 'normal-yet-hot-twenty-something' was not it. That was for sure. She hopped in the shower to wash off the stench of sleep that had covered her during the course of the night. She dried herself off, put her long brown hair up into a bun on the top of her head, and wrapped a towel around her to run to the closet. She threw on her favorite pair of jeans, a thin, teal sweater, and a cute pair of brown, suede heels. She grabbed her bag of makeup off the bathroom counter and ran out her bedroom door.

"I figured I'd put my makeup on at your place while you're getting ready, if you don't mind," she said as she grabbed her purse and headed to the door. "Oh yeah, don't forget your stuff on the side table."

Rogue wasn't sure what he had expected, but Lissie certainly wasn't filling the behavioral role of 'modern woman' he had come to think of all twenty-first century females being. She had taken five, maybe six minutes to shower, fix her hair and dress. She was now standing by the door, waiting for him to get *his* stuff together. She also had no qualms that he was looking at her beautiful face, untouched by makeup. *You certainly are an enigma,* he thought about Lissie, as he finished his coffee and walked to grab his things from the bedroom. He wondered if she would try to snoop in his wallet and phone—as he had seen women on television shows and in movies often do. But his things were completely untouched. *Trustworthy,* was the thought that permeated his head.

He fixed his clothes and collected his things. He headed back out into the living room and saw Lissie had already grabbed his keys from the kitchen counter and was waiting excitedly.

"Does that mean you're driving?" Rogue asked with a nervous smile.

"Ha! Are you kidding me? You couldn't pay me to drive a car that nice in this city," she replied as she tossed him the keys.

I like her even more now, Rogue thought with a smile as he took Lissie's hand and walked out the door.

Twenty-Three

As Matthew drove into the garage at his building, Lissie looked around at the wide open space in confusion.

"There are only three cars in here," she said questioningly. Matthew laughed and wore a guilty look.

"As you saw last night, I have a rather close relationship with my cars," he said. "And when I started looking for an apartment here in Chelsea, I decided I would have to find a space where I could have my own garage." He looked around at the large parking garage and let her do the math.

Lissie's eyes flared in surprise, "So you just bought all the rights to the parking spaces from the other tenants?"

"No," Matthew laughed again, "I bought the entire building so I could clear the garage out for my personal use. I made a deal with a nearby public garage to pay for two years of parking for all of my current and future neighbors in the building. They were initially unhappy about having to walk a block to get to their vehicles, but were a little less hostile after I told them about the financial arrangement."

Lissie stood, dumbfounded. She was pretty sure her mouth was fixed in the open position.

"You …" she was having trouble formulating coherent thoughts. "You just … bought the whole building?"

"You know I have money to spare, Lissie. If I'm going to own a space of my own, I can afford to be picky," he replied nonchalantly.

Suddenly Lissie felt sick. How had she actually believed he liked her apartment? It was now obvious he was only being polite. There's no way he could actually have liked her six hundred square foot apartment. It was huge in her mind, but for billionaire Matthew McCloud, it was probably the smallest apartment he had ever stepped in. She wanted to run away, hide in a closet, and drown in self-pity. She tried to gulp down her emotion and continue on the tour without revealing she had discovered his deception.

"I didn't think about that," Lissie choked out. Why did she look ill?

"Are you okay?" he asked, worried she might need a doctor.

"I'll be fine," she responded with a bit of emotion in her voice.

This is really strange. What could have prompted this change? She knew I was wealthy, Rogue pondered.

"Well, let's go on up to my apartment," he said, feeling exasperated by the confusion he was feeling over her mood swing.

They entered the elevator, and Rogue could have sworn Lissie rolled her eyes when he swiped his key card and selected the top floor of the building.

"What is going on? Are you truly upset that I have my own building with my own garage and live in the penthouse? Because I don't think it's fair that you knew my financial situation yesterday and acted like there was nothing abnormal before you actually saw where I lived," he said, exasperated.

"I don't know, Matthew. I just feel … insecure and frustrated. I'm feeling insecure that you spent the night in my tiny apartment and acted like you were comfortable there when it's clear you're accustomed to a much nicer—and *way* bigger—space," she confessed with an irritated tone. "And I'm frustrated that you throw away an irrational amount of money on worthless things like your own *parking garage* while there are people starving to death in the world!"

"What?" Rogue was extremely confused about how she came to this conclusion. "First, I loved your place. Truly. It was modern and cozy and felt like home. If I'm being honest, I was jealous of your space. That's why I asked you to redecorate mine. It feels like a tomb up there. Believe me when I say you have no reason whatsoever to feel insecure." *Did I somehow give her that impression? This female's mind feels like a landmine waiting to explode. How am I supposed to know how to navigate her brain? Ugh. I am completely useless when it comes to women ... or maybe this woman in particular.* "And second, I donate money to all sorts of charities. All over the world. I can show you receipts from the transactions if you're that upset," he offered, worried that she wouldn't believe him. *She must think I'm a spoiled, selfish brat. Do I really come off as that much of an asshole?* he wondered with consternation.

His distressed inner dialogue must have shown on his face because Lissie was immediately apologetic.

"I'm so sorry. I don't know where that came from. Sometimes when I'm upset about something, I bring completely unrelated matters into the conflict—things that have nothing to do with what I'm upset about. It was unfair of me to imply that you're uncharitable. I really am just insecure about my apartment in comparison to your *building*. I worked really hard for my tiny space, so when I saw this," she motioned around like she was referring to the entire building, "I just couldn't envision a scenario where you could possibly be comfortable in my space. But I believe you. I think. And I'm really happy you like my home," she finished with a smile.

"Well, I can certainly guarantee you that last night was the best night of sleep I've gotten in years. I'm not sure if it was the apartment, the company, or a mixture of both. But I know for sure that living alone in my apartment hasn't been great for my health," Matthew assured her.

They exited the elevator straight into a massive apartment. *His penthouse is the entire floor*, she thought in awe. The walls that previously separated the four apartments that once shared this floor were gone—and whoever took them down did an amazing job at making the space feel natural and whole rather than reconstructed. The floors were a beautiful white marble. The walls were painted stark white, and the black furniture with sharp square edges made the space feel uninviting and sterile. Everything in the room was black or white—nothing to soften the space or make it feel homey. *There is so much untapped potential in here,* she thought with excitement. The massive space had floor-to-ceiling windows on three sides. There was an incredible view of the city from almost every angle. The only thing she couldn't see from this room was the Hudson. The original designer created designated spaces for the television viewing area, reading area, and dining area. There were at least four thousand square feet of open space in this room alone, and this was just the living area. She turned away from the east-facing windows and walked to the huge kitchen. The island alone had seating for six. Unfortunately, the designer maintained the 'boring' theme through the kitchen as well. All the counters and cabinets were plain black with no detail whatsoever. The cabinet and drawer pulls along with all the appliances were stainless steel. *At least I can keep the appliances,* she thought smugly. Even the lights above the island were simple, round, black metal.

"What do you think?" Matthew asked with genuine curiosity on his face.

"Well the good news is, the floors and appliances can stay," she grinned.

"When can you start?" he wanted to know.

"Why don't you let me see the rest of the place so I know just how extensive this job is," she said as she walked toward the hallway behind his kitchen.

Matthew led her into a nicely sized guest bedroom that housed nothing more than a queen-sized bed and side tables. She couldn't believe he had paid this so-called 'interior designer' any money at all. With a disapproving shake of her head, he chuckled and led her into an office—smaller than the other rooms, yet still larger than her own master bedroom. It was stark like the rest of the apartment but contained a large black bookcase on one entire wall that made the room less offensive.

"You have almost as many books as me," she teased.

"Ah ha, but you haven't seen the libraries at all my other homes. My library in Paris is *really* something to see," he countered.

Now *that* was something she wanted to experience.

"I guess I'll have to see the others someday," she playfully added, amazed by her own flirtatiousness.

His wide smile showed Lissie he approved of that idea, and she returned the smile, grateful for his reaction. He led her back into the hallway and into a massive room with floor-to-ceiling windows on two sides.

"I'm going to take a shower. Feel free to scrutinize my bedroom while I'm away," he teased.

The lonely king-sized bed and two dressers looked small and desolate in the giant room. The lack of any window treatments made the room feel unfinished.

When Matthew re-emerged from the bathroom a few minutes later looking debonair in another fitted suit, Lissie continued where she had left off.

"Wow. Your bedroom is just … sad," she said with a chuckle. "Your designer was even worse than I imagined." Matthew looked like he was relieved he wasn't the only person that felt that way. "I guess I'll have to get started right away," she finished.

"Not this weekend though." Matthew came to stand beside her, "Your culinary adventures have scarcely begun. It's almost one o'clock and we need to grab lunch. We're going to have Indian, and my favorite place happens to be within walking distance."

Lunch was a success—as Rogue had expected. He had gotten Lissie to try six different dishes—she loved four of them and tolerated the other two. Her favorites were naan, lamb kebab, chicken tikka masala, and the handmade cheese dessert soaked in sweet syrup. Every time she took a bite of something she liked, her eyes opened wide and she exclaimed her appreciation. She was such an adorable creature, full of joy and life. She reminded him in so many ways of his Anamaria, but she was cut from a much more predictable mold. It seemed like it wasn't until he entered her life that she even considered actually *living* her life. She was an unadventurous workaholic with no close friends or family, with the exception of her brother. Rogue felt a sense of responsibility to open Lissie's world to adventures that lay awaiting discovery. If he needed to start with cuisine, he would.

"That was *amazing*!" she exclaimed. "I feel like I ate about ten times more than I should've, and I'm already curious where we're going for dinner."

"We're actually going shopping now," he said with a smile. "We have to get you something that will be suitable for our plans this evening."

"I feel a little like Julia Roberts in *Pretty Woman*," Lissie admitted. That got a huge laugh from Matthew.

"Not even close," he replied, "You're way better looking than her."

She giggled as he took her hand and led her north. *I wonder where he's planning on taking me for this. I can't believe he's spending so much money. I mean, I know he has it, but it's like he's never had to think about money in his whole life. What an amazing way to live.* She continued thinking about the lifestyle he could maintain as they walked toward what Lissie considered the worst part of the city—Midtown. She normally avoided it at all costs. There was no stability in that part of the city. Tourists swarmed the streets, and new restaurants opened and closed every week. It went against every fiber of her being to be a party to that kind of fluctuating madness. Just as she thought those words, she and Matthew rounded the corner onto 5th Avenue—straight into a swarm of people. Somehow the crowd seemed less overwhelming with her hand in his.

She looked around at the famous department stores they were walking past. *He's taking me shopping on Fifth Avenue?* she thought with nervous excitement. Never in her wildest dreams would she have expected to have the means to shop anywhere on 5th Avenue. Truth be told, she'd rarely had time to go shopping in a physical store in the past ten years. She almost always ordered her clothes online to avoid long lines for dressing rooms and checkouts. But *this* ... this she could handle. They entered Saks Fifth Avenue, and Matthew marched her straight to the designer dresses.

"Stay here while I grab someone to help us," Matthew ordered. She did as she was told with a smirk on her face. He returned a few minutes later with an eager-looking salesperson. Lissie was certain the woman had just been handed a wad of bills to drop whatever she was doing and help Matthew.

"What size dress do you wear, dear?" the salesperson asked.

Really? In front of Matthew? Well, this sucks. "A six or eight depending on the designer," she reluctantly answered.

"We're going to go pick out a few dresses—and no objections. I want to do this for you," Matthew said with a wary look, already anticipating her protests to their choices.

What an intriguing man, she thought as she looked around at the other patrons milling around the store. *I wonder what kinds of dresses he'll choose for me. I doubt he'll come close to anything I would actually wear*, she thought smugly.

About ten minutes later, the two returned without any garments. "I've already put the gowns in the dressing room for you. Follow me, and I'll show you to the room," the salesperson said.

Lissie followed with a sense of dread at what the two could have possibly chosen for her. The last time she had worn a gown was for her junior prom— which ended up being a terrible night. She hoped she would fare better with a new dress on.

"I'll sit right outside the dressing room so you can show me the dresses you like," Matthew said hopefully. Lissie could tell even he was worried about his selections.

She walked into the large dressing room that had obviously been set up for bridal fittings and saw the two dresses he had selected for her. She gasped at how incredibly perfect they both were. The first was a navy gown with deep blue sequins sewn in a beautiful pattern over every piece of fabric. It was strapless with a sweetheart neckline and a ruffle around the waist. It sat at exactly the right length for her to need three or four inch heels. The second was an all-black sleeveless gown with a high neck and a trumpet skirt. The top of the dress was covered in black lace, the bottom flared with taffeta ruffles. It was finished off with a thin belt patterned with a crystal and black bead design. These were the exact two dresses that she would have chosen for herself. *How on earth could he have known? He's only known me for a day*, she thought with amazement. She tried each dress on but ultimately went with the sequined gown. *Much more sophisticated,* she decided. She did not let Matthew see either gown on her. If he was buying her all these ridiculous things, the least she could do would be to surprise him when she put the full outfit together. Matthew could not have been more disappointed at her secrecy—she could tell by the look he wore on his face—but he didn't complain aloud. He took her over to the shoe department where she found a beautiful pair of silver heels to accompany her dress. To top it all off, Matthew insisted on buying her jewelry to match. She decided that the detail on the dress was so intricate, she only needed a necklace and earrings to complete the outfit. She found a Kenneth Jay Lane set that was absolutely perfect. By the time they left the store, Matthew had spent over fifteen hundred dollars on one outfit for her. She was feeling overwhelmed with guilt at the extravagant gifts so powerfully that she had to keep reminding herself not to hyperventilate.

"Only one more stop," Matthew said as he led her away from the store.

"You cannot be serious!" she demanded as she roughly pulled him to a halt.

"You have been more than generous. I feel I'm inadequate for this kind of attention. And I have absolutely nothing I can give you in return," she finished, with her breath quickening at the panic she felt rising within herself.

"That's not even remotely true. You recently agreed to remodel my massive apartment, and you refused to accept payment for the job. Therefore, I'm going to treat you like a queen until I feel you've been properly repaid. And by then we'll both be so used to the treatment that I'll have to continue on with it," he finished with a huge smile.

She was dumbfounded. He was right about the remodel, and she knew it. And she was just fine with his long-term relationship implications. For a moment, she allowed herself to live in the fantasy where she ended up with Matthew. She smiled at the thought.

"Well, just this once," she conceded. But she could tell from the look on his face he was enjoying his victory.

They walked past a few shops before entering a salon that felt more like a modern home than a salon. There was a designer rug on the floor of the waiting area. The receptionist had apparently been expecting them, because she immediately called Matthew over to talk about the timing of the appointment and to make sure they could fit Lissie in. Matthew sat in the seating area at the front of the salon while Lissie was immediately taken to a chair in the back. Her stylist asked to see her dress and jewelry for the evening. The woman beamed at the ensemble, complimented Lissie's good taste in fashion and men, and got right to work. When she was finished, Lissie had a large braid framing her face that started at a part on the left side of her head and ended in a low bundle of loose curls directly behind her right ear. The stylist curled her hair in a way that made it gently sit in perfect waves against her head. It was beautiful. The stylist finished her look with a full face of makeup—including dark smoky eyes, long lashes and natural lip gloss. Lissie had never felt this pampered in her life.

"Come with me," the stylist motioned as she took Lissie to a room in the back of the salon. Lissie's dress was hanging on a hook, waiting for her, and her shoes and jewelry were carefully laid out on a small table next to the dress. "Take your time getting dressed, and let me know if you need any help at all," she added as she closed the door. *God, this is overwhelming. That's the first time anyone has offered to help me get dressed since I was seven or eight years old. I feel like I'm in a romantic movie. How am I supposed to act? I don't know how to be in a romantic movie! Just get dressed, and you'll get through this night*, she told herself, hoping the self-motivation would calm her nerves.

Rogue was tired of waiting—he wanted to see his gorgeous date all dressed up. He had absolutely loved pampering Lissie today. *I could really get used to treating her like a queen*, he thought. When he looked towards the back of the salon to check for the fifteenth time if she was finished yet, he nearly blacked out from the vision walking toward him.

Lissie looked absolutely stunning. And at least for tonight, she was his date. The last time he felt this much pride at the opportunity to stand beside another person was … *let's not*, he told himself. *This moment is far too perfect to ruin with the memories of a dead woman.*

His eyes were glued to the picture of perfection now standing before him.

"You are, without a doubt, the most beautiful thing I have ever seen," he said with the shock of realization that he actually meant those words.

Lissie's cheeks turned a beautiful shade of rose. He could tell she wasn't accustomed to this kind of attention, but he could also tell she was enjoying it. *Get used to it, Lissie*, he thought with satisfaction.

Twenty-Four

THERE WAS A BLACK sedan waiting outside the salon when they exited. Lissie had been confused this afternoon when Matthew selected a suit to wear after telling her to wear jeans; but now everything made sense.

"We're going to see *A Midsummer Night's Dream* at Lincoln Center," he revealed excitedly. "Have you ever seen it?"

Lissie could hardly contain her joy. Shakespeare stole a piece of her heart when she was in junior high, and she could not have envisioned a more perfect way to spend an evening. She forced herself to remember not to tear up for fear of her makeup smearing. "Oh my goodness, Matthew," she said, flinging her arms around him. "You could not have chosen anything that I would have liked more."

He smiled widely at her obvious pleasure. As they rode across town, Rogue thought about his relationship with Anamaria … or lack of a relationship. His time with her was cut short. He was never able to dote on her, take her to plays, or make her feel like the princess she was. He began thinking about his relationship with Lissie. *I want this relationship to be different. I want to spend time getting to know her—inside and out. I want to let go of everything from the past and move forward with a clean slate. And hopefully, someday, I'll be able to tell her about me and my Family*, he thought with slight consternation. He hadn't considered the idea of dating a woman in so long that he'd completely forgotten the complications of being in a relationship with a mortal. But that was a bridge he would cross later. Much later.

"We're here!" Lissie squealed in delight.

Rogue got out of the car first and helped Lissie exit without incident. It was obvious that she wasn't exactly comfortable in her new dress and heels, but she certainly wasn't complaining. Every time he caught a glimpse of her from the corner of his eye, he suppressed the urge to gawk at her beauty. She looked more like a supermodel than an executive assistant. With the four-inch heels on, she stood almost six feet tall. Rogue, standing at six foot four, liked the minimized distance between their heights—mostly because it was less obvious when he stole glances at her. The way the dress fit her body was criminal. She wasn't a stick figure, but genetics had blessed her with a trim waist. Her chest and bottom were full, and as he looked over her build, he thanked God for crafting her perfectly. Rogue couldn't find a single flaw on her. The way her hair was fixed, along with the strapless dress, and her impeccable posture gave him an amazing view. Even her skin was flawless. Looking at her neck made him want to lean over and kiss it, but that would have to wait. *Take it slow, you idiot*, he reprimanded himself. He slipped an arm carefully around her waist and walked her inside.

"Welcome to Lincoln Center, Mr. McCloud," a member of the Lincoln Center staff said as soon as they entered the building. "Here are your tickets. Let me show you to your seats," she said, walking toward the theater.

"Do you always get this kind of service?" Lissie whispered to Matthew.

"Only when I offer to make a donation to the theater in order to get the best seats in the house at the last minute," he whispered back with a smile on his face. Lissie wondered exactly how much of a donation he had offered.

When they arrived at their row, Lissie realized that their seats were in the very center of the first row of the mezzanine. This was the first time she had attended an event at Lincoln Center, so she wasn't sure what Matthew meant when he said 'best seat in the house'. But when she arrived at her seat and sat down, she understood *exactly* what he meant. She could see everything from here. And honestly, she felt like a child on Christmas morning getting ready to open her gifts. Except this whole day was better than any Christmas she could remember. She turned to Matthew who was staring at her with a mixture of joy and admiration—*damn, he's easy to read*—and placed a hand on his cheek.

"This has been the most wonderful day. Thank you so much," she softly spoke as she leaned in for a quick kiss.

As soon as their lips touched, Matthew wrapped one of his arms around her lower back and the other held her neck gently as he pulled her in for a deeper, longer kiss.

I'm going to die. Right here, right now. This has to be heaven, she thought as she melted into his arms. He released her almost as quickly as he grabbed her, but took extra care to keep his hand on her skin as he traced it all the way from her neck down to her hand. Lissie shivered at the gentle caress but maintained a smile the whole time to show her approval of the action. As soon as he had grabbed her hand, the lights dimmed so the production could begin.

The dimming of the lights brought Lissie out of her fantasy like a bucket of cold water being thrown in her face. *Everyone around us just watched that whole exchange!* Her eyes darted around without her head moving to see if the entire room was staring at her. When it seemed the people to the left and right of them were paying no attention, she decided they had probably only given the guests directly behind them a show. *Oh well,* she thought, *it's probably the most romantic display they'll see today.* She glanced back at Matthew to find he was still staring at her, enamored, and she decided that it wouldn't bother her one bit if he stayed that way through the entire play.

At that moment, the stage lights came up and the Duke of Athens began the play.

Twenty-Five

When the black sedan that had been waiting for them after the play dropped them off at Matthew's apartment, Lissie still felt like she was floating on air. The performance was incredible. After the performance, he had taken her to an elegant French restaurant and ordered four different dishes to share; she loved every one. Lissie knew she would be dreaming about this day for months. Matthew took her hand and walked her into his building.

"Hello, sir," his doorman greeted, "Here's the package that was left for you. The man making the delivery said you would be expecting it."

"Thank you," Matthew said with a nod as he took the large box and headed toward the elevator.

"What's in the box?" Lissie asked, intensely curious.

"You'll have to wait and see," he responded with a playful smirk.

When they exited the elevator, Matthew told Lissie to pour them a couple of glasses of wine while he took the box back to his bedroom. She could hardly contain her excitement at the thought of another surprise, but when she opened the cabinet doors that held his wine collection, she forgot all about the box. *Wow*, she thought. *There are bottles in here that have to be worth well over one thousand dollars.* She grabbed one that she hoped might be in the forty to sixty dollar price range and poured two glasses.

"Okay," he said as he emerged from his room, "Come on back."

He looked nervous, which only made Lissie more intrigued about the surprise. He led her into the bedroom, where she saw no fewer than ten complete outfits laid out around the room. There were clothes for lounging around, clothes for going out on a date, casual clothes, shoes along with the other dress that she had tried on earlier today. She looked at each outfit, confused.

"When, how and why?" she asked, unable to get anything else to come out of her mouth.

"Well, today I told the salesperson to look at how you were dressed and keep an eye on anything you glanced at for more than a few seconds. She knew your sizes, and they're well trained to look at a body style and know what kind of fit you might need. I had the clothes packaged and shipped here after we left the store. They were quite gracious about everything. And why? Well, I figured I'll probably be taking you to more events in the months to come. And since you may want to stay over on occasion, I thought it might be nice if you didn't have to pack a bag when you come over. She even brought you socks and undergarments—though I saw no need to lay any of those out. You can go through those on your own," he finished with a laugh.

Whoa. This is fast, Lissie thought with her jaw slightly open. *I mean, things are going well, but it's been, what? Thirty hours since our first date? He just bought enough clothes to fill an entire closet. That's super weird, right? Now think about this, Lissie. You like this person right?* she asked herself. *And you can see yourself with him in the future? Yes to both. But wow. I don't know if this is desperation or if he's just a giving person who really wants to make me happy. He admitted he's rusty here. Just say something.*

"Well ... okay," she said, "Thank you."

She hates it! Rogue thought with uneasiness. You can't buy a girl a closet full of clothes and declare that she now has a drawer in your apartment after one day! My God, you truly are an idiot.

"I'm sorry. I've been trying not to rush things. But this is too much, isn't it?" he asked quietly.

"Well," she paused for a moment, "I can't say I was expecting it. But it's not necessarily unwelcome. Just, really ... fast."

"I can send it all back. Really, it's not a problem," he added quickly.

"Stop it, Matthew. I like everything. I just need you to understand that I'm excited about this relationship, but I have to take it slow. I'm an absolute mess when it comes to dating—because I haven't ever dated anyone seriously. This is the first time in my entire life that I can remember feeling like I actually have time for this kind of thing. And I don't want to rush into anything and lose it before it's even begun. Do you know what I mean?" she asked.

"More than you know," he accidentally said aloud, but quickly added, "I've been far too busy to devote myself to a long-term relationship. And right now the timing of this relationship is perfect. Yes. I do understand. And I'm sorry about the closet full of clothes. Really I am. I got caught up in pampering you today, and I didn't even think of the implications of buying you a separate wardrobe to keep at my apartment. You can take everything back to your place if you'd like. That wouldn't hurt my feelings," he finished with an apologetic look.

Lissie walked over to him, set her wine glass on the side table, and wrapped her arms around his waist.

"I think you're the most giving person I've ever met. And I would be foolish not to appreciate your thoughtfulness. I'm going to keep them here. And you," she said as she brushed his lips with her own, "are going to stop overthinking this."

She kissed his bottom lip in a way that sent shivers down his spine. *What an incredible woman*, he thought.

"Now get out of here so I can change into sweats and a t-shirt," she announced as she pushed him away. "Which drawer do you keep them in?"

Lissie felt much more herself when she dressed in comfortable clothes. She had loved playing dress-up today, but that was a once-in-a-while kind of thing. She pulled nearly fifty hair pins from her hair and ran her fingers through it to get the knots out. *Oh wow, that feels better,* she thought with relief.

She grabbed her glass of wine and headed into the living room. There Matthew sat, looking as handsome as ever, still dressed in his suit. *He looks as comfortable in that suit as I feel in these sweats.* Right as she thought that, he popped up off the couch and said, "I'm going to go change into something as comfortable as what you have on." He disappeared for a few moments before reemerging in a nearly identical outfit to what Lissie was wearing. *How is it possible that he looks just as gorgeous wearing sweats as he did wearing a suit?* she thought in amazement.

"Who knew you could look as amazing in sweatpants as you did in that dress?" Matthew said.

Lissie was so surprised by his statement that she choked on her wine and had to hold a hand over her mouth to keep from spitting it all over his pristine white couch. She looked over at him like he was insane and laughed, "You have got to be kidding me! I look like a makeover gone wrong with my hair let down from that up-do!"

Matthew grabbed the bottle of wine and sat down next to Lissie on the couch. "I think you're gorgeous this way."

She smiled and tried to brush it off as the flattery of a new relationship. "What does a normal daily schedule look like for you?" Lissie asked.

"Well," he began as he refilled both glasses of wine, "I usually spend the better part of each day in my apartment. I remain fairly tied up in my work. I sit back like this with my laptop here and paperwork covering the coffee table."

"And what exactly is it that you do?" she continued.

"That's complicated. But mostly my family deals in consulting and contract labor. We all have specialized knowledge, and individuals or corporations contract us when they have a specific need that can't be met from within their own organizations. It's quite lucrative," he finished.

"Sounds like it," Lissie replied, confused by his vague description. *Well, that was avoidance if I've ever seen it. Maybe he's just private about the family business? He hasn't given me the impression that he's a private person up to this point. But maybe it's the business stuff,* she thought.

"I can't believe I have an entire Sunday left until I have to go back to work. This weekend has already felt longer than a normal work week," Lissie said, but quickly added, "in the best possible way."

"I know what you mean," Matthew agreed as he scooted closer to Lissie so he could put his arm around her shoulders.

She leaned in against his muscled body, closed her eyes and felt herself melt a little. *Can this all really be happening? I feel like I'm living out some kind of crazy fantasy. But he definitely feels real enough,* she smiled as she drifted off into sleep.

Rogue carried Lissie to his bed and gently tucked her under the covers. With the conversation they had had a moment earlier, he figured it would probably be smart to take the couch for the night. He grabbed a pillow and blanket from his closet and walked back out into the living room. He didn't shut the door behind him—he worried that something might happen to her if he couldn't keep an eye on her while she slept.

As he nestled down for the night, he thought about the day. *She didn't seem satisfied with my answers about work,* he worried. *Perhaps I'll have to come up with a more elaborate response. I was hoping to escape using lies. But it seems that may be unavoidable.*

He could feel himself relax and knew sleep would soon be upon him. He thought only of Lissie's beauty until sleep took him.

Twenty-Six

MATTHEW HEARD the faint sound of a phone ringing as he slowly woke up. The clock on his DVR said it was one a.m.—he had slept for a total of fifteen minutes. He swore as he grabbed his cell phone and saw that his Uncle Samuel was the caller. *It's going to be one of those kinds of nights.*

Samuel was the youngest of Rogue's uncles and somehow always in need of a helping hand. They maintained a lopsided relationship over the past several decades—one in which Rogue received regular phone calls from the uncle either asking Rogue to bail him out of a difficult situation or teach him how to use technology he didn't understand. Rogue had never seen a person more inclined to misfortune. Most of the Family changed their identities once or twice a year to avoid recognition or suspicion. Samuel had changed his identity over twenty times in the past six years alone by getting into car and boating accidents, having regular hospital visits, and landing on no-fly lists. Incidentally, the occurrences were rarely connected to contracts.

Rogue was relieved when his uncle called him for advice in the early 2000's before replying to an email from King Mutumba of the great nation of Africa offering him millions of dollars. He couldn't understand how the king had gotten his email address, and it had taken nearly twenty minutes for Matthew to explain how spam emails worked.

During the Middle Ages, the uncle's identity was nearly found out during three consecutive contracts—all because of a slip of the tongue while visiting brothels. After his third mistake, he was branded with a black mark on his record nearly as dark as Rogue's. Both the youngest of their siblings, Rogue and Samuel felt a kindred connection that sparked their present relationship.

"Hello?" Rogue mumbled, hoping the call would end quickly.

"Rogue," his uncle whispered in Italian. "I'm on the roof on the twenty-ninth floor of the Woolworth building, and I'm trapped."

Rogue groaned in frustration. He didn't even know his Uncle Samuel was in the city. Now, he was in trouble and Rogue would have to once again bail him out.

"Why are you on the roof of the Woolworth building?"

"I'm finishing a contract that began in India. I was planting some information in one of the offices on the twenty-sixth floor when a security guard walked by. The guard was not supposed to make that route for another forty-five minutes. I think I might have been caught on the security cameras," Uncle Samuel admitted.

Perfect. Not only do I have to plan an escape for him, I also have to wipe the security footage of his little visit. What a wonderful way to spend the middle of the night.

"You have no escape plan?" Rogue asked, agitated by his uncle's oversight.

"I had *three* escape plans, but I didn't take into account that I would get caught on the security footage," his uncle said loudly, upset that Matthew was questioning his preparation.

"I'm on my way to you. Keep checking your phone for my text," Rogue ordered as he ended the call.

He quickly changed into an all-black outfit—complete with baseball cap and sunglasses. He hated dressing like a criminal from a movie, but without any prior knowledge of what he was up against, he knew this was his best option.

He drove his Escalade downtown and parked several blocks away from the building. He opened a hidden compartment under the floorboard in the back of the SUV and grabbed a briefcase that held his laptop for hacking into any security system. His first order of business was to delete the footage of his uncle from the security cameras.

He climbed into the back seat of the Escalade and opened his laptop. Within a matter of minutes, he had complete control over the Woolworth's security system. He scanned through the footage and found that three separate cameras captured his uncle during the initial information plant, and another fifteen cameras captured him during his escape to the rooftop. Rogue groaned, exasperated by the man's recklessness, while he deleted each section of footage. When the footage from the evening exported to a remote server, there would be no remnant of his uncle's escapades.

His second order of business was to shut down the entire security system. He wanted easy access into the building and free movement throughout. He left his laptop running while he made his way in. With security down, the lock was a breeze to pick.

Once inside, he heard two guards screaming back and forth about their system not working. They were on the verge of calling the police, which sent Rogue into action. He ran to the room where the men were yelling and quickly knocked both of them unconscious. He dragged their limp bodies into the closet that housed the security server and placed a chair under the door handle so they couldn't escape. At least one more guard was upstairs, searching for his uncle. He prayed it was only one.

As he entered the elevator, he sent a text to his uncle.

I'm on my way up. The footage has been erased. Stay hidden.

I'll be there in five.

When he reached the twenty-fifth floor, he exited the elevator and found the nearest stairwell. He didn't want to announce his presence to the guard, so he quietly climbed each flight of stairs, checking every floor on the way up.

The guard had flipped on all the lights on the twenty-eighth floor and was checking every corner for the intruder. Rogue exited the stairwell and stayed crouched to avoid detection. He crept closer and closer to the guard, pausing at intervals to make certain he remained undetected. As soon as he was within striking distance, another voice called out from behind him.

There were two guards. Rogue was out in the open. And there were two guards.

"Damn it," he heard himself say as the first guard turned around. The man's eyes grew wide as they took in the huge figure before him, dressed completely in black. Rogue swung his foot around and kicked the man in his temple. The man's body crumpled to the ground in a matter of seconds—he was alive, but wouldn't feel great when he woke up.

The other guard was now screaming and running toward Rogue with a sidearm pointed directly at his head. Rogue ducked behind a wall and held his breath. He listened to the footsteps as the second guard closed in on his location. *One, two, three, four,* he counted each step, knowing exactly how far away the man had been when he began his chase. Rogue knew that an average-size man would run a distance of one and a half meters with each stride. He knew that the man had first seen him from approximately twenty meters away. He knew that in ten seconds, the guard would foolishly stand too close to the doorway—which would allow Rogue to round the corner, relieve the guard of the gun with his left hand, and knock the man unconscious with his right ... all in one fluid motion. People were always predictable in these situations. And eleven seconds later, the man lay unconscious on the ground. Rogue took the clip out of both guards' guns and unchambered the remaining bullet. He couldn't help but feel a little smug over the quick work he had made of the guards.

He pulled out his phone and called his uncle.

"The guards are taken care of. Come back inside so we can get out of here. I took out four guards, but if there are any more, I don't want to run into them. I'll meet you in the stairwell," he said.

"There were only supposed to be three guards on duty tonight!" his uncle yelled before he hung up the phone.

"I don't even know why I bother with reconnaissance," Uncle Samuel said as he walked down the stairs from the twenty-ninth floor.

Rogue could only laugh. *Another story to add to the ever-growing list of Samuel-isms.* His poor uncle was still upset as they exited the building and headed to Rogue's Escalade.

"Thank you again, Rogue. I owe you. Again," Uncle Samuel said begrudgingly, as he embraced his nephew.

"I'm always here for you," Rogue promised. He shut down his laptop—returning control of the security system back to the Woolworth's security center—and waved goodbye to his haphazard uncle.

By the time he made it back home, changed into his sweats, and laid down on his couch, it was three a.m. He passed out from exhaustion in seconds.

Twenty-Seven

Lissie awoke to yells coming from another room. *Where am I?* she wondered in a haze of sleep.

"No! You can't be dead! This is impossible! NO!" she heard as she groggily climbed out of bed. It finally registered that she was in Matthew's bed, alone. How had she gotten there? She heard more yelling and suddenly worried that Matthew had just found out something horrible from a friend or family member. She worried that her presence would be an intrusion of his privacy, but was too intrigued by his screams to not find out what was going on.

The bright light of a full moon filled the living room with enough light for her eyes to see everything clearly. Matthew was thrashing around on the couch yelling—obviously having a nightmare. She ran to him and shook his shoulders to wake him up. It seemed whatever dream he was having had a strong hold over him.

"Matthew!" she yelled with a twinge of panic as she continued to shake him, "Matthew, wake up!"

"No! Lissie!" he screamed as he jolted awake with tears streaming down his face. He grabbed her shoulders with a crazed look of intensity in his eyes and pulled her close. He hugged her tighter than she had ever been held. "I thought they killed you too," he sobbed into her hair. "I'm so happy you're alive."

Lissie was dumbfounded. Whatever dream Matthew had awoken from must have taken a page straight from a horror flick. She hugged him fiercely and shushed him softly, hoping to calm his racing heart. She grabbed his face with both of her hands, wiped his tears with her thumbs, and forced him to look her in the eyes.

"I'm here, Matthew. It's okay. You were dreaming," she said quietly.

Matthew's mind seemed to register there was no danger or need for alarm.

His eyes flashed with recognition, and he visibly calmed himself.

"I'm sorry, Lissie. It was only a nightmare. They can get pretty brutal for me sometimes."

"It's fine—don't apologize. Just come into your room and lie down," she said as she grabbed his hands and stood. He followed her compliantly to the bedroom and lay down next to her. They lay awake facing each other in silence for quite some time. They had not touched since lying down. Lissie reached out and gently rested her hand on his cheek. He turned his head to kiss her palm.

"Thank you," he whispered.

"Of course," she said as she closed her eyes, yawned, and fell back asleep.

Twenty-Eight

When Matthew woke up the next morning, he felt like his head had been cracked open in the night. Between the lack of sleep and the dream, he worried his entire day would be ruined.

He always seemed to have a lingering headache after a night full of the dreams he loved and hated so much. He had gone months or even years without those precious dreams—dreams that helped him see his Anamaria with perfect recollection. It was as if some latent part of his brain locked away his memories of Anamaria's perfection and would only allow them to come back to him in his sleep.

He had always been conflicted when he had awoken from past dreams. He was happy to see Anamaria in perfect recollection, but horrified that he was forced to relive her death over and over. This time, for the first time in his life, the dream changed. Upon entering Anamaria's room, instead of finding Anamaria dead—as he had hundreds of times before—he found Lissie sprawled and bleeding on the floor in her place. She was wearing the gown he purchased for her, still dressed from the night before. It was more than he could endure. He reacted with fury unlike he had ever known. The only two mortals he ever cared for, both stripped away from him? He would never allow such an unspeakable horror to happen.

He checked the clock on his side table. 11:09AM. He couldn't believe he'd actually fallen back to sleep after his dream. Lissie really had a way of calming him with one touch of her hand. He thought back to how Lissie had awoken him and how perfectly she'd responded. He resisted the urge to turn over and stare at her. He snuck a quick peek as he climbed out of bed and saw she was still sleeping peacefully.

He crept to the bathroom to take an aspirin in an attempt to rid himself of the pain in his head before tiptoeing into the kitchen. He started a pot of coffee and checked his fridge to make sure he had some of the creamer Lissie liked. He was pleased to find that he did. He grabbed eggs, bacon, cheese and tomatoes as well. *This morning, Lissie is going to taste my world-famous omelet,* he thought with pride. It had been years since he had been able to cook for anyone. He and his brothers always cooked when they were together, but the last time that happened was over five years ago, and it had been a rather short visit. Apart from his brothers—and on the rare occasion, his Uncle Samuel— no one else visited his New York home.

By the time he began preparation for breakfast, his headache was gone. He didn't know whether he should give credit to the aspirin or to his giddiness about the prospect of cooking for Lissie.

He cracked and whisked the eggs, diced the tomatoes, and began to cook a few pieces of bacon in a skillet. Once the bacon was crisp, he set it aside to cool so he could break it into small pieces to sprinkle into the omelets.

"Good morning," a groggy voice said from behind him.

He spun around with a smile on his face and said, "Good morning!"

Lissie chuckled and added, "Well, aren't we chipper this morning?"

"You have no idea. I actually fell back asleep last night and didn't wake up until about twenty minutes ago. That's the first time that's happened in years," he chatted ecstatically. "I'm making omelets. What would you like in yours? I have bacon, cheese, tomatoes, and I can chop up some mushrooms or spinach if you'd like," he said with a smile.

"Bacon and cheese would be wonderful," she replied. "Oh! You've already made coffee. Is it ready?" she asked as she marched towards the coffee pot.

"It should be," he said without looking. "The mugs are in the cabinet on the left."

She prepared her coffee and sat down at the island to watch him work. Matthew loved the audience. Cooking had always been one of his favorite pastimes. He spent as much time finding and trying new recipes as a young girl spent obsessing over the newest celebrity heartthrob. He rarely repeated a meal, so it was almost a game for him to find inventive ways to prepare food. But breakfast omelets were a staple in his life, and this was the first time he was making one for a woman. He threw in a little olive oil for a rich flavor, then added some freshly chopped basil and a dash of garlic salt and pepper to spice it up.

"All finished," he announced as he plated the meal and slid it across the island.

"Thank you," Lissie said, clearly amused by his temperament.

He waited on edge for her reaction, and was thrilled when she made a delighted sound at her first taste.

"This is delicious," she said with a full mouth before taking another bite. "I don't usually have time for breakfast in the morning. This really is a treat."

She could not have given him any greater pleasure than those words. He got to work on his own and sat down next to her when it was finished. They ate in contented silence. It was nice to be in the company of another person without the burden of feeling like every moment needed to be filled with conversation. Sitting here, with Lissie, felt so … comfortable. He picked up the dishes when they were finished and took them to the sink. Lissie continued to work on her coffee, but her look changed from one of blissful contentment to concern. *Uh oh*, he thought, *something unpleasant is on her mind*.

Lissie sat for several moments trying to decide whether or not she should bring up the nightmare episode. It had been such an intense moment, and he had called out to her by name in the dream. She decided it was a subject that needed to be broached.

"Do you want to talk about last night?" she asked timidly. She wasn't sure if he would try to brush it off or actually be willing to talk about it with her.

"What part of last night?" he asked, refusing to make eye contact with her.

"The nightmare," she said, confused about what else they might talk about.

He looked relieved as he turned off the faucet and dried his hands. Lissie had no clue how to respond to such strange behavior, so she simply observed and listened.

"I suppose," he said as he refilled both cups of coffee and walked over to the couch where his pillow and blanket were still crumpled on the couch from the night before.

Lissie followed him and sat a few feet away. She didn't know what compelled her to maintain distance, but she felt more comfortable with a few feet between them. She waited patiently for him to begin—it took him some time to organize his thoughts.

"When I was much younger, someone that I held very dear to my heart was murdered. Since then I've had nightmares ... or 'nightmare', I suppose I should say. Sometimes I go for years without it, other times I'll have it every night for a month straight."

Lissie let out a gasp. She had not expected his response, but decided to push for more details.

"Who was murdered? And why? Did they ever catch whoever was responsible?" she pressed.

"I can't say any more," he said with a tone of finality.

Lissie was hurt. She knew she didn't have any right to know the specifics, but she had been the one to wake him up from last night's nightmare. And it had been *she* that he had said was murdered in last night's dream. It gave her a sense of entitlement to know more than he had admitted to her.

"Please don't be upset. I can see the unhappiness on your face," Matthew pleaded. "My family is incredibly tight-knit, and no one outside my family even knows the whole story. We rarely talk about the incident ourselves. Please believe me when I say it's not a slight against you. It's something we've kept private for a long, long time," he finished with his face clothed in grief.

Her heart was softened by his confession and his pleading. She decided that he had revealed more to her than he had likely revealed to any other person outside his family.

"Okay," she said as she reached over and grabbed his hand. "If that's all you can say, then thank you for telling me that much."

His face showed relief that she was letting it go, and Lissie knew she made the right decision. She was determined to ease the tension in the room and change the subject back to their weekend.

"Well, you have me all to yourself for another twelve hours. What do you plan to spend them doing?" Lissie really was curious about his plans for the day.

"Well, I already cooked you breakfast. That was a big part of today's 'to-do' list. If you're amenable to walking, I thought we could take a stroll down the High Line. And we could grab a snack at Chelsea Market after our walk if you'd like," he finished.

"That sounds wonderful. And since I have a whole new closet of clothes and shoes to dress in, I don't even have to go home!" she said with a playful hint of sarcasm. Matthew's face changed to an adorable shade of pink with embarrassment, and Lissie couldn't help but laugh a little. "You didn't, by chance, have an assortment of makeup bought for me did you?"

Now Matthew looked even guiltier than before.

"You did?!?" she shrieked in surprise.

"Well, you see, I bought all the makeup that the stylist at the salon used on you. She said ... it was something ... people often did ... for formal events—in case you needed it ... to touch up your makeup that night ... so you would have all the right shades," he stumbled over his words.

Lissie smirked and put her hands on her hips in feigned irritation. "Well, if it's all here, you better hand it over so I can look like a living person instead of a zombie when we go out."

Matthew laughed at her joke and retrieved the bag. "Don't take too long," he said as she walked toward his bathroom to get ready for the day. He laughed again at his own words and added, "Please, fair maiden, do not leave me alone and deprived. I shan't know how to live in thine absence!" he said in a perfect Italian accent.

Lissie laughed so hard at his last plea, she had tears in her eyes. She could hear him joining her in the other room. *Yup*, she thought, *I think this one's a keeper.*

Twenty-Nine

As Matthew and Lissie walked hand in hand through Chelsea Market, he thought of how easy this relationship felt. *I feel like I've known her for years, not days*, he mused. *And for the first time in what seems like forever, I'm actually thinking of myself as 'Matthew' instead of 'Rogue'. It's nice to feel like a person again rather than an entity.* He was grateful for the quiet afternoon he'd planned for them. The conversation all day had been effortless. As they had walked along the High Line earlier, they talked about the joys of spending time outside, how much they both loved to walk, and how they felt like they needed to explore the city more. They made tentative plans to venture into other parts of the city in the coming weeks and months. Not once did they experience the awkward break in conversation that generally plagued new relationships. *Being with Lissie is effortless*, he thought with satisfaction. Even the periods of silence during their walk felt natural. He stole a glance at Lissie and was happy to see she returned his gratified expression.

"What did you decide to eat?" he asked. They walked through the entire market and checked all the menus.

"I think I've made up my mind," she started, "and I'm going to order for both of us if you don't mind." He gave her a small nod of approval before she took off down the corridor and headed straight for Bar Suzette. She ordered a gruyere, black pepper and thyme crepe first. Then she walked to the Doughnuttery and ordered a dozen assorted doughnuts. Next, she made a beeline to Hale and Hearty for a large bowl of soup. Finally, she ended at Los Tacos No. 1 and ordered all four varieties of tacos. With their hands full of a myriad of choices, they sat down at a table and spread all the food out in front of them.

"I feel like you made some great decisions here," Matthew said approvingly. "I think you should get the first bite of everything."

Lissie didn't need any more encouragement as she dug into the amazing food in front of them. She took a single bite of each dish and made sure she savored it before moving to the next. Matthew watched her, excited to see her reactions to each new food. She was especially interested in the grilled cactus taco—it took her three or four tiny bites before she decided she didn't like it and handed it over to Matthew. Her favorites were the crepe and the doughnuts. His favorites were the tacos and the doughnuts; but he kept that last part to himself so she could enjoy as many as she wanted without worrying about saving any for him. By the time they were finished, they were both stuffed.

"I'm not sure I'll be able to stand," she groaned as she sat back in her chair and placed a hand over her bloated stomach. "I ate entirely too much food for one sitting. Why did you let me do that to myself?" she asked accusatorily.

Matthew let out a short laugh and replied, "I had to. You were having a love affair with your food. At one point I was certain you were going to stop eating and start kissing one of those doughnuts." Lissie sat forward, reached across the table, and slugged Matthew in the arm.

"Ow!" Matthew shouted with laughter. "That really hurt! You're a lot stronger than you look." Lissie looked offended for a second before returning the laughter.

They walked back to Matthew's apartment—Lissie was adamant that she needed to walk off all the food she had just eaten. When they arrived it was already six p.m., and neither felt the inclination to go out again after the busy weekend they had spent together.

"Would you like to stay in and watch a movie?" Matthew asked.

"That sounds perfect. Do you have popcorn and candy and soda? We could make it into a true movie theater experience!" she said excitedly.

"I think I might," he replied sneakily. At that, he walked into the kitchen and pulled a Whirley Pop and a butter dispenser from one of the cabinets.

"You've got to be kidding me?" Lissie exclaimed. "I haven't seen one of these since I was a kid!"

She helped him measure out all the kernels and salt with precision. It was obvious to Matthew at this point that Lissie was one of those people who *always* followed the recipe—exactly as it was written with no deviations whatsoever. He giggled a little at her attention to detail, but made no comment.

While she was melting the butter to go on top of the popcorn, Matthew snuck into his office and returned holding a large box. As soon as he set it on the counter, Lissie ran over and asked to open it. He smiled as she tore into the box like it was her birthday. There were M&Ms in every variety, Runts, Nerds, Crunch Bars, Rolos, Junior Mints, Skittles, and Kit Kat bars inside. Lissie's eyes were as big as a kid's on Christmas.

"And I can eat any of it?" she asked as if he'd given her the greatest gift of all time.

"Anything you want, it's yours," he replied. "If I had known how much you liked candy, I would've skipped the rest of the weekend and merely given you this box!"

She rolled her eyes and gave him a disgruntled look, but quickly returned to the task at hand. She grabbed a box of each kind of candy and took them to the coffee table while Matthew finished buttering the popcorn.

"So why on earth do you have a huge box of candy sitting around in your house?" she asked.

"Well, every year on Halloween in our building, we have a sign-up sheet so all the children know which apartments they can come to for candy. I pride myself on always having full-size boxes. And the kids always race for my apartment first because they know I have the best candy selection," he answered.

"Well I think that's great. Maybe I'll have to come over to help hand out candy this year. What movie should we watch?" Lissie asked with a flirtatious smirk.

God, she's an adorable woman. Already making plans for the two of us months in advance. I like her more every minute, he thought before answering her question. "Anything you want. Take a look at the collection I have, but keep in mind we can also order one from On Demand." He paused for a moment before adding, "And I would love for you to come over and help me hand out candy on Halloween."

Lissie looked over Matthew's collection of over four hundred films. He organized all his movies into sections—action, war, comedy, horror, cartoons, romantic comedies, science fiction, fantasy, and classics. She glanced over the action, war and horror sections—those had never been her kinds of movies. She reluctantly moved past the romantic comedies—her regular movies of choice. She decided comedy would be a good section to look in—there were only one or two movies in the entire section that she had seen. She spent several minutes reading the backs of boxes and finally decided on *The Darjeeling Limited*. She handed it to Matthew, and he looked at her with an odd expression.

"I've never heard of it, but it sounds like a funny concept," she said quickly.

"Well I think you've made an excellent choice. This is one of my favorites," he told her with a smile. "But I'll warn you, it's a different kind of movie. People either love it or hate it, and I'm not sure we can be together if you hate it," he jested.

Matthew put the movie in and situated himself on the couch right next to her. She leaned into him as he placed his arm around her shoulders. The low back of the couch was the perfect height for her to lean against his arm without having her neck in an uncomfortable position. She felt his lips brush her forehead, and she let out a contented sigh. *This has been such a comfortable weekend*, she thought as he fast forwarded through the previews. *I wonder if he feels the same ... like we've known each other for months instead of a few days. What will we do during the work week? I suppose we'll talk about that tonight.*

I don't even know what his work schedule looks like! she thought with alarm. *The fact that he has apartments all over the world could mean he'll be gone months at a time.* At that thought, she sat up, reached over Matthew, and hit pause on the controller.

"Already regretting your decision? We're not even through the opening credits," Matthew said with playful accusation. His expression grew serious when he saw the look on her face. "What's wrong?" he now asked with urgency.

"What does your work schedule look like, Matthew? Because I know you have apartments all over the world. And I'm not sure I can handle a relationship with someone that's gone more often than he's here. I mean, I'm not trying to sound needy, but I'm new at this. And I don't want to start a relationship without knowing what I'm getting myself into," she finished, on the verge of getting emotional.

He turned to face her and grabbed her hands in his own. "Lissie, I have the freedom to stay wherever I like for as long as I like."

"So what does that mean?" she asked, frustrated by the ambiguity of the response.

"My work trips last one to two weeks tops, and those are few and far between. If you want, I could probably be in town for at least three weeks out of each month. Is that what you want?" he asked softly.

"I think ... I think, yes," she said timidly.

"You think?" he teased. "Because if you're unsure, I can stay away for much longer periods of time."

She slapped his chest and laughed. "I'm sure," she said with finality as she relaxed back into his side. "And you can start the movie again."

Thirty

AS SOON AS the movie ended, Matthew nervously turned off the TV and looked at Lissie.

"Well?" he asked.

"I'm trying to decide what that was," she sounded thoughtful. "Because there were parts that were so hilarious I was in tears. But I'm not sure how to gauge how much I enjoyed it, because I haven't watched anything like it before."

Matthew chuckled at her statement. "As long as you thought it was funny, that's all I needed to hear." He gave her a quick kiss.

She smiled back at him and finished her box of Runts. She burned through four boxes of candy during the movie, and Matthew was certain she would be in a sugar coma in a matter of minutes.

"What would you like to do tonight?" he asked. "Because I'm happy to have you stay or drive you home. I'm not the one who has to wake up for work in the morning."

She thought for a moment before responding, "I *want* to stay, but it's probably best for me to go back to my place. You really don't have to drive me home though. The subway is only a few blocks from here, and it takes me straight home."

Matthew tried to hide his disappointment, but he figured she knew what he was thinking because she hadn't had any issues reading his emotions the rest of the weekend. "Well I'll at least walk you to the station then," he said, resigned to her departure.

She grabbed her things and waited for him to join her by the front door. As they silently rode down the elevator, they held hands. The mood was clearly one of despair for both of them.

"This is ridiculous," Matthew began. "I'm not leaving on my next trip for three weeks, but I feel like I'm saying 'goodbye' for good. If you would like to see me in the next few days, give me a call and I'll come over. I hope you don't mind, but I programmed my number in your phone and yours in mine."

Lissie smiled, "I don't understand why it feels like this either! But you'll definitely be hearing from me soon. And the same goes for you—if you want to see me, just call."

When they arrived at the subway stop, Lissie reached her arms up around Matthew's neck and gave him a long hug. He wrapped his arms around her waist and rested his chin on the top of her head. When she began to pull away, Matthew pulled her close again and kissed her fiercely. He hadn't allowed himself to be physical with her when they were alone in the apartment, but out in the open air it somehow felt safer. He was happy to feel her return his kiss with equal ferocity, and when he finally pulled away, he could hear her breathing had quickened.

"I'll see you soon," she said as she turned and walked down the stairs into the subway station.

Matthew stood there for a long time after she left. Her scent still lingered in the air around him, or maybe it was left on his clothes from their embrace. All he knew was that he needed to spend more time with Lissie Renaud. At some point during the course of the weekend, she had stopped being Anamaria's reincarnation and had begun to simply be Lissie. She was funny, brilliant, creative, and adventurous despite her previously innocuous life. It had taken one tiny push in the right direction for her to dive in head first—to want to live a life of adventure. In his experience, if a person was desperate for adventure after such a small push, she would undoubtedly change her entire life to accommodate the need to *live*. He decided right then and there that he would be responsible for showing her adventures she had never dreamed. He walked home feeling gratified by the notion.

When he entered his apartment, he realized a voice message was waiting on his cell. He was overjoyed at the prospect that Lissie had already called. As he entered his password and listened to the message, he grew serious.

"Rogue. The contract will be fulfilled tonight. Stein is in his office."

When the message ended, Matthew abruptly snapped back to real life. Gregory Stein would die tonight.

Thirty-one

LISSIE SLEPT so soundly the night before, she hadn't even messed up the sheets on her bed. She hadn't dreamed a single dream all night and was disappointed when she woke up. She really wanted to dream about that kiss Matthew left her with the previous night. In fact, she was hoping she would relive that kiss sooner rather than later.

She quickly dialed her brother on the phone and was once again met with a voicemail. "Hey, John, it's Lissie. Call me as soon as you get this. I have SO much to tell you! EEE!" she squealed as she ended the call. She couldn't wait to tell him about her weekend.

She grabbed her thermos of coffee and rushed out the door for work, disappointed that she hadn't gotten a delicious breakfast like the past two mornings. All the way into work, she reminisced about her perfect weekend. There was not a single moment during the weekend that didn't resonate in her memory with bliss.

She glanced around at the other passengers boarding the subway and realized she was the only one who looked ready for the day. Every other rider looked like a sleepwalker dreading the week ahead. She couldn't help but be excited at the idea of calling Matthew in a day or two and scheduling another date. Work would at least take her mind off him—hopefully—until she felt the appropriate amount of time had passed before she could call him without seeming desperate. She entered the lobby of her building with a smile.

"Hello, Ms. Renaud," the receptionist said.

"Hello, Susan! Has Mr. Stein arrived yet?" Lissie asked.

"When I got here this morning, the system log showed that he came in late yesterday and hasn't left," the receptionist replied.

"Oh no," Lissie said with a bit of gloom. *That means he's been in another fight with his wife. My job description today will involve lots of coffee runs and writing down angry messages from Mrs. Stein.*

The receptionist gave her a sympathetic look as Lissie walked to the elevator. *Welcome back to real life,* she told herself as she ascended to her office on the forty-fifth floor.

She exited the elevator into a dark lobby. *He must have fallen asleep last night and still not woken this morning,* she thought as she flipped all the office lights on. She tucked her purse under her desk and listened to the messages on the office phone. Mrs. Stein had already called three times this morning and was furious that Mr. Stein had left the previous night. *He might be sleeping here for the next few nights,* Lissie thought sadly. Their relationship had been rocky for the last four or five years. Mr. Stein dived into planning his new investing strategies when he first came up with the idea six years ago. It was right after his plan received approval by the Stein Securities Board of Directors that Lissie had been hired as his new executive assistant. Three months later, Mrs. Stein came into the office convinced that Lissie was having an affair with her husband. It had taken months of daily check-ins with his wife for Mr. Stein to prove he wasn't cheating. After that, things were never the same between them. Lissie was sure that Mrs. Stein hadn't been too thrilled that her husband was more interested in developing a new investment model for his business than spending time with his wife. And who could blame her? *Thank God they never had kids,* Lissie thought with a shake of her head.

After she had taken notes on all the messages from the weekend, she decided it was time to wake up her boss. She walked to the door and knocked quietly. "Mr. Stein?" she said, hoping not to startle him too badly from his slumber. No response came. She knocked more loudly. Still nothing. "Mr. Stein!" she yelled as she tried the door handle. It was locked. Thankfully she kept a spare key to his office door in her desk. As she searched her drawers for the key, she began to feel a twinge of panic. *What if he had a heart attack in there and was all alone? Or what if he choked to death? Oh, God! I really don't want to find him dead in there,* she thought as she found the key.

She ran back to the door, turned the key and slowly opened the door.

Her heart stopped. Mr. Stein was sitting in his reading chair with the lamp on. A book splattered with blood lay spine-up on the ground at his feet. His right hand hung lifelessly over the arm of the chair. The entire right side of his head was blown off, and blood and brains covered the wall next to him. The amount of blood on his clothing, on the chair, and on the floor beneath him was incomprehensible. Lissie stood rooted in the same spot for either minutes or hours—time seemed to stand still. She heard wind coming from the glass to her right and realized one of the windows behind Mr. Stein's desk was cracked. The window was still intact, but a small hole in the center finally made it clear to Lissie what exactly had happened here:

Mr. Stein had been murdered.

After the initial shock wore off, Lissie screamed at the top of her lungs and didn't stop screaming until she felt herself blacking out from the lack of air. She let go of the door handle and realized her hand was in pain from the death-grip she had maintained from first opening the office door. She ran to the phone and called security downstairs. When the guard answered the phone, Lissie's mind couldn't put intelligible words together. Her breath was coming in and going out far too quickly, but she finally screamed, "Mr. Stein is dead! Come fast!" She heard panic on the other line, but in a matter of seconds, she passed out from hyperventilation.

Thirty-Two

MATTHEW WAS PACING the floor. He knew, without a doubt, that Lissie had found out her boss was dead at this point. He checked his phone so often that he forced himself to put the cursed thing down. Surely she would call. He wanted so badly to be the person she called … the person she would rely on for comfort in this time of loss.

This contract was different. Someone he cared for deeply was in the middle of this one, and he didn't know how to handle the situation.

Matthew had knocked out the building's electrical system for the kill, and by the time the power was back on in the building, he was long gone. Matthew had no idea what kind of scene was left to find. He was even more worried that Lissie might be the one to find it. He swallowed back the bile that rose in his throat as he pushed away the mental image his brain concocted. He began pacing faster.

Please call, he thought as noon rolled on by.

Thirty-Three

LISSIE WAS STILL in shock. She kept reliving the morning in her head. After regaining consciousness from her earlier fainting episode and giving her statement to several detectives, she sat, silent and unmoving, for several hours. Her mind was immersed in a heavy fog, and the world around her was a blur of sounds and motion. Every once in a while a single word would slip through the fog. "Stein." "Secretary." "Blood." "Assassination." When that last word slammed into her mind, she blinked a few times and looked around. *This is something out of a book or a movie—this doesn't happen in real life. People aren't actually assassinated!* her mind screamed in protest to the word. But the memory of her bloodied, lifeless boss forced her to admit it could be a possibility. Police were everywhere in the office. Her desk had been commandeered by a detective making calls on the phone. There were three board members talking with other detectives near the entry to Mr. Stein's office … or what used to be his office. As soon as the detectives were finished questioning them, Lissie jumped up and walked to where they were standing.

"I'm not sure who we should call about this," Mr. Callahan, the CFO of Stein Securities was saying. "Maybe we'll just make a call to the Times and give them an exclusive."

"A reporter? You're worried about making this into a news story?" Lissie was disgusted. *Of course the board is going to try to turn this into something profitable. Free publicity is the best publicity.* She thought for a moment as the men stared at her, shocked that she was once again speaking. Or maybe they were shocked that she had just reprimanded the board? She didn't care.

"If you're going to bring anyone in, it better be Jason Luce at the Journal. He knew Mr. Stein personally and wrote that piece that ran earlier this month on the new investment strategies he was implementing in the company. I believe he'll honor Mr. Stein's memory while keeping the company's appearance clean," she advised them.

The men seemed to appreciate the suggestion and began giving nods of approval to each other. "Thank you, dear. The Wall Street Journal would be the perfect paper to run this story," Mr. Callahan said. "Once Mr. Luce has your statements about the incident, you can have as much time off as you need—weeks, even months if you don't feel up to coming back. And of course, it will be paid leave, so don't worry about your finances."

Dear? Lissie thought derisively. *Which means 'receptionist-whose-name-I-never-bothered-to-learn'.*

"And keep your statement to the journalist PG. The last thing we need is a bunch of employees panicking about the possibility of getting shot through their office windows," Mr. Callahan added in a hushed voice.

Lissie wanted to grit her teeth at the request.

"Thank you. As soon as I've given my statement to Mr. Luce, I'll get out of your hair," she said as she turned and walked angrily back to the chair where she had spent most of the day.

I'm supposed to gloss over the details of a murder? Not likely. She wanted to yell in the man's face. She wasn't going to lie to Jason. She knew Mr. Stein deserved better than that. He was the CEO of the company, and his story shouldn't be lessened because of a worried employee.

There were other upsetting issues on her mind as well. *Paid leave with nothing to do is awful,* Lissie thought with distress. She required a full-time work schedule to maintain joy in her life, and she wasn't about to quit her job just because of this incident. *But I suppose I'll have more time to invest in Matthew's apartment,* she mused.

An hour later, Jason finally showed up and made a beeline for Lissie. He had a grim look affixed to his face as he sat down next to her.

"I'm so, so sorry," he started. "I was interviewing someone else when I got the call."

"It's fine, Jason. You don't have to apologize," Lissie said.

"No. I feel awful that you've had to go through this. I heard what happened. You found him?"

"Oh. Yes. I unlocked his office this morning and walked into … a bloodbath. I'm sure that's a bit too strong for a single murder, or assassination as my mind continues to scream. But it looked like a bloodbath. His brains were on the wall." She stopped talking to calm her breathing and keep from getting emotional.

Jason looked more upset at the fact that she was a witness to the horror than anything else. "Can we do this somewhere else? A coffeehouse or a bar? I want to get you out of here," he said.

Lissie couldn't ever remember feeling more grateful for a change of scenery. "Yes, please."

Jason hoped that something good might still come from this horrible incident. He had been interested in asking Lissie Renaud out on a date since his first visit to Stein Securities three months earlier, and he took her request to use him as the exclusive reporter for this case as a good sign. His friendship with her hadn't gone as deep as he would like over the course of his visits, but he could undeniably call her a friend. He once had to wait six hours at Mr. Stein's office for an interview, only to have it rescheduled for a later date. Lissie spent most of the six hours answering his questions and trying to keep him entertained. Despite his frustration over the postponement, he walked away feeling that the day had been a success. As he now sat across the small café table from her, he only wished the circumstances for this outing were different.

"Umm …" he began, unsure of how emotional she was, "… would you like to talk about what happened today? We can stay off the record for a while if you just need to talk."

Lissie gave him a wry look as if she was thinking that nothing was ever 'off the record' with a reporter. *Smart girl*, he thought with a smirk.

"Where do you want to start?" Lissie asked.

"How about this morning," he said as he took out his tape recorder.

She told him the same story she told the detectives three times earlier in the day. She was a professional—never stuttered, never got emotional. She simply told the story as if she were reading it from a newspaper.

Jason admired her resolve to stay calm. He had been around tragedy enough in his career to see beneath the façade people put on for these interviews. But he realized Lissie was determined to remain impassive.

"I really do consider you a friend, Lissie," he said when she finished her recounting of the day's events. "Please tell me you're going to be okay."

Lissie gave him a sad smile. "I'm sure I'll be fine. I have someone in my life who I think will be happy to help me through this," she said with a barely noticeable smirk on her downturned face. "But I'm not sure what to do about my job. I doubt I'll have one for much longer," she said thoughtfully.

Jason wasn't sure if she was talking about him being the person to help her through—though he wildly hoped that was the case. And he hadn't previously thought about her job situation. He decided not to push either subject any further.

"Part of my article will hopefully include some info about the responsible parties—in the event that they're caught. Can you think of anyone who could have possibly had problems with Stein?" he asked.

"Well," she thought for a moment before continuing, "Mrs. Stein always had problems with her husband, but isn't that most marriages? Their issues seemed fairly normal to me. And I don't think she's capable of murder. There are some competitors in the investment business that expressed disapproval over strategies we were planning to implement into the new company design, but mostly that was because they were frustrated about losing high-end clientele. There were never any threats toward Stein or the company—just complaints. Then there were some employees that were pretty upset about the restructuring of the company. But again, they were distraught about having to learn a bunch of new programs when they had already been in upper management for ten or twenty years. Honestly, I can't see a cause for any of them to have Gregory Stein murdered. I just don't understand who would."

Jason was worried when her professional façade would shatter and her grief would come pouring through. But Lissie was tougher than most women would be in the same situation. He wanted so badly to reach over and grab her hand—to comfort her in this time of loss. But he knew she was teetering on the edge of an emotional breakdown, and he was too much of a gentleman to take advantage of a woman who just experienced such trauma.

He tried to make small talk as they sat in the café, drinking their coffee. But Lissie's downturned face and one-word answers were evidence of her true desire. She wanted to be alone.

"Well, here's my card. I really would love to grab a bite to eat or another cup of coffee with you sometime soon. And don't hesitate to call if you need a shoulder to cry on—I have really, really comfortable shoulders," he said, hoping his untimely flirting wouldn't come across as offensive.

Her returning grin was small but beautiful. He stood and gave her a quick hug from the side—wishing he could wrap his arms around her tightly and never let go—and left the coffeehouse with a backward glance. From what he had learned about her during his interviews at Stein Securities, and now with her ability to stay calm during this high-stress situation, he decided she really was his dream woman. He just wasn't sure how to attain that dream.

Thirty-Four

LISSIE CHECKED her watch. *Four p.m? My God, I've been here too long*, she thought as she reached for her purse and grabbed her suit jacket. She wasn't ready to go home to a lonely apartment, but didn't have anywhere else to go. She reached into her purse, grabbed her phone, and dialed the only person she was willing to see at the moment.

"Hello?" Matthew said with a calm voice.

"Matthew," was the only word Lissie could seem to choke out. It was as if just hearing his voice set her emotions off like a bomb.

"What's wrong?" he asked, now with urgency in his voice.

"I need ... I need to meet you for a drink. Where can I meet you for a drink? Somewhere near your place?" she asked, desperately trying to keep from weeping.

"Absolutely. The Ale House on 7th between 27th and 28th. I'll be there in twenty," he said as he ended the call.

She walked out of the coffeehouse and let the warm afternoon air wash over her. She knew she would remember this day for the rest of her life—how she found him, her confused emotional state, the temperature of the air outside, the way her coffee tasted. She turned to head toward the subway but quickly decided she needed to walk all the way to the bar. The temperature was so pleasant; she hoped it would help calm her emotions by the time she looked into Matthew's face.

As she headed up 6th Avenue, she looked around. People dressed in their business attire walked up and down the streets, oblivious to the dangers that surrounded them in the world. A family passed, children giggling. Lissie felt none of the joy she would usually experience on a day like today. She felt ... cold. Not scared or worried. Just ... cold. As if all the warmth and happiness in the world had been sucked out of her life, and she only existed as a walking, breathing shell of a person. Everyone around her was acting as if nothing tragic had happened, which, when she thought about it, was true for most of the people in the city. Moreover, Stein Securities wasn't going public with the murder until Jason ran the story—which could be anywhere from two days up to a month. She turned her head down and decided that walking was only making things worse for her. She hailed a cab and got in. When the driver asked where she was going, she couldn't think straight.

"Where to?" the cabbie asked a second time as he turned around. When he looked her over, he quickly added, "And if you're going to throw up, let me know so I can pull over. No puking in the cab."

"7th Ave. Between 28th and 29th," she finally whispered. The driver, still uncertain about whether she was going to get sick during the ride, reluctantly turned and headed north toward the bar.

She dialed her brother once again, but this time he actually answered the phone. "Hi, Lissie!" he said excitedly. "I'm sorry to do this to you—and I really want to hear about your weekend, I promise—but I'm about to run into a meeting. Can I call you back in a few hours?" Lissie forced as much of the emotion out of her voice as possible before answering. "Sure! I'll talk to you later. Hope you have a good meeting," she said as she hung up the phone. Well at least she would get to talk to Matthew. It was probably better that John hadn't been able to talk. There was no way she could've explained everything to him before she made it to the bar—or with the cab driver listening in on the conversation. She heaved a sigh and stared out the window.

The cab arrived at the bar ten minutes later. Thankfully, what she saw when she walked through the front door was that Matthew had already gotten them a secluded booth and held two drinks in his hands. The bar was exactly what she hoped for from an Irish pub—dark wooden countertops, pillars, booths and benches. The bar felt old—like it had been there for decades—which suited Lissie just fine. She always felt more connected with things that were old, established, and stable. Because of the time of day, the place was mostly empty, for which she was entirely grateful. God only knew she would be an emotional mess here, and she had enough trouble getting emotional by herself in the comforts of her own home. As a child, crying had been frowned upon by her parents. They told her time and again that she was going to have to develop thick skin in order to survive in the world. She learned only to cry in the company of her brother or by herself. Crying in public was going to be a whole new level of strange for her. Matthew turned to the door as she walked in, put the drinks back down on the bar and raced over to her. *I must truly look awful if this is his first reaction*, she thought. He gently grabbed her shoulders and looked deeply into her eyes.

"Please tell me what's wrong," he said with a command in his tone that she had not heard from him before.

"Drinks first," she replied as she brushed his hands off her shoulders, headed toward the bar, picked both glasses up, and marched toward the table where Matthew's jacket was lying.

As she sat down, she threw back the first drink and held the empty glass up to Matthew. "I'm gonna have to drink more of these before I talk about this day."

He nodded, eyes filling with dread, and headed to the bar with the empty glass. When he returned, he set three full glasses in front of her and kept one for himself. He gently sat down across from her, seemingly worried that if he made any fast movements she might be scared and run away.

She gave a small laugh at what she supposed were his intentions, and Matthew looked up at her, wide-eyed, as if she were insane.

"I'm not going to run away if you move too quickly, Matthew," she said with a humorless smile.

Matthew was uncertain on how to proceed in this situation. The last time he had come face to face with a victim's family, he had been mourning the loss as much as they had. And he had never encountered one of *his* victims' relations. This ... this was uncharted territory. He'd been trained for almost every situation, but where was the handbook for falling in love with a victim's assistant?

As she finished off her third drink and placed her hand on the forth, Matthew decided it was time to step in. He laid his hand over hers and held it in place so she couldn't take another drink.

"Please. You're going to get sick before you even realize you're drunk. Slow down and talk to me," he pleaded.

He could tell she wanted to swat his hand away by the defiant look in her eyes. But it quickly softened as she stared into his concerned eyes.

"Okay," she said as her hand relaxed on the glass. He took her hand gently in his and brought her palm to his lips for a brief moment. That was apparently too much for her to handle right then. Her bottom lip began to quiver with the threat of sobs. A single tear rolled down her right cheek as she took a deep breath to calm herself.

"This morning, I got to work and found Mr. Stein had locked himself in his office and was asleep." She took one small sip from her glass before continuing. "I knocked a few times to try to wake him up, but when he didn't respond, I knew something was wrong. So I unlocked the door with my spare key." At that point in the story, she paused to finish the rest of her drink. She wiped her mouth with a shaky hand which Matthew quickly captured and caressed to try to calm her.

Damn it, damn it, damn it! Matthew's mind screamed. *She found him. She's the one who found him dead.* He didn't know what to do. He didn't know how to take care of her. He desperately hoped this incident wouldn't scar her for the rest of her life.

"I don't ... I don't even know how to tell you this," she said with a slur creeping into her speech. "He was dead."

"Oh my God!" Matthew exclaimed with what he hoped sounded like true surprise (though at this point he wasn't sure she would know the difference). "Was it a heart attack? Or a stroke? Men his age always have to worry about those things."

"A bullet to the head," Lissie quietly said without any emotion or quiver in her voice. She looked straight into Matthew's shocked eyes—which were truly shocked at her delivery of the news—and told him every detail. "The bullet struck his left temple. The entire right side of his head was blown off. Brains, blood, and bits of skull were stuck to the wall and all over the floor." She started to cry softly as she continued. "I felt like I was in a TV show or a movie. It was horrible, Matthew. Absolutely horrible," she finished as her tears began to flow more freely. Her posture sank almost into a crouch over her drink, as if she were fiercely protecting the only thing that mattered in her world at that moment.

"Oh my God," Matthew proclaimed. "I'm getting us more drinks," he said as he walked back to the bar.

"Make all the rest virgins," he said to the bartender as he handed over a few hundreds. "And can you get us some food as well?" The bartender nodded and handed him two glasses of coke.

When he returned to the table, he slid into the seat next to Lissie and put his arm around her waist.

"I'm so sorry you had to see that," he said softly as he kissed her temple. She slumped into his side, and he felt her body shake with emotion.

Matthew was grateful that he had picked this establishment for them to meet. Apart from one table in the back and a few patrons sitting at the bar near the entry, the place was empty. But he supposed that would be normal for most bars at this time of day. He knew business would soon be picking up due to happy hour. The pub was run by an efficient set of bartenders—not too intrusive yet somehow always attentive. It was exactly the environment they needed in this situation.

The waitress brought over a platter of appetizers and eyed Lissie with worry. *Is she okay?* the woman mouthed to Matthew. He nodded, and she walked away to give them back their privacy.

Lissie continued to quietly cry into his shoulder. And he was particularly satisfied that she had chosen his shoulder over anyone else's.

"Would you like to talk about the rest of the day?" he asked her softly.

"Well," she began with a not-so-subtle slur in her speech, "Jason came to interview me—he's a report … porter … reporter," she managed to say after several attempts.

Matthew was less than thrilled at the first name basis she seemed to be on with this 'Jason' person.

"And we got coffee together so he could get me out of the office for me."

Matthew wasn't quite sure what she was trying to convey with this statement, so he tried to clarify. "He took you to get coffee so you didn't have to talk in front of the detectives?" he could only hope.

"No. He's worried. So I got coffee with him," she answered as if it was the most obvious thing in the world.

"Umm … so he got you out of the office. So that you could get away from the crime scene," he said with a slight question.

"Isn't that what I said?" she nearly yelled indignantly. She was upset that he was having trouble following her 'very clear' train of thought.

"Yes. I suppose that is what you said," he said with a twinge of amusement. "What did you talk about with this *Jason*?" he asked.

"Nope. Uh uh." She turned to face him with a scowl and pointed her finger right in his face. "You don't get to play jealous boyfriend today. Nope. You just be happy a friend had me," she finished as she grabbed a mozzarella stick off the platter and took a bite.

"I am happy you weren't alone. But you could have called me. I would have come to get you, and I would've taken you home—either to your place or mine," he said wistfully.

"The boss told me I had to get interviewed and then take months off to recover. Which basically means to go home and not come back. I doubt I even have a job now," she let out a quick sob ... or hiccup ... Matthew wasn't sure which.

He thought about what she had revealed to him and immediately felt sick. *She's losing her job? How did I not think of that before? Surely I can fix this? She's not the kind of woman who would accept money for nothing. I have to get her to work on my apartment immediately. And pay her a lot for it.*

After a long pause, Lissie continued the story as if she had been telling him all along. "So then I told him how I don't know who murdered him. There are so many weird people in his life—competitors, employees, and especially his horrible wife. Anyone could be the one. I don't know why he had so many people hating him. He was a brilliant man. And now he's just ... dead." She stopped talking, and the look on her face grew grave.

Matthew was sure the reality of the situation was sinking in right at this moment.

"My glass is empty. And that makes me feel like crying," she said.

Nope. No reality check. Merely the absence of a drink.

He caught the bartender's eye and motioned for the check. He really needed to get her home.

"So," he wasn't sure how to ask this of a very drunk Lissie, but decided to broach the subject nonetheless. "What do you say to working on my place for a while? While you're taking time off from your job?"

She whipped her head around to look him in the eyes, and it appeared she was searching for something in his face.

"You're making me charity," she said with accusation in her tone.

"No! Honest to God. I asked you to redecorate my place before all this, remember? How can it be charity if I asked you over the weekend?" he scolded her.

She looked at him for a long moment before placing both hands on her hips and slightly lifting her nose in the air. "Fine. I'll do it. But I'm not cheap. And I'll have to come look at everything and take measurements before I can give you an estimate."

Matthew wanted to laugh but decided his life was more precious to him than that. "Okay," he replied. "I expect you to start this week."

"Deal," she said as she grabbed Matthew's left hand that had previously been resting on the table and forced him into an awkward handshake.

"Now finish that drink so I can get you home," he commanded. "Would you like to go to your place or mine?"

Now Lissie looked like she was going to really start sobbing.

Oh no, Matthew thought nervously. *What did I say?*

"You're going to leave me alone?" she yelled as he tried to calm her quickly.

"No! No no no. I'm going to go with you. I only wanted to know where you would feel more comfortable," he tried to explain calmly.

My God ... It's like she's a four year old! he thought with a little humor.

"Oh. Well then, I choose my place. It's more cozy. And there are books. *My* books," she said emphatically.

Matthew was completely confused why the presence of books had any bearing whatsoever on the location where Lissie would be sleeping, but he knew better than to question an emotionally unstable drunk woman.

Lissie abruptly stood, nearly falling over as she tried to exit the booth by sliding over the top of Matthew. He slid out and steadied her as she grabbed his jacket.

"Let's go," she announced with finality.

Matthew walked quickly to the bartender, handed him more money, and thanked him for the attentive service. By the time he was finished, Lissie was halfway out the door, and he had to run to grab her before she walked right out into traffic. As soon as he placed a hand on her arm, she screamed, "Get off me!

I'm a grown-ass woman! I can walk by myself!"

Matthew let go of her and threw his arms up in the air, sparing a glance at the passersby who were eyeing him suspiciously.

"I am only trying to help you," he whispered firmly. "Please don't yell. I promise I'm merely trying to help." He only hoped she would calm down.

"Fine. You can help me," she said as she straightened her shirt and put her arm through his. "But if you talk to me like I'm a child, I'll scream for the police to help me."

Oh my God, Matthew thought with dread. *Hundreds of years of avoiding police recognition, and a drunk woman could undo everything in a second. No more heavy drinking for her. Ever.*

"No problem, Lissie. You're an adult, and I'm going to treat you as such," he agreed.

"Good," she nodded. "Now can we get a cab? My heels are going to shred my Achilles if I have to walk in them any longer," she said, as she nearly fell over trying to remove her high heels.

Matthew was grateful she had grabbed onto his arm, or she would now be lying face-down on the sidewalk. He kept her upright and managed to hail a cab at the same time.

"67th between Broadway and Amsterdam," he told the driver as he helped Lissie into the cab. By the time they reached her house, she was almost asleep on his shoulder.

"Lissie?" he asked as he helped her lift her head.

"Huh? Are we already home? That took like, three minutes," she said in awe.

More like twenty minutes, but Matthew knew better than to argue with her.

As they stepped out of the cab, Lissie fumbled through her purse for her keys, and Matthew paid for the trip.

"Found them!" she yelled as she stumbled toward the front door of her building.

"Hello, Miss Renaud," the doorman said to her with a look of confusion written plainly on his face.

"Thank you so much for letting us in!" she began. "I just found my keys!"

The doorman's eyes cut to Matthew with a look of fatherly protectiveness. "Miss Renaud, you call down if you need anything. Anything at all," he finished, still staring down Matthew.

"Sure, sure," she said dismissively. "But if you're worried about this guy, you shouldn't be. He's one of the good guys. The bad guys shot Mr. Stein in the head. Matthew just helped me get drunk," she finished as she entered into the elevator and waited impatiently for Matthew to join her.

The doorman's eyes grew wide, and he shot a questioning look at Matthew. Matthew nodded to the man to convey his own protectiveness. Apparently, the message was received because the doorman smiled tightly and returned to his desk. But as the elevator doors closed, it was obvious that the issue would be plaguing the concerned man for the rest of the night.

As soon as Lissie set foot into her apartment, she dropped her purse and headed straight to her bed. She knew one thing and one thing only—it was time for her to fall asleep. She jumped onto her queen-sized bed, fully clothed, and started to doze off. She suddenly remembered there was someone else in her apartment.

"Matthew?" she yelled into the other room.

"Hold on, Lissie. I'm shutting and locking your front door," he replied.

I forgot to shut the door? That's weird, she thought in her drunken state.

When Matthew entered the room, he took her high heels from her grip and helped her take off her suit jacket. She turned onto her side in a sudden movement he wasn't expecting and nearly kicked him in his gut.

"Are you comfortable?" he asked softly.

"Mmhmm," she replied as she rapidly fell asleep.

Lissie's phone began to ring in the other room. He quickly found her purse on the floor and pulled out the phone. *John ... I wonder if I should get this.* He walked to her doorway, hoping she wouldn't be angry if he woke her up.

"Lissie?" he asked as she looked up groggily at him from the bed. All he heard in return was a grunt. "Do you want to talk to your brother?"

"You talk to my brother. He's the one you're gonna have to get past," she said as her head hit the pillow again.

Matthew shook his head and answered the phone. "Hello?"

"Umm. Who is this?" John asked, unprepared for a male voice on his sister's phone.

"My name is Matthew McCloud. I'm your sister's boyfriend," he answered with a smile. He couldn't help the joy he felt when he said those words.

"Boyfriend? Wow. I knew she was going on a date, but I never expected that. Now I know why she sounded so happy in her messages. I might go into shock," John said.

Matthew laughed in response and said, "It was a whirlwind weekend."

"I can see that. Well ... if she's serious enough to call you her boyfriend, then I feel I have a brotherly responsibility to tell you that if you ever break her heart, I'll break your nose. I've officially warned you. And I'm sorry if that seems cheesy to you, but I've been waiting to say that to someone since she was fourteen years old." Matthew heard John chuckle a little before asking if he could talk to Lissie.

"Lissie? Your brother wants to talk to you. Can you talk?" Matthew asked as he walked to her bed. She grabbed the phone that he held out and said something—though Matthew wasn't sure if she had actually formed words. She held the phone up to him and began snoring as soon as it left her grasp.

"She had a really bad day at work, but I'll let her tell you about that tomorrow," Matthew told him.

"Whoa. She not only has a boyfriend, but she's drunk as well? This early? I have no idea who my sister has become," John said, worried. "Okay. Please tell her to call me first thing when she wakes up."

"I will," Matthew said as the call ended.

He placed her phone on the side table and sat on the bed next to Lissie as she began to breathe more deeply. He bent down to kiss her on the forehead and whispered, "I love you. I know it's crazy because I've only known you for a few days, but I needed to say it out loud. I love you."

He pushed her hair out of her face and pulled the comforter up around her shoulders. He felt so much despair when he thought of the emotional turmoil she was experiencing in her life. He decided in that moment, he would be there for her. No matter what she needed. Even if it meant saying 'no' to a job from the Family. He would do anything for her.

Thirty-Five

THE NEXT MORNING, Lissie woke with the worst headache she had ever had. She sat up slowly and looked down at her crumpled work attire. *Uhh. What the hell happened?* she thought as she raised a hand to shield her eyes from the light seeping in through her curtains. At that moment, Matthew crept in from the other room with two cups of coffee in one hand and a glass of water in the other.

"How are you feeling?" he whispered. Lissie's hungover heart melted. *Seriously. He is the best. He's even whispering! Be still my heart.*

"Yes," she tentatively whispered. Even that small sound made her headache worse.

Matthew handed her two aspirin and a glass of water first. Once she had taken the medicine, he smiled and handed her the coffee.

"I laid out some clothes for you on the bed," he continued in a hushed voice. "You're not going anywhere today. Doctor's orders. And I had a nice conversation with your brother last night. But you should probably call him and let him know that I am, in fact, your boyfriend and not a serial killer," he said with a laugh as he left the room to give her some privacy.

Lissie remained sitting on the edge of her bed in shock for a few minutes. *How did I miss that phone call?* she vaguely wondered. She picked up her phone and dialed her brother.

"Lissie?" he said with worry in his voice.

"Shhh! I have a horrible hangover. Please talk quietly," she begged.

"I've been worried sick about you. Are you okay? What happened?" John asked.

"Well." *Where to begin? I guess I should start at our first meeting.* "I was a work on Friday, and a new investor was coming in to meet with my boss. When he came in, I almost had a heart attack because he's young and gorgeous—and most of our major investors are old and fat. And he kept staring at me. So after the meeting, I was giving him all the paperwork he needed to fill out, and he asked me out on a date! I was so shocked that I actually said 'yes'. We went to dinner, and then he spent the whole weekend doting on me. Like, *really* spoiling me. He took me to all these amazing restaurants and took me dress shopping at Saks. He got us tickets to see *A Midsummer Night's Dream* at Lincoln Center," she said, emphasizing every word.

"Whoa. Sounds suspicious. And rich," he worried.

"He's a millionaire ... possibly billionaire. And he's amazing. You of all people know how hard it is for me to trust anyone. And I really trust Matthew. I don't know why, but it just feels ... right," she said with a smile.

"Well, good. But I'm a little upset he let you get so drunk you passed out," he responded.

"No, no. That was all me. You have to promise you won't tell this to anyone, okay? I'm not supposed to talk to anyone about it until the information is publicly released by the police," she begged.

"Alright, I promise," he agreed.

"Yesterday when I got into work, I found my boss dead. Shot in the head," she said, worried that her emotions would kick into high gear once more.

"Oh my God. Are you serious?" he asked.

"Yeah. When I say 'getting drunk was all me', I mean it. Matthew basically babysat me all night. Poor guy." She felt awful because of her hangover, but even more so because she couldn't imagine what she had put Matthew through the night before.

"Well, I'm happy he was there to take care of you. He couldn't have shown up at a better time," John said.

"Okay. I'm gonna go eat some breakfast. I love you, brother. Thanks for worrying," she said, happy to know he would always be looking out for her.

"Love you too. I'll talk to you soon," he said as the call ended.

Lissie was grateful to have one person in her life she could always depend on. *Maybe two now,* she thought hopefully.

She finally worked up the courage to stand up and change clothes. Every movement made her feel like she was about to pass out from dizziness. She gingerly grabbed the mug in one hand so she could use the other to reach out and steady herself against the wall. By the time she made it to the couch and sat down next to Matthew, she was ready to lie down and fall asleep again.

"I'm never drinking alcohol again," she said with a groan.

His responding chuckle made her heart feel lighter somehow. Despite what happened the day before, his presence alone made her feel less despondent about everything.

"You drank a lot. And not a lot for you—a lot for anyone," he said, still smiling at her with his gorgeous lips and teeth.

Since when did a hangover make a person horny? she thought with humor. All she could think about when he smiled at her like that was ripping his clothes off and taking advantage of him. *Stop it!* she chided herself. *He's here to be a good boyfriend. And you're an emotional wreck. Shut up and drink your coffee.*

"Are you okay?" Matthew asked. "You have a strange look on your face."

"Yes!" she said way too loudly. She squinted her eyes and grabbed her temple as the pain subsided. "Yes, I'm fine. Just ready to eat some food," she said in the tiniest whisper she could manage.

Right on cue, Matthew jumped up and went to the kitchen. He listed out her options in as quiet a voice as he could. "You can have scrambled eggs with cheese and bacon, an omelet, pancakes, or a bagel with cream cheese. Your choice."

Lissie was confused. She had missed her regular routine of shopping on Sunday, so she knew her fridge was empty. "But I don't have any of those things."

"Well you do now," Matthew responded matter-of-factly. "I went shopping for you this morning."

This morning? What time is it? she thought as she looked at the clock on her wall.

"Oh my God! It's noon? I haven't slept this late since I was in middle school!" She felt as if she could pass out. "I am *deeply* sorry, Matthew. I can't believe you're still here," she said in an apologetic tone.

Matthew walked back to the couch and sat down next to her. He wrapped both arms around her and kissed the top of her head. "Where else would I want to be? I promised you I wouldn't leave, and I didn't make that promise for your sake. If you were alone right now, I would be a wreck worrying about you."

Lissie's eyes began to fill with tears again. *Stop it! You are not this emotional. Dry it up, little girl.* But it seemed her emotions didn't want to listen. She sank deeper into his arms and wrapped hers around him as if he were the only life preserver on a raging sea.

"Thank you so much," she said as the tears poured from her eyes. "You have no idea how much I needed you to be here. And honestly, *I* had no idea how much I needed you either."

Matthew held her a bit longer then said, "Okay. Let's get you fed. What would you like?" He stood and walked over to the kitchen.

"I'll take pancakes and bacon," Lissie said, already starting to feel better from the medicine and caffeine. She walked over to her kitchen and leaned against the island while Matthew got started.

"What do you have going on this month?" she asked him, hoping he would be around for a while.

"Well, I'm supposed to fly to Asia in a few weeks for work. But if you need me to cancel I'm happy to oblige," he answered, still working on the pancake batter.

"Absolutely not," Lissie said, determined to keep her composure despite the panic she began to feel. "You're going to go on your trip, and I'll start working on your place while you're away."

Matthew seemed to study her face for any hint of distress, but apparently was satisfied with what he found. "Okay then. I'll be here with you for the next three weeks, and then I'll go. And I should only be gone for four days. I'll be leaving an international cell phone you can use to call or text me if you have any questions about the remodel or if you simply want to talk."

Lissie could see she had persuaded him that she would be okay and felt a smug satisfaction.

The rest of the day was spent lounging around the house so Lissie could recover. For dinner, Matthew had Thai delivered, and as a late night snack, they popped popcorn and ate chocolate while they watched Lissie's favorite movie —*You've Got Mail.*

"This movie is one of the reasons I moved to the Upper West Side," she said with a smile. "But I just can't help it. Every time Meg Ryan says, 'I wanted it to be you. I wanted it to be you so badly', I lose my mind and just have to cry."

Matthew laughed at her sentimental heart, but he found her love of romantic comedies endearing. "Well, I don't mind at all. You cry all you want. I think it's sweet."

Lissie looked embarrassed by his words. "I'm sorry you've seen me cry so much. It always makes me feel a little stupid when other people see me cry."

He was confused by her confession. Because he came from a family of emotional men, to see a woman cry didn't seem odd or wrong to him. He faced her and made her look him in the eyes. "Don't ever feel like you need to be embarrassed about showing your emotions. Growing up, my mother, father and brothers all cried at times. I have an emotional family, and I really mean it when I say it's sweet, not stupid."

He was happy to see that her smile was real—which hopefully meant she heard and believed him.

When it was clear Lissie was tired, she went into her room to get ready for bed. Matthew wasn't sure if she wanted him to stay until she came out with an extra-large pair of sweat pants and a toothbrush.

"Now I'll have you know these sweatpants mean a lot to me. My college roommate was in the athletic training program at our school, and she stole these for me from one of the football players. They are the only stolen good I've ever owned—and I cherish them. So be gentle," she finished with a chuckle as she handed them over.

Matthew loved that instead of asking if he wanted to stay, she gave him clothes to sleep in—or pants. She may not have owned a shirt that would fit him, but it was possible she was simply interested in a better view of his body. He had no problem whatsoever with the idea of getting halfway undressed with Lissie, or even all the way undressed for that matter. But in her emotional state, that probably wasn't the best idea.

Matthew walked into the room as soon as Lissie turned off her light; he slid into bed beside her, and Lissie snuggled into his side.

"Thank you for today," she said in a relaxed tone. "I honestly don't know what I would have done if you hadn't been here."

Matthew couldn't help himself. He placed a lingering kiss on her forehead. Any lower and he knew the evening would be taking a turn in a direction quite different from sleeping.

"I had a wonderful time with you," he said. "I think we should do it again tomorrow."

Thirty-Six

THE NEXT DAY, Lissie woke up at eight a.m. She was grateful to be back on a normal schedule despite having no job to go to. As she put the coffee on, she decided that she and Matthew needed to go to his apartment to get started on the redecorating plans. She wanted to have everything measured and planned out before Matthew traveled to Asia.

It was comforting to know that although she was still upset about her boss's murder, she could live a somewhat normal life. She would be working essentially the same hours as before—doing something she actually loved instead of a desk job that simply paid the bills. *This could really be good,* she thought. *If I take before and after photos of each room, I'll have a pretty solid start on my portfolio. Maybe I can even open a business in the city after this job.* She had already taken all the before and after photos from Mr. Stein's office and her own apartment. She bought a professional camera and wide angle lens specifically for that purpose. Her level of excitement rose with the prospect of doing a job she actually felt passionate about. *Don't get ahead of yourself,* she scolded. She poured both cups of coffee and walked into the bedroom to wake up Matthew.

This was the first time she had seen him with his shirt off. When he crawled in bed the night before, the lights were already off. He looked gorgeous and peaceful lying on his back with his left arm up over his head. She walked closer to look at a tattoo inked on his left forearm. The three inch square had an intricate design that Lissie thought was amazing. His tattoo was done only in black ink, but the artist had given it incredible depth. The background was a detailed 'X' with several intersecting lines. In the foreground—or what the tattoo artist had designed to look like the foreground—were the outlines of two smaller intersecting squares. She realized that the design matched the ring Matthew always wore, but she hadn't paid any attention until now. She would have to ask him about it later.

"Good morning," she said quietly as she sat on the bed next to Matthew's perfectly sculpted body. *God, he's gorgeous.*

As he stirred awake, he smiled sleepily and wrapped his arms around her waist to pull her closer.

"Be careful!" she scolded as she placed both mugs on the side table. She laughed at his grunt of impatience and slid back into his arms.

"Did you sleep well?" he asked groggily.

"I did. And you?" she replied.

"Excellently. I could really get used to sharing a bed with you," he said as Lissie's face turned red. She had never slept with a man before Matthew. She had engaged in casual sex a time or two in college, but never slept with them afterwards. She suddenly realized just how deeply she cared for Matthew. Rather than feeling dread or panic as she would have felt with anyone else, she felt comforted. She had opened up to Matthew in a way she hadn't even opened up to her own parents. He made her feel like it was finally okay to be vulnerable with someone besides her brother. And she was completely happy with the idea of being candid with him.

"I could get used to it too," she said as she leaned in for a small kiss.

"That was a dangerous action, young lady," Matthew said in a seductive yet playful tone. "You're lucky I have terrible morning breath, or I would have captured you and kept you in bed for the rest of the day."

"Oh yeah?" she replied with a laugh. "I'll have to brush your teeth before I wake you up next time."

In a matter of seconds, he grabbed her waist and tossed her over his body onto the other side of the bed with minimal effort. He rolled on top of her and gave her a serious look. Lissie wasn't sure what was coming next, but she felt her heart beat faster and her breath come more quickly.

"Very dangerous," he said as his lips found her cheek. Then her neck. Then left a lingering kiss behind her ear. Lissie was certain her heart would explode from beating so hard.

Matthew smiled widely and jumped out of bed as if nothing had happened. Lissie stayed paralyzed on the bed for several more minutes as Matthew threw on a t-shirt he dug out of one of her drawers. She wasn't sure how he had found the only extra-large shirt in her home, but she was in a haze. A few moments later he grabbed her off the bed with little effort and threw her over his shoulder, laughing all the while.

"You know you deserved that," he said, still laughing. Now Lissie was aware enough to fight back.

"Oh yeah?" she asked with a jab to his side. "Well you deserve this too," she said as she began searching out his ticklish spots.

Matthew began to squirm and nearly dropped her as he tried to grab her hands to keep them from tickling his sides. He put her down on the couch and threw his hands up in surrender.

"Truce!" he yelled. She looked at him as if it wasn't going to be that easy.

"Truce?" he asked sheepishly, which brought on laughter.

"Okay," she was barely able to gasp in between laughs.

Matthew looked like maybe he was ready to recant on his truce, so Lissie quieted her laughter and put on the most serious face she could muster. She stood to shake his hand.

"Truce," she declared. "Why don't you tell me about that tattoo? I noticed it matches your ring."

"Nice change of subject," Matthew teased. "But you're very perceptive. It's a family thing. All the men in my family have them. One of my uncles designs one for each of us, and when we come of age, we get our tattoo and signet ring."

"Huh. That's a really cool family tradition. But the women don't get to join in the fun?" she asked, worried at the chauvinistic implications.

"There really aren't very many women in my family. And none have ever asked for a tattoo of their own. I'm sure my uncle would happily comply if any of them wanted one," he assuaged her fears.

"Well I would definitely want one if *my* dad and brother both had them. Especially if it was that intricate," she said as she looked at Matthew's ring. She suddenly realized she was staring and forced herself out of her daydreams.

"Now finish your coffee so we can head to your place," she ordered.

"My place, huh? Sounds good. Any specific reason?" he asked.

"Well, I figured I should get a lay of the land over there before I start work. I'm going to try to come up with a game plan today. Plus you have to show me how to access your high security lair," she said with a smirk.

"Well okay. I suppose we have a lot on the day's agenda then," he agreed.

When they arrived at Matthew's apartment building, he introduced her to his doorman and told him that she would be over frequently to redecorate his apartment. He also gave her the spare key card for his elevator and a set of keys for his SUV so she would be able to transport any supplies she might buy. His last order of business was to give her his personal debit card and pin number so she could make purchases directly to his account.

Never in a million years would he have thought he could trust someone outside the Family so unequivocally. But this beautiful woman had proven otherwise.

Lissie brought her laptop and measuring tape, and as soon as Matthew was finished giving her his debit card information, she set off to work. He could tell she was the kind of person who loved a project. She was glowing with excitement … and it was hard for Matthew to look away from her as she worked.

"What?" she asked as she caught him staring at her.

"Nothing," he said clearing his throat. "I was simply admiring the way you use that measuring tape."

"That is the most ridiculous thing I've ever heard," she laughed. "Now go order us some food so we can spend the rest of the day eating and watching movies. I plan to utilize our time over the next three weeks. We shall stay wrapped up in mindless entertainment until you leave."

Matthew had to keep his mind from imagining all the wonderful kinds of mindless entertainment he wanted to wrap Lissie up in.

Forty-five minutes later, three delivery men arrived at his apartment with food from three different restaurants. He ordered a rack of lamb, fresh hummus with pita, and a Mediterranean salad from one restaurant, barbeque brisket sandwiches and fries from another, and a massive schnitzel with butter noodles and German potato salad from another.

"I have to keep reminding myself that you're a billionaire. You don't act like a spoiled brat. Most of the time," she added.

His face twisted into a wicked grin as he placed the bags of food on the counter and headed straight toward her. He locked her wrists behind her back with one hand, and with the other he began to tickle her sides until she was laughing and begging him to stop. She stretched up on her tiptoes and planted a kiss firmly on his lips, which immediately stopped the torture and turned his mind toward her incredible full lips.

"Ah ha," he said when she broke away. "You've found my weakness."

She laughed and sat down on the couch.

"My choice for which movie we watch? Since you picked our meal?" she asked.

***

Lissie was delighted with the food Matthew ordered. She had forgotten how wonderful a simple barbeque sandwich could be after all the fancy food he had been feeding her over the past several days. Lissie decided to watch *Die Hard* for Matthew's sake. She had forced him to sit through a chick flick the night before and thought it would only be fair to pick out an action film for him. She was enjoying the movie, but she couldn't concentrate on it long enough to follow the storyline. She loved the feeling of lying back against Matthew's beautiful body with his muscular arms wrapped around her ribs. All she could think about was the intense relationship she had forged with Matthew over the previous week. They hadn't even had sex, yet she had inadvertently grown accustomed to waking up next to him in the morning and falling asleep in his arms each night. She was not the kind of person who needed a significant other in her life to be happy, but she could feel herself changing more each day into a woman who desperately needed this man. And the notion terrified her.

"Are you alright?" Matthew asked, somehow aware of the change in her emotional state.

"I think so," she responded without further explanation. Without knowing what she was doing, she turned toward him, ran her hands through his beautiful dark hair, and leaned into him for a full long kiss. He returned the kiss passionately and pulled her over onto his lap. They remained locked in that position for some time until Matthew, without breaking the kiss, turned off the TV, picked her up in a fluid motion, and carried her into the bedroom.

An hour later, Matthew propped himself up to study the woman he had fallen in love with. He couldn't believe how natural it felt to make love to her. There was no fumbling for what to do next, no pausing in the heat of the moment, no worrying about what the other wanted. They fit together perfectly, and Matthew felt even more strongly for her in that moment than he had only hours before. She stared up at him with the most beautiful flush in her cheeks and a magnificent smile plastered to her face. She was perfect in every way—gorgeous, creative, intelligent, curvy, complex, and independent. He wanted to stare at her for hours on end, but he knew that their evening plans were quickly approaching. He checked the pocket watch he always left on his side table, and smiled down at his lover.

"What?" Lissie questioned suspiciously.

"You have to take a shower. Someone's going to be here in a few minutes, and you're going to want to be all cleaned up."

Lissie stared at him—her face a mix of worry and delight. He knew he had created a monster. She loved these surprises, and he couldn't wait to come up with all sorts of ways to indulge her new found fascination.

"Do I need to do my hair and makeup?" she asked as she headed toward his bathroom.

"No. You only need to take a shower," he replied as he battled the urge to follow her into the bathroom and join her under the water. *We would never leave the apartment. Do not go in there*, he commanded himself. *Please lock the bathroom door, Lissie. Please.* He heaved a sigh of relief when he heard the lock click into place. He took a hurried shower in the guest bathroom and found Lissie dressed and waiting for him when he emerged.

The intercom buzzed and Matthew told his doorman to let the guest come on up. When the elevator door opened, a woman who looked like she popped straight out of the 1950s emerged, carrying a dress bag and a large rolling suitcase. Matthew glanced at Lissie with a smirk on his face.

"What in the world?" Lissie asked, confusion written all over her face.

"This is Peggy. You two can use the guest bedroom," Matthew said as he walked to his room to get ready for the evening.

"Hi," Lissie said with an outstretched hand. "I have no idea what's going on."

"Don't worry about it. I'll explain everything," Peggy replied as she shook Lissie's hand.

An hour later, Lissie felt like she had walked right out of a glamorous 1940's movie. Peggy first made her choose from several vintage dresses. Lissie tried each one on, and ultimately decided that a sleeveless green and white striped dress would do nicely in the summer heat. The more formal satin, long-sleeved gown was impractical if she wanted to keep from sweating. And the full-length Grecian chiffon gown was too formal for her to feel comfortable. Two of the other dresses she decided against were just too casual for a night out on the town. The dress she chose was tea-length and flowed out from a fitted waist. The neckline plunged from her neck down to her breasts in an almost seductive manner. But all the important parts were fully covered. She loved the way the dress fit her body. Peggy had even brought matching green heels from the same era.

Then she proceeded to fix Lissie's hair and makeup exactly like a 1940's movie star. Her long, dark hair was curled in waves and pinned into place. And though her hair was down, there were so many hidden bobby pins in it that she knew it was just as secure as an up-do would've been. The makeup made her skin look like a porcelain doll—a doll with bright red lips. As Lissie looked at her reflection, she barely recognized the woman staring back at her. Peggy was a genius.

"I love it," Lissie breathed.

"And now you need to go show your man. He was adamant that you look perfect. It's his approval I'm worried about," Peggy said with a wary look.

Lissie couldn't help but giggle as she emerged from the bedroom and saw the look on Matthew's face.

"You look like Rita Hayworth. But even lovelier," he said, awed by her appearance.

"Thank you, sir," Lissie said with a curtsey.

Matthew thanked Peggy several times as he escorted her to the elevator to leave. And she wished them a good evening as the doors shut.

"What are we doing tonight?" Lissie squealed as she turned to Matthew. She looked at him closely for the first time since she came out of the bathroom. He was wearing a vintage three-piece suit and tie. The dark gray suit was baggier than anything she'd seen him wear before, but it somehow still fit him perfectly. His shirt was white, and his tie was maroon with a blue paisley pattern. He had a matching maroon pocket square, and even his wingtip shoes looked vintage.

"When did you have time to go shopping?" she asked, amazed.

"Oh, I've had these for a while. I like to hang onto vintage suits in case of emergency," he said with a mischievous gleam in his eye.

Unbelievable, Lissie thought. *He has a 1940's suit lying around. Why not?* She had to laugh at the absurdity of the notion.

Matthew pulled his pocket watch from the pocket of his vest to check the time.

"We have to leave if we're going to be on time."

"On time to what?" Lissie asked again.

Matthew only smiled and held out his arm for her to hold.

Thirty-Seven

As they walked arm in arm, Matthew was nervous about taking Lissie to this performance. He didn't think she was too fragile over Stein's death, but a few gruesome parts of the performance might send her over the edge. He would need to keep an eye on her to gauge her reactions.

They arrived at the McKittrick Hotel at exactly six p.m. They ate a wonderful meal at The Heath while listening to a live jazz band in the corner. Lissie still had no idea what was going on, but she was enjoying the intrigue nonetheless. Matthew leaned in close to his gorgeous date.

"You like Shakespeare's *Macbeth*, right?" he asked.

"Of course! I love Shakespeare," she answered excitedly.

"Because you know the story, you're really going to enjoy tonight. We're going to *Sleep No More*. It's an interactive performance of *Macbeth*, but it's not actually the play," he tried to explain. The look on Lissie's face was pure confusion. *I should've thought harder about how to explain this.* "The performance takes place over six floors of this building, and the actors are portraying different characters from *Macbeth*. But rather than act out the play, they're just living life. It's difficult to explain, but I believe you're going to love it."

Lissie smiled widely. "It sounds fun. And I'm very intrigued." She leaned in for a short kiss, but their passion from earlier in the day hadn't yet subsided. When they pulled away, Lissie's eyes burned with desire, and Matthew was sure that his own desire was evident to her as well. He breathed deeply before speaking again.

"There are some graphic scenes in the performance. If you feel uncomfortable at any time, let me know, and we can leave."

"I will," she promised.

Once they were outside where all the other guests were congregated, Lissie's stomach started to get butterflies.

"I have no idea what to expect," she whispered.

"That's half the fun," he responded with a smirk. "They're going to separate us and put all the guests in masks, but I'll find you," he promised. He bent down and gave her a kiss that overpowered her senses. She grasped the back of his neck to pull him in closer, wishing she could magically transport them back to Matthew's bed for another round of their earlier exploits. As soon as he pulled away, they were ushered into a dimly lit hotel lobby. Each guest received a playing card from an old deck—she drew an ace of hearts while Matthew drew a four of spades. She held tightly onto Matthew's hand, hoping she could maintain the contact throughout the night without anyone noticing. They were ushered to a bar where they ordered drinks while awaiting their turn to enter. The atmosphere seemed to buzz with excitement as guests waited for the next step in their journey.

"Aces," a man dressed like Frank Sinatra said over a microphone.

Matthew leaned down and gave her a quick hug. "I'll find you," he whispered again as she left his side.

The separation made her feel like she was walking into something dangerous. When Matthew was by her side, she always felt protected for some reason. As soon as she received her mask and was told she could no longer speak, she felt her adrenaline start to pump. She and ten others entered an elevator that looked like it could break down at any moment, and when it came to a stop, Lissie and two others stepped off. As she turned around further instructions, the elevator doors closed and took the remaining guests to another floor.

Lissie was disoriented. She had no idea what to do or where to go. When she looked around at the other guests she was grouped with, her stomach lurched in fear over the terrifying white-masked faces beside her. *Everyone feels the way you do. It's all part of the show,* she told herself as her nerves calmed back to a manageable level. She followed behind the other two people, hoping that they would have some clue of how to proceed. But it seemed they were as lost as she was.

The first room they came upon was a dark hospital ward. Lissie shivered and passed quickly through the room. The others seemed to want to stay there for some reason, but Lissie couldn't get out of there fast enough. The next room was full of baths. One of the characters was washing a shirt repeatedly in one of the tubs. *This room isn't any better. And shouldn't I be able to understand what's going on? This is Macbeth, right?* she worried, hoping she wasn't the only guest feeling that way.

When she walked out the next door, she found several large groups of people observing different parts of an outdoor scene. She strolled along, sometimes piecing together bits of the story, other times feeling completely lost. When she finally came to a staircase, she headed down to the next floor, hoping Matthew would find her soon.

She passed through an eerie laundry room and a long passage, only seeing a few other guests before she happened upon an empty room set up to look like a bar. Lissie approached the bar, and a door flung open as a barkeep walked out of a back room and began wiping down the counters. Guests flocked to characters as soon as they spotted one, so Lissie decided to sit down and see what he would do. He was a good-looking man, probably in his early thirties, with his hair fixed the same way Matthew fixed his each day. His tan skin, dark hair and dark brown eyes were mysterious as he kept glancing at her from the corner of his eye. He spent a few seconds wiping down the bar before he poured a shot from a whiskey bottle and slid it down to where Lissie sat. She nodded to him, knowing she wasn't allowed to voice her thanks, and sipped at the liquid in the glass. She nearly gasped when it hit her throat. *This is real whiskey! I expected soda or juice. But holy crap, that's strong,* she thought as she gathered her composure and took another sip. That was when the bartender started flirting with her. She was dumbfounded. *Is this really part of the show? I'm so confused.* A few people trickled into the room and began gathering around to watch the barkeep's performance. The man eyed the guests then looked back at Lissie for a short moment. She had no idea what happened next—everything was a blur. But somehow the man had grabbed her wrist and yanked her back into the room where he had appeared from. Lissie let out a small gasp as the door slammed behind her and locked, closing her in with the flirtatious actor.

Matthew was let out on the third floor. He made his way through each room, not paying much attention to what the characters were doing. His only goal now was to find Lissie. The 'no cellphone' policy hadn't bothered him on his first visit to the show. He had been alone then. But this time, he wanted to find Lissie as quickly as possible. He looked through each group of guests closely, hoping she would be there. But when he rounded the corner to the stairs, he realized she wasn't on the third floor.

He headed up to the fourth floor, feeling a small welling of panic in his chest. He felt more protective of her than ever today—their earlier activities gave him an even greater sense of responsibility for her. She was *his*, and he intended to protect her—even if only to keep her from being scared by a harmless performance. He wanted nothing more than to have her in his arms in case she was alarmed by any of the scenes.

He found his feet moving more quickly as a sudden urgency came over him. Each time he searched a room without finding her, he grew more distressed. Regret was creeping into his head. *I should never have brought her here. This was a mistake.*

He *needed* to find Lissie soon.

The second the door locked, the man slammed Lissie up against a wall and ripped the mask from her face. Her eyes went wide with shock as he looked up and down her body.

"My God, you're beautiful," he spoke vehemently as he stared into her eyes.

She could hear her heart pounding in her ears. *Is this supposed to happen? Where is Matthew?* she kept repeating in her mind.

"Sit down," the man commanded. She immediately sat down on the whiskey barrel next to her, her hands grasping the mask she was supposed to be wearing. The room felt like a small stable. There were hay bales around the edges of the room, and hay covered the floor. A single light hung from the ceiling, barely giving off enough light for Lissie to see the corners of the tiny room. There was one small table that separated her and the man—and on that table were two glasses and another bottle of whiskey. He poured the contents of the bottle into a glass and pushed it toward her.

"Drink it." His command was dark and dangerous.

She immediately took the glass and drank it all. She didn't dare disobey his command while she was locked in this room with him. *Where is Matthew?*

The man pulled a deck of cards from his pocket and started doing flirtatious card tricks. Lissie felt relief when she finally understood that this was the character he was supposed to play. The more tricks he did, the closer he moved to her. *Maybe he's not just playing a character,* she wondered as her heart began to race again.

Matthew entered the bar on the fourth floor where a small group had congregated and were talking in hushed voices.

"They've been in there for a long time."

"Who?" Matthew demanded with urgency. The guests' faces were covered, but he could feel shock through their masks.

"It was just the bartender and some lady in a vintage dress. But that was like, ten minutes ago," the woman whispered.

Matthew was mortified. A man was with Lissie. *His* Lissie. In a locked room. He immediately pulled off his mask and headed for the door. By his estimation, it would take him approximately ten seconds to pick the lock.

The man's face was only a few inches from hers now.

"What's your name?" he asked as his hand pushed a stray piece of hair out of her face.

"Lissie," she whispered, barely able to speak her own name. She knew the rules. She wasn't supposed to talk to any of the characters. He had broken the rules by speaking to her, though, and now she really started to worry.

"You smell amazing, Lissie," he said as his lips nearly brushed her cheek.

In the next ten seconds, Lissie's trepidation turned to jubilation. She heard the handle to the door jiggle and the lock pop open. When the door flung open, Matthew stood—looking terrifying and amazing—on the other side. He pushed the very surprised barkeep away with his right hand and pulled Lissie into his body with his left. Matthew glared at the petrified barkeep as they left the room.

He pulled Lissie around the corner into a dark hallway and pushed her up against the wall. His furious eyes looked her over several times before he roughly kissed her, using his hand to pull her close to his body.

Lissie was in heaven. Only moments before she had been like a terrified child, but under Matthew's protective stare, she felt foolish for having worried at all. He had rescued her.

"Are you alright?" he asked, his voice still tinged in anger.

"I'm wonderful," she breathed, staring into his beautiful green eyes. "You … you rescued me. I'm not sure I could be any better," she whispered, admiration flowing through her entire being. He kissed her deeply again before replacing her mask.

"We can leave if you want," he offered.

"No. As long as I'm with you, I want to stay until I've seen everything."

It took nearly two hours for Matthew to calm down again. He had the inclination to return to the bar and punch that barkeep hard in the face. He knew the man was simply acting out the character he was hired to play, but where Lissie was concerned, no other man would ever get to touch her that way.

By the time they made it through each floor of the production, Lissie was dead on her feet. She pulled Matthew from room to room, trying to figure out the symbolism behind each setting and character. She loved the performance and kept thanking Matthew for the experience. But all he wanted from the moment he found her was to take her home and make love to her.

The walk back to his apartment took far too long, but once they were inside his elevator, he realized Lissie's thoughts were similar to his own.

She turned to face him and pushed him roughly against the back of the elevator. His eyes widened when she quickly unbuttoned his jacket and vest. It took him nearly half a second to understand what she was doing. He grabbed her hair, pulling her closer for a kiss while her hands continued to remove clothing as quickly as possible. By the time the elevator reached his penthouse, they were down to just their underwear. She jumped up and wrapped her legs around his waist as he carried her into the bedroom.

Once they reached Matthew's bed, the rest of their clothes were thrown to the ground, and they blissfully spent the rest of the night enveloped in the intense flames of one other.

Thirty-Eight

For the next three weeks, Lissie and Matthew fell into a relaxed routine. Matthew cooked breakfast for Lissie every morning. Days were full of Lissie deciding on color palettes for each room and looking at fabric swatches, while Matthew worked on his laptop in the living room. Lunches were delivered from a different restaurant each afternoon, and Matthew took her to unique restaurants for dinner each evening. It was as if they had been together for years. Every night, no matter how much of the day they had spent together or apart, they always seemed to end up naked and entwined in another round of passionate lovemaking. And every morning, they both awoke feeling more rested than the night before.

"I can't believe you have to leave tomorrow," Lissie pouted, head resting on Matthew's bare chest.

"It's only for a few days. I'll be back before you know it," he said as he kissed her temple softly. "But I'll be an emotional mess without you," he tacked on. She was happy to know he was as upset about the temporary separation as she was.

"Are you packed?" she asked sadly.

He pointed to a briefcase sitting next to the bedroom door. She looked at him, questioningly.

"That's it?" she asked.

"My apartment is waiting for me. It's fully stocked for my visits, and my housekeeper always fills my refrigerator with food the day before I arrive. I'm all set."

Lissie stared at him, bewildered.

"Wow," she whispered.

"I'm looking forward to taking you to all my other homes. And hopefully introducing you to my ridiculous brothers," he said as he ran a hand through her long dark hair. She felt her heart lighten at the idea of traveling with him and meeting his family. It was comforting to know that he was as serious about her as she was about him.

"I would like that very much," she said smiling up at him.

For the first time in a month, she had trouble falling asleep. All she could think about was Matthew leaving her in the morning. She didn't know what kind of sleep to expect during his absence. She didn't know what kind of communication she should expect. When she finally drifted off, the sleep was restless. Even in her dreams, she couldn't seem to shake the singular emotion she felt each time she thought about Matthew's trip: dread.

Thirty-Nine

As Matthew boarded the direct flight from JFK to Dubai, he daydreamed of Lissie, lying in his bed, curled up in his arms. Her hair, her lips, her smile, her beautiful neck. He had done a full study of every inch of her during the weeks leading up to this trip. He discovered that he not only loved her personality and her beautiful face, but also the soft skin that stretched across her stomach, her back, and her legs. He loved her slight inhale when he moved her long, dark hair to the side and kissed her neck. He loved that when he first looked her over, she seemed embarrassed about her body, but at some point over the past month, she realized that he worshipped her curvy features and gave up her discomfort.

Matthew was happy he slept during most of the flight—he hadn't gotten much sleep the night before. He reclined his seat completely flat and closed his eyes. He needed to rest so he could focus on the job before him. The one benefit to this trip was that he would be spending some much needed quality time with his brothers. It had been over five years since the three of them were able to spend more than one day together. The timing of their contracts was constantly overlapping in a most inconvenient way. He was excited to tell his brothers about Lissie, but worried about their reaction. The last time he fell in love, the Family had nearly fallen apart. Hopefully, history wouldn't be repeating itself.

Lissie awoke alone in Matthew's bed, completely nude. She inhaled the scent of Matthew's pillow with her eyes closed. The remnant of the night before sent her memories—and her heart—racing. She had experienced casual sex before. But with Matthew, it was the first time she actually *made love*. And it was the most incredible feeling she had felt in her twenty-eight years of life. At first she was wary of being naked in front of a man whose body was something that could have been painted during the Renaissance. But he made it apparent that he found her body ... exquisite ... that she allowed herself to relax and live in each moment. And she had never felt so alive in all her life.

Matthew woke her for a kiss before he left at six a.m., but she had fallen right back to sleep. She glanced at Matthew's cold pillow and found a note waiting for her.

> *My dearest Lissie,*
>
> *I will miss you every minute that I am away. Please call me on the cell phone I left with you if you need to reach me at any time. I cannot wait to hold you in my arms again.*
>
> *Yours,*
> *Matthew*

She felt the dread from the previous night lessen as she read his note. "Yours," she read aloud with a huge smile on her face. "I like the sound of that."

She rolled over as her cell phone began to ring and realized it was one p.m.

"Hello?" she answered as she frantically threw herself out of bed. How had she slept so long?

"Hi, Lissie. This is Jason Luce. Do you have any time to get together today? I have a thirty minute break between meetings and want to go over a few things with you."

"Absolutely. Let's grab a coffee. When and where do you want to meet?" she asked.

"Four o'clock. And I could meet you at the Starbucks on 6th and 47th," he decided.

"Sounds great, Jason. I'll see you in a bit," she said as she hung up the phone.

Lissie rushed around Matthew's apartment as if she was in a hurry to go somewhere. The truth was, she always felt she was missing out on the day if she slept past ten a.m. And though she knew there was nothing important on her agenda, she wanted to get started on Matthew's apartment as soon as possible. While the coffee brewed, she took her shower and got dressed. Though she originally thought it was strange that Matthew had bought her a full set of clothes to keep at his place, she now found them incredibly convenient. She called several stores to check on the orders she placed weeks earlier for Matthew's bedroom furniture and window treatments before she realized it was time to head to her meeting with Jason.

She took advantage of the lovely weather and walked to the meeting. When she arrived, Jason was overjoyed to see her. They greeted each other with a short hug, and sat down. Jason had taken the liberty of buying her a latte, for which she was grateful.

"How are you holding up?" he asked, concerned.

"I'm good. Great, actually. I've been staying busy to keep my mind off of what happened," she replied. It amazed her that her answer was completely honest. Matthew had come into her life at just the right time to pick up all her broken pieces and put her back together. He had even given her a job. *He really is my knight in shining armor*, she thought with a smile.

Jason seemed to be bothered by her answer, but pushed past his concern to get back to the questions about Mr. Stein's murder.

"I'm getting frustrated because I'm hitting dead ends at every avenue," he said solemnly. Lissie knew Jason wasn't used to writing stories that required this much digging. His normal articles revolved around new financial trends, investment advice, and up-and-coming investment firms.

"I'm feeling a little out of my depth with this story. I asked you to meet me here so I could pick your brain about some other possibilities," he added.

"Go ahead. I'm happy to help in any way I can," she said encouragingly.

Jason sighed in relief and began.

"All the possible suspects have alibis for the time of the murder. But that doesn't mean they didn't have anything to do with it. The way the kill was carried out would suggest a hired professional. But they would have had to collect some pretty sensitive information about Mr. Stein's office and schedule. I think it's possible that the killer had some sort of relationship with Mr. Stein. I've now extended my list of possible killers to people who work in the building and all of his new clients," he said as he looked at Lissie questioningly.

"You already have access to all the company employees though, right?" she asked, confused. Jason's guilty nod made her understand what Jason was really after.

"You want me to give you a list of all the people who recently invested their money with Mr. Stein? That's against company policy, Jason. I can't give you any of that information," Lissie said, irritated that he would even suggest it.

He paused for a moment, and she could see the wheels turning in his head. He opened his mouth several times to try to argue, but ultimately let the issue drop. "I understand," he said, clearly dejected at yet another dead end.

"Are the police even okay with you digging into this investigation? I thought you were just supposed to be running a piece on the murder to make it look less horrible for Stein Securities," she pressed.

Jason closed his notes and sat back in his chair with a feeling of defeat. He didn't know what he expected to get out of Lissie. One of the things he admired about her from the first time he met her was her attention to detail. She was a consummate professional. He had hoped that maybe she would have enough of a soft spot for him to bend the rules a little. He should have known better.

"The police have told me to stay away from this investigation until they can give me something concrete. They don't want any speculation to run in my article. And of course I would never do that—I'm not a writer for a tabloid. I think things are moving too slowly on their end, and I thought maybe I could do a little digging to help find the culprit faster," he admitted.

"Well you won't get any client information out of me. And I think you knew that coming into this meeting. So what is this really about?" she asked.

Jason felt his cheeks reddening. He only dated a few girls in high school despite having a lot of girls chasing him. He had always been too wrapped up in baseball to spend his energy on dating. At the end of high school he had gotten serious with a girl—and the relationship lasted all the way through college. But the summer after they graduated, a rejected proposal caused him to lose his nerve. It wasn't that women weren't interested in him, but he was terrified of getting attached to a person that he feared might eventually break his heart. There were several women in his office and gym that had shown interest. Unfortunately, it seemed as if Lissie barely noticed he was an attractive male.

"I was going to ask you out on a date," he admitted sheepishly.

He could see Lissie hadn't expected this admission. Her face was confused at first, then thoughtful, then kind. Which could only mean one thing: rejection. Jason regretted asking her out even before hearing her predictable response.

"Jason. You're a great guy. Really, you are. But I'm ... unavailable at the moment. I started seeing someone last month. And I think it's going to last."

As she finished talking, it was written all over her face that she was smitten with this guy. Jason wanted to swing a baseball bat at a large piece of glass and watch it shatter into a million pieces. He knew that he would replay the months since he first met Lissie over and over again in his mind. *I missed my opportunity. I waited too damn long, and now she's with someone else*, he scolded himself.

"Well, I'm happy for you. I can tell you really like the guy. I hope that means he's treating you right. Where did you two meet?" he asked, curious why he wanted to continue to torture himself by talking about Mr. Right.

"We actually met at the office. He was planning on working with Mr. Stein to help him diversify his family's money. But that was before ..." she trailed off.

Jason's mind started to churn. The mystery man came into the picture right before Stein's murder. *Too convenient*, he thought. *And he just happened to be there to help Lissie through this difficult time in her life*. He would be doing some serious digging later.

"Does this guy have a name?" he asked in what he hoped was a playful tone.

"Matthew," she said with a smile that lit her entire face from the inside out. She almost said his name with reverence. She adored the guy. "Matthew McCloud, billionaire." She let out a small giggle, and then apparently realized she was talking to Jason—the guy who just asked her out—about Matthew—the reason she turned him down. She abruptly grew quiet and took a sip of her coffee.

"I'm sorry, Jason. I wasn't trying to be insensitive."

"Don't worry about it at all. But I do have to run. I have some work to get done tonight. It was great seeing you again." He reached out to shake Lissie's hand.

"You too," she said as she returned the handshake. "And let me know if you need anything else for the article."

As he exited the coffee shop, he turned the corner and hid in a loading dock until he saw Lissie exit. He knew it was wrong, but he needed to know where she was headed. He maintained a safe distance, and in a city with this many people, he was confident she would have no idea he was following her.

Nervousness churned in his stomach as he watched her cheerfully stroll down the sidewalk. *I really hope I'm wrong about this,* he thought. When she entered the apartment complex in Chelsea, Jason wrote down the address and hurried back to his office. This night would be a long night of research.

Forty

MATTHEW EMERGED from the plane feeling refreshed. He slept for the majority of the trip, completely stretched out on the fully reclining first-class seat. *I really don't understand how people can fly internationally in an economy seat*, he thought, feeling sorry for the miserable looking passengers exiting the plane behind him.

He sent a short text to Lissie:

Made it safely.

Dreamt of you the whole time.

I'll be home before we know it.

Only few seconds passed before he received a response:

Miss you. Be safe.

He smiled and thought about Lissie's lips and laugh as he waited in line to pass through Customs. As soon as he made it through, he saw his brothers waiting for him with smiles on their faces.

"Antonio. Marcus," he said as he hugged each. "I cannot believe it has been so long, my brothers."

"You have been avoiding us, I think," Marcus said suspiciously in his heavy Italian accent. As the eldest, he always acted as if he was responsible for keeping his younger brothers in line.

"Of course he hasn't been avoiding us," Antonio said as he punched Matthew's shoulder playfully. "He has so many *amantes* around the world that he does not have time for his own brothers anymore. Yes?"

"You are both ridiculous," Matthew said with a laugh. "I've been working, as I know you have as well. And we all know *you're* the one with too many lovers around the world, Antonio," Matthew said with a jab to Antonio's shoulder.

The three walked out of the airport where Matthew was surprised to see the SUV from his Dubai apartment parked near the entrance.

"You idiots broke into my home and stole my car?" he questioned accusingly.

"You really should tighten your security, Mattia. It only took the two of us an hour to break into your security system and power it down. I cannot believe you installed a system that poorly made. You are better than that," Antonio laughed.

Matthew wanted to laugh at them. The security system was low enough in quality that he could have broken through the firewall in a matter of minutes. But he kept that tidbit to himself.

He sat in silence for the rest of the trip while his brothers bickered back and forth about who had been responsible for breaking through Matthew's security system.

His family constantly stirred up his memories of the past. When he was around them, his nightmares grew more frequent and more detailed. And the fact that his brothers called him 'Mattia' rather than 'Rogue' or 'Matthew' made everything worse. After his grandfather branded him with the name 'Rogue', he begrudgingly became used to hearing it. Now, each time someone called him 'Mattia', his memories were transported back to Anamaria. He feared that while his brothers were close by, his sleep would be stricken with nightmares of losing Anamaria *and* Lissie. He prayed it would not be so.

Matthew was one of the few in the Family to take on an English name in order to maintain his American persona. The Family had been set in their traditional ways for millennia, and they mostly spoke with a heavy linguistic influence from past ages—usually in Italian. His brothers had mastered the English language, but when they spoke, it was obvious—especially for Marcus—that they were born in Italy. Matthew had adapted to the New World as well as he could manage. It was likely because he had chosen to relocate to New York shortly after the incident, while most of the Family was still scattered across Europe. But he always felt that he was an outcast, a rogue, for leaving the old country and adapting to all the current technologies and languages as easily as he had. He hadn't surprised anyone with his European exodus. And he didn't think anyone in the Family blamed him for needing the change. Priest and Saint quickly learned that they could use his abilities of adaptation to their advantage and never made complaint. And if neither of them put up a fight, the rest of the Family was happy to stay quiet.

One thing he was always grateful for when he was with Marcus and Antonio, was their ability to read his mood. He decided it was time to break out of his dreary funk. This was a time of celebration. He was with both of his brothers, he had good news to give them, and he had every intention of telling them about his love over lunch. In an Italian family, food, wine and good news go hand in hand—and that was a tradition he was grateful would never change.

As soon as they stepped into his apartment, Matthew announced it was time to cook. His mood changed from quiet and solemn to boisterous and joyful. The brothers' favorite activity to engage in together, apart from fighting, was cooking.

By the time they finished cooking their Caprese salad, bruschetta, homemade gnocchi, and tomato sauce, the kitchen was covered in the remnants of tomatoes, flour and crumbs. All three men were laughing and ready to talk about their lives. Matthew poured wine for his brothers and sat down.

"I have something to tell you," he finally confessed.

His brothers barely took the time to look up from the food they were devouring to give him nods that they were listening.

"I … I am in love," he announced.

As he had expected, both brothers stopped eating, wiped their mouths, and stayed silent. They looked at him as if he had told them he no longer wished to be their brother. Matthew refused to say more until one of them broke the silence. Minutes passed while he watched the wheels turn behind his brothers' eyes.

"Congratulations," Antonio finally said with a smile as he leaned over and smacked Matthew's shoulder. "When do we meet the lovely lady? Or is it a man?"

Matthew laughed and answered, "No, no. It's a woman. Her name is Lissie. And I'm hoping that you'll come to New York and meet her sometime soon. Even though I don't need your approval, I would like it all the same."

Marcus, who Matthew wasn't sure had even taken a breath since his admission, finally spoke. "If you want us to meet her, we'll plan a trip. Absolutely." And he went right back to eating his food.

Matthew knew there was much more his brother wanted to say, but for now he decided it was better to enjoy the food they had joyfully prepared.

After a quiet lunch—mainly because the food was so delicious that none of them wanted to take the time to talk—the brothers entered the sitting room and each poured themselves a drink from Matthew's dry bar. *Now comes the real conversation*, he thought, worried about what they would have to say.

"So, Mattia," Marcus began, "how did you meet your woman?"

"She was the executive assistant at my last job," he explained. This caused both brothers to raise their eyebrows. "I took her out on a date after a meeting at her office, and I was there for her when she found her boss murdered three days later." Matthew wasn't happy about Lissie's involvement in the matter, but it had allowed him to meet her, which made everything worthwhile.

"And she simply caught your eye? It has been hundreds of years since you allowed yourself to get entangled with anyone associated with your contracts," Marcus pushed.

Matthew knew he looked guilty because his brothers both wore confused looks on their faces.

"She looks ... she has similar features ... umm ... she *may* share some DNA with Anamaria," he finally admitted.

"Are you insane?" Marcus yelled as he stood and began pacing around the room. "You cannot be this stupid. Surely you are joking."

Matthew readjusted in his seat and glared at his brother. "I've checked the family records. There are more generations between them than I can count on both hands. And it was Isabel Serrano, Anamaria's sister, who is actually her ancestor. Isabel ended up marrying a conquistador and having several children. Lissie is one of many descendants. And let me assure you that Lissie is an entirely different person than Anamaria. Her looks drew me in, but Lissie's exquisite personality and sense of humor are what made me fall in love. And she's always ready for an adventure. And she speaks her mind …" Matthew trailed off. *She is much more like Anamaria than I recognized,* he suddenly realized. He smirked, amazed that he would end up with two women so similar yet centuries apart. "She really is extraordinary."

Marcus stared out the window, unmoving. "Her connection to the target will not complicate anything? There is no suspicion of involvement?"

"Do you really think I would be with her if there was?" Matthew asked, offended.

"Please be careful," Marcus said with finality. Matthew knew he would not be arguing any longer on the issue.

"I'm just happy that you're with someone," Antonio said as he walked to Matthew and embraced him in a firm hug. "It truly has been long enough for you to grieve. I have been worrying about you for a hundred years. This brings me more joy than you can possibly know."

Matthew knew Antonio was getting emotional and decided to pour all three brothers more alcohol to lighten the mood a bit.

The rest of the evening was spent talking about Antonio's latest female conquests—a French girl he couldn't remember the name of, and a Russian model he had seen three times (which was proof he was growing up). His regular dating regime included a one night stand with a high chance of finding out he would be fathering a child at some point down the road … which apparently happened yet again. His most recent son came to him from Japan. His short stay there in the '80s had produced a son who recently entered the training program to join the Family's ranks.

Marcus was still grieving Sera, the wife he lost nearly seventy years earlier. He had fallen in love with her when she was a young woman, but was forced to watch her age as he remained young. She passed away at age eighty-four, but to the day she died, he loved her as much as when they first met. His two sons were now grown and in training at the Family's facility in Tuscany. He filled Matthew in on how the training was going and scolded Matthew for not being a more involved uncle.

"You have technological skills that would be invaluable for my boys. Your knowledge is far superior to the rest of the Family's. Surely you must see how you could help them," Marcus said, petitioning him for his help in their training.

"As soon as they've finished their physical training, you send them to New York, and I'll teach them everything I know," Matthew agreed. This brought a smile to Marcus's face, but as he took a sip of his drink, Marcus grew serious again.

"You bore witness to what happened with my Sera," he began. "Are you sure you are willing to commit to that life? Especially after the way your last relationship ended. I am only worried about *you*, brother. I do not want the Family to lose you again. You ..." Marcus seemed to have trouble finding the words, and Matthew braced himself for what he knew Marcus was going to say. "You disappeared, Mattia. Even though you were alive and present, we mourned you as if you had died. You were an empty shell. Please do not put us —or yourself—through that again. If there is any chance that we may lose you, stop now," he finished.

Matthew was nearly overcome by Marcus's admission. No one in the Family had ever expressed their feelings to Matthew; probably because they were afraid that he would push them away or that they would be responsible for sending Matthew back into the downward spiral he had finally pulled through.

He walked to Marcus, gripped both of his shoulders, and spoke with conviction. "I will never go back to that place, brother. I am truly sorry for the pain I caused. I promise this is different. And though I know I will someday mourn her as you mourned Sera, I promise I will try to handle it as you did. Lissie is ... she's worth it. She's worth the pain of watching my soul mate grow old and pass away. She's worth the stress of worrying whether or not she's safe every time I leave for a contract. She's worth everything." His brothers both nodded to him in approval of his promise, and the time for talking about past sorrows came to an end.

The next morning, after the brothers cooked breakfast together, it was time for them to get down to business.

This contract was more complicated than usual, which is why all three brothers were required to carry it out. Usually, jobs only called for one or two of the Family to fulfill a contract. But on the rare occasion, three or four were needed to take care of specialized tasks within one assignment. Matthew's previous six contracts had forced him to work with his uncles, which was never high on his list of 'fun things to do in life'. He much preferred to work with his brothers, cousins, nephews or great-nephews—now that several of them had joined the ranks of the Family. But more often than not, he found that Priest— he refused to acknowledge the man as his grandfather—wanted to send his spies to make sure Matthew was behaving.

This particular contract was to remove a Saudi military threat. The Family contracts were never sent with an explanation for why the target was being removed, but in cases like these, the danger was fairly obvious. Matthew realized years earlier that many of the contracts came from governments who were unwilling to get their own hands dirty. And with the money they were paying for the use of the Family, there were only a few governments in the world that would have the disposable income to hire them.

It was clear that Matthew and his brothers had been chosen for this contract specifically for their specialties. They had each been blessed with more natural talents than the others in the Family, and Priest and Saint took advantage of their gifts whenever possible. This Saudi leader was locked in a bunker somewhere in the desert with heavy artillery cover and an incredible security system that Matthew would actually have to think through to hack—it usually took him only a matter of minutes to hack a system.

Marcus was somewhat of a firearm specialist. He would be taking out any personnel he could find with his sniper. Marcus was a surgeon with long-range weaponry. Matthew was certain he had no match.

Antonio was a hand-to-hand specialist. He would be the one to actually fulfill the contract. He was a surgeon when it came to knives. He could kill someone with a knife a hundred different ways and never get a drop of blood on his hands. And his ability to kill a person with his bare hands before they became aware he was anywhere near them was beyond Matthew's understanding.

They would be driving in through the desert to keep a low profile, which meant they would be driving for hours on end to get to the job site. Antonio complained that they should just take a helicopter if the plan was to take out all the personnel anyway, but Marcus was adamant that they not draw any unwanted attention from surrounding areas by announcing their presence with a noisy helicopter. Matthew was so grateful to be working with both of his brothers again after five long years that he had no preference about any of the particulars. He sat back and watched his brothers bicker, amused and relaxed by their mere presence.

"That all sounds fine," Matthew said when they asked if he was happy with the plan.

"Damn it, Mattia!" Antonio shouted with a pouty lip. "You always side with Marcus."

Matthew let out a loud laugh. "I'm truly happy with any plan that doesn't involve an uncle spying on me to report back to Priest," he confessed.

His brothers joined in his laughter and agreed that the plan was set.

Forty-One

JASON WAS CERTAIN that there was some correlation between Gregory Stein's murder and the appearance of Matthew McCloud at Stein Securities. He couldn't put his finger on it, but he could feel it in his core. He'd spend several hundred dollars to bribe one of the security guards at Stein Securities, but the video footage he received in exchange had allowed him to see the man's face from several angles. He couldn't place it, but he knew it was connected with some memory from his past—an unpleasant one, to be sure. He stared at the photo for hours, begging his subconscious to reveal how he knew this man. Jason wasn't sure whether to tip off the detectives on the case to his hunch or just stay silent. But because he had no physical evidence, he ultimately decided to keep it to himself. And though his article had already run in the Journal without revealing the death was a murder, he still felt a responsibility to solve the case. He wanted to write a follow-up piece that would reveal the killer to the public.

Jason never had to be so secretive about his stories. His latest articles entitled, 'Preparing for the Worst' and 'Rethinking the Cost' were his regular types of articles since he began working at the Journal. 'Murder on Wall Street' was not only outside of his professional comfort zone as a writer, but it left him secluded from his peers in a way he had not experienced in years. He usually bounced ideas off his coworkers and made sure they felt he had a strong piece before he submitted it for publication. He wasn't even allowed to talk about his current assignment until it hit newspaper stands.

Despite yesterday's rejection, he wanted to see Lissie again. Even if it was just to bounce ideas off her for the article. She was the only person in the world he could talk candidly to about the murder.

As he prepared to call her, he decided it was in her best interest to try to sway Lissie into falling for *him* instead of this McCloud guy. Something wasn't right about him, and she deserved to be with someone *good*. Someone who didn't have the threat of danger surrounding him.

"Hello?" he heard on the other line.

"Hi, Lissie. Sick of me yet?" he asked jokingly.

"Not at all! What's up?" she responded with a smile in her voice.

"There is literally no one else I can talk to about this article. Would it be terrible of me to ask you out for dinner? I want to bounce some theories off of you," he pleaded.

"Uhh," she said.

"Not like a date or anything. I really need to talk to someone, and I can't talk about the story with any of my coworkers. They're under the impression that Mr. Stein passed away quietly in his office," he quickly added.

"Sure. I can meet for dinner," she said.

"Are you coming from your place? 'Cause I could meet you halfway," he asked, hoping her answer was "yes."

"No, I'm coming from Chelsea. You want me to come to Midtown?" she asked.

"How 'bout if we meet at Chelsea Market?" he suggested. That was a nice, big public place. He hoped she wouldn't feel uncomfortable meeting him there.

"That's perfect," she agreed. "Six o'clock?"

"See you then," he said as he hung up.

Jason's background check on Matthew McCloud was spotty at best. The information he found on the man and his family left him with more questions than answers. He supposed that billionaires could afford the luxury of erasing their family histories if they so desired, but this was different. It almost seemed that the family had sprung up from nowhere. Like six generations of the McCloud family had been created overnight. Jason had never seen a family history like this in all his years of researching and writing. The family didn't have any connections to other families from the same timeframes and locations, which was never the case. There were no photographs of any of them. Jason had even gone so far as to call a few residents of the cities listed as the McCloud family's previous residences. Nothing. No one had heard of them. No one had met them. And Jason couldn't find any information on the family's current whereabouts.

He felt like this story would cause his hair to turn prematurely grey. He had been frustrated like this only once before. But that was when he was fresh out of college and writing for a small newspaper in Portsmouth, New Hampshire. The publication was such a tiny operation that any time a story came in, the next available writer who wasn't already working on an article would take it. Six months into his employment, he happened to be the lucky winner of the biggest story in the town's history. A college student disappeared after wrecking his car into a tree off of US-4. The boy had not told any friends or family where he was headed or given them any reason for the disappearance. Four months writing story after story about the newest developments and latest evidence had equated to nothing. The police never found the kid. Jason had always felt like a piece of the story was missing. The one detail that nagged at his psyche from the beginning was that the rag from his roadside emergency kit had been stuffed into the tailpipe of his car. He talked to every witness, friend, and professor who was remotely connected to the boy and come up with nothing. For months, he walked around feeling the stares of the town residents—he knew they were judging him for not discovering the truth about the disappearance.

Jason made the decision to apply for jobs in New York City one year later. Fortunately, his uncle had a connection at the Wall Street Journal that paid off with an interview. A month later, he moved to the city and started a research intern. With serious dedication, the internship turned into a career and he had been with the Journal ever since.

He was determined to discover the truth about Gregory Stein's murder. Even if he needed to bend a few laws to do so. Furthermore, a part of him hoped that discovering the truth would help him win Lissie's affection.

Right at six p.m., Lissie walked around the corner in front of the market.

Jason always felt such joy when he saw her. She hadn't given him any reason to feel this way, but he still pictured her in his arms when he closed his eyes. He wanted so badly to be the one who made her smile the way she smiled when she spoke about McCloud.

"Shall we?" he asked as he opened the door to the market.

"Thank you!" she said with a beautiful smile. *God, that smile*, Jason thought wistfully.

Lissie purchased a crepe and a box of doughnuts for dinner. He wasn't sure what to make of those selections, but thought she must be grieving. Jason decided to order a crepe as well so he could pay for Lissie's dinner more easily.

He wasn't sure how to approach the issue on his mind, so he started the conversation on a lighter note.

"What have you been filling your days with?" he asked.

"Well," she said as she finished chewing the bite in her mouth, "I'm actually redecorating Matthew's apartment. It is awful right now. Seriously. Feels like a tomb in there. I'm going do my best to make it more homey and comfortable while maintaining the modern feel. It's tricky, but I'm up for the task."

"That's great!" Jason said with forced enthusiasm. A job like that could take months to complete—months of time spent alone with the owner of the apartment. *So great*, he thought with despondency.

"So what part of the story do you need to talk about?" she asked as she took another bite.

"I just can't key in on the murderer. After looking through all of Stein's files along with interviews of employees and close relations, I have to believe that the assassin was hired by one of the suspects you gave me. What I really don't understand is how the murderer knew Stein would be in his office. They would have needed to get into Stein's office prior to the murder to know how the office was laid out. And they certainly would have had to do extensive reconnaissance to know the perfect vantage point to take the shot while Stein was sitting in that particular chair. And on top of that, someone would have had to tip off the assassin to let them know Stein was in his office that night. Because there was probably a short window of opportunity where the assassin would be able to shoot Mr. Stein from the building they used. And I say 'they' because there could easily have been more than one person involved. The building has security in place for an alarm to sound if one of the external windows or doors is shattered. And a bullet would definitely set off the alarm. Either someone with access to the alarm system or someone who has advanced technical skills had to be involved.

"My gut is telling me that it's one of two possibilities. One: Mrs. Stein hired a professional killer or group of professional killers. She sent them into the office to pose as potential clients so they would have a working knowledge of the layout of the building and know which buildings would have the best vantage points to take the shot. Then Mrs. Stein would need to inform the killers that Mr. Stein was in his office. It's possible because she made several calls to his office the next day to voice her frustrations over his not coming home the night before. But I've heard the messages and I've met with the woman, and she's either a really good actress or she wasn't involved. The other possibility is that an employee hired the assassins and used someone on the security team to inform them of Stein's presence in the building so they knew when to strike. The employee would've had to have access to Stein's office to either take photos of the layout of the room, or have access to the building plans to give to the assassins. But the security cameras and the building's alarm lost power for an hour during the night of the murder. I'm leaning toward the first theory," Jason finished and caught his breath.

Lissie sat, staring at him with a look that made him feel as if she thought he was insane.

"Umm ... wow," she said quietly, still staring.

"You think I'm crazy, don't you?" he asked, slightly embarrassed.

"No. I think you've gone above and beyond the call of duty. You've already written the story you were assigned, and you're writing a follow-up *and* trying to catch the killer on your own time. Are you sure you're not working for the wrong newspaper?" she asked with a chuckle.

"I actually hate this kind of story. I once followed a small-town murder for months on end, writing story after story about new theories and evidence. The murder was never solved, and I swore off that kind of writing. This is the only time I plan on breaking my rule. And the only reason I'm breaking it is because I was told that you specifically requested I be the reporter for this case." His cheeks reddened. He had probably revealed too much, but if he ever planned on winning her away from McCloud, he needed to seize every opportunity that presented itself.

Lissie looked bewildered by his confession but didn't respond. Apparently there would be no more talk of a relationship between them, that much was clear.

"I wanted to get that list of clients because I think one of the newest clients is involved." He paused for a moment before quietly adding, "And I'm worried about you."

She looked like she was processing the information he had presented to her. She looked down at her own folded hands, her face shifting from thoughtful to concern to anger before looking up at Jason with wide, understanding eyes. She leaned forward with a scowl on her face.

"Are you implying that *Matthew* could somehow be involved here?" she asked in a hushed yet intense whisper.

"I'm sorry, I can't place his face in the photographs, but I recognize him from somewhere," was all Jason could say.

"How on earth did you get photos of him? Did you have him followed? I was wrong. You *are* insane. Don't call me again," she said as she got up in a huff and stormed away.

Well that went well, Jason thought. "This was fun! Let's do it again sometime," he said cheerfully to the empty chair across from him. Several passersby looked at him as if he was crazy. He took the opportunity to get up and leave the building. He still had work to do if he wanted to prove his theory.

Forty-Two

MATTHEW AND HIS BROTHERS arrived at the GPS coordinates after a tedious nine hour drive through nothing but desert, desert, and more desert. They had listened to the radio the entire way, and Matthew hoped he never had to listen to Saudi radio ever again. About two miles east of their destination, they parked their SUV just off Route 75, gathered their bags of weapons and tech gear, and headed on foot to the target's location. They planned their arrival perfectly so they arrived at the site as dark set in. As they came upon the site, the three brothers realized there would be more complications than they previously expected. The terrain was even and flat. For Marcus to have the opportunity to snipe the guards above ground, they had counted on a few rolling hills—which their geographical map had shown them were present in the area. The brothers lay down on the ground where they could avoid detection while discussing the plan.

"I need to be within one hundred meters of the bunker in order to find their power sources. I'd put money on everything being run by generators out here. It would be easy for me to cut the gas lines to the generators if you could take out the ground forces," Matthew said to Marcus.

"Unfortunately, we need to use our night-vision goggles to find a good spot for me to set up camp. I cannot stand what those things do to my eyes. I always feel like I'm in Oz with them on," Marcus said as his brothers laughed. "The only issue I can foresee is that there may not be any ground forces. And once we get underground, we'll be dealing with winding tunnels—which would mean hand-to-hand for all three of us," Marcus sighed, frustrated that his skills might be rendered useless.

Antonio's wicked grin grew to a full smile. He loved hand-to-hand combat. And in underground tunnels, his knives would be put to good use. He didn't have to say anything. Matthew and Marcus both knew what the new plan would be if there were no signs of forces above ground.

"Let's hope it doesn't come to that. It would make this mission ten times more dangerous, and we simply aren't prepared for that kind of change." Marcus's concern was written all over his face.

"Oh yes we are. You don't think I knew this scenario might be a possibility?" Antonio asked, offended at Marcus's implication. "I brought enough knives for an army," he laughed as he unzipped the large bag he'd been carrying on his back.

Marcus and Matthew exchanged wary looks. Neither of them was as skilled with knife combat or hand-to-hand as Antonio.

"Don't worry, you dumb pricks. I'll take the lead. You probably won't even have to make a kill," he said, still smiling.

"We should wait until daylight," Marcus said. "If they're staying below ground at night, there's a possibility they'll come up during the day for supply runs or shift changes."

Matthew hated any deviation from the plan. But this change could mean a longer stay in this Godforsaken desert. The job was supposed to have happened at night to ensure there would be fewer guards awake and aware. If no one came out during the night or into the morning hours, they would literally be knocking on the enemy's door in order to get into the bunker. He grabbed his phone and waited for it to power on. He sent a short text to Lissie to let her know he may be out of the country an extra day, then turned the phone back off.

The brothers found a good spot to set up camp behind a small sand dune about two hundred meters away from the entrance of the bunker. They took turns keeping watch through the night, but as dawn broke, their suspicions were confirmed—there was no activity above ground. All night they monitored radio channels, but there wasn't a single peep. The brothers' intel suggested that supply shipments were irregular at best—seemingly unplanned. But when supplies did arrive, they came between four a.m. and six a.m. They had hoped to use a supply shipment as their 'in' when they discovered the lack of above-ground security. But all hopes of an easy entrance were now gone.

"I guess we're all going in," Matthew announced sullenly.

Antonio threw his brothers their flak jackets, each equipped with over twenty throwing knives and a few grenades. They still hoped to keep their presence quiet as they moved through the tunnels. Matthew and Marcus exchanged glances and then looked at Antonio as if he were insane.

"For good measure!" Antonio said guiltily.

They were suited up for combat within minutes. Marcus chose an assault rifle as his weapon. Matthew grabbed two silenced pistols on the off-chance there was a way for them to make it through the bunker undetected. Antonio carried only his knives—which all three hoped would be the only weapons in use today.

They stayed low to the flat, sand-covered ground while they ran to the thick, metal, in-ground bunker door. They slowed when they neared the door and tiptoed the last few yards.

"Ready?" Antonio whispered. Both brothers nodded in agreement. Antonio grabbed Marcus's gun and rammed the butt of it into the metal three times as a way of knocking.

They heard a series of shouts from below.

"I believe they think we're the supply shipment," Marcus whispered as he listened to the men yelling. All three brothers spoke Arabic fluently, but the sounds were so muffled through the metal door, they couldn't be certain if they were hearing correctly.

A sound came from below—as if someone was grinding metal on metal to open the door.

"Here we go," Antonio smiled.

Forty-Three

LISSIE WAS CONFUSED when she heard the strange beeping coming from her purse. She was deep in thought at the hardware store, picking out paint colors to test on Matthew's walls. *What's that sound?* she thought as she dug around in her purse.

"Oh!" she said excitedly when she realized it was the international phone Matthew had given her. She looked at the text she received and was confused by the abruptness. It only said:

May get delayed an extra day. Miss you.

Let you know when I'll be home as soon as I know.

Weird, she thought. Ever since her conversation with Jason, she had been doing her best to stay as far away from his line of thinking as possible. *He's not a murderer. He's the love of your life and a wonderful man. But what do you really know about him? I mean, you've only spent a month with him. Could he be out there right now, killing people? He only said he needed to go to Asia for family business. What does that even mean? He didn't even tell you what country he was going to. What if it's all a lie? He could be anywhere and you wouldn't know it. He could be ... STOP THIS, LISSIE!* she scolded herself as she snapped out of her thoughts and realized there were tears in her eyes. She ran a hand through her hair and dried her eyes. *Paint colors. You're thinking about paint colors.*

Forty-Four

JASON SAT in his apartment, unmoving. All the research he had done was sprawled out before him on his coffee table and living room floor. He had been over everything so many times, his brain stopped functioning properly.

Normally on a weekend with weather this nice he would be back in Pennsylvania with his parents. Fishing with his dad on the lake behind his parents' house was one of his favorite pastimes. Fishing, playing baseball on the Xbox with his dad, watching Pirates games—that's what he wanted to be doing. Instead, for the past month he'd been sitting in either his office or his apartment staring at all the same pieces of information and all the same photos of Matthew McCloud.

His strict daily workout regimen had suffered. He had missed the last two games of his summer league softball team. Even when his friends convinced him to put his work away so they could drag him to the bar for a few drinks, he had been so absentminded that they knew better than to ask him again. When he was isolated with his work, he became focused to a fault.

How do I figure this out? he wondered.

He looked around his apartment. Well, it wasn't really *his* apartment, but it was the apartment he had lived in for the past ten years. His very rich uncle—the same uncle that had gotten him the internship, and subsequently his job, at the Journal—kept an apartment in New York City for business trips. After he retired, he only kept it for when his wife and kids wanted to take trips into the city. He graciously offered Jason the apartment—rent-free. Jason, of course, accepted the generous offer, and hadn't paid a dime of rent the entire time he had lived in the city.

He hadn't changed a single thing about the apartment since he moved in. He was dedicated to keeping the place spotless in case his uncle decided he needed it back some day. The only improvement he made was to the television.

For a man who loved sports the way Jason did, a forty-two inch screen just wasn't enough. He looked up at the sixty inch screen and grinned at his one and only piece of personal property in the apartment.

He picked up his beer and took another drink. He decided after his meeting with Lissie that he was bound to die a bachelor. He already lived in a bachelor pad and maintained an entire group of friends that he just knew would be spending the rest of their lives as bachelors. *As long as I have a few one night stands a year I can live alone,* he tried to tell himself without much luck. He knew he only concocted the lie to ease his frustration. *Why, when I finally find a woman I'm interested in, is she unavailable?*

His daily routine of getting off of work, eating dinner, watching SportsCenter with a beer, and going to bed was getting tiresome. He didn't really want his routine to change. He simply wanted to share it with someone.

He turned off the TV and stepped out onto his balcony. The city beneath was still alive. He sighed, walked back inside his silent apartment, and finished the daily routine.

Forty-Five

As soon as the bunker door opened, all hell broke loose. Antonio killed the first three guards with ease, but the tunnels were filled with an endless stream of armed men. Antonio jumped down into the bunker and kept swinging and throwing knives with precision and ease. As soon as Marcus dropped down behind him, shots rang out. Matthew's heart began racing and he jumped in, rolling to the side as he landed to avoid getting hit. The dark bunker stretched out in all four directions. The metal walls made him feel as if he were in a prison rather than underground in the middle of the desert. It was good they went down at dawn rather than waiting for full sunlight—it would have taken his eyes much longer to adjust to the darkness.

"Go left," Antonio shouted above the sounds of gunfire. All three brothers dove into the left hallway as soon as the command was given. In under thirty seconds, Antonio had taken out no less than fifteen men—each killed by a knife.

"Mattia—stay here and guard the entrance. If anyone tries to escape, take them out. Marcus—we're going in back-to-back. We'll have to stay low, but the sound in these tunnels is reverberating in a way that I think we'll be able to navigate. Use your knives first. And trade weapons with Mattia. I want to keep as low a profile as possible while we're moving through these tunnels. It doesn't matter if they know Mattia's at the front door because they already know we're in here."

The brothers nodded to each other and a few seconds later Matthew was alone. He held the assault rifle tightly to his shoulder and found a stack of boxes he could easily hide behind but still see the exit. He knew his back was exposed to a long hallway, but no one seemed to be headed toward the exit. In his experience, the soldiers in Middle Eastern cultures did not run and hide in the face of danger—they protected their leaders. He always found the practice honorable. Even now, as he heard gunshots fired in distant tunnels, he was impressed that not one soldier was trying to escape. Ten minutes later the gunshots came to an abrupt halt, and Matthew allowed himself a moment of worry for his brothers' well-being. Unfortunately, he chose the wrong moment to let his mind wander.

The pain in the back of his skull was intense, and he felt something hot running down the back of his neck and spine. He tried to reach behind his head to see what struck him, but he quickly realized his hands were tightly bound. He was in a kneeling position. As he quietly struggled to release his hands from their binds, his right arm sent a searing pain all the way through his body. His eyes flew open when his mind registered the cold metal circle pressed to his right temple. Around him, several men spoke quietly in Arabic about where the other intruders might be. Matthew heard them radio another group of soldiers about the other intruders getting away. *Thank God my brothers are alive,* he thought with relief. *At least they don't know I can understand them,* he thought with pleasure. The men talked about the death of their leader and how they weren't sure how they should continue their coup without his guidance. They chattered about who might step up and take the reins in his absence. Matthew counted four voices and could see only one other man standing guard at the entrance to whatever room they dragged him into. *Five in all. I think I can handle them. I just need to figure out where they're all standing.* He decided he needed to take action soon. If his brothers came charging into this room, at least one of them would be hit by a bullet. Matthew wasn't going to wait for his brothers get ambushed.

He rolled to his right and swung out his legs, taking down two very surprised men. He lifted his legs high and dropped them straight down into the closest guard's forehead. The man stopped struggling immediately. The other four guards regained their composure and trained their weapons on him, all shouting for him to stop moving. Matthew stayed as still as possible and closed his eyes. If he was going to be shot and killed, he would be envisioning his beautiful Lissie with her perfect body pressed against his and her bright blue eyes smiling up at him. This was his heaven. He knew the afterlife held nothing for him. Lisette Anamaria Renaud was the only heaven he would ever know.

He heard four grunts. And four men drop to the ground.

"It's about time," Matthew said before he opened his eyes.

"My God, Mattia. Were you playing 'tea party' instead of guarding the exit?" Antonio said with a forced humor as he cut the ties binding Matthew's hands together.

Antonio's tone was off. He only sounded that way when something was horribly wrong. Matthew knew his injuries had to be pretty awful.

"Let us get you back to the car, Mattia. We're going to need something to carry him on," Marcus said quietly to Antonio.

Matthew looked his brothers over—neither had a scratch on them. He hated being the only liability. They needed to get back to the car and out of the area as fast as possible. They had no idea if any of the guards in the bunker radioed for backup before being killed.

"I can walk fine on my own. It's my arm that's broken," Matthew said, frustrated.

"You can try. But I don't think you'll get very far. Let me at least wrap your head so you don't bleed to death," Antonio replied.

The brothers wrapped his head tightly with a piece of a canvas tarp and brought along the rest of the tarp in case he needed to be carried. Matthew stood, and although the pain ripped through his body like a serrated knife was sawing up and down his back and limbs, he did not complain once. His brothers pushed him up the bunker's ladder, then placed their arms around his waist and ran toward the SUV. Two miles straight they ran without a break—and Matthew stayed conscious the entire time.

As soon as they laid him down on the tarp in the back of the SUV, Antonio went back to retrieve the bags they left near the bunker. Half an hour later, Antonio emerged in the distance with all three bags slung over his back.

Matthew wanted to make a joke to lighten the mood, but he could see Marcus was in no mood for a joke. Matthew was never supposed to enter the bunker, half the guards should have been shot above ground, and Antonio should have been the only brother to enter the underground tunnels. Marcus was responsible for planning this mission. And they had been forced to improvise so completely off-plan that it was clear he was shouldering the full responsibility for Matthew's injuries.

"Stop what you're thinking right now, Marcus. I let my guard down when I heard the bullets stop. If I had been aware of my surroundings instead of worrying about you two, I would be fine right now. Stop beating yourself up. This one's on me," he assured his brother.

Marcus showed no signs of relief from Matthew's speech, and Matthew decided it would be useless to talk any more.

On the nine hour drive back to Dubai, Marcus kept pressure on a gash across the back of Matthew's head and the deep cut on his right cheek. He applied medical tape to the rest of the cuts to minimize his blood loss. When they arrived back in town, Antonio first went to Matthew's apartment to grab fresh clothes and wet towels so the three could walk into the hospital without too much suspicion. The brothers helped Matthew change clothes—though the pain was so intense in his arm that he nearly passed out twice.

When they finally got to the hospital, Matthew was immediately taken back to have his arm set. He was told that his arm was not broken severely, but it could take up to six weeks to heal. He also had three cracked ribs, a dislocated shoulder, and thirty stitches sewn in various places around his body. Matthew was frustrated with the diagnosis, but mostly he was thankful that he was alive. He was on such a high dosage of pain medication, that by the time his brothers got him back to the apartment, he was out cold.

Then next day he woke up in excruciating pain. All he could think of was Lissie. He grabbed his phone from the side table where his brothers had graciously left it for him and turned it on. He'd missed three texts from Lissie.

The first read:

> Okay. Just let me know if you're alright. It's weird being here without you.

The second was sent right before midnight in New York:

> I'm spending the night at your place. Today was weird. I need to talk to you when you get back.

The final text was sent an hour earlier:

> Can't sleep. If you get this, call me.

Matthew felt a slight panic welling up inside him. Lissie had shown no signs of being a needy person since he met her. If she needed to talk to him on the phone, something serious was going on. He dialed her number immediately. After three rings she picked up.

"Hello?" she said groggily.

"Oh no. Did I wake you up?" he asked, worried.

"No ... well yes. But I'm happy you're calling. The past few days have been really weird, and I needed to hear your voice," she said.

"Are you alright? What happened?" He was bothered that she was upset about something, and he couldn't be with her to make her feel better.

"I can't really talk about it over the phone. But I just needed to hear your voice and know that you were okay. I had the weirdest feeling that something was wrong. I know that probably makes me sound like a clingy girlfriend who can't deal with life if she hasn't heard from her boyfriend, but this was different. I could've sworn something horrible happened. I even prayed! And I'm not even religious!" she said, giggling. "Can you believe that?"

Yes I can, he thought gratefully. "I'm coming home as soon as I can. I'm going to try to catch the next flight. I'll let you know if I get on it, okay?"

"That's perfect. I'll talk to you soon," she said as the call ended.

Matthew crawled out of bed and realized that every muscle in his body ached, and the back of his head felt like it was still split open.

"There's our brother," Antonio said as he and Marcus entered the room.

They handed him pain medication, a large glass of water and a hot cup of coffee. "We waited to cook breakfast until you woke up."

Matthew felt emotions welling up inside him and swallowed them down along with the pain pills. He was grateful for these two men. They were skilled in the art of 'making you feel like nothing is wrong when something is terribly wrong'.

"When's the next flight to New York?" Matthew asked quietly.

"We're booked on the two o'clock to JFK," Antonio replied.

"We're?" Matthew said confused. As far as he knew, his brothers were both heading off to other contracts.

"We spoke with Saint, and he agrees that your condition requires additional care. We will be staying with you until you have healed enough to stand on your own," Marcus said with a furrowed brow.

"I can stand on my own right now," Matthew said as he tried to stand too quickly and nearly blacked out, "or maybe not."

His brothers laughed and helped him walk into the kitchen. By the time they had cooked, eaten and readied themselves for the day, it was time to head to the airport.

In his whole life, Matthew had never been so grateful to board a plane.

Forty-Six

LISSIE WAS THRILLED that Matthew's delayed schedule allowed her to finish redecorating his bedroom. The room no longer felt like an empty cave. She couldn't wait for him to see it. She knew he would be home soon, so she finished placing the décor she purchased and decided to take a quick shower.

As she scrubbed paint and grime off her skin, she couldn't quite understand the mix of emotions she was experiencing. Jason had planted the seed of doubt in her head about Matthew's 'career' or whatever you called it. She was afraid of what Matthew might actually be. She knew he would never hurt her, so that wasn't where the fear came into play. But if he really was an assassin … a killer … how could she allow him to be a part of her life? She had never felt this connected with another person—and she was scared to lose him. But what scared her most of all was that she was so completely in love with him that she wasn't sure it actually mattered to her what his job was. Did that make her a horrible person? Surely there was something wrong with her for feeling this way. Matthew didn't look or act like a murderer. She wandered if those feelings made her a sociopath or just a woman who was desperately in love. She couldn't decide.

She heard footsteps in the living room, and her stomach churned with the nervous butterflies a woman felt right before seeing the love of her life. She finished her shower, threw her long hair up into a bun, and wrapped a towel around her. She knew she should get dressed, but was certain Matthew would enjoy her towel-wrapped 'welcome home'.

She smiled widely as she rounded the door into the kitchen and stopped abruptly. There were two unfamiliar men standing in the living room by the couch. Her heart was pounding so hard she was certain they would hear it. Before she could stop herself, a shrill scream escaped as she threw her hands over her mouth and stumbled backwards into the wall. She meant to back into the bedroom where she could lock herself in, but she missed and was now off balance.

"Lissie?" she heard a voice say from behind the two men. She knew the voice, but her panic was so thick that she couldn't place it. She planted her feet, ready to run if the men approached her.

"Lissie! Don't panic! These are my brothers," Matthew said with concern as he leaned forward on the couch.

That was when she really saw him. The right side of his face was swollen, purple and blue with several cuts that had been stitched up. His right eye was slightly shut because of the swelling. And his right arm was resting on the arm of the couch—in a cast. Her heart sank as her panic shifted from terror for her own life to concern for Matthew's. She ran to the couch and dropped down to her knees in front of him. He smiled at her lovingly, but she could see even that small effort pained him.

She didn't know where to touch him that wouldn't hurt, so she started checking each part of his body—lifting his sleeves, his shirt, his pant legs. After a few moments, she found her voice.

"What happened to you?" she asked in a gentle tone. Matthew's responding silence infuriated her. "What the hell happened, Matthew?" she asked angrily. "Because you didn't mention anything about this on the phone! Couldn't you have given me a little warning? About your brothers coming? Or about this?" she shrieked as she motioned up and down his body with a quivering hand.

No one answered her. They just remained still, looking like children who had been caught doing something wrong. She turned sharply to glare at the brothers, hoping they would answer her.

"Don't look at us," the one on the right said as he threw his hands up. "This is his issue to explain."

The other brother turned to Matthew and announced they were going to head out to grab some stuff they needed for their visit. *That's right*, Lissie thought with irritation. *Get the hell out of here so I can get to the bottom of this.*

She felt certain they heard her thoughts because they nearly tripped over each other trying to get to the elevator door.

Lissie stood slowly, adjusting the towel that she just realized she had been cloaked in the entire time, and glared at Matthew.

"Can you grab my pain medication out of that bag? I'm due for another dose," he said with a grimace.

Lissie was unmoved by his plea. She stayed firmly planted. No amount of pain or discomfort was going to soften her heart towards him right now. She knew he was trying to pull at her heart-strings. And she was having none of that.

"I'm really in a lot of pain. I have three cracked ribs too," he said with a small moan.

"And I'll be happy to get that medicine for you as soon as you tell me what the hell happened in Asia. If that's even where you were," she tacked on at the end.

Confusion was clearly written across Matthew's face. *Why in the world would she think I was lying to her about being in Asia?*

"I was in Dubai. It's in the Middle East, but technically it *is* in Asia. Why would I lie to you?" he asked, shocked by the implication.

Her expression was a combination of hurt and distrust. Matthew didn't know what to think of her reaction.

"What am I supposed to think?" she began, anguish thick in her voice. She was so upset she couldn't even express her displeasure. She kept her face blank while screaming at him in her mind. *You tell me you're going to be taking care of family business for four days in Asia—Asia is a continent, Matthew. You didn't even tell me what country you were heading to! Then I get one short text telling me you're going to be delayed. And when you actually get home, you're not only accompanied by your brothers—who you didn't manage to mention were coming with you, but you also didn't mention that you are beat to a pulp with a broken arm!* She took a few deep breaths before quietly asking, "How, exactly, were you hoping I would react to this? You're beat to a pulp!"

Matthew hadn't really thought this through. He knew she would be concerned about him, but hadn't thought that his omission would cause her to doubt him. He struggled to scoot to the edge of the couch and took Lissie's hand in his left hand.

"I'm sorry, Lissie. I didn't think any of this through. After this happened, I was on so much pain medication that my brothers took me to my apartment to sleep. And when I woke up the next morning it was time to head to the airport. I only called to tell you that we were heading back into the country, because my brain was so cloudy from the oxycodone. That was the only thing I knew I was supposed to tell you. Please. Please forgive me," he said pleadingly.

Lissie's expression softened a little, but it was clear she hadn't gotten over her distrust.

"*What* happened, Matthew? You just said, 'after this happened,' but what is the 'this'? What happened to you?" she asked, her voice soft and pleading as she knelt down in front of him again.

Her hands held tightly onto Matthew's left hand as her expression begged for him to tell her the truth. Matthew was at a loss. He wasn't sure she was ready for this yet. And he still hadn't talked to Marcus about how, exactly, to reveal the truth to the person you love. Marcus had somehow kept Sera in his life after he divulged all the gory details of his life to her. Matthew desperately needed his help if he planned to reveal his true identity to the woman in front of him.

"I need you to trust me," he begged. "I will tell you what happened. But I honestly can't do it right now. Please. Trust me."

Lissie's eyes reflected the deep pain he had inflicted. She let go of him, dropped her hands to her side, and stood. Walking silently to his bag, she grabbed his pain medication and filled a glass with water. She took him the pills and water and retreated to the bedroom without saying a word.

Matthew didn't know what to do. He wasn't prepared to tell her the truth. This secret was an all-or-nothing kind of thing. He couldn't simply tell her one part without revealing everything. But his heart was breaking. The last time he loved a woman this way, she was murdered before they could even develop their relationship. If he lost Lissie now, he didn't know if he would have the will to live any longer. He had already come to grips with the fact that someday she would die. But that was years away. He planned to spend every day with her for the rest of her life.

Lissie returned to the room, fully dressed, with her purse thrown over her shoulder. She looked at Matthew as if she wanted to say something but instead wiped a tear from the corner of her eye and turned to leave.

"I can't lose you, Lissie. I can't lose the love of my life."

She stopped in her tracks without turning to look at him and shook her head.

"That's not fair, Matthew. You can't just pull out 'love' for the first time just because I'm upset with you," she stopped to gain her composure. "That's not fair," she whispered as she entered the elevator and left.

Matthew didn't know which hurt worse: his body or his heart. He let out an enraged cry. His only thought over the past thirty-six hours was that he needed to get home to Lissie. He wanted to hold her and kiss her. He wanted to thank her for being his only reason to live. He hadn't done any of those things. And moments before, he watched her walk out of his apartment—and possibly out of his life. He lay down on the couch and placed a hand over his face. His eyes seemed to produce an endless stream of tears, though he didn't have the energy to let out the sobs or screams he felt in his tormented soul. "How many times do I have to die before you'll let me live?" he screamed angrily toward heaven. Hundreds of years of immortality. Endless years of solitary, meaningless life. Yet the only time he had truly *lived* was when he was with Lissie. For the second time in his life, he thought it might be better to die than to live with this kind of pain.

As soon as the elevator doors closed, Lissie lost it. She cried so hard she was hyperventilating. She tried to straighten herself and calm down as she reached the lobby to leave. When the doors opened, Matthew's brothers were standing there, talking to each other. They looked at Lissie, surprise registering at her red face covered in tears. The taller one started to speak, but Lissie cut him off with a finger pointed in his face.

"No! When he's ready to tell me what happened, he knows where to find me," she yelled as she stormed out of the building.

She refused to look back. She hailed a cab and headed towards midtown. There was only one person she needed to talk to at that moment. She quickly typed out a text:

> I think you may be right. I'll be in the lobby of your office in five.

She took a deep breath and hit 'send'.

Forty-Seven

JASON RACED to the lobby as soon as he received Lissie's text. He hoped desperately that this tormenting story would finally be coming to a close so he could get back to his regular routine. Lissie walked in, tears dripping down her face and wetting her clothes. Her expression was that of a woman who just lost a part of her heart. He was so excited about the possibility of unravelling this mystery, he hadn't even thought about what Lissie might be going through. He wasn't sure what to do, so he opened his arms to embrace her. She almost fell into him, bawling, and buried her face in his shoulder.

"What happened?" he asked quietly.

"Is there an office we can use? Somewhere private?" she asked in between sobs.

He led her to the 7th floor, took her to an interview room, and shut the door behind them.

"There are no recording devices in here. You're just talking to me," he explained.

Lissie sat quietly for a few minutes, calming her breathing so she could speak intelligibly.

"What do you need to know about Matthew to figure out for sure if he's ... what you think he might be?" she whispered.

"Umm ..." he thought for a moment before running to his cubicle and grabbing his research. He closed the door and began to spread out everything he found on assassinations in the past ten years. "Because I figure he's in his late twenties or early thirties, I only went back ten years. I've been gathering all the intel I can find on recent unsolved murders or possible assassinations. What can you tell me about his personal life?"

Lissie took a moment to look over a few of the articles and police reports Jason had gathered. Hundreds—maybe even thousands—of possible assassinations were laid out on the table. Lissie looked like she might be ill.

"There's no possible way he could've done all of these, Lissie. These are all the unsolved cases that fit the same profile—assassinations and high-profile murders." His words seemed to calm her a little, but she still looked paler than normal.

"He has apartments in New York, LA, Paris, Tokyo, and Dubai. At his apartment in New York, he has a flashy sports car, a black SUV, and a black sports car—but less expensive than the flashy one. He implied that he has the same types of vehicles at each of his apartments. He purchased his apartment building so he wouldn't have to share the parking garage with any other tenants."

Jason was writing as fast as possible to take down every detail. He never knew what info could be the piece that gave him a break in the story. She slid a cell phone across the table to him.

"He was out of the country for the past five days. He told me he was in Dubai, but I don't know what to think. He came home with his face stitched up and swollen like he had been beaten, and his arm was broken," she said with a quick sob. She was trying to collect herself.

"I'm sorry, Lissie," he tried to console her.

"I'm so worried about him. And he won't tell me what happened. He asked me to trust him. But he's given me no reason to! Before he left, I felt like I knew him inside and out, but now I feel like maybe I never knew him at all!" She began to cry again.

Jason knew Lissie could give him more info, but he allowed her some time to recover by making a call to his tech buddy. His friend agreed to track the origins of the texts and phone call Lissie had received while Matthew was away. By the end of the evening he would know where they were generated.

As soon as he finished the call, Lissie started again. "He has two brothers. Both seem to be around the same age. I met them today. They're definitely related by blood—they all share similar features and they're staying with him right now."

Jason immediately thought of a private investigator one of his friends worked with when he thought his wife might be cheating. The investigator had done such a thorough job that Jason had saved his number in case he ever needed extra help for an article. Jason decided to call him if nothing fruitful came from Lissie's information.

"His family is from Italy. I don't know anything else that would be pertinent to the story. I wish I knew more," she said as she hung her head.

"This is amazing, Lissie. I think we're going to figure out if he's involved or not based on this info. Do you want to stick around while I work on this?" he asked, hoping she would say yes.

"Thanks. Yeah. I just need to be someplace where everything doesn't remind me of why I love him. I'm on the verge of running back to his apartment to tell him I'm sorry and make sure he's okay," she confessed guiltily.

Jason's heart sank further than he thought possible. *She loves him.* "Well you can keep hoping that he's not involved. This could all be a bad hunch," but he wasn't sure how convincing that sentiment was.

As Lissie sat quietly with her eyes downturned, Jason looked over the latest stack of possible cases to see if anything turned up near Dubai. There had been fifteen incidents over the weekend that fit the profile he created. Only two were in the Middle East, but one was within driving distance of Dubai.

> *The Saudi desert*
> *Thirty-eight Saudi military and one high-ranking Saudi commander were slaughtered in a hidden bunker in the southern desert of Saudi Arabia. The commander was rumored to be organizing a coup against the Saudi King. The slaughter was performed by a small group of two to four individuals. One survivor who was stabbed in the stomach and received*

severe damage to his face told officials that he heard the men speaking Italian.

Jason was elated. He called his tech guy to see if there were any breakthroughs on the origins of the texts or call, but he was met with mocking laughter. Jason checked his watch and realized he had given the guy only thirty minutes to work. He apologized and hung up. There was nothing to do now but wait.

"You want to grab dinner?" he asked Lissie.

"Why not," she said with a forced smile.

Dinner sucked. Lissie could only think of Matthew. He was wounded, and she screamed at him and left. What if he wasn't really a murderer? What if he had been mugged and felt like she would think he was weak if she knew the truth? She excused herself from the table for a moment and vaguely noticed that Jason was staring at her with concerned eyes. He was such a nice guy—and an amazing friend—but he entered the picture too late. If he had asked her on a date before she met Matthew? Maybe. But now she wasn't sure any other guy would ever be as perfect for her. If, after all this research, she found out that Matthew was an assassin, would she stay? Would he change his career for her? She thought maybe he would. Or hoped.

As soon as she locked herself in the restroom, she pulled out her phone. She'd received a new text from Matthew. As soon as she opened it, the waterworks started up again.

> I'm sorry about today. Springing everything on you like that wasn't fair. I swear to you I'll tell you what happened. I only need a little time. And I meant what I said. I really do love you.

Lissie was even more upset than before. How could he use the word 'love' now? It seemed like he conveniently pulled it out of his bag of tricks only when he was afraid she would leave. And *that* application of the word was rarely a truthful one. She thought for a moment before responding.

> I have to figure out some things. I feel like you've been keeping secrets from me, and I'm not sure how to deal with that. I think I just need a little space.

Her phone lit up seconds later.

> I can give you space. But you should know I'm an absolute wreck without you. No matter what, I'll never stop loving you.

Lissie took a few deep breaths to calm her racing heart. *He'll never stop loving me. Is that true? Because if it is, I could be making a huge mistake by sharing all this information with Jason.* She felt her pulse race again and splashed her face with cold water. She needed to calm down.

When she returned to the table, Jason had a renewed look of intensity on his face. He had an idea that could absolutely confirm whether or not Matthew was an assassin. They paid the bill and raced back to his office. Lissie prayed the new evidence would prove Matthew was innocent.

Jason couldn't believe he hadn't made the connection before this moment. He was elated. He searched the internet for the Portsmouth Police Department and dialed as quickly as he could.

"Chief Heller?" he asked when a man answered the other line.

"Yes. Who am I speaking with?" the chief answered.

"Jason Luce. I was the reporter at the Herald that wrote the story on the Wilson boy ten years ago," he said, hoping he wouldn't be met with disdain.

"Oh yes. How have you been? Enjoying life in the Big Apple?" The chief let out a laugh.

"I've been alright. But I actually have a favor to ask. During the Wilson case, do you remember the photos that the ATM snapped of those two guys no one had ever seen in town?" Jason prayed that the pause on the other line meant the chief was remembering.

"Of course I do. I think they're filed away in a box in the back room somewhere. But I don't think you need to keep worrying about solving this case, Jason. I know how hard you took it when it went cold," the chief said, concern thick in his voice.

Jason had never heard anyone from Portsmouth worry about him before. He felt a little of the burden he had carried around with him for ten years lift off his shoulders. Then he remembered the purpose of his call.

"I need you to fax me those photos. I'm writing a story on an assassination, and my gut is telling me that I've seen one of the suspects before. Those photos are the only thing I can think of that might explain the connection. I'll let you know if I find anything," he said as he gave Chief Heller the fax number and thanked him for his willingness to help.

Jason's phone lit up with a text—his buddy had sent over the traces from Matthew's phone. Jason looked over the paper he removed from the fax machine as it once again turned on and printed out another paper.

Lissie walked slowly to the fax machine and stared down at the low quality image that had been taken from a crappy ATM camera ten years earlier. Her heart stopped. She immediately recognized the man she loved ... and he looked exactly the same.

Jason held up the fax he was looking at and pointed to one line. The first text she received had originated in the southern Saudi Arabian desert. Matthew was a murderer. The man she loved was a killer. For the second time in her life, Lissie passed out from hyperventilation.

Forty-Eight

MATTHEW WAS SULLEN and withdrawn from his brothers. He had barely been home for twenty-four hours, but without Lissie, it felt like a lifetime. He had only moved from his couch to use the guest bathroom—which was closer than going to the bathroom in his own room. He wanted nothing more than to be alone in his apartment. But his brothers were here, doing their best to cheer him up—cooking delicious food and listening to his favorite music. Matthew wanted to kick them out, but somewhere in the back of his mind he knew they were helping the situation.

Matthew's phone beeped with a new text message. He grappled with the phone—his worthless right hand was making everything difficult for him. It was going to take him a long time to grow accustomed to not using it.

> Could your brothers step out for a little bit? I have to come over and grab my things.

Matthew immediately barked at his brothers to get out of his apartment. He made them promise to spend the night in a hotel and not come back until the next afternoon. They reluctantly agreed and left him alone. Fifteen minutes later, the elevator opened and Lissie emerged. She looked terrible. And incredibly beautiful. He was still confused about what had brought on this emotional turmoil. But whatever it was, he wanted to fix it.

She barely stepped out of the elevator and was standing still, looking at him like he was a stranger. He tried to stand up to go to her.

"Don't. Please don't," she begged, clearly on the verge of tears.

Matthew sank back into the couch and nodded. "I don't understand, Lissie. Why are you so angry with me that you won't even let me come near you?"

Lissie's eyes filled with grief as she took a step towards him. She set her purse down on the kitchen counter and walked into his bedroom. When she came out a few minutes later, she carried a bag full of the things he had gotten her. She placed it next to her purse and leaned wearily against the counter, never taking her eyes off of him. It was almost as if she expected him to lunge at her or something.

"Why?" he finally choked out, the pain in his chest pouring out through his words.

Lissie dug through her purse, held up two pieces of paper and placed them on the counter. Without another word, she grabbed her things and stepped on the elevator. "I wish you had just told me," she whispered as the doors closed and she left.

Once she was gone, Matthew buried his head in his hands and sat unmoving for several minutes. When he finally found the strength to move, he struggled over to the kitchen counter and looked at the papers she left.

His was sure his heart stopped beating. *How? How in the world is this possible?* He read the words on the paper ten times before his brain registered that something needed to be done. He dialed Marcus's phone and waited.

"How did it go?" Marcus asked.

Matthew took a deep breath. "Get back here now. We have a problem."

When his brothers arrived, he was standing in the kitchen, staring at the elevator. They rushed to him, but he simply held out the paper he had been gripping in his hands for the past half hour.

"What? This is impossible. I made sure there were no survivors!" Antonio screamed.

"How did she get her hands on this?" Marcus asked, deadly serious.

"That's what I've been trying to figure out since I called you. We have a lot of work to do," Matthew said as he made his way back to the couch. "I need my laptop. We need to know who accessed this information. I know Lissie has a reporter friend who's writing the story on my last job. I have a terrible feeling he's the culprit. We have to erase this report from the international database. And one of you needs to call Saint and tell him to send someone to that hospital in Saudi Arabia to finish the job. This is a disaster," he said, aggravated that his injuries had made them careless. "And it's my fault if this goes public," he added.

"You are *not* taking the blame for this," Antonio yelled at him. "Marcus and I were in charge of the bunker operation. And if I had properly done my job, there would be no evidence that the three of us were ever there."

Antonio grabbed his phone and walked into the back bedroom to call the Family. Saint and Priest would be furious, but the survivor would be dead within hours. That much was certain.

"What is this date?" Marcus asked while looking at the second paper Lissie left behind.

"I have no idea, but I figured this was more pressing," Matthew barked in frustration.

He hacked into the Interpol database where the report was filed and erased it with ease. He then ran a reverse search from the database's mainframe to get a list of I.P. addresses that had accessed the information. There was only one in New York City, and it was at the Wall Street Journal headquarters in Midtown. *Perfect*, Matthew thought sarcastically.

"We have our guy," he said to his brothers. "His name is Jason Luce. He's a writer for the Wall Street Journal, but was selected to write the story about Gregory Stein's death for Stein Securities. I have no idea how, but he somehow drew a link between me and Stein's murder."

"Jason Luce ..." Antonio said quietly. "Why does that name sound familiar?" He looked at the brothers for a moment before his eyes went wide and he grabbed the other paper sitting on the island.

"Give me the laptop!" he ordered as Matthew slid it to him, confused. After a few moments of typing, Antonio looked up, slowly shaking his head in disbelief. He turned it around for Matthew and Marcus to see.

"You have got to be kidding me," Matthew whispered, annoyed. "Eight million people in Manhattan and she befriends the only one who has any connections with us." He pushed his hands through his hair in irritation.

"What am I missing here, guys?" Marcus asked, still confused.

Antonio, still in shock over this turn of events, paused for a moment before answering. "This is the date of a story that ran ten years ago. Jason Luce wrote several articles about a contract that Matthew and I were assigned up in New Hampshire—it was that college student who we had to make disappear. Luce would not let it go. We watched him for months to make sure he never found any tracks we may have left behind. Matthew hacked his computer so we could read every story he wrote before he submitted them. The guy was fixated on the rag we shoved in the boy's tailpipe—to keep the fumes in the car after we ran him off the road. We didn't think he would ever let it go. But once he stopped writing stories about the kid's disappearance, we thought it was over and quit tracking him."

"Unbelievable," Matthew shouted as he paced around his living room. The pain in his body had disappeared beneath the adrenaline pumping through his veins.

"He must have found out from Lissie where I was this weekend and gotten a hold of her phone to run a trace. You don't have to tell me I'm an idiot, but I texted Lissie from the desert to tell her I might be delayed."

"You're an idiot," Marcus yelled with a bit of venom in his voice.

"How would Luce have known I was connected at all? Lissie doesn't seem like the kiss and tell type of girl to me. She barely talks to anyone besides her brother," Matthew wondered aloud. "I don't understand how I could've been linked to the Stein murder in the first place," Matthew said, his head spinning. He went over every detail of his visit to Stein Securities with his brothers. Neither could understand how Matthew had been implicated.

"Why don't you hack into Luce's computer to see what he's got on there," Antonio suggested.

Within a half hour, Matthew was scanning the contents of Jason's work computer.

"Whoa. Here it is," he announced as his brothers rushed over. Right before his eyes was a fuzzy photograph of him and Antonio. The date on the image matched the Portsmouth contract. Next to it was a photo of Matthew from the security cameras at Stein Securities.

"Wow," Antonio said, impressed that Luce had matched the images ten years apart. "You have to admit that's impressive."

"Ugh," Matthew groaned as he walked to the couch and lay down. "Lissie must hate me." His brothers said nothing, which Matthew took as a confirmation of his fears.

Within the hour, Marcus and Antonio received a new contract. "You have orders to stay out of this," Marcus said as he pointed to Matthew.

Matthew let out a bitter laugh. He had no problem staying out of Family business. Ever since Anamaria's murder, he had been trying to find a way out. Maybe this was finally it. He had nothing to prove to his lunatic of a grandfather. Half of his relations wanted nothing to do with him. The other half were completely indifferent. He was not eager to secure the respect of any of them. After this, he was even more determined to make an exodus from the Family. His only concern was that he wouldn't disappoint Saint or his immediate family.

"You better get to it then," Matthew said to his brothers, who were already going over the details for their new contract. He decided there was no reason for him to stay in the living room. He wasn't needed there. He made his way into his bedroom to change clothes and work on his own plans for winning Lissie back.

As soon as he stepped into his bedroom and flipped on the light, he froze. Had he walked into a different apartment? No. No, this was his room. But this was his room transformed—lovingly filled with his personality and style.

The wall of windows where his low-profile bed previously rested was transformed. Wide, vertical strips of dark brown wood stretched from floor to ceiling, creating a massive headboard over his king-sized bed. His boring, black bed had been replaced by a deep brown platform bed that matched the stain on the wooden headboard exactly. Sheer, white, linen drapes were pulled all the way to the side walls, which allowed daylight to pour in through the windows. Before the transformation, any light coming through the windows made the simply-designed room feel vast and lifeless, but with the addition of the white bed linens and the massive natural jute area rug, the space now felt inviting and homey. The bed was accented with feminine touches like white linen euro pillows and white leather bedside tables tailored with brass studs and accented stitching. Atop each bedside table was a restored antique brass task lamp. His walls were painted a light beige color similar to the finish of the lamps, and ornate, white crown molding had been added around the ceiling. Across from the bed was a new, dark walnut set of drawers that replaced his old dresser, with a wall-mounted television centered above and framed in the same horizontal wood strips Lissie used for the headboard. The room felt complete with his books and half-burned candles sitting atop his new set of drawers. On the wall to the left of the windows, square black and white photographs of the city, finished with white mats and metallic gallery frames, spanned the space that had previously been a blank, white canvas. The overall transformation was truly a work of art with hand-crafted furniture and stylistic accessories. As Matthew looked around, he thought the room could have been featured on the cover of the latest Restoration Hardware catalog. Every item had a purpose, and every color was carefully chosen to complement the rest of the room.

He sat down on the end of the bed in awe. For the rest of his life, he would have a piece of Lissie here in this room. He would never change a thing. She captured his style perfectly. He wanted her to be with him in this moment even as he feared he was losing her forever. He wanted to tell her how brilliantly she had done this job. He wanted to kiss her in appreciation. He wanted to tell her everything. He wanted *her*.

He could smell her on his bed—she had slept on these sheets. He walked to the bathroom. The towel she had used was hanging on the hook next to the door. He sunk his face in the towel and breathed in deeply. Her scent was everywhere. He prayed it would never disappear.

He returned to his bedroom and closed his eyes, yearning for Lissie to come back to him. He longed to hold her in his arms—if not in real life, maybe his dreams would suffice. He sat down on the edge of his bed and sent one last desperate text to Lissie's phone.

> I walked through the bedroom for the first time a moment ago.
> I can't believe how incredibly talented you are. You truly are the perfect woman. I'll never get over you. I love you. For eternity.

Lissie was confused past the point of words. She knew she was in love with Matthew. She felt a deeper connection to him than any other person in her life. But the fact that he had kept such a huge part of his life hidden from her was not something she could just get over. What confused her more than anything was the fact that his profession didn't really bother her. Shouldn't she be more upset that he was an assassin rather than the fact that he had hidden it from her? Maybe it made her a little insane, but she just didn't care.

Lissie spent the next week in her apartment. She had food delivered so she didn't have to go out in public. She wasn't ready to face the world yet. Jason had called her a few times to make sure she was okay, but he gave up a few days earlier—*probably because of my indifference to his attention*.

Today, she decided, it was time to venture out into the world. She drank her coffee, showered, and dressed. *What day is it again?* She wasn't sure. She hadn't returned her brother's calls. She hadn't even watched the news or checked a paper. World War III or the zombie apocalypse could've been happening outside and she wouldn't have known.

Lissie mustered her courage as she rode down the elevator. *I'll just start with something small. Maybe buy a paper and have a drink at a café. Yes. I can do this.* She always felt better after a pep talk, even if it made her feel foolish.

After grabbing a paper from a nearby stand, she headed to her favorite neighborhood café, purchased a coffee and pastry, and sat down to catch up on the latest news. As soon as she opened the paper to page two, she gasped and forgot how to breathe for a moment. Her heart may have stopped as well, but she was so caught up in the feeling of suffocating, she couldn't dwell on the heart issue. The big story on page two read:

Reporter Found Dead in Home

She quickly read the story under the headline, hoping that her worst fears hadn't been realized.

> *On Thursday afternoon, thirty-one year old Wall Street Journal reporter Jason Luce was found dead in his home. A coworker, who wishes to remain anonymous, went to his home after Luce missed two consecutive days of work. The coroner reported that Luce was killed by an electrical shock. Police are investigating further ...*

Lissie couldn't read any more. She knew this was because of the story. Matthew killed Jason because of the story he was going to publish. And she had been the one to hand over the information to both parties. Jason would not have been able to come to his conclusions without her cell phone records. And Matthew never would have known about Jason's story. Until the story ran. In which case Jason would likely have been killed anyway. But she still felt responsible for the whole catastrophe. She jumped up from her table, threw away the paper and remaining coffee, and walked back home. *It is not safe for me to be out in the world right now*, she thought with panic.

As soon as she was in her apartment, her emotions shifted from panic to rage. *How dare he? He knew Jason was my friend. Couldn't he have just threatened him?* The longer she reflected on it, the angrier she became. After a week of silence, Lissie had to speak her mind to *someone*. Even if it was her murderous ex-boyfriend, Matthew. She grabbed her phone and texted him.

> You are worse than I ever imagined. Not just a liar. Not just an assassin. But you HAD to go and kill my only friend. Did you even TRY to talk to him? Or did you realize somewhere along the way that he felt something for me and you just couldn't handle it? Are you gonna kill me too now? I just ... I cannot believe this. You are unbelievable.

She hit 'send' and cried. She fell into bed and cried some more. And after a few hours, the crying stopped, and she stared into nothingness.

Over the course of the next two weeks, Lissie tried to adjust to her new life. During the first few days, she felt accomplished just crawling out of her bed to eat breakfast. She didn't know what she grieved over more—losing the presence of Matthew in her life, or knowing that he murdered her only friend in the city. She refused to dwell on the grief for long enough to figure out the answer to that nagging question, but after a few days, she realized she needed to accept that both griefs were a part of her life.

On the fifth day, she forced herself to leave the apartment for groceries. She walked around the corner to the nearest bodega, hurriedly gathered the food she needed, and returned to the safety of her apartment.

"You're going to start eating three meals a day," she firmly told herself.

She knew she would never recover from everything that had happened since she met Matthew, but she decided it was time to try to live *despite* what she had been through.

Each morning, Lissie drank a cup of coffee and ate a bowl of cereal. After breakfast, she would search the internet for jobs—though she never submitted her résumé because she was still receiving paychecks from Stein Securities, and no job ever seemed quite right for her. Every day at noon, she made herself a sandwich, and after her lunch, she allowed herself ten minutes to cry for the friend and the love she had lost. From then until dinner, she usually laid on her couch in a haze of nothingness—she discovered it was easier to think about nothing at all than it was to try to think about anything besides Matthew and Jason. She cooked dinner each night while distracting music blared from her television. When she crawled into bed each night, the loss of having someone big, warm, and safe beside her made her weep.

"At some point, you're going to have to let him go. At some point, you're going to have to leave the apartment for more than buying groceries around the corner. At some point, you're going to have to forgive yourself for Jason's death. At some point, your life has to go on," she repeated every night.

Unfortunately, her head told her that 'some point' was completely out of her reach.

Forty-Nine

Two weeks. Two weeks without a single word. Matthew was despondent. He would choose another angry text message over this silence. At least he could envision her face as she screamed at him with a text message. He would give anything to hear a word from her beautiful mouth. He wanted to tell her that he had nothing to do with Jason's murder. He needed her to know that he would never allow anything to happen to her. He and his brothers made sure no one else in the Family knew about her involvement. She was safe. He needed to make Lissie ... not hate him—even if she never liked him again. He simply needed to know that she didn't hate him.

She knows what you do for a living. Do you think there's any chance in hell that she won't hate you forever? he asked himself bitterly. He hated asking himself that question. The answer was always 'no'.

Marcus and Antonio were still trying to nurse him back to health. Of course, he didn't want to be nursed back to health. He made it his mission to become the worst patient in the history of health care. He tried to refuse proper care of his broken arm. He barely touched the food they prepared for him—no matter what he tried, it all tasted flavorless. They even forced him to take a shower—it would've been helpful if they weren't both as strong as he was. Two against one is an unfair advantage when all three people are the same size and build. This was not how he wanted to live his life. Without Lissie, he wasn't certain if he was willing to live at all. But with his brothers constantly watching his every move, he had no choice but to carry on. His depression was worsening by the day, and the more he thought about losing Lissie, the more convinced he became that she would never take him back.

"It's been three weeks for Christ's sakes," Antonio groaned. He wasn't sure Mattia would recover this time. After Anamaria, he was depressed and viciously angry at the Family. But that was the extent of it. Never once did he shut down completely. Antonio feared that Mattia would live out the rest of his long life in a state of complete emptiness—unwilling or unable to allow any semblance of happiness back into his life.

"We have tried everything. It's like he isn't the same person anymore," Marcus said with tangible emotion in his voice. Antonio refused to look at him. He had been on the verge of tears for the past week, and he knew Marcus was feeling the same way.

"We have to do something, brother," Antonio said as he cleared his throat of the emotion that was threatening to surface. They sat, unmoving for hours. They needed a plan.

Lissie began her day as she had for the past four weeks since ... *no Lissie. You're moving on.* She had to stick to the new routine. Up at eight a.m. Shower. Dress. Downstairs. Grab a paper. Go to the café. Look at job openings.

She forced herself to read the paper every day for more information about Jason's death. No one contacted her for information, which she thought was odd, but it was relieving to not have to speak about it with anyone. Today's headline was interesting, to say the least:

> *Wall Street Journal Admits to Server Crash on Night of Reporter's Death*

It wasn't a fluke that no one had contacted her. All the information connecting the two was missing. *Along with all Jason's personal computers, hard drives and notes, I'm sure. You are thorough, you piece of ... ."* She stopped her train of thought. She had caught herself mentally yelling at

Matthew—or at no one—on more than one occasion and decided the best course of action would be to identify her problem and stop herself immediately. There was no reason to continue to act like a psycho if you could identify the behavior and put an end to it quickly. Unfortunately, it hadn't lessened over the weeks since Matthew's 'omission of truth' or *lie*, as she liked to call it.

She threw away her paper and empty coffee cup and started to walk out the door when her arms were each gripped by large strong men who seemed set on escorting her out the door quickly.

"Don't scream, Lissie. We're not going to hurt you," one voice whispered in her left ear.

Oh sure you're not, she thought sarcastically. But for some reason, a part of her believed the man was telling the truth. She didn't make a sound or try to turn around.

As soon as they were outside, the men steered her toward her apartment. *Excellent. They know where I live*, she mused without humor. Her unconcerned reaction to the situation at hand was startling to her sensibilities. She *should* be alarmed and screaming for help. But the only thing she wanted to do was text Matthew to come free her from her captors. Like *that* would put her in a better situation. The men released her arms before they arrived at her apartment.

"We do not want to alarm anyone. Try to look normal," a different accented voice whispered in her other ear.

Her doorman smiled at her as he opened the door, knowing better than to try to engage in conversation after weeks of brooding silence. He merely nodded and went back to reading his paper.

Lissie finally gathered the courage to turn and face her captors as soon as they'd entered the elevator. What she found chilled her to her core.

Matthew's brothers stood before her. But instead of looking like the murderers she knew them to be, their faces were pleading and drawn. Something was terribly wrong.

"What? What happened?" she asked urgently. She had never felt so much despair before that moment. And she knew in the pit of her stomach that something horrible had happened to Matthew.

The brothers said nothing until they were safely within her apartment and the door was locked behind them.

"Sit down," the shorter one with the stronger Italian accent said. "I am Marcus." He put out his hand to greet her.

Lissie was dumbfounded. *What in the world?* She slowly reached out and shook his hand, confused by the whole situation.

"And I am Antonio," the taller, louder brother said, also shaking her hand.

"Why exactly are you here?" she questioned, though she wasn't sure whether she really wanted them to answer her.

"Mattia. Matthew," Marcus began. It was clear both brothers were in serious emotional pain.

"Tell me right now, and tell me quickly. What is going on?" she demanded.

"We think …" Antonio choked out, but was unable to continue.

"Mattia is deeply depressed. He has become a shell of the man we have known our whole lives. We've watched him closely, and we fear our brother might never recover from this," Marcus finished.

Lissie looked back and forth between the brothers and tried to hold in the tears that were fighting to escape. Questions swirled violently around her head as she processed Marcus's words. *How can I fix this? Can I take him back after all the lies? After he killed Jason? I still love him, don't I? Is he this depressed over me? Didn't I already decide I would love him no matter his job description? Why do I even have to think this through?*

I love him.

"How can I fix it?" she said as tears started to roll down her cheeks. The brothers perked up at her response.

"You care if he is alright?" Antonio asked.

"What? Of course I do! I mean. I'm angry with him, yes. But I'm in love with him. I've been in love with him since the second day I knew him. I just can't be with a person who refuses to tell me who they are. I can't handle secrets. Never have," she said as she wiped her tears away.

Marcus and Antonio looked absolutely confused. They kept looking back and forth between her and each other. Marcus looked at her with a furrowed brow.

"You are not upset with him because he is an assassin?" he asked in disbelief.

Lissie took a deep breath. She was actually going to admit this out loud, wasn't she? She took another deep breath and cleared her throat.

"No. Not really. Actually … not at all. I know that's crazy. I'm probably crazy. Okay, I *am* crazy. But no," she took a breath. Not only was she rambling, she had just repeated herself enough times to prove she was crazy to anyone who heard.

"Perfect!" Antonio shouted with a smile on his face. "Let us get you to Mattia so he can explain everything. He turned to Marcus. "I think she is ready. Do you agree?"

Marcus stared at Lissie with an intense look plastered on his face for several moments. Lissie wasn't sure what he was hoping to find, so she just stared back.

"Yes. She is ready," he said.

Lissie was so elated by the idea of seeing Matthew that she momentarily forgot how angry she was with him. But when she remembered the pain-stricken faces that his brothers had worn at the beginning of their conversation, she wondered if she would even recognize the man she had fallen in love with.

Antonio hailed a cab for them, and they set off toward Matthew's penthouse.

"He's a hairy disaster," Antonio said with a snort of laughter.

Lissie slowly turned her head toward him, perplexed by his ability to laugh at a time like this. He saw the look on her face and continued.

"He refuses to shave his face and fix his hair. He stays in sweatpants and tshirts all day long. He barely eats any food—and no longer finds joy in preparing it. His body is withering away, and he doesn't seem to care a thing about it," Antonio finished with a grimace.

Lissie couldn't fathom that she was the root of his depression. She only heard him say he loved her after he thought he had already lost her. And wasn't that a sign of a man just trying to save face? *Surely he hadn't meant it.*

"After all these years," Marcus said under his breath.

Lissie didn't understand what he meant. Though she had never asked him his age, she was positive he was no older than thirty. But what if he was one of those people who aged *really* well? How old could he be? Thirty-five? Forty maybe? Surely no older than forty. But the idea of being with someone thirteen years older than her made her feel strange. *Are you really stressing about the age gap here? He's a murderer, and all you can think about is whether or not he's too old for you?* She shook her head at her own absurdity, but the age issue still hung in her mind. *No, no. He can't be more than thirty*, she told herself with a sigh.

The three got out of the cab in front of Matthew's building, but neither brother made a move toward the front door.

"We're not going with you," Marcus said with finality.

Lissie's heart began to race. She was going to have to face Matthew alone.

"Please. I don't know if I can be in there with him alone," she pleaded.

"Tell him we brought you. And that we want him to tell you *everything*," Antonio said with an encouraging smile.

She didn't feel encouraged. But she nodded, entered the building, and ascended to Matthew's apartment.

Fifty

She slowly exited the elevator and glanced around the huge apartment. One of the brothers was living in the guest room while the other was apparently sleeping on the couch. The aromas surrounding the kitchen hinted that delicious food had recently been cooked there. Fresh fruits and vegetables were scattered on the counters, and a new machine for making homemade pasta was sitting next to the sink. Usually kitchens like this were a sign of a happy home. Lissie thought maybe Matthew's brothers were using the cooking as a method to cope with the problems they were understandably ill-equipped to deal with.

She walked to Matthew's closed door and knocked quietly.

"Oh my God, guys! Go home already! How long are you going to keep this up?" Matthew yelled.

Lissie squeezed her eyes shut as she turned the knob and opened the door as quietly as possible. There, on the bed she created for him, was Matthew. She was conflicted with emotions. She wanted to run and throw herself onto the bed beside him and hold him. She wanted to slap him in the face. She wanted to yell at him. But mostly, she wanted to kiss his incredible lips.

He was curled into a ball, lying on his right side, facing away from the door. He wore only sweatpants. How long had it been since she'd seen him? She counted the days in her head. No more than four weeks. But the man on the bed looked like he had been sickly for months. His muscles were less defined. The skin on his back looked paler than she remembered. And she could see a thick layer of facial hair matting his exposed left cheek.

She walked to the side of his bed and reached out to touch his back softly. At the lightest touch, Matthew sprung from the bed. He grabbed her by the neck with his right hand and pinned her against the wall, holding her right hand with his left. Her eyes went wide with surprise. It took her a moment to realize she couldn't breathe. As soon as she gasped for air, Matthew's crazed eyes snapped to recognition. He stumbled backward, falling into a seated position on the side of the bed. He buried his face in both hands and began to weep.

"Even my dreams have turned against me," he muttered into his hands. "I do not want to live without you. Is that so much to ask?"

The tears spilled out from between his fingers, and Lissie held a hand over her mouth to contain the sobs that now racked her body. The man before her was *broken*. 'Broken' was not a word that she ever pictured in the same sentence with 'Matthew'. But here, before her, was the epitome of a broken-hearted man. She walked slowly toward him, tears running down her cheeks. She knelt down in front of him and pulled Matthew's hands away from his face. His half-closed eyes stared into hers for a long moment before he lay back down on the bed and curled up the way he had been before she walked in. She stood, resolved to snap him out of whatever this was.

"What do you need to tell me?" she asked.

Matthew laid flat on his back and stared at the ceiling angrily.

"I am not going to leave until you've told me everything. My life has been a wreck for the past four weeks. And I deserve an explanation from you. Talk to me, Mattia," Lissie said, growing more and more frustrated with his inability to differentiate dream from reality.

"My dreams are muddling everything. You stand there looking like Lissie, but you call me 'Mattia'. Decide which dream you want to be and stick to it!" he yelled angrily.

Lissie was going to force him to acknowledge he was awake, one way or another.

"Your brothers basically kidnapped me from my café, brought me down here, and made me come up here alone so you can explain whatever it is that you're supposed to explain. I am *NOT* a dream. So explain, Matthew," she said angrily.

About halfway through her impassioned speech, reality sank in. Lissie was standing next to his bed. He had choked her against a wall, yelled at her, and ignored her plea for him to talk to her. Now she was even angrier than he'd heard her before. What a way to start out this conversation. *But at least she's here,* he thought with relief.

He sat up on the edge of the bed and stared at her lovely face. He felt an urgency to study all of her breathtaking features. He didn't know what look he wore on his face, but Lissie's softened upon seeing his expression. He felt something hot on his skin and realized there were tears running down his cheeks. He quickly wiped them away and took a deep breath. This was going to be a long and difficult conversation.

"I have to ask you, would it be terrible if I took a shower before we do this?" he asked guiltily.

Lissie looked around the room, shaking her head. Then she threw a hand into the air and said, "Why not? I'll be waiting right here."

Matthew glanced back at her as he hurried to the bathroom, worried that if he left the room, she might disappear again. She was sitting on the edge of the bed, staring down at the floor as he closed the bathroom door. He prayed she wouldn't leave and turned to look at himself in the mirror. He was usually a well-groomed man. After hundreds of years of living, he didn't even recognize the person staring back at him. He thought about the woman in the other room —the woman he was in love with—and felt shame for the first time in his life. He had given up on his relationship without even trying to explain himself to her. He realized that Lissie needed to hear *everything*. And if she still hated him after hearing all the gory details, maybe he could try to live with himself. He stood up straight, looked at himself, and spoke firmly; "All right, let's get this over with."

Everything took him longer because of his cast, but by the time he walked back out of the bathroom, he felt more himself. His hair was fixed, face shaved, and he smelled wonderful. He emerged feeling more confident, but he still worried that this could be the last time he ever saw or spoke with Lissie. This was his final chance to win her back.

When Lissie looked up at him, he caught a quick spark of something before she masked it with a carefully blank expression. Love? Passion? He could only hope.

"Do you mind if we talk in the living room?" He held out his hand so he could lead her into the kitchen. She eyed it as if she were making a huge decision by choosing to accept or dismiss it. Thankfully, she took his hand and walked with him to the open room. Before he released her, he brought her hand to his lips and nearly kissed it. He stopped only millimeters away, realizing Lissie might not be amenable to any acts of love. Matthew could not remember doubting himself this intensely. He questioned every move, every word, every glance exchanged. And he did not like the person he had become.

They sat down a few feet away from each other on the couch, and Matthew took a moment to gather his thoughts.

"I'm going to start from the beginning. And I know you're going to think I'm lying. Or that I'm insane. But I promise you I am not, and I can back up everything I'm about to tell you." He shut his eyes and breathed deeply. This would be the first time to tell anyone about his true self. He was opening himself up in the most vulnerable way possible. *She's worth it*, he told himself as he calmed his racing heart.

"I was born in Milan, Italy ... in 1575," he began. He stopped for a moment to let Lissie comprehend what he had said. Confusion and disbelief were plastered all over her face as her eyes darted around the room beneath her furrowed brow.

"I come from a Family of immortals. My father's father was the first immortal. He and his brother were born mortals, but they somehow became immortals. They have never revealed the true origins of our immortality to the rest of the Family, but the gene is passed on to each new generation. We cannot die from natural causes—sickness, disease, old age, etc. We actually cannot even get sick. Our cuts and scrapes even heal faster than a normal human's would because our bodies are completely resistant to infection. We can, however, die from mortal wounds, fire, and drowning. One of my cousins drank himself into a stupor a few hundred years ago and ended up dying when the bar went up in flames. It's always a shame when a crazy accident ends up getting one of us killed. Others have died on the job. But the most frequent type of death in my Family is suicide. After a thousand years, some people cannot abide the idea of living any longer."

Lissie's mouth was now slightly opened and her face showed she wanted to protest his claims and ask questions about what he meant all at the same time. He decided it would be best to continue and let her ask questions at the end.

"My Family—which is what we call ourselves, 'The Family'—has been contracting ourselves out as assassins since the beginning. My grandfather—who we call 'Priest'—and his brother—who we call 'Saint'—officially formed the Family sometime in the 7th century. No one knows why they started offering their services as assassins, but the two have been training the sons of the Family in hand-to-hand combat, knives, weaponry, surveillance, and strategy ever since. They actually have an academy in Tuscany where each son trains for sixty to eighty years before they advance to on-the-job training. I specialize in technology—something I actually taught myself. Each member of the Family has a different specialization."

Lissie cut him off. "You're actually telling me that you're immortal. And I'm just supposed to believe you?" she asked incredulously.

"Yes. I think if you listen, you'll see that there's no way a person could come up with a lie this elaborate. Honestly. It only gets worse," he laughed without humor.

Her look was wary, but she nodded for him to continue. He wasn't sure how to communicate everything to her. This was the first time he had ever tried to explain his Family or his life to anyone.

"Only sons are born to immortals. If there were any daughters, we've never found them. The men in the Family that sleep around have to actually keep a written account of the women they've slept with in order to find their children later on." He thought through the strange pieces of his life to make sure he wasn't leaving anything important out. "And we stop aging around twenty-seven or twenty-eight. Our theory is that it's the age when men are at their physical prime. I think that's the basics of the history of the Family."

Lissie was speechless. Her mouth still hung slightly open—in a way that made Matthew want to reach out and touch her full lips.

He paused, awaiting a flood of questions that he knew would come at some point. But she sat silently, thinking through the things he had revealed. After a few minutes of deafening quiet, he decided to continue talking.

"Now comes my story." He heaved a long sigh as he collected his thoughts. "As I said before, I was born in Milan in 1575. My given name at birth was Mattia—which my immediate family still calls me. After training for sixty years and aiding other Family members on their missions for an additional eighty-six long years, I was finally given a contract of my own in Madrid in 1749. I was given notice by my father that I would be receiving the contract, so I became acquainted with as many people at court as possible. In the first one hundred fifty years of my adult life, I was somewhat of a ... womanizer ... I guess you could say."

Lissie cocked an eyebrow at him, but remained silent.

"In order to prepare for my contract, my brothers encouraged me to act more like an adult. Because of the nature of the contract, we were under the impression that I would likely be killing the King of Spain. I felt it was necessary to make connections with his closest advisors, and my brothers helped me realize that I needed to ignore the women of the Spanish court to focus on my task. Unfortunately for me, there was one woman in court who was blessed with the laugh of an angel. After I heard her laugh, I simply could not ignore her any longer. And once I beheld her beautiful face, I knew my soul would be forever lost without her." He paused and glanced up at Lissie. She was captivated by his story, her eyes begging him to continue. He looked straight into her eyes and spoke with an unfaltering tone.

"Her name was Anamaria Serrano, sister of Isabel Serrano, who was the wife of the Spanish conquistador, Juan Bautista de Anza."

Lissie couldn't believe what she had just heard. She couldn't really believe *anything* Matthew had just said, but her ancestors' involvement in the story put her over the edge. After a long stretch of silent disbelief, she finally found her voice.

"Are you actually telling me you knew my ancestors?" she squeaked.

"I am," Matthew began. "I'm telling you that the only other woman I have ever loved was the sister of one of your great grandmothers—I believe it is eleven 'greats' removed, but I did not want to say it that many times."

Lissie sat unmoving, dumbfounded by his confession. Did he seek her out because of the connection? Did he have some sort of sick, twisted reason for getting close her? She needed to know.

"Wait. Did you find out I was related to your long lost love and come to find me? Cause that is just weird … and disturbing." She had to know the truth.

"No. I swear to you. I did not seek you out at all. But when I walked into your office and saw your face, the reason I fainted was because of your resemblance to Anamaria. My only thought was that it was not possible for you to exist. Then I lost consciousness," he admitted.

"I … I really don't know what to think of that. It's really, *really* strange. And disconcerting. And … I don't know what else," she added, still completely confused by the entire conversation.

"Well, you keep processing that, and I'll continue the story," Matthew said.

Lissie stared blankly at Matthew. Or Mattia. Or whoever he actually was. After a long moment, she gave him a small nod to continue.

"I fell in love with Anamaria, and she fell in love with me. I received permission from her father to marry her, and we spent two weeks privately betrothed. The day we decided to announce our engagement was the day I received my first contract. I was supposed to murder the entire Serrano family and frame my only friend in the Spanish court for the murders."

Lissie gasped. "But you didn't do it right? Because, I mean, I'm sitting here!"

Matthew smiled bitterly and shook his head. "No. I told my brothers the situation, and they immediately called a meeting of the Family Council to address the worth of the contract. Unfortunately, my conniving grandfather sent my Uncle Sergius to fulfill the contract while the meeting was in session—so he would ultimately get his way regardless of the outcome. He doesn't like to be questioned. Nor does he allow accepted contracts to go unfulfilled. In this case, however, my uncle only murdered the three Serranos that were home during the meeting—which included Anamaria, her younger brother, and her mother. When I arrived at the house, Anamaria's father and sister were weeping over the dead bodies on the floor. I never fully recovered … until I met you."

Lissie's eyes filled with tears that threatened to spill from her eyes. Matthew wanted to hold her. She was the first woman he had truly looked at since Anamaria's death. And he needed her to know she was his only reason for living now.

"What happened to your friend? Was he framed for the murders?" she asked as she wiped the tears from her eyes.

"No. He wasn't framed. I left Madrid immediately, but several years later I went back to check on him. He died a few years after the murders. I think from a broken heart," he said quietly.

"Broken heart?" she asked.

"He was as in love with Anamaria as I was," he admitted.

"Oh." She thought for a few minutes before whispering, "What did you do after she was killed?"

"First, my grandfather stripped me of my name. He declared that I defaulted on my very first contract and was therefore unfit to be called Mattia by the Family. He renamed me 'Rogue' and declared that all the Family should call me by that name from that time forth. Then he began assigning me contracts only with other members of the family. I have never been assigned a solo contract since," he admitted, rubbing the back of his neck.

"I'm so sorry," Lissie said, grief tangible in her words. "I can't believe your grandfather would strip you of your name! How could he do that?" Her volume grew, anger seeping out through her words. "He sounds like a horrible man," she concluded.

"Yes. I would agree. He is a horrible, controlling, arrogant manipulator who I refuse to call 'grandfather' any longer. I simply refer to him as 'Priest' ... which I think he prefers anyway," he said with a snort of derision.

"Well I don't think he deserves that name either. Maybe we could come up with something a little more truthful," she said, smirking.

Lissie is taking this surprisingly well. And I think she actually believes me. Could telling her the truth really be the solution to this situation? She is even smiling from time to time. It is possible that she could come out of this without hating me, Matthew hoped.

"What happened to Mr. Stein?" she asked seriously.

"He was shot with a sniper rifle. We are not given the details about any contracts. Priest and Saint are responsible for receiving proposals for contracts and negotiating specifics. When we are assigned a contract, we are responsible only for carrying it out according to the details we are given. I do not know who hired the Family for the task. I do not know why he was killed. But I came in to scout out the building in order to know the layout of the office and which buildings had the best vantage points to make the kill depending on where Stein was in his office."

"What about Jason?" she asked as she stared him straight in the face. Her temper was threatening to break through when she asked the question, and her eyes searched his face for any insight into the answer.

"Honestly, I am still amazed over this one. He was a reporter on one of my contracts ten years ago in New Hampshire. He never figured out what happened, obviously—or he would have been dead ten years ago. We thought we had seen the last of him. Then, he showed up here as the reporter on the Stein case and somehow recognized me from a blurry image captured ten years earlier. It's astounding, really. He should win a posthumous award for 'Most Intuitive Reporter of All Time'. We are all trained to wipe our trails clean. It would have been the first story leaked about any of us in over two millennia," he admitted. "And I am certain Priest blames me for the entire mess," he added in a dejected tone. "Someone in the Family was given a contract to eliminate the threat. And as I said before, you do not refuse a contract from Priest." He was unwilling to tell Lissie that his brothers carried out the contract. She did not need any motivation to dislike his brothers, and there was no reason for him to divulge that information.

Lissie wasn't sure how to respond. She walked to the couch, sat down, and buried her head in her hands. *Matthew is from a family of immortal assassins. They killed Jason. They've killed countless others. I actually think he's telling the truth about the whole thing. And I'm not running away screaming. Does that make me crazy?* "Is any of this possible?" she asked herself aloud.

"I assure you it is," Matthew answered. "It is all true, and I have family to testify to its truth if you do not believe my word."

She was happy to know the whole story. But at the same time, she wasn't sure she could comprehend it. Her mind was spinning, and her hands were shaking. She knew he was a killer, but she was positive he could never harm her. Matthew had been gracious enough to give her space through his full explanation, but all she wanted in that moment was for him to wrap his arms around her tightly so she would stop shaking. As if on cue, Matthew walked to her and knelt before her.

"Why am I alive?" she asked, realizing that she knew as much as Jason.

"I would never allow any harm to come to you. We did not tell the Family that you were involved in any way," he said with an intense expression of ferocity on his face.

Lissie felt her heart soften at his admission. She knew *he* wouldn't harm her, but now she knew to what lengths he would go to protect her. A horrible thought came crashing into her head.

"When you came home from Dubai … had you almost been killed?" Lissie shrieked.

"I know I've shocked you with all of this, and I know you're still angry with me, but can I please touch you?" he pleaded.

"Please. Please just tell me. I can handle it," she begged.

"Yes. There were several men that knocked me out and were about to blow my head off, but my brothers came in and killed them before they could do any permanent damage," he said with his head hung, embarrassment clear from his body language.

Lissie couldn't stand the thought that he had almost died four weeks earlier. She wanted to kick herself for reacting the way she had. Matthew still had a cast on his arm, and the remnants of his wounds were still visible. But there was still one thing that Lissie needed to know before she made her decision.

"Why did you wait until you realized you might lose me to tell me you loved me?"

"I didn't," he quickly replied.

"Yes you did! The first time you told me was when I was walking out your door," she countered indignantly. "Believe me when I say I would have remembered you saying that to me."

"I said it to you twice the night you found out Mr. Stein was dead. You were passed out on your bed. I kissed you on the temple and told you that I love you," he admitted.

Emotion overtook her entire being, and she felt like she might pass out. She threw herself into Matthew's body, knocking him slightly off-balance, and wrapped her arms tightly around his waist. She began to weep uncontrollably into his shoulder. He shushed her and ran his hands through her hair to try to calm her, but she continued to weep for several minutes.

Matthew was relieved to have finally told Lissie the truth. He felt as if a massive weight had been lifted off his shoulders. He held the love of his life in his arms; and she was using him as her shoulder to cry on.

He hoped this would be one of the greatest moments of his existence. To allow someone to know your darkest secrets and most horrifying experiences and to have them accept you despite them … there was no greater joy in the entire world. He was sure of it. He merely hoped that she really would accept him, and that they could go back to the way they were before this mess.

He held her tightly for as long as she would allow. After a few minutes, she stopped crying and calmed her breathing. He felt his heart break a little as she pulled away, but she only pulled back far enough to look him in the eye. She wiped her tears away with her right hand while continuing to cling to Matthew with her left. She took a deep breath before speaking.

"Okay," she said with a firm yet quiet voice.

Matthew wasn't sure what that meant, and he knew his puzzlement was written on his face.

"Okay?" he asked guardedly.

"I believe you. And I accept who you are," she said with more determination. "I've been angry with you all this time because you were hiding your life from me. Lying to me."

"But I told you I'm an assassin. And all of my Family are assassins," he said questioningly.

"And when I first realized that might be a possibility, I sat down and asked myself what I could and couldn't live with. I found out about your possible involvement with Mr. Stein's murder while you were in Dubai. But once you came home all beat up and refused to tell me what happened, I was devastated. I can love an assassin that's forthcoming about his profession. I will not love a liar. That was the decision I came to. That was why I left you. And now that I know everything—that you were acting out of preservation for your family and your ... your kind—I can't really think of a reason to *not* be with you," she admitted.

Matthew was speechless. He stared at her blankly for several minutes, waiting for her to get up and leave or admit she was playing a cruel joke on him. But she sat motionless, stared at him with her kind blue eyes, and gently placed a hand on his cheek.

"I love you," she said passionately. "I've loved you since the second day I knew you," she giggled.

Matthew knew life would never be any more perfect than this exact moment. He smiled widely, cupped her face with his hands, and pulled her in for a long, passionate kiss. This was how he wanted his life to be. He desired only Lissie. He thought back over his hundreds of years of existence and understood how every decision, every path, led him to this moment. To Lissie.

He never wanted to be away from her.

He realized what he needed to do. He pulled away from Lissie, who had an openly disappointed look on her face.

"I have to make a call," he said.

Fifty-One

I STILL DON'T UNDERSTAND why he's being so secretive! Lissie thought as she looked down at her massive luggage.

Without giving her a single reason, Matthew told her to pack for two weeks in Europe. He forced her to purchase fancy clothes she was sure she would never wear. He also gave her instructions on what kinds of outfits she needed to take from her own closet. Though she didn't want to admit it, she was unbelievably thrilled.

Europe had been on her bucket list since she was ten or eleven. The idea of traveling to Europe was enough to delight anyone with half a brain. But to go with the man she loved—who also happened to be a billionaire? That was just unfair to the rest of the world. On top of that, prior to Matthew's entrance into her life, her fear of the unknown would have kept her from taking the leap and traveling overseas. He had given her a new perspective on living life to the fullest, and she loved the person she had become.

He had only given her a week to prepare for the journey, but she welcomed the challenge. Her bags were packed, and she dragged them to her front door.

She heard a quick knock before Matthew and his brothers barged into her apartment with huge smiles on their faces. All three were absolutely gorgeous. They could have been models if they weren't so busy killing people for a living. But Marcus and Antonio paled in comparison to Matthew. Lissie knew no other man could hold a candle to his perfection.

They had spent every night together since she made the decision to stay with Matthew. He was so attentive that he barely let her out of his sight. She knew she would eventually grow tired of his unerring attentions, but for now she was thrilled to have him and wouldn't dream of complaining that he was around too much.

"Are you ready?" Matthew asked.

"I think that's everything," she replied as she pointed to the two large suitcases by the front door. It had gone against every fiber of her being to pack one, let alone two large suitcases. It was her personal policy to only take carry-on luggage on flights. But with all the clothes Matthew made her bring, she had no choice.

"Your cast is off!" she squealed, realizing that both of Matthew's arms were hanging down to his sides.

"Yes it is. That's why we're leaving today. I got special permission to have it taken off a week early. And the doctor said it was perfectly healed." He moved his arm around to prove his point.

"Alright then! Let us get you two to the airport," Antonio said.

Antonio and Marcus grabbed the suitcases and headed toward the lobby while Matthew stayed behind. As soon as the door closed, he swept her up into a long, sultry kiss. Lissie felt the compulsion to wrap her legs around Matthew's waist and ask him to take her back into the bedroom for a few minutes. But before she could follow through on her evil plan, Matthew released her and checked his watch.

"Our flight leaves in two hours. And *without* traffic, it could easily take us forty-five minutes to get there," he looked disappointed.

Lissie knew she wore a matching expression, but she was so excited for the journey, she didn't want to delay any longer.

"Let's get out of here then," she said as she grabbed her coat and let Matthew lead her out to the car.

Once they arrived at the airport and began the check-in process, Lissie finally found out where they were headed. They were on a direct flight from New York to Milan. Lissie fought the urge to jump up and down screaming, but the look on her face was enough to give Matthew and the ticketing agent a good laugh.

"First time to Milan?" the man behind the counter asked.

"First time to Europe," Lissie beamed.

"I hope you have a wonderful trip," he smiled as he handed her the tickets and returned their passports.

As they walked toward their gate, Lissie glanced down at Matthew's Italian passport and was perplexed when she read 'Mattia Galli' as his full name. She held it up and gave him a questioning look.

"Ah. My mother's last name. You see, the Family has never taken a permanent last name. Priest and Saint are convinced that we would gain too much notoriety if the whole family traveled around, doing jobs under the same surname. We all choose our own surnames and are supposed to change them periodically. I am currently alternating between McCloud, Galli, and Bernard. It depends on where I'm travelling, but I have passports for all three," he answered in a hushed voice.

"Well that's ... something," Lissie said thoughtfully. *So if we were to get married, would I have no last name? Or would I just keep mine? Or would he want me to take his mother's? Probably too soon to be talking about marriage ... or even thinking about it. God, I'm obsessed with him.*

"You okay?" Matthew asked, probably concerned by the expressions that had crossed her face while thinking about the name conundrum.

"Of course! I'm going to Europe!" she squealed and did a little hop/dance move.

Matthew laughed so hard he had to catch his breath.

"Did you like my dance?" she asked.

"Absolutely. It would have been award-winning if you were in a competition," he said, still laughing.

The flight to Milan flew by faster than Matthew expected. He spent the first two hours talking to Lissie about Italy. She was beside herself with the idea of spending time in Europe, and Matthew was happy to tell her a little about Milan on the way over. He let her believe they would only be visiting Milan, which simply was not the case. He planned the trip around a Family meeting, which would not happen for another two weeks. Before the meeting, they would get to spend a few days in his favorite city in the world, Interlaken, Switzerland, before visiting Lucerne and Venice. Then they would end the trip right outside Florence for the Family meeting. He thought it best to keep the meeting from Lissie so she could enjoy the splendors of Europe without uneasy anticipation. Matthew, on the other hand, was a nervous wreck about the meeting. It had been over five hundred years since a Family gathering of this magnitude was called, and he was not alive for the last one. He forced himself to push all those thoughts from his head in order to get some rest.

When he woke up, he realized that he and Lissie slept for almost the entire remainder of the flight. The flight attendant brought them two breakfast trays, and they only had enough time to eat a few bites before it was time to land.

"Where are we staying?" Lissie asked as she looked out the window of the plane.

"We're going to stay at Marcus's villa just outside the city. It's the home where he and his wife lived for their entire marriage. They raised their children there, so I have spent quite a bit of time in that home—especially when the boys were little," he explained.

"Wait. How long was Marcus married?" she asked.

"He met Sera when she was seventeen. They married when she was eighteen. And she passed away at age eighty-four. I guess they were married for sixty-six years. His sons are in training now," he answered.

"Wow. I am not going to get used to that, am I? When did she pass away?" Lissie pressed.

"It was sometime between 1940 and 1950. I don't remember the exact year, but it was a difficult time for our whole family. We all loved Sera, and to watch Marcus go through that loss was excruciating."

"Wasn't it strange for a man in his twenties to be married to a woman in her eighties?" Lissie asked, troubled by the mental picture of the complicated relationship.

"It isn't strange for the men in our family. When we fall in love, we quit seeing age—we only want to utilize the time we have with the ones we love. None of us ever saw Sera as an old woman. She was Marcus's great love. And when she passed away, we all felt the loss of a family member."

Lissie didn't ask any more questions on the issue, and Matthew was grateful for the end of that conversation. He was not keen on thinking about losing anyone right now. He stopped that line of thought and dwelt on the fact that he had Lissie in his life—permanently. She was enough for any lifetime.

After they exited the plane and made it through Customs, the driver Matthew hired was waiting for them with their luggage already loaded on a cart. Matthew put matching tags on all four suitcases so their driver would be able to identify them and pick them off the baggage claim without any help.

"I'm not sure how to deal with this first class service," Lissie admitted. She was an economically-minded woman to the extreme. Matthew made it his mission to get her used to this kind of treatment. He would break her by the end of this trip, he was sure of it.

"Well you're going to get used to it. And then you will wonder how you ever lived without it," he teased.

Marcus's home was a thirty minute drive from the airport. Lissie couldn't refrain from gasping and pointing at each lovely villa they passed. Apparently Marcus's villa was south of the city in an area called Basiglio. As they entered the gate to the property, Lissie couldn't breathe. It was magnificent. She had imagined something more majestic, but this was simple and old and picturesque. The villa could have come straight from a story book. The land on the property was green and filled with fruit trees and flowers. A brook wound through the length of the property, complete with stone bridges. The main house was old brick with rounded doorways and massive wooden doors. Even the tops of the windows were arched. Each window was fitted with a planter box filled with beautiful pink, red and purple flowers that looked as if they had been growing there for decades, untouched. Attached to the main house by a large covered courtyard were a second house and a garage. Lissie couldn't tell what the second house looked like because the entire exterior was covered by ivy. Only the windows and doors were trimmed free of the ivy that encompassed the walls. It was idyllic. The three garage doors that opened like double doors were made of weathered wood and maintained the arched theme present throughout the home.

Lissie couldn't wait to walk through the courtyard and nearly jumped out of the car before the driver stopped.

"Do you like it?" Matthew asked, clearly amused by Lissie's reaction.

"How could I *not*? Come on! I want to see the rest!" she said as she grabbed his hand and pulled him out of the car.

Matthew yelled to the driver to take their luggage inside. Lissie was entranced by the grounds of the property.

They passed through a small brick courtyard and emerged onto a giant brick patio with old stone benches. Behind the house was a sprawling yard with narrow paths twisting and turning through fruit trees and low bushes. The stone fence around the property looked like it had stood in the same place for the past five hundred years.

"How did Marcus find this place?" Lissie asked in awe.

"Umm ... he built it. Back in the 1700s he was ready to settle down, and since he has always been more of a homebody than me and Antonio, he decided to put roots down in Milan so he was only a few hours from the Family estate in Tuscany. Plus, Milan is where we were raised."

Lissie worried that her jaw was on the ground.

"He built this? Oh man. I'm really not going to get used to that. He built it in the 1700s. You just say that like it's a common thing!" she laughed.

"Well it is for my family." Matthew chuckled at her astounded response to the property. "You are the first non-immortal I have spent substantial time with for over fifty years. I am not used to this seeming strange to anyone."

Lissie continued looking around at the architecture and age of the property. It was really going to be difficult to not treat every part like it was a hallowed antiquity. She turned to Matthew and looked hard into his face.

"For an old man over four hundred years old, you sure do carry your age well," she teased.

Matthew grinned the evil grin he always wore before he did something devious. He ran up to Lissie and picked her up.

"We're going inside now, young one. I have a few matters I am going to have to clear up about my youthfulness. It seems I am going to have to prove my stamina to put an end to further 'old man' comments," he said as he carried her inside.

Lissie was sure she was blushing. But as soon as they stepped across the threshold of the home, she was distracted by the beautiful interior of the entry.

"Not right now. Nope. We are heading straight to our room. You can marvel at the age and architecture of the interior later. We have more important things to … discuss," he teased as he headed straight up the beautiful wooden staircase and into a large, but simple room. She was going to study each piece of furniture in the room, but quickly realized Matthew was removing her clothes at a new world record pace. She completely forgot whatever it was she had been doing and turned her full attention to Matthew.

He laid her down on the bed and kneeled over her. He bent in for a soft kiss on her lips, but pulled away when she tried to hold him there longer.

"You spent far too long in the garden," he whispered softly in her ear.

All he had wanted to do since he woke up on the plane was make love to Lissie. She was the best part of every day. His reason to wake up in the morning. His motivation to get through each day. He was desperately in love with her.

And now he was going to punish her for those old man remarks.

He laid his lips lightly on her right temple. Then her ear. Then behind her ear. He slowly moved down her neck to her shoulder. Then he started on her left temple and made the same pattern on her other side. He began to stroke the soft skin on her stomach and sides with his right hand. Her breath came faster while her eyes watched his every move.

"I waited all day to do this," he said as his mouth placed a kiss right above her belly button and continued to work his way south.

Forty-five minutes later, Lissie lay sprawled on the bed next to Matthew. They were both breathing heavily and were coated in a thin sheen of sweat.

"I'm so glad you didn't let me dawdle downstairs," Lissie said, still trying to catch her breath.

Matthew laughed and turned onto his side to marvel at Lissie's beauty.

"I could stare at you all day long and be perfectly content. I would never have to move from this spot," he said reverently.

"But we're in Milan!" she shouted, jumping from bed. "Can we take a shower and get ready to go out? It's lunchtime, right?"

"Yes it is. And I am going to show you how the locals live," Matthew said blissfully. He was delighted to show his love where he spent his years as a child —along with all his favorite spots in the city. He was going to show her a few places not even his family knew about. He was ready to share his life with her in its entirety.

Fifty-two

Lissie spent the next three days on a back-roads tour of Milan. Matthew took her to several tiny restaurants where the recipes had been passed down for hundreds of years. The food was remarkable, but the owners of the restaurants were the highlights of each meal. They told stories that their grandparents had passed down while Matthew interpreted for her. She sat, engrossed in each story, while eating amazing food. But the food was only half of her journey.

Matthew knew every historical landmark to take her to—and spoke about each one's history as if he had either lived through it himself or someone with first-hand knowledge told him about it. He kept including little nuggets of information that were left out of the tourist pamphlets at each landmark.

Her favorite story was at the Castello Sforzesco. Galeazzo Maria Sforza, the son of the man who built the castle during the fifteenth century, was assassinated by four of Matthew's uncles. The contract was one of the most intricate contracts the family had ever accepted and took months of preparation. The uncles had to kill Galeazzo just as he arrived at his church for mass. Uncle Gregorius and Uncle Elias created a distraction for the gathering churchgoers while Uncle Demetrius stabbed Galeazzo with four knives to make his injuries look as if he had been stabbed by several men. It was imperative that the murder be pinned on three high-ranking officials from the Milanese court. The men were already in attendance at the church, and Uncle Felix ran inside to gather them while Galeazzo was being killed. As soon as the three men reached the church steps, Demetrius thrust the knives into their hands and began screaming for help. The men were so dumbfounded, they dropped the knives and ran from the scene. Matthew's uncles paid a hefty price to spread the circulation of the lie—and all three men were quickly caught and 'brought to justice'. To this day, that assassination is one of the Family's greatest achievements, and they regularly talk about it at Family gatherings.

Lissie loved that she was getting a grittier version of the history most people accepted as truth. She hung on Matthew's every word as he lit up with excitement over stories of intrigue and murder at each landmark. By the end of the third day, Lissie decided that a murder had somehow happened in every square inch of the city during one century or another.

On their fourth morning in Milan, Matthew woke Lissie with a macchiato and two packed suitcases.

"Are we going somewhere?" Lissie asked groggily.

As she took a careful sip of the macchiato, Matthew smiled and replied, "That's for me to know and you to find out. Now come on and get ready. We have somewhere to be in an hour."

As soon as Lissie readied herself for the day, she heard a knock at the front door.

"That will be the driver!" Matthew called up from the foyer.

She hopped down the stairs with excitement in each step and took Matthew's outstretched hand. She realized that his secrecy was going to be a common theme for this whole trip, which made Lissie's heart flutter with anticipation.

Before Matthew, Lissie's life was centered around stability and routine. But ever since he stepped through the doors at Stein Securities, her life had been a whirlwind adventure. At some point in the past few months, Lissie unconsciously decided that stability was boring. Now, she lived her life day-to-day, hoping for the next adventure to present itself to her at any moment. *This is what life should be*, Lissie thought as she watched Matthew gather the bags to embark on the next leg of their journey. *Life should be a whirlwind adventure shared with the person you love most in the world.*

The driver dropped them off at the train station where they boarded a train to Spiez. Lissie had never heard of the city, but she knew she would get no answers from Matthew. He looked smug during the two and a half hour ride but gave no hints about their destination. It wasn't until they switched trains in Spiez that Lissie saw their actual destination: Interlaken.

She had been gawking at images of Interlaken on travel websites for years but hadn't dreamed she would ever get to experience the city herself.

Interlaken was breathtaking. Nestled between the snow-capped Swiss Alps and a beautiful turquoise lake, the small town looked more like a painting than an actual physical place.

Lissie could see that Matthew was enjoying each of her reactions, and she was happy to give him that small pleasure. He had given her a gift so far beyond her wildest imagination, it was only right that he glean some enjoyment out of the trip as well.

"When I was a child, this was my family's favorite summer retreat. Me, my brothers and my parents. We kept a very small home in the village and would go swimming and fishing in Lake Brienz. This place holds some of my fondest memories," he said wistfully.

Lissie looked out over the lake and tried to imagine Matthew and his brothers playing as children, splashing in the lake. She smiled as her imagination gave her a glimpse of how he might have looked as a child. She wished she could have seen photographs of Matthew when he was young.

He reserved a room for them on the third floor of a tiny bed and breakfast. It looked exactly like a Swiss cottage from a story book. The home was made completely from wood, the roof extending all the way down on both the left and right sides of the home to the bottom of the second floor. The second and third floor balconies had flowers covering every inch of railing. Each window on the first floor was adorned with its own flower box, and more flowers hung from planters off the balconies. The shutters and doors were painted a lovely shade of green. The room Matthew reserved was the smallest room in the bed and breakfast, but it was the only room on the third floor. The bed was dressed only with a fitted sheet, two feather pillows, and two down comforters folded neatly where their occupants would be sleeping later in the evening. Lissie walked to the doors and opened them widely to a private balcony. The view was magnificent—the lake directly in front of them and mountains on either side. She breathed in the fresh, unpolluted air and sighed in delight. Matthew walked up behind her and wrapped his arms around her waist, nestling his chin into the crook of her neck.

"Do you like it?" he asked softly.

"I don't know how I could like anything more," she said as she relaxed into his perfect arms.

After two peaceful days of lackadaisical walks through the city and delightful meals at tiny restaurants, Matthew woke her with a cup of hot chocolate and packed bags.

This time, they headed to Lucerne. Lissie was, once again, overwhelmed by the quaintness of the city. The city was hugged by mountains and a bright blue lake—much the same as Interlaken. But somehow, Lucerne felt much more ancient and medieval. The most incredible covered walking bridge—the oldest of its kind in the whole of Europe—ran across the narrow river that cut through the town, making it easy for pedestrians to access both parts of the city. Cobblestone streets barely wide enough for a small car twisted through the entire town. The buildings were picturesque—each unique and colorful with flowers on most windowsills. Spires and turrets from the Middle Ages could be spotted throughout the city.

Lissie fell in love with the tranquility of the tiny Swiss cities. She was so used to the busy streets of New York that she had forgotten just how calming the peace and quiet of the country could be. She knew she would eventually miss the hustle and bustle of New York, but this visit was exactly what she needed at this precise moment in her life.

The morning Matthew woke her up to leave, Lissie was expecting the announcement. She knew more adventures were awaiting them.

They arrived in Venice the same afternoon. There were certainly more tourists in Venice than in the Swiss cities, but she wasn't deterred. Venice was another city she had dreamed about while she was growing up. Matthew booked them a room in a small hotel that was situated on a tiny canal. The room he reserved was on the second floor with a tiny balcony that opened right over the water. Lissie insisted that the door be left open at all times while they were in the room just so she could hear the quiet waters lapping up against the stone walls of the canal.

They went out onto the streets late at night—when everyone was asleep and the town was completely empty of tourists and residents alike. Matthew pointed out where various assassinations were carried out during the Renaissance. He showed her buildings that he climbed to gain vantage points for surveillance. He explained how everything was essentially the same as it had been since his first trip to Venice over two hundred years earlier.

"It is one of my favorite cities in the whole world," he told her. "Not only is it one of the most beautiful cities, but it's the only one that has remained essentially untouched. I can walk anywhere here and find the same landmarks, buildings, and bridges that existed hundreds of years ago. It is refreshing to know that there is always one place I can come—no matter how long it has been since my last visit—that I can navigate as if I were here yesterday."

Lissie was engrossed by his words. The city was unchanged. She began looking around, studying every building and street. If Matthew felt most at home here, then she wanted to spend as much time here as his schedule would allow.

"Show me your favorite place," she begged with a gleam of excitement in her eyes.

Matthew smiled widely at her enthusiasm. He grabbed her hand and took off in a hurried pace. Lissie had to jog to keep up with him, but she didn't mind one bit. Seeing Matthew like this brought her joy.

"I'll probably have to help you climb," he said as he looked up the side of a tall building. "But it's not too difficult," he said, worried that Lissie would be afraid.

"I'll be fine!" she said with determination as she grasped the nearest windowsill and hoisted herself up. After an initial struggle, Lissie swiftly learned where to place her hands and feet for an easy grip. She was pleased that she had made the climb with very little help from Matthew. He stopped her on the top balcony and turned her around. Lissie's breath caught as she realized she could almost see the entire moonlit city from the vantage point.

"It's incredible," she said in awe.

"I absolutely agree." Matthew's tone seemed to match Lissie's.

He pointed out a few parts of the city where he had lived at one time or another, delaying their inevitable descent as long as possible. Fortunately, Matthew was able to easily pick the lock on the balcony so they didn't have to climb down the way they came up. They tiptoed through the residence without alerting anyone to their presence. It seemed Matthew had been in the house so many times before that he knew exactly which floorboards to step on and which to avoid.

"Thank you for going up there with me," he said as soon as they were away from the home. Lissie heard a tone of respect and desire in his voice—a tone she liked very much. "Before you, I have never known anyone who I wanted to share that spot with."

Lissie blushed and wrapped her arms around his waist. "I'm honored that you wanted to show it to me. And I'll climb back up there any time you want."

They spent the next two days enjoying Matthew's favorite churches and historical spots in and around Venice. He rented a boat for their personal use, and they spent hours just going from island to island to see what each had to offer. Lissie knew their time there was coming to an end, but desperately hoped they would come back soon.

On the third morning, Lissie awoke to packed bags and a macchiato. But unlike the other mornings that were filled with enthusiasm for the upcoming change of scenery, Matthew wore a look of weariness and concern on his face.

"What's wrong?" she asked urgently. "Did you get a call for a contract? Do you have to leave?"

"Am I that easy to read? No, no contract. But we have to go to Tuscany," he said sadly.

Lissie racked her brain for any reason that Tuscany might be a bad thing but came up short.

"And that's upsetting you because … ?" she asked

"We are going to attend a Family meeting. With my entire Family," he whispered.

Lissie's heart skipped a beat as she felt the blood draining from her face.

Fifty-Three

MATTHEW WASN'T SURE what to do with Lissie. Since he told her about the meeting with the Family, she had barely spoken. He couldn't tell if she was angry with him for keeping the meeting a secret, or if she was simply terrified at the idea of meeting his family.

He stared at her as they rode on the train to Florence. On the trip from Milan to Interlaken and all the trips thereafter, Lissie had been glued to the windows. She gasped in delight at each new mountain, town or lake. Now she sat staring wordlessly down at her hands, her face unreadable. After a solid hour of silence on the train following the two hours of silence leading up to the ride, Matthew couldn't take it anymore.

"Lissie, please. I have to know what you're thinking," he pleaded.

She looked up at him, eyes wide.

"I'm sorry," she said with a small laugh. "I didn't realize I was making you uncomfortable. I just don't know what to think or how to act around them. I mean, I'm getting ready to meet all the immortals in existence. Do you realize how daunting that is? I don't even know how to act properly in a setting like that. And you've only told me it's a meeting. Is it a business meeting? Or a formal evening? Or a trial? My head is spinning. I don't even know what questions are appropriate for me to ask you. I mean, they *are* your family … and I've always found that staying silent is the best way to avoid offending someone."

Matthew smiled and heaved a sigh of relief. "You are not going to offend me, my love. I don't think you are capable of it, no matter what you say. Ask me anything. I promise."

Lissie looked thoughtful for a few moments before starting her questioning.

"What kind of meeting is this going to be?" she asked, concerned.

"Well," Matthew began with a long pause, trying to figure out how to answer her. "It's a formal meeting of the Family. We will all be in ceremonial dress. But any women present will be in very specific formal attire. The long sleeved dress that I purchased for you in New York is for the meeting. I guess you could say it's a cross between a business meeting and a trial. But it doesn't really work that way. I'm honestly not certain myself how the meeting will be run. I have never actually been to one," he admitted.

Lissie didn't look consoled.

"And why is there a meeting? If this is such a rare thing, what's the reason for it?" she asked.

"I ... actually called the meeting," he admitted sheepishly.

"What? So you knew this was coming? Why didn't you tell me?" she shrieked in alarm.

"Because I didn't want to burden you with anxiety on your first European excursion. And I knew you would be worried about the meeting the entire trip if I told you before we left."

She looked at him with narrowed eyes before continuing.

"Why did you call the meeting?" she asked as she studied his face for her answer.

"You're just going to have to wait find that out," he answered with the hint of a smirk around the edges of his mouth.

Lissie crossed her arms and sat back in her seat, pouting at his avoidance of the question.

"Am I expected to stand silently in a corner somewhere?" she asked in frustration.

Matthew reached for her hand and rubbed it gently between his. "You are going to be at my side. And my brothers will be close by as well. No matter what, you will have me beside you," he smiled reassuringly. "Plus I would not allow you to be pushed aside by anyone, regardless of the circumstances. My immediate family places a high emphasis on the care and respect of the women in our lives."

Lissie's expression softened at his reassurance, and he placed a soft kiss on the palm of the hand he had captured.

Lissie stood from her seat and curled up on Matthew's lap. She kissed him deeply, then nestled her head into his chest. Matthew loved her dearly. Her actions were so openly loving. He had never been in a long-term relationship before, but he liked to imagine that most women were not this affectionate. He had always craved a physical affirmation of love, and Lissie provided exactly what he needed.

"I love you," he said quietly. "Don't worry about anything. I promise I'll take care of you."

"Okay," she said. "I trust you."

When they arrived in Florence, there was a black SUV waiting for them. Matthew stiffened as a man walked around the front of the car; Matthew grabbed Lissie's arm and pulled her behind his body. Lissie knew the man was dangerous just by looking at him, but Matthew's reaction was enough to give her a panic attack. Her heart was racing as she peeked around Matthew. The man was approaching slowly with an odd look on his face.

"Rogue," the man said brusquely.

Lissie's blood boiled at the use of the name Matthew's grandfather had given to him so long ago. *How dare they call him by some awful nickname?*

"Uncle Sergius," Matthew said with a tight nod.

Lissie's eyes snapped up to Matthew's face. *Uncle Sergius? As in the uncle that killed Anamaria? No wonder he's freaking out.*

"I am your driver while you are being here," his uncle said in a rough Italian accent. Lissie was positive that the man rarely spoke English. She thought it was interesting that he chose to speak English for her sake.

"I do not believe we will require a personal driver for the duration of our stay," Matthew said in an irritated tone.

The two began to bicker back and forth in Italian that was so fast, she couldn't make out a single word. She was completely lost, but both men looked exasperated.

"I understand," Matthew said as his body relaxed. "This is Lissie," he said as he pulled her closely to his side. His posture was still protective, but he didn't seem to be worried about his uncle pulling out a knife and stabbing her to death.

"Nice to meeting you. You can calling me Sergius," he struggled to say to her.

Though she was nervous about the man before her, she knew Matthew would never let anything or anyone do her harm. She straightened up, walked up to Uncle Sergius, and extended her hand.

"It's nice to meet you," she said with a smile.

Uncle Sergius looked surprised and amused, but he gave her a tiny smile and shook her hand. He glanced over Lissie's head and said something to Matthew in Italian. She looked back at Matthew with a questioning look, but he only smirked.

The trip to the Family house was a short drive to the east through mostly residential areas. When they finally reached the end of the neighborhoods, they turned onto a narrow road that commenced their climb through the hills of Tuscany. Italian cypress trees and low stone walls were scattered across the countryside. The properties grew larger and larger as they climbed the hills. For most of the drive through the hills, Lissie could see only the beautiful, thick foliage, but every once in a while they would come upon a break in the trees where she could glimpse an incredible view of the rolling hills dotted with villas and vineyards. They came around a sharp turn, and slowed to a crawl. Matthew rolled down the window and breathed deeply.

"It has been too long. Far, far too long," he said pensively.

Lissie saw a long unpaved driveway lined with enormous Italian cypress trees. The long, straight driveway led to what could only be described as a castle. Her eyes grew large, and she looked at Matthew for confirmation.

"Yes. This is the Family castle," he verified.

As they drove slowly down the path, Lissie tried to remember how to breathe. They came to a stop in front of a massive stone building, and Matthew had to pull Lissie from the car to get her to move.

"Priest and Saint built it in the 12th century to create facilities where the Family could train. We have a church, a farm where we grow most of our food, a mill, a winery, a forge and an armory. We have goats, sheep and chickens. And of course a small vineyard. What Italian castle is complete without a vineyard?" he asked with a chuckle. "Then there is the main house. It has twenty bedrooms—which makes family meetings quite easy. And of course there are underground barracks for the trainees." Lissie looked around in amazement.

"This isn't just a castle. It's a fortress!" she exclaimed. It was breathtaking. There were five main buildings in all, but there were several smaller structures dotting the edges of the land. The stone property looked like it fell straight from the pages of a history book. The top of the main house was built with battlements all the way around. A large brick staircase led to a huge porch that spanned the entire side of the castle facing the hills. The walls were covered in ivy that had likely been climbing the stones for centuries. Clay potted plants lined the parking area—which seemed out of place in the ancient setting. Lissie had to keep reminding herself that many of Matthew's family members outdated the castle. There was a narrow tower on the front of the church that used to house a bell which was now missing. The mill, forge, winery and armory were all housed in the same large building, and if Lissie had to guess, she would bet that the barracks were in there as well.

"You live in history," she said in awe. Matthew nodded and pulled her to him.

"Don't we all?" he asked as he leaned down and kissed her on the cheek. She laughed quietly and held him more tightly.

"Are you alarmed by all this?" he asked, his voice revealing worry.

"Not at all. It's mind-blowing. Unfathomable. But truly amazing. *You* are a piece of history," she said as she reached up and placed her hands on either side of his face. She was about to pull him in for a kiss when Uncle Sergius called to them from the front door.

"I have to sit down with my father and brothers to prepare for tomorrow's meeting. Uncle Sergius will show you to our room and take you anywhere around the castle grounds that you might like to go," he said as he hugged her.

"You're leaving me with him?" she asked in a hushed whisper. "Not fifteen minutes ago you were protecting me from him as if he was going to kill me. Now you're okay leaving me alone with him?"

Matthew leaned his forehead against Lissie's and spoke quietly, "He really likes you. And he apologized for his involvement in Anamaria's death. I have not seen him since her murder. He said he's been hoping to apologize to me ever since. And he is not the kind of person who would lie about something like that. I believe him. I promise you will be safe with him."

Lissie didn't want to leave Matthew's side, but if he needed to prepare for the meeting without her, she would make the best of her time.

"Okay. Go prepare for the mystery meeting. And come find me as soon as you're finished. I'm not eating dinner alone," she said with determination.

"I wouldn't let such a dreadful thing happen," he said as he gave her a short kiss and headed toward the church.

"I will showing you to your room now," Uncle Sergius said with an outstretched hand toward the front door. He carried both of Lissie's suitcases and dragged Matthew's behind him. She walked through the massive doorway into a grand foyer. He led her up the large stone staircase that hugged the left wall. She followed him down a dark hallway lined with closed doors on both sides. The chandeliers that lit the hallway were the original wooden ones with candles. It seemed that the family forgot to put electricity in the hallways.

"This is Rogue's room. And for you also," Uncle Sergius said as he opened the last door on the right side of the hallway. He placed the luggage on the twin bed that sat against the right wall. An old, wooden, king-sized bed sat on the opposite wall. *At least this room has lights,* she thought as she flipped them on.

"Antonio and Marcus stayed here with Rogue when young. But it is for you and Rogue now," Uncle Sergius said. "I will waiting in the hall." And with that he exited the room and shut the door behind him.

Lissie looked around the room, taking in every detail. There were handmade swords and knives carved from wood—*the toys that the boys played with as children,* she thought with a smile. On the dresser that was pushed against the left wall were three small framed paintings. Lissie placed them side by side and looked closely at each.

"The boys!" she exclaimed. The portraits of Marcus, Antonio and Matthew had been painted when they were each roughly ten years of age. It was obvious which portrait belonged to each brother. Lissie picked Matthew's up and sat down on the edge of the bed. She couldn't help her wide smile. He was adorable as a child. His hair had grown darker as an adult, but his bright green eyes still glimmered with the mischief the artist captured in the painting.

Lissie set the portrait back down and changed her clothes to something a little less casual. She put on a long coral skirt, a white tank-top, and a tan three-quarter sleeved leather jacket. If she was going to meet any of the other family members, she wanted to look good. She pulled her hair into a high ponytail and checked her makeup before opening the door. Uncle Sergius turned toward her as if he was waiting to follow her lead.

"Can I look around the castle?" she asked.

"I will show you," he said with a serious tone as he briskly walked down the hallway.

Lissie felt a little rushed because of his pace, but she got to see most of the castle—even if it was at a slow jog. He ended his tour of the main house in the dining room—which was larger than any dining room she had ever seen. The room had three long tables set up in a U-shape. There were no less than one hundred chairs set around it. Lissie vaguely wondered if this would be where the meeting was held. There were two larger chairs for Priest and Saint at the head of main table. Overhead was a massive, ancient wooden chandelier that was electrically wired so dinners could be eaten at any time of the night.

"Any times you are needing food, you go to the kitchen and take what you want. Or if there is Family around, just asking for food. We all loving to cook," he said with a nod.

Lissie smiled tentatively at him. She hadn't been sure how amiable he would be towards her up to this point, but his returning smile was reassuring.

"Would you like to cook with me now?" she asked.

"Prego!" he responded as he headed back to the kitchen.

The two made a lemon basil cream sauce and homemade pasta for their lunch. Lissie decided she could happily live in a house where everyone felt as passionately about cooking and eating homemade food as she felt about decorating. They barely talked while they cooked, but by the end of the meal, she knew she liked this uncle. He was gentle and kind—and he didn't get upset with her when she messed up the first batch of dough for their pasta. He simply laughed, threw it away, and started again. After they finished eating, he offered to show her the smaller buildings around the estate. She specifically wanted to see the animals and the vineyard, and he was happy to oblige.

This man gives off the appearance of a terrifying killer, but he's just a gentle soul who loves to live in the country and cook his own food, she mused as he led her to the stables. She spent hours making friends with the sheep and goats. Most of her afternoon was spent laughing at the way the goats played with each other, which in turn made Uncle Sergius laugh at her amusement.

After her time with the animals, she realized that a small crowd of men had gathered outside the main house. They were doing their best not to stare at her and failing miserably. She felt incredibly self-conscious, but tried not to show her embarrassment.

Right then, Matthew emerged from the small church. He glanced at the group and followed their gaze straight to Lissie. He barked out some harsh-sounding Italian before heading straight to Lissie, scooping her up into his arms, and planting a long, passionate kiss on her lips. She thought she heard whistles and hoots from the group standing behind them, but she was so overcome by Matthew's intensity, she could focus on little else.

"I guess you had a good time with your brothers and father?" she asked as soon as Matthew pulled away from her to take a breath.

"I suppose you could say that. My father thinks the Family meeting will go well, and that is enough assurance for me. Have you eaten anything?" he asked.

"Yes! Uncle Sergius and I made pasta and a lemon basil sauce. I had a wonderful afternoon, by the way," she added.

"I told you he likes you. He's a hard man, but if he likes you, you'll know it," Matthew said with a smirk.

Matthew asked Uncle Sergius to take him and Lissie into town for the rest of the afternoon and evening. He dropped them off on the edge of town and agreed to wait until they were ready to go back to the castle. Matthew showed Lissie the Duomo, the Paradise Gates, and the Medici Chapel. For dinner he took her to an upscale restaurant right on the Arno River. Their table was next to one of the large windows that overlooked the river. She ordered a delicious steak—sirloin with cream brandy and green peppercorn sauce. That, mixed with the bottles of champagne Matthew ordered for them, made for the perfect night. She was grateful Uncle Sergius had driven them into the city. There was no way Matthew could've driven back to the castle after the amount of alcohol he consumed.

Upon their return to the castle, Lissie was exhausted.

"Is it alright if we go to bed? Between the long day and all that champagne, I'm not sure I can stay up for another five minutes!" she said with a slight slur in her speech. Matthew laughed, but agreed they could go to sleep.

"I'm so happy I got to see you as a child," she said as she caught another glimpse of the three brothers' portraits while crawling into bed.

Matthew looked confused for a moment, but followed her gaze to the dresser.

"Ah yes. My mother painted them," he said quietly.

"She was quite talented," Lissie was barely able to say before drifting into a deep slumber.

Fifty-Four

MATTHEW STAYED IN BED beside Lissie until he was certain she would be asleep for the rest of the evening. He needed to know where his uncles and cousins stood with regard to the next day's meeting. He threw on a t-shirt and sweatpants and headed toward the sound of his Family arguing. He wanted so badly to enjoy being surrounded by his boisterous Italian Family, but he was wary about the greeting he might receive. He took a moment to listen to his Family speaking only in Italian. He had not realized how much he missed speaking his native language until that moment. He took a deep breath and walked around the corner.

As soon as he entered the dining room, everyone went completely silent and turned toward him. He scanned the room, trying to decipher the looks he was receiving, and he was happy to find most of them determined but amenable. He was met with several small nods—which he took as a sign of allies and friends.

Uncle Sergius walked up to him first and extended his hand. Matthew took his hand firmly as his uncle spoke, "I would like to begin calling you by your given name, Nephew Mattia. I would have stood beside you long ago had I known the situation. If you will allow it, let me stand at your side now. Give me this chance to rectify my past offense."

"I am honored, Uncle. All is forgiven," he replied as he clasped his uncle on the shoulder with his other hand.

Uncle Samuel was the next to approach him. The pair had been friends for so long, Matthew knew he could always count on the man for support. Several others came over to shake his hand in a sign of unity, while some watched with disgust. After the initial greetings, the Family broke into several small groups with arguments materializing in each. There were those that thought Matthew was out of line. There were those that thought each member of the Family should be able to go his own way. After about an hour, the conversations turned more serious. The hard alcohol was brought out and the men sat down around the table to have a discussion as a group. Thomas, Matthew's father, started.

"I fear for what the Family has become. I do not know if you feel the same," he swept his hand around the room, "but my contracts have been of less and less worth over the past five centuries." The men around the table grunted and nodded their agreement while Thomas continued. "I fear that Priest no longer concerns himself over which contracts he accepts or denies. His respect for human life is dwindling. We cannot afford to abide a leader who willingly accepts contracts from evil men. From the beginning we have sworn ourselves to our leaders and to our Family. But I have not seen evidence that Priest returns that faithfulness to any of us. I feel it may be time for a change in leadership," he finished.

"And who would be fit to take on that responsibility?" Uncle Gregorius yelled angrily.

"To even speak of such a thing outside of an official Family meeting is treacherous!" his twin brother, Elias added.

Matthew made a mental note that those two would not be on his side in the coming meeting.

"I have sat by quietly for hundreds of years. But I cannot abide a leader who has no desire to *lead*. It seems that Priest has given up trying to sort contracts for their merit. I had not noticed until my son was given orders to murder an entire family who was wholly unconnected to the reasoning behind the kills. Father would never have accepted such a contract a thousand years ago. He has transformed into someone I do not even know!" Thomas yelled angrily.

Matthew's brothers and cousins sat quietly, carefully weighing the information that their elders presented. As he looked around the table, Matthew could see battle lines being drawn. He knew the Family could easily be at war with themselves in a matter of years.

Uncle Paulus stood calmly, and everyone quieted immediately. "I think we can all agree that this meeting never happened. We will never discuss this again outside of an official Family meeting—not as a whole or in groups. Someday, a time will come where we will address the issue. But this is not that time. Now be off. The meeting begins at nine a.m. tomorrow."

The Family silently exited the dining hall and made their way toward their rooms. Matthew's brothers gave him a signal to follow them to their room.

As soon as the three were behind closed doors, they spoke about the events of evening in hushed voices.

"I am confident you will be alright tomorrow," Antonio said.

"I believe you have the support of most of our uncles. Surely, Priest and Saint will have sought their counsel," Marcus added.

"I feel more at ease than I have since I first called the meeting," Matthew admitted. "But the decision is ultimately up to Priest. And we all know how well he thinks of me," he said with his eyes downcast.

"Sleep well, brother. Tomorrow is approaching rapidly and you will need your rest," Marcus said as he opened the door for Matthew to leave.

As he entered his bedroom and saw Lissie sleeping peacefully on his bed, he felt dread for the coming day. *She is worth it,* he told himself as he climbed into bed beside her. And he knew he was right.

The castle was eerily quiet when Lissie awoke. She had seen the large gathering of men in the home, but it seemed everyone was either still asleep or out of the house this early morning. She checked her phone—7:30am. *Way too early,* she thought as she rolled over and realized Matthew was not beside her.

A tray of breakfast with an accompanying note was placed where he slept the night before. A few baguettes with butter and jam, a glass of milk, and a macchiato made her stomach growl. She picked up the note and read:

My dearest Lissie,

I wanted you to wake up in my arms, but my brothers forced me out of the castle for some shooting. Please enjoy breakfast and ready yourself for the meeting. I will be back to get ready around 8am. The meeting begins at 9am.

Yours,
Matthew

Her stomach churned with nervousness over the secretive meeting. Lissie felt like she was the only one in the dark. She had no idea what to expect. He hadn't even given her an idea of what the subject matter entailed.

She ate her breakfast quickly, and took her delicious macchiato with her while she got ready. She decided to keep herself calm by imagining she was back in Interlaken. She focused on the silent hills and peaceful lake as her heartbeat slowed to its normal rhythm.

She dressed slowly while taking lots of deep breaths. The gown Matthew bought her specifically for this occasion was a long-sleeved, black, lace gown. It was fitted, but the bottom flowed out just enough for comfortable walking. The back zipped up to the waist but had a button at the bottom of the neck so there was a small slit up the center of her back. He bought her matching lace flats—which were incredibly comfortable. She decided to wear her hair down in loose curls. Completely ready, all she had left to do was sit and wait for Matthew to get back. She sat down on the edge of the bed and stared at the clock on the wall.

As eight o'clock passed, Lissie grew more and more anxious about the meeting. She checked the clock on the wall every two minutes. *Where is he?* she wondered as panic began to creep in. *He's never late!* Finally, at eight-seventeen, she heard the bedroom door open.

As Matthew entered the room, he looked at her as if she were a goddess.

"Wow. You look amazing," he said as he crossed the room to kiss her.

"And you smell like the great outdoors!" she said with a laugh.

Matthew hurried to the bathroom to clean off the stench, but when he emerged it was evident his mind was troubled. It was unlike Matthew to show any signs of stress or discomfort, but at that moment he looked like a young boy unsure of his father's approval.

"The meeting will be held in English, per my request. I want you to understand everything that is going on. And Sergius is one of the few who never became fluent," he said as he dried himself off.

Lissie nodded and stood waiting, ready to help Matthew prepare himself for the meeting. His outfit was a simple pair of tan pants with a loose, white cotton tunic. His final addition was a dark brown three-quarter length cloak. Lissie helped him with each part of his ensemble, and when he was finished dressing, it was apparent that the outfit was from the Medieval period.

He checked the time and engulfed Lissie in a tight hug. "No matter what happens, stay by my side unless I tell you otherwise." He kissed her fiercely, then pulled away and led her out of the room and down the stairs.

Fifty-Five

MATTHEW'S STOMACH was churning with anticipation. He had no clue how this meeting would end. For all he knew, he could be shot and killed tonight. But he thought that was unlikely with the presence of his immediate family and the backing of several uncles. He had played in the large underground meeting chamber as a child, but had not dreamt of attending a meeting in it, or *calling* a meeting in it for that matter. He told himself time and time again over the past two weeks that he was making the right decision. He had wanted to make this decision for hundreds of years, but before Lissie entered his life, he hadn't been able to come up with a good enough reason to follow through. The time he spent with her in Switzerland and in Venice only further confirmed his decision.

They entered the large stone chamber quietly, and hundreds of pairs of eyes were immediately trained on them. The circular chamber was built in a half-circle amphitheater. Rows of marble benches lined each tier with the eldest sitting at the ground floor closest to Priest and Saint's thrones. One set of stairs in the center of the room led down to the ground level of the room. Matthew's nine uncles and his father sat oldest-to-youngest on the benches on the ground floor. His twenty eldest cousins sat on the next row up. The next thirty younger cousins—including his brothers—sat on the third row. The fourth and fifth rows had the fifty or sixty youngest of the family—most of whom were still in training and living in the barracks at the castle. Sitting on benches to the right of Priest and Saint were fourteen women dressed in long-sleeved black gowns.

Lissie wasn't sure what to think. She had hoped for some sort of differentiation between the oldest and the youngest of the group, but before her sat an army of assassins who were all exactly the same age as Matthew. There were no differences between uncles and nephews, grandfathers and grandsons. Lissie's mind spun with the realization. Only Priest and Saint appeared to be older than the others. She imagined Priest was in his mid-thirties, and Saint looked as if he might be over sixty. On the ground-level to the right of Priest and Saint were a group of ten or fifteen women, all dressed in long black gowns. *Well at least I'm dressed appropriately,* she thought with relief. She was desperate to understand the nature of this meeting. She glanced at Uncle Sergius who gave her a reassuring nod, but she didn't understand what it meant. She found Marcus and Antonio on the third row, and they each gave her a tight smile—which she knew was intended for encouragement but only made her more nervous. She looked up at Matthew, hoping for some clue about the reason they were here.

Matthew looked down at Lissie, who seemed overwhelmed by the situation, and gave her a quick nod. She smiled bravely up at him and followed his descent down the stairs to the center of the amphitheater.

You are doing the right thing, he kept telling himself. He squeezed Lissie's hand a little tighter. *She is worth it. She is worth everything.* The thought calmed his nerves completely. They came to a halt at the bottom of the stairs. Because Matthew's father was the fifth of his ten brothers, he sat directly to the left of where they stood. Matthew glanced down at his father and saw that the man stared up at him with a look of determination. Matthew took a deep breath and turned back to face Priest and Saint directly. *I'm not in this alone.* Out of the corner of his eye, he saw Lissie look directly at his grandfather. She was not the kind of woman who would be intimidated, and he loved her immensely for that. Priest stared straight back into her face for a few moments before rolling his eyes and looking away.

Saint stood, and as soon as he did, all the men at Matthew's back stood in unison. Lissie jumped a little and turned with wide eyes to make sure they were still safe. Matthew gave her a nod of reassurance.

Saint proclaimed, "I call this meeting of the Family to order," and the entire group spoke together:

> "We stand united, Family of Immortals. Plagued by life. Cursed by the hand of God. We pledge our lives to the Family, the Priest and the Saint."

Again, in unison, the men behind them sat down, and the silence of anticipation was thick in the air.

"Mattia, son of Thomas, son of Priest," Saint began, "you have called this meeting together with a petition of unprecedented nature. Priest and I have spoken at length about your appeal. We have consulted with our sons. We have studied your history. But before we grant or deny your request, your grandfather has a few words he would like say."

Saint returned to his throne with a wary look in Priest's direction. Priest stood, looking enraged as paced back and forth in front of his throne. Matthew could tell his grandfather was fighting the urge to kill him. Priest turned and glared at Matthew with anger shining through his eyes, marched right up to him, and thrust his finger into Matthew's face.

"YOU ARE NO GRANDSON OF MINE!" Priest screamed.

Lissie held Matthew's hand tightly. He could hear her breathing quicken and feel her hands shake—whether with anger or fear he was not certain.

"I stripped you of your name hundreds of years ago. When Saint refrains from using the name I gave you—*Rogue*—I am provoked to dangerous levels of anger. When you refused your first contract so many years ago, I denied you your name, your family lineage, and your right to fulfill a contract on your own.

I mistakenly believed you would learn your lesson and grow into a better man from the punishment. But you only grew *weaker*," he said with a sneer. "I am shocked that one of our kind is capable of becoming less valuable than a mortal. But you have proven it is possible. You are a disappointment. As a child you showed such promise. Even in your training, you were one of the best I had ever seen. But one *female* in your life and you throw away everything!" Priest was pacing the floor, using wild gestures and spitting out angry curses in ancient dead languages that none present could understand. He carried on that way for several minutes before coming to a halt in front of his throne, staring down at his seat in a dead silence. After some time, he turned toward Matthew with a scornful glare affixed to his face.

"Not one," he said quietly with a shake of his head. "NOT ONE KILL!" Priest screamed at the top of his lungs. "In nearly three hundred years of fulfilling contracts, you have never performed a *single* kill. NOT ONE! It is disgraceful. You. Are. A. Disgrace!" He punctuated each word to emphasize the depths of his disappointment, but Matthew was unmoved. It had been hundreds of years since he had relinquished his yearning for Priest's approval.

Lissie had been shaking with excitement and fear since they entered the chamber. But upon Priest's declaration that Matthew never made a single kill, her entire body went still. She stopped breathing, her heart stopped beating, and her mind stopped spinning. She had never felt so much adoration for another person. Not once had Matthew downplayed his role in the contracts he had been part of. He took full responsibility for the assassinations despite the fact that he had not actually performed one. She was sure in this moment that there was no better man in the world. And he was *hers*.

Matthew glanced at Lissie, who was staring up at him with wide, adoring eyes. He never mentioned that he hadn't performed any of the kills because he had long since decided that any involvement in the planning or execution of the murder made him equally as culpable as a murderer. But he saw now in Lissie's eyes that it made a world of difference to her.

When he looked back at Priest, the man was scowling at him with narrowed eyes. Matthew grew concerned for his well-being for the first time since he entered the room. The saying 'if looks could kill' took on a whole new meaning when the look came from someone as deadly as his grandfather. Lissie apparently didn't like the look on Priest's face either—she took a tiny step toward Matthew that put her body slightly in front of his. Priest's glare shifted from Matthew to Lissie as she moved.

The next three seconds were a frenzy of movement. Priest rushed at Lissie, pulling a knife from inside his cloak. He grabbed Lissie by the throat and pressed his blade against her neck. In the same moment, Matthew's father pulled his own knife from a sleeve and moved behind Priest, the blade coming to rest on the skin that protected his carotid artery. Matthew's own blade was pressed firmly against center of Priest's ribcage—one forceful thrust and the knife would enter the man's heart.

Women shrieked as the rest of the men jumped from their seats—apparently everyone decided to bring their knives to this meeting. Most of the men knew from the previous night's gathering who stood on each side of the battle lines, but no one expected the fracture to run so deep. The entire room was in a silent deadlock. No one was willing to make the first act of betrayal toward the Family.

Matthew's eyes locked with Lissie's. He would kill every man in this room to keep her alive. *You are my life. You are worth dying for. I love you more than anything in the world. I will die to protect you.* Her terrified gaze relaxed as he thought the words he was desperate to speak aloud. She had always been able to read his emotions, and he knew even without hearing the words, she felt their truth.

"Enough," Saint said quietly as he rose from his throne. He was the only man in the room who was neither threatened by a knife nor threatening another with one. No one budged from his position—they were trained so well with the placement of their knives, that if anyone decided to strike out, it would be a killing blow.

"I said ENOUGH!" Saint yelled. Everyone's eyes went wide, and knives were put away with expediency. It was the first time anyone had ever heard Saint raise his voice. No one was willing to push him further. Priest released Lissie's neck, and Matthew examined her closely to ensure she was not injured. He grabbed her hand again and held on tightly.

"Return to your seats so we can finish this meeting," Saint commanded. The men obeyed, and within ten seconds, the room returned to silence.

Priest sat down on his throne to reclaim his regality. He ran a hand through his hair and over his throat where his own son had pressed the edge of a knife. A glimmer of disappointment flashed across his face before he leaned over to confer with Saint.

Matthew was disgusted that his own grandfather was disappointed there hadn't been any bloodshed. The Family's pledge swore allegiance to Priest, Saint, and every other member of the Family. But this night had shown Matthew that Priest's allegiance was to Priest and Priest alone. Matthew could not fathom how anyone in the Family could willingly follow a leader so self-serving.

Saint and Priest whispered back and forth for several minutes while everyone awaited their decision. When their discussion was finished, Priest looked as angry as he had at the beginning of the evening.

"In light of your horrendous record, your *absurd* request to be released from active service is permitted," Priest said with a sigh.

There was a small gasp of relief from a woman sitting on the bench to the right of Saint's throne—which he knew could only be one person.

Priest continued, "Unfortunately, Saint persists in reminding me that you have unparalleled technological skills which are vital to our Family. Therefore, instead of being banished from the Family or killed as I would see befitting of your actions, you will serve as an instructor for the trainees in the most recent technological advancements. You *will* accept a post here two months out of each calendar year. This is non-negotiable, so do *not* try to dispute the decision," Priest warned.

"I accept," Matthew said loudly. He could not believe that he was offered a job he would actually enjoy. He was excited to finally work with a generation that grew up with technology in their lives. Trying to train men that had been without electronics for hundreds or even thousands of years had proven an impossible task. The younger generations would already know the basics.

"I am grateful for the mercy you have shown unto me. I will gladly accept the post you have assigned. And I will happily consult with my brothers, nephews, cousins and uncles whenever there is need," he finished with a nod to the men seated behind him. They all gave a small synchronized nod back to him, grateful for his offer. Saint looked smug, and finally stood to speak.

"We are pleased to have an expert in your field as an instructor here. This is a position we should have created for you long ago. As an instructor, your name and lineage will also be officially reinstated. Welcome back to Castello San Romolo, Mattia, son of Thomas, son of Priest. It has been far too long since your last visit," Saint said as he held his arms out for an embrace.

His words marked the official end of the meeting, and the room's silence broke into several tense conversations.

Lissie was still trying to process what had happened when Matthew released her hand to embrace Saint in a friendly hug. *Matthew is free from further contracts.* She was having trouble wrapping her head around the extraordinary news. Her arm was grabbed from behind, and she was spun around and swept into a giant hug from a jubilant Antonio. Lissie couldn't help but laugh in her shock. Marcus, too, gave her a small hug and a smiling nod. The brothers almost looked ... grateful. But she had absolutely nothing to do with this meeting. She hadn't even understood the nature of it until Priest spoke. Uncle Sergius came over next to kiss her cheek and give her another of his small grins.

Without warning, Matthew picked her up and swung her around, kissing her passionately before placing her back on the ground. She looked at him with a glare of accusation, which was met only with laughter.

"I told you to trust me, and you did. You inspired this whole thing!" he said, beaming. "I have wanted a way out of fulfilling contracts since Anamaria's death. But I had no other reason to live. If I had simply killed myself, I would have broken my family's hearts. But when you came into my life, everything changed. You are my reason to live. You are my reason to be free. And for that, I love you more than ever," he said as he planted another long kiss on her lips.

Lissie didn't know what to say, so she just smiled. Matthew looked over her shoulder, and his smile changed from one of jubilant adoration to one of respect and honor. She turned around to see the man who had pulled his knife on Priest during the altercation—he looked exactly like Matthew. He was accompanied by a young woman in her early twenties.

Matthew rushed to the two and embraced them in a firm hug. He kissed the young woman on the forehead and cupped her face in his hands. Lissie was confused by who the woman might be, but she was certain she recognized her from somewhere.

"Lissie, I would like to introduce you to my father, Thomas." The man embraced Lissie the same way Marcus had.

"And to my mother, Caterina," Matthew added with a smirk.

Lissie's shock was palpable. Matthew had said that no immortal daughters existed. How was it possible that his mother was still alive? The woman smiled and grasped Lissie's hands in her own.

"I am honored to meet you. And very excited to have another woman in our family. I do hope that you plan to spend time with me and Thomas in Milan?" she said with a questioning glance at Matthew.

"Of course!" Lissie said as she embraced Caterina in a hug.

As Matthew's immediate family gathered in a corner of the room, dozens of other men came over to express their apologies about the altercation. Most of the apologies were directed toward Lissie, but she was shrewd enough to know the men were really voicing their agreement with Matthew's stand against Priest.

Two men in particular unabashedly declared they would stand beside Matthew's family if a civil war broke out within the Family—Uncle Sergius and Uncle Samuel. Lissie thought it was interesting that the eldest and the youngest of the uncles were so dedicated to dethroning Priest. She had never spoken with Uncle Samuel before but was immediately inclined to like him. He was relaxed and informal—the polar opposite of Uncle Sergius. But both men seemed to adore Matthew, and in kind, adore her for loving Matthew. *I think I could get used to this Family,* she thought as the conversation continued.

About an hour after the conclusion of the meeting, the Family finally began to exit the amphitheater for what smelled like an incredible meal above. Matthew took Lissie's arm and smiled widely down at her.

"Isn't there something you need to explain?" Lissie asked.

"I'm not sure what you mean," Matthew said with the wicked grin he always teased her with.

"How is your *mother* alive? And why on earth does she look so familiar?" Lissie asked quietly. Matthew and his brothers began to laugh at a joke she had somehow missed.

"That, my love, is a very long story for another time," he said as he kissed her gently on the forehead. Lissie was unsatisfied with the response, but decided she would approach the issue later.

"So are we heading home from here?" she asked, knowing that their two-week trip was coming to an end.

"Home? Home is wherever you and I are together. And I believe our job situations have cleared off our calendars for the time being. I think we're due for our next adventure. Imagine all the places in the world you have ever wanted to visit, and tell me where you would like to go," he said excitedly.

Lissie hadn't realized that Matthew's new job would allow them this freedom. Her mind raced at the possibilities.

"Anywhere in the world?" she asked.

"Anywhere you want," he confirmed.

She thought for a moment before answering.

"Have you ever been to the Tianzi Mountains?"

Acknowledgements

FIRST, I have to thank God for giving me the ability to write and the passion to do everything with one hundred percent of my heart. I know He's the reason I'm able to do what I love.

Thank you to my husband, Caleb, who has stayed up with me brainstorming, reading my work, and encouraging me to keep going. Because of him, every day of my life is a new adventure.

Thank you to Melissa—my incredible friend and editor. Without her, this book would still be stuck in a very sad first draft. Thank you to Carin, Stacey, and Jake for your invaluable input in so many different areas of the book. And thank you to Julia for being the greatest proofreader of all time.

Thank you to my family and friends for supporting me on this journey and being almost as excited as I am for this novel.

Thank you to Bill Canning—my favorite teacher of all time—who showed me that reading could be more than just an assignment in school.

Now, I have to thank the people who made this book possible financially. I am still blown away by the outpouring of love from all of you and will forever hold each of you in my heart: Kendrick Rozelle, Emily and Jason DeCoursey, Rachel and Caleb Arthur, Wayne and Daniel Bonner-Bell, Christopher and Nancy Nolan, Stacey and Justin Breezeel, Chris and Kayla McElmurry, Keera Jung, Bill and Amelia Carwin, Sarah and Devin McBride, Kate and David Fullerton, Mario and Melissa Luna, Mandy and Terrance Avery, Amanda and Tracy Cook, Sonya Schwader, Taylor Singleton, Scott and Heather Lacy, Ron and Tonya Nichols, Becca and Drew Godsey, Chris Venable, Ashton and Trevor Portman, Missy Schwader, Ian Johnson, Liz Snoap, Carlie Lott, Brigid DeCoursey, Jerron and Tiffany Nichols, Daniel Bright and Caroline Holt, Ward and Shari Clark, Melissa Harlow and Kerry Cissell, Rebecca Craft, John and Kendall Youngman, Matthew Overturf, and Nicholas Norfolk.

Finally, thank you to my readers. I hope you're excited to see what happens in book two of The Plagued Trilogy!

Family Signets
of introduced characters

Sergius 615 C.E.	Claudius 628 C.E.	Samuel 610 C.E.	
Paulus 620 C.E.	Felix 630 C.E.	Marcus 1568 C.E.	
Gregorius & Elias 620 C.E.	Alexander 631 C.E.	Antonio 1572 C.E.	
Thomas 625 C.E.	Demetrius 633 C.E.	Mattia 1575 C.E.	

Priest
birth unknown

Saint
birth unknown

KEEP READING FOR A SNEAK PEEK AT GHOST, THE SECOND BOOK IN THE PLAGUED TRILOGY...

Ghost

Prologue

She had never been so terrified in all her life. She had known tragedy, loss, and terror. But the sorrows of her past seemed like a small splatter of paint accidentally spilled on an otherwise perfect painting compared to what now stretched dauntingly before her.

She knew it was the right choice—he had convinced her that the consequences of staying would be dire. But for all the wisdom in his advice, she still felt a pit of fear in her stomach.

She stepped aboard the ship and spared a quick glance backward. She felt as if she were a prisoner being released after a lifetime locked in a prison cell—alone, scared, unsure of how to live outside the boundaries of her familiar cell and bars. She knew how to live with the difficulties of her former life. Surely the hardships of the life ahead could not rival those of her past.

One step at a time, she told herself in a small, terrified voice. She turned back to the ship and breathed a heavy sigh. She could not look back again, could not dwell on her former life, could not question the decision she had made.

As the ship set sail, she gazed toward the sea—toward the life that lay ahead. She wished she could paint this moment to capture the depth of her emotions. The vast, terrifying sea that lay ahead would be beautiful if only she had a way to capture the vision before her. *There is no turning back now,* she thought as a tear escaped from the corner of her eye. *There is only what lies ahead.*

KARI NICHOLS

was inspired to write after moving from Arkansas to the colorful and energetic city of New York. Her passion for creating art was developed from the time she was a child. Her artistic endeavors have ranged from music composition to photography to fashion design, but writing novels is far and away her favorite artistic outlet. She can often be found wrapped up in her favorite blanket, writing her next novel with a cup of hot tea in hand. She is a self-professed nerd, and when she isn't writing, she loves to play video games, read romance novels, and go on international adventures with her charming husband.

You can visit her online at

WWW.KARINICHOLS.COM

or on Twitter (@TheKariNichols)